D0480365

ANTONIA

"Obey, believe, fight." These are the words with which Benito Mussolini rallied his supporters—but to little Antonia they have a different and special significance. This is the story of a little Italian peasant girl who rises superior to the squalor and poverty of her background, and, endowed with a special talent and with unusual strength of character, makes of her life something splendid and successful. It is the story of how she comes to know love and heartache—of how, twice in her life, she touches the heights of happiness, but of how, also, she experiences the extremes of grief, and learns to carry herself at such times with self-control and fortitude. Naomi Jacob's gift for characterization finds full and delightful expression in the character of Antonia Trolli, with her simple and loving heart, her quaint and engaging dignity; in Francis Winnerton, the young English artist who becomes so important in Antonia's life, and in John Trevor, Marquis of Rivermead, the loyal friend of Francis and of Antonia herself. The life of the little Italian village where Antonia is brought up is depicted with a faithful and loving pen, and no less convincing are the French and English backgrounds against which the later part of the story is set.

NAOMI JACOB

has also written

POWER
JACOB USSHER
ROCK AND SAND
THE BELOVED PHYSICIAN
THE MAN WHO FOUND HIMSELF
"SEEN UNKNOWN . . ."
THE PLOUGH
ROOTS
PROPS
POOR STRAWS
GROPING
THE LOADED STICK
"HONOUR COME BACK——"
BARREN METAL
TIMEPIECE
FADE OUT
THE MORNING WILL COME

THE LENIENT GOD
NO EASY WAY
STRAWS IN AMBER
THIS PORCELAIN CLAY
THEY LEFT THE LAND
SALLY SCARTH
UNDER NEW MANAGEMENT
THE CAP OF YOUTH
LEOPARDS AND SPOTS
WHITE WOOL
HONOUR'S A MISTRESS
A PASSAGE PERILOUS
MARY OF DELIGHT
EVERY OTHER GIFT
A LATE LARK SINGING
SECOND HARVEST
ANTONIA

One-Act Plays:

THE DAWN

MARY OF DELIGHT

Autobiography and Biography:

ME: A CHRONICLE ABOUT OTHER PEOPLE
"OUR MARIE" (MARIE LLOYD)
ME AGAIN
MORE ABOUT ME
ME IN WARTIME

ME OVER THERE
ME IN THE MEDITERRANEAN
ME AND MINE
ME LOOKING BACK
ROBERT, NANA—AND ME

General:
ME IN THE KITCHEN

THE GOLLANTZ SAGA

Volume One
comprising

FOUNDER OF THE HOUSE

"THAT WILD LIE . . ."

YOUNG EMMANUEL

Volume Two
comprising

FOUR GENERATIONS

PRIVATE GOLLANTZ

GOLLANTZ
LONDON, PARIS, MILAN

ANTONIA

NAOMI JACOB

THE BOOK CLUB
121 CHARING CROSS ROAD
LONDON, W.C.2

Printed in Great Britain
by The Anchor Press, Ltd.,
Tiptree, Essex

For

TINA CECI

the bravest woman I have ever known, with all my
affection and admiration
MICKIE

"Wherefore to you, my friend, I dedicate
This so indifferent bookling."

Translation from *Catullus*
by JAMES ELROY FLECKER

Part One

CHAPTER ONE

THE first thing that Antonia remembered clearly was sitting in a little wooden chair, looking out through the open door. She could see the trodden patch of earth outside, a tree and the old well head. Sometimes hens advanced to the open door and put their heads round the doorposts, nervously like visiting spinsters who are not certain of their welcome. Antonia liked the ducks better, they walked right up to the door, and if you kept still, came in and paddled about the kitchen, picking up crumbs, bits of green vegetable, and fruit skins. The two lambs ran in and out, once or twice the old sow came, and Antonia screamed for her mother to drive the sow away because it smelt so nasty.

There was a profusion of smells in the cottage; Antonia thought that everyone had their own special smell. Her father, who worked in the quarry, smelt of sweat and dust, her mother of oil, and sometimes garlic. Her brothers, Franco and Marco, smelt of—well, smelt of "boy". Her sister, Carolina, smelt of some soap she used which she said was the scent of roses; it didn't smell like roses to Antonia, it was too sweet and sickly.

She remembered later being able to walk alone easily, and with certainty. She went down on all fours to climb over the doorstep, and then scrambled to her feet again. She could see beyond the tree, right over the vineyards, away to the mountains; she felt that she could see the whole of the world. She suddenly felt very small, afraid, and turning back to the cottage rushed to her mother, burying her face in Maria's skirts.

Antonia must have been about seven when she realized that they were very poor; later she was to discover that almost everyone in the village was very poor. The streets were not properly paved, the houses were very old, in bad repair and exceedingly dirty. Carolina, who was fifteen, worked in the only factory in Morano. She was a big, well-developed girl with a shock of curling dark hair, brown eyes which noted everything, and a full red mouth. Antonia suspected that she was lazy, for she was always unwilling to help her mother in the house, and would climb the ladder which led to the upper story, where she slept, and remain there for hours, combing her hair, rubbing some white stuff on her hands, and staring at herself in a little spotted mirror in a cracked wooden frame. At the factory they made cardboard, and Carolina brought some sheets of it home, and Franco made a wall of it to divide their room from the one where Carolina and Antonia slept.

Franco was almost grown up, Antonia thought. He went to the barber once a week and came back with his face very smooth and shining a little; sometimes his hair smelt really like flowers; if you rubbed your fingers on it, they smelt also. Franco was a carpenter, and when furniture was broken he could mend it so that it looked as good as ever. Marco worked for a farmer; he was a year younger than Franco, and his skin was burnt quite brown. He tied the vines in the Spring, and in the Autumn picked and packed apples to send away by the train in boxes. When Franco was given the order to make a great number of these boxes he was delighted; Marco said that they paid more for the boxes than the apples were worth.

Pietro Trolli worked at the quarry where you could hear the bangs and rumblings when they were blasting rocks. He was a big, heavy man, with a large moustache, and immense hands. On Saturdays he drank too much wine, and came home walking unsteadily. His wife always said that it was no wonder they were poor, when he drank the money. Antonia wondered how anyone could drink money, and what it tasted like.

She could never remember that she loved her father very much; he frightened her, his hands were so big, and he had lost the third finger of his left hand in an accident, and the sight of the stump made Antonia shiver. Her mother was kind; true, she flew into terrible tempers, and hit everyone within reach, even Franco if he were at home. Those sudden tempests were soon over, and she would return to being her slow, rather bovine self. She moved slowly, was hopelessly untidy, and the words "It doesn't matter" were perpetually on her lips. She cooked *polenta*—they had *polenta* almost every day; she bought the cheapest *tagliatelli* at the grocer's—the kind which is very hard and a greyish white, the kind that poor peasants eat. She used to send Antonia out to gather dandelion leaves to make a salad, which they ate with oil and vinegar. They never actually bought vinegar, they put all the dregs of the red wine into a bottle, stood it in the sun with the cork left out, and it changed to vinegar very quickly. They had meat once a week, and then most of it was given to Pietro, Franco and Marco. Antonia used to be given a slice of bread soaked in gravy.

One day Pietro said to Antonia, "How old are you, *cara bella*?"

She said, "I think that I'm seven."

He stared at her owlishly, she thought that he had been visiting the *osteria* on his way home. "You ought to have some schooling."

Her mother, who was mixing *polenta* on the kitchen table, demanded, "How can she go to school? The nearest school is at Trepasso, and that is nearly eight *kilometri* away! Can she walk, tell me?"

He wagged his head. "Ah, here is my wife who knows everything! She should be a minister of state, a judge, perhaps the editor of a newspaper. Listen! Today I was talking to the priest, he is concerned that the children get no schooling. He has spoken with the Reverend Mother at the convent. She will take the girls; he will interest himself in teaching the boys. Antonia will go to the convent."

His wife said, "And who pays for this, please?"

He answered with dignity, "It is arranged. I shall make an offering to the priest."

Pietro Trolli was a religious man, and never more religious than when he was in his cups. At such times he would tell Antonia long, involved stories of the Saints, often tears would pour down his cheeks as he was moved by his own eloquence. No matter how drunk he had been on Saturday night, he always went to Mass on Sunday, and Franco and Marco, each giving a hand to Antonia, went with him. Carolina went irregularly, and their mother protested that she had no decent clothes—which was true—and that she must clean the house— which she never did.

The church was a very large building, not beautiful, and the altars and Stations of the Cross were tawdry, for the parish was very poor and the priest always looked as if he did not get enough to eat. His clothes were shabby, his boots patched, and his collar was made of some substance which could be sponged clean when it became soiled. Age had caused it to crack in several places. He was a small, desiccated-looking man, with scanty grey hair, and a chin which except for two days in the week was covered with stubble. His eyes behind steel-rimmed spectacles were very bright, and there were tiny wrinkles at their corners because he was always ready to smile. He lived in a small grey stone house next to the church, where an old woman called Anna Bellafiore was supposed to cook and clean for him. She was an unpopular old woman, for it was believed in the village that she robbed the priest, and even—it was whispered—extracted coins from the offerings of the Faithful when the priest brought them home to count and lock away.

The farmer for whom Marco worked once said to the

priest, "Father, that old woman is robbing you! Send her packing!"

Father Dominic smiled at him. "My friend, how can she rob me? There is nothing for anyone to take. I have only two shirts, one is always being washed, the other is on my back! I have only one pair of boots, and when they are being mended," he laughed, "I serve Mass wearing my cloth slippers!"

The farmer, who was accustomed to eat well, drink generously, and possessed plenty of shirts, stared at him and ejaculated, "Humph!" The next morning a parcel came to Don Dominic, and he became the owner of various articles of wearing apparel, all in the very best possible condition.

The villagers both liked and respected their priest; they were poor, many of them grindingly poor, but from time to time they sent him small presents—a cheese made from goat's milk, a few eggs, sometimes a fish which they caught in the roaring river Saroli. He never mentioned his donors by name, but always from the pulpit offered thanks to "the kind giver of six eggs" or "the faithful servant of God who was prompted to send me a cheese".

Father Dominic baptized the babies, married the young people, and buried the old ones; he offered three services every day in the week, and on Sunday was added another. He tramped the country round to visit the sick, he gave advice to those who were puzzled or in trouble; he trained his altar boys meticulously, and saw that his church was kept spotlessly clean. It never occurred to him to wonder why His Grace the Bishop of the Diocese did not come and find out what means might be employed, what machinery set in motion, in order that one of his parish priests might have at least an extra pair of boots, and sufficient fuel to keep him reasonably warm during the bitingly cold winters.

When Mass ended Pietro took his daughter's hand and led her to the vestry. Father Dominic was gazing ruefully at the cotta which he had just removed, shaking his head. He greeted Pietro:

"Ah, Pietro, you have brought the little one. It is indeed necessary that our girls shall be taught to sew. Look!" He pointed to the cotta. "Mother Lucia assures me that there are more darns, more patches, than original material! Like me." He laughed. "These cottas grow old in the service of God. So, my child, you will go to the good nuns, and learn all that they teach you, eh?"

Antonia dropped her little curtsey. "Yes, if you please, Father."

"Tomorrow, Pietro, at nine o'clock. There, God bless you and make you a good child—always."

For the remainder of the day she was terribly excited. True she had been to the convent once or twice, with messages for Father Dominic, and once to take some ripe figs to the Reverend Mother, but now she was to go every day, to learn, to see how the nuns worked and kept their convent shiningly clean. Even Carolina was interested and washed her hair for her, using a raw egg, which made it very soft and fluffy, so that it stood out all round her small, neat head.

The next morning Franco took her to the convent. They were shown into the parlour. It was a simply furnished room, the floor-boards were bare, and scrubbed to the whiteness of milk; there were two or three brightly coloured hand-woven rugs. Such furniture as there was shone with much polishing, and there were two pictures—one of Our Lord pointing to His Sacred Heart, the other of an old gentleman wearing a white skull-cap, his hand upraised in blessing, and a wide smile on his lips. Antonia decided that she liked him.

She whispered, "Who is that gentleman?"

Franco said, "His Holiness—I'm not sure if it is this Pope—but he is called, or was called, for I am not sure if he is dead or not, and if he is, then God rest his soul—Leo the Thirteenth."

She said, "Thirteen—a lucky number, no?"

Franco pursed his lips. "S-sh, you mustn't talk like that about a Pope."

When Reverend Mother came, Antonia squeezed herself nearer to Franco, she felt suddenly shy and frightened. The nun was a tall, spare woman, with the long, melancholy nose of the Lombards, and eyes which seemed to see everything. They saw the poverty of Antonia's clothes, the shabbiness of her shoes, she saw also the shining hair which was more golden than brown, the wide eyes of such dark blue that they were like the flowers of the gentian. She noticed the fine clear skin, the small determined chin, and the well-formed body of the child. She held out her hand and said, "Come here, my child."

Antonia went forward. The hand the nun offered her felt cold and dry. Antonia knew that her own was warm and soft. She looked up at the calm, rather hard face of the Reverend Mother.

"You want to come here to learn?"

"Yes, if you please, Reverend Mother."

"You will try to learn hard, you will be good and attentive?"

"Yes, I promise, Reverend Mother."

"Very well, come with me to Mother Angelica." She turned back to Franco. "She will be sent home at four this afternoon. She will have a bowl of soup and some bread at midday."

"Thank you, Reverend Mother. Good day to you."

"And to you, go with God."

Antonia's first day at school had begun.

The Order was a poor one, the nuns were vowed to poverty and, even had they wished, it would have been impossible for them to disregard their vows. The convent was completely without any real comfort; Reverend Mother, in

her lighter moments, used to tell her nuns that their only
luxury was complete cleanliness.

"If cleanliness is indeed next to Godliness," she said, "then
let us win our way to God, and come near to Him with
scrubbing and polishing."

So Antonia learned to read and write, to do simple arithmetic from Mother Angelica; she learned to do fine needlework from Mother Lucia; polishing, yes, and how to make
the polish from Sister Isobella. Later to her great joy she was
allowed to help in the kitchen. Even if she were only set to
peel onions, Mother Anna Maria demanded that there was "but
one way—the right one, all others are waste of time, waste of
good food". She had come from a French Order, and still
loved to recount to Antonia the mysteries and beauties of
French cooking. Their convent had been in Paris, where they
had taken boarders who were members of the French aristocracy.

"Old ladies, you understand, but they had still retained
their love and appreciation of good food. They paid well—ah,
how well—to the enrichment of the Order! They might eat
simply, my child, but whatever they ate must be"—she
bunched her fingers, kissing them lightly—"perfect. They had
their own rooms, a wing of the convent, you understand, and
they brought their own furniture with them. Ah, such
furniture! I have nothing here to teach you with. How shall I
show you the method of making exquisite sauces? Of cooking
with fine wines? Of stuffing young chickens with grapes?
Alas, where can I get sufficient butter, cream, fine wine? I can
show you what this *polenta* should taste like, I can show you
the proper way to make *pasta*—but, for the rest! Each day I
offer my skill—which I cannot exercise—I offer my knowledge—of which I cannot take advantage—to Our Lady as a
sacrifice. I tell her—today I make *polenta*, but imagine that I
am preparing for You, dear Mother of God, Soufflé Pole

Nord, or Crêpes des Gourmets, perhaps Tournedos Rossini or Poularde Polignac. Ah!" She sighed gustily, for she was a stout woman with a large amount of chest development. "I only hope that Our Lady enjoys the thought of these dishes as I enjoy—almost with tears—the careful preparation. In my mind only, remember, Antonia."

Antonia did not learn cooking which held any great variety, but she learnt exquisite cleanliness, a knowledge of flavouring—no matter how simple the dish—and she knew that she longed, almost passionately, to know more.

When she went home on Friday nights the state of her own home horrified her. She had been filled with a love of cleanliness, her nostrils had absorbed the fresh, sweet smell of beeswax, and she had come to have a great respect for fine linen no matter how old and worn. She loved the orderliness of the convent; the quiet, the tranquillity. True, there were times when Mother Lucia grew irritated and even spoke sharply to any girl who could not make the stitches sufficiently small and regular as she deemed necessary, but these were rare occasions, and the small storms never lasted for more than a few moments. She had learned something of dairy work from Sister Maria Pia; she could churn butter which the nuns made and sold to such people as could afford to buy it. She could milk, she had been taught that hens, geese, and even pigs throve better if they were kept clean and fed regularly. She had learnt to make jam, and to preserve fruit, beans and mushrooms, and the sight of the big cupboards, their shelves filled with jars all neatly labelled, never failed to delight her.

On week-days she was tired when she got home, for slowly she had come to stay at the convent later than the other girls, helping this nun, or doing some work for that sister. When she arrived home she longed to get to bed, to stretch her limbs and relax. Her mother laughed at her on account of the time she spent brushing her hair, on her insistence that she must carry water and soap into the outhouse, strip to the waist and wash before she went to bed.

"They're making a fine lady of you, my girl," she would say. "Giving you ideas too high for your station of life. Remember that after all you're only a peasant. You don't see your father and me washing all the good oil out of our skin, do you?"

Antonia had no feeling of being drawn to the religious life. She enjoyed going to Mass; she said her prayers in the firm conviction that, if it were for her good, they would be answered. The nuns never suggested to her that she should contemplate embracing the religious life. They realized that the child was happy with them, that she enjoyed working and that she was eager for knowledge. Not particularly for knowledge which was imparted to her by Mother Angelica, but for the knowledge of cooking, mending, cleaning and tending the animals.

Reverend Mother, speaking to Mother Angelica one evening after Benediction, said, "Mother, what of the little Trolli girl? How old is she now?"

"Antonia, Reverend Mother? She must be nearly twelve. A good child, not over-fond of learning—that is, book-learning —but as ready to absorb anything concerning housework and the kitchen as a sponge absorbs water."

"Might it be possible that she has a vocation, think you?"

Mother Angelica shook her head. "I doubt it, Reverend Mother. Mind, the child is good, says her prayers regularly, is attentive when Father Dominic gives his lessons on religious practice and precept, but she shows no particular devotion. Have you noticed, Reverend Mother," the nun asked tentatively, "that she grows quite remarkably pretty?"

"I have, Mother," the Superior's tone was a little grim, "and it disturbs me a little. Her family—oh, good enough people, but living in a haphazard way, from hand to mouth I gather. The sister—she came here you may remember for a few months, then tired of learning and never came again—is, so I hear from Father Dominic, not quite as steady as she might be. Without the benefits of religion how can we hope for her to be? The father told Father Dominic that he was worried about her; she stays out late, and spends all the money she makes at the factory on cheap finery. Not a good example for little Antonia. Still," she sighed, "we must trust that Our Lady will protect her."

Antonia was growing to like her home less and less. Lately there had been scenes between her mother and Carolina; once Maria had beaten her daughter, and Antonia had been terrified. Her father looked disturbed, and her two brothers made no attempt to hide their contempt for their elder sister.

Carolina was defiant and impudent. "No good staring at me like that, Marco! I earn my wages, I've a right to spend them where I wish."

Marco returned heavily, "From what I hear, you spend them *on* whom you wish. You'll get yourself into a mess one of these days."

Carolina swung her skirts and turned her back. "Mind your own business!"

"It'll be our business if you come home with a bastard. That Luigi's no good to anyone. He landed a girl over at Severoni with a baby, and her father kicked her out!"

"Oh, shut up! You judge others by yourself, I suppose."

Franco, who was growing broad-shouldered and heavy like his father, who worked honestly and was gaining the respect of the whole village as a good workman, said, "That's sufficient! Marco's right, Luigi Penachi wants girls for one thing only. Once he's got what he wants, he's off like a rabbit. Better watch what you're doing, Carolina."

She tossed her head so that her thick hair swung and danced up and down.

"You know a devil of a lot about everything, don't you?"

"No, but I know a devil of a lot about Luigi Penachi."

Antonia listened, and wondered. She knew Luigi, a tall, thin fellow who was said to travel in something mysterious, something which was forbidden by the law and the Church. She had never discovered what the commodity was, and suspected that it might be lipstick and scent. She didn't like him; she had met him once on her way from the convent and he had smiled at her, and offered her a *caramella*.

Mother Angelica had told them all in class that they must never accept sweets from men, because there might be poison in them, and so Antonia had shaken her head and walked on quickly. Luigi had thrown back his shining brilliantined head and laughed. He had said in a loud voice, "Better take some lessons from your sister, no?"

How did you "land" a girl with a baby? If you were married it seemed quite easy to have babies, and what was this "one thing" for which Luigi wanted girls? Antonia was not completely ignorant; few girls whose lives bring them into close contact with the farmyard and its inhabitants are ignorant, but she had never applied what she had seen and learnt from birds and beasts to human beings.

Mother Angelica had said, "Remember that Saint Paul says there are some things which should not be even spoken of among you." And when Maddelena had told her that she knew something which was most exciting, Antonia listened to an account of the propagation of the species which was half solid commonsense and half pornography.

She pushed Maddelena away, saying, "Oh, go on, you dirty thing!"

"It's true, I promise it's true, 'Tonia."

"Well, I don't want to hear it." She wrinkled her straight small nose. "It's—as you tell it—just dirty."

Maddelena flushed, looked sulky and said, "All right—ask your sister Carolina. She'll know," and giggled.

Antonia knew that her own face went scarlet, because she had an uneasy feeling that Carolina would know about all this nastiness, and that she had no right to be in possession of the information. When she went home on the Friday evening which followed she found her mother with her head in her arms weeping noisily.

"Mama, what is the matter? Mama, why are you crying?"

Her mother raised a drenched and blotted face, and between her sobs told her that Carolina was a wicked girl, she had run away from home, and it was said that she had not gone alone.

"Who has gone with her, Mama? Her friend, Celia Manzoni?"

"No, indeed, she has gone with Luigi Penachi. She left a note, she says that he is going to marry her when they get to Milano. She has taken all her new clothes, and two hundred lire which I had hidden away in a box for your father's new trousers. Oh, *Dio mio*, oh, *Santa Maria Vergine*! What will happen to her!"

When Maria told her husband, Antonia watched his heavy face flush to a dark, ugly red, he clenched his hands, and the veins on his neck stood out like cords. He seemed incapable of speech, and sat there silent, while his eyes grew more and more bloodshot. Suddenly he stretched out his hand and caught Antonia by the shoulder, dragging her to him. Instinctively she tried to hang back, but he drew her close and she could smell the scent of *vino* on his breath.

"Listen," he said, "listen to me. Your sister has gone to walk the streets of Milano. She will sell her body for money to men she doesn't even know! This man will never marry her, never! No man goes to buy a cow when he can get milk cheaply from the milkshop—aye, and clean milk too. Hear me!

There may be fathers who would go to Milano to bring her back. I am not one of them. We don't want her back. I would not waste money on the train fare to go and find her! Remember, my girl, keep yourself clean, behave yourself, for if you followed your worthless sister—I would kill you myself, with these hands. You understand?"

She whispered, "Yes, Papa," and he let her go. Her mother was still sobbing, and her father sank back into his sullen silence. Antonia did not feel very much; she disliked seeing her mother cry, she had hated the way her father had spoken to her, but she had never been very fond of her sister, and if she had gone to "walk the streets" in Milano, well, that was what the streets were for, surely?

Later that evening, when she stood outside the cottage in the stillness of the purple dusk of the evening, her brother Franco joined her. They stood there together, looking out over the wide valley.

A fox barked away on the hillside. Antonia heard a rat rustle through the long grass; a bird gave its sleepy evening call, and sank into silence again. Over the tall cypress a star shone suddenly, very bright, steady and clear. There was a scent of newly-cut grass in the air, and from the sawmill the sharp tang of sawdust came to them. Antonia drew a deep breath.

"It's nice, isn't it?" she said.

Franco answered, "Yes, fields, and rivers, pasture, hay and such things are all right. It's people who make everything dirty and disgusting, people like our precious sister!"

"Franco, what has she really done?"

"Done?" he echoed. "Done? She ran off with Luigi Penachi. To Milano."

"But what for? She could have been married to him here."

Franco gave a barking laugh, not unlike the sound which

the fox away on the hills had made. "Marry him! He doesn't want to marry her, he wants to sleep with her, you foolish girl. He'll get tired of her and leave her, then she'll have to find some-one else to go to bed with her—someone who'll pay her!"

Antonia sighed. She felt that she ought to understand, and in some vague way she realized that—right at the back of her head—she understood that the whole thing was disgraceful. It was puzzling, though, disturbing and puzzling at the same time.

"Does she love him, Franco?"

"Love!" Again he gave his barking laugh. "Love! Her kind don't love men, and men don't love them. They just—want each other! It's like animals—cocks and hens, sows and boars! Love is something different. I'll tell you something, 'Tonia. I'm in love, yes, in love with Giselda Zanbrini. Her father's rich, but he knows I'm a good workman, and when I can keep her properly he's going to give me a share in his timber mill. I shan't much like telling him that my sister's run away with Penachi! Curse Carolina! Oh, Giselda will under-stand; she loves me, believes in me. You don't think that we would go on like Carolina and Penachi, do you?"

She answered eagerly, "No, Franco, no, of course not!"

That night, lying in the bed which she had always shared with Carolina, she thought how pleasant it was to have the whole bed to herself, even though the sheets might have been cleaner, and the stale scent of Carolina's brilliantine still hung about the pillow. She wondered where her sister was; if she was happy with her Luigi, if she loved him—in spite of what Franco had said? What was this being in love? She had seen young men and girls walking out in their Sunday clothes, looking rather stiff and self-conscious; she had been told that they were engaged to be married, that they were in love with each other. They never looked particularly happy, she thought; generally they seemed rather oppressed with what lay before them.

Franco had said that he and Giselda would never go to bed

together. Antonia was not surprised, for Giselda was a heavy-featured young woman with a sallow complexion, and, although Franco was good and hard-working, he didn't wash a great deal, and only shaved once a week. Perhaps they would just live in the same house, and Giselda would do the cooking, and have babies and wash Franco's shirts.

Her mind ran on, she was growing drowsy, and her thoughts came disjointedly. One day she would be in love; she would get married and have a cottage. She would see that the sheets were beautifully clean, and that the pillows didn't smell of stale scent and brilliantine. It was strange how fresh, new smells were pleasant, and old, stale smells nasty. Like the flowers in the brass vases on the altar at the convent and in the Church. While they were fresh, when she and Sister Monica Mary did them every Saturday, they smelt beautiful, but after a week, when the next Saturday came round, the flowers and the water were horrible! Slimy, sticky, and smelling like the stagnant pond near Farmer Vicini's lower field.

The smell of a wood, that was pleasant. The wild herbs which were crushed underfoot and sprang up again when you had passed; the smell of violets which you couldn't see because they hid under broad leaves, even the smell of the garlic—such a pretty flower it had—was fresh and sweet in the open air. One day she would walk through a wood, perhaps without shoes so that she might feel the dew on her feet, and she'd meet someone—not someone who offered her sweets, and had hair which shone with grease, but someone who was young and kind, someone with a smile, someone who liked clean, fresh things as she did. Someone who liked the sting of cold water, the tang of the air in the early morning, the shine of copper pans—and so she fell asleep, lulled by the deep breathing of her two brothers in the room separated from hers by a partition of thick cardboard which Carolina had brought home from the factory.

CHAPTER TWO

To Antonia it seemed that everyone was talking about war. Carolina as a subject of discussion was abandoned; instead, her father, Marco and Franco sat talking, talking, talking about this terrible thing called war.

She asked questions, and her father rumbled out answers which did not make things much clearer to her. She stood listening, her small face with its bright blue eyes intent and serious, trying to understand what it all meant.

"The Germans," her father said, "are greedy. Maybe they learnt to be greedy from the English, who have always wanted land and more land. Well, now the Germans want some. Then this Archduke has been killed. I don't know that he lived a very Christian life—but that doesn't give men the right to murder him, no?"

"Did the English murder him, Papa?"

Pietro scratched his head. "Well, no—no, most emphatically they didn't. Friends of theirs did, it would appear. This makes the Germans very angry—and the Austrians also."

"Did the Germans and Austrians like this man who was murdered?"

Again Pietro scratched his head. "Now what is this—like? I think not; not much, anyway. Germans like no people except themselves. So now they will all start to fight. What a thing!"

Franco asked, his broad hands spread on his knees, "Do you think Italy will fight, Papa?"

"Ah, who knows? War, my son, is like a weed in a garden; once it starts, once it gets hold of men's minds, it is difficult to get rid of. I can't see into the future, huh!"

Father Dominic preached about this war; he said that the dead Archduke had been only a pawn. Marco said that pawns were used in a game called *scacchi* (chess), and that it meant someone who didn't matter a lot. That seemed strange to Antonia, because if he didn't matter much why did all these countries want to go to war about him? Mother Angelica said that they must all pray that there would not be a war at all, but Marco and Franco seemed rather excited at the thought of it. Mother Angelica said that of course the Austrians had behaved very badly to Italy, and that indeed they still held parts of Italy which were not theirs by right at all.

"Who gave those parts to them, Mother?"

"They took them, my child."

"Then they're thieves, no?"

Mother Angelica clapped her hands. "Enough of this talk of war. We must pray that it will be averted. In England they have wise men who will do whatever is possible; in France also. Now, let us return to our studies."

Antonia lay awake at night and thought about the war. Since Carolina had gone she had cleaned the room. The sheets smelt of pleasant herbs, and when she laid her head on the pillow the sweet scent of rosemary filled her nostrils. Here, safely in bed, she could think quietly. In the room downstairs there were too many distractions, too much noise, and the general disorder which she hated.

Her father washing his feet, and sometimes cutting his corns with an old razor, always made her shiver; so did the sight of her mother skinning a rabbit on the table where she made *polenta*, and which Antonia knew she never scrubbed properly; of Franco sitting unwashed and unshaven reading a torn newspaper—he only shaved when he was going to see Giselda or when he was going to Mass; Marco cleaning the pelt of a fox which he had shot in the mountains, and which he was going to sell to a man from the next village—it smelt horrible, and Antonia would feel her small stomach heave as she passed the board where the pelt was nailed. Added to these things were the hens picking about the floor, the old disused things—rusty rat-traps, worn-out brushes, pieces of rag, which were never thrown away, but lay about in corners, offensive to the eye and the sense of smell. How she hated that atmosphere!

She had tried, crying, "Now, Mama, today you shall rest and I will clean the house! You shall see how I will make everything shine."

Maria had stared at her. "What's wrong with the house? I have swept the floor. No, no, I understand what it means—this cleaning and shining. I shall never be able to find anything again! No, leave it; this is how I like it. I have so much to do that I am obliged to know where everything is—ready to my hand. You have too many convent ideas, 'Tonia."

In her own bed, even though the mattress was terribly lumpy, she could lie and stare out of the little window and watch the stars come out, twinkling at her in a manner which was friendly, reassuring. This war . . . Of course she understood what it was all about now, it was because someone had killed an Archduke, and because England had taken all the land in the world and now Germany wanted some. It seemed that they were strange people, these Germans. Melena had told her that they had two heads and ate new-born babies for breakfast. Antonia did not believe it; there must be many Germans and the supply of new-born babies would not be sufficient to feed them all. Francesca, who had an uncle who had been a waiter at places with curious names such as Rizz, Charton, Savoia—which was very curious, for Savoia was in Italy—and Clarich, said that all the English were very rich, they ate curious things too—raw beef, and a terrible drink known as *thé*. Not the infusions you took as a purge, or for colds or headaches, but a dreadful infusion which they drank from large bowls, each person taking at least two litres every afternoon. The French were very gay and loved dancing and singing, though they did not sing as well as Italians. And to think that while she lay in bed, with the whole valley sleeping, with the birds nestling their heads under their wings, and nothing stirring except the foxes who were slinking about in the mountains searching for food, that men—somewhere—were killing each other. Shooting guns, throwing things of which Franco had told her, called bombs, firing cannons, and being killed. She shivered.

Father Dominic had said, "Don't be afraid. Even if the Austrians got into Italy—which God forbid—they would most certainly come down the Adige valley, and the Altro—Adige, Vicenza and the city of Verona. Why should they come here—here is nothing!"

He asked them to look at the big map which hung on the wall, and Mother Angelica showed them all the places he had mentioned. He smiled and rubbed his hands, saying, "So here, please God, we shall all be safe. We must pray—pray for all men who are fighting, and always remember that though the world may be dark, there is in each church a light burning always, always before the altar. The world can never be quite dark while those lights burn."

Italy had joined in the war, again Papa explained, and Antonia again tried to understand. This time it was a little easier, for he made it quite plain that Austria had a big mouth, and having swallowed part of Italy was anxious to swallow the remainder. This, he said, the Italians could not allow, so they were going to kill every single Austrian and send their Emperor to an island, as the English had done with Napoleon Bonaparte.

For the first time in her life she felt an admiration for her father. She told the girls at the convent that she understood everything about the war. "My papa is very clever," she boasted. "He tells me what it is all about, and what will happen when it is over and Italy is the greatest nation in the world."

ii

Franco drank his soup noisily, then pushed away the bowl, and leaned back in his chair. He stuck his thumbs in his belt and announced, "I am going!"

Marco also leaned back and plunged his hands into the pockets of his trousers. "I also am going!" he said.

Their mother stared at them, then threw up her hands, exclaiming:

"*Mama Mia! Santa Maria Vergine!*" she began to cry, then suddenly her grief turned to fury, she railed at them both. "You would go and leave me here? On what shall I live? On what your father earns—and drinks! First your sister deserts me, then you two must go as well. And for what, tell me that? To walk about the cities wearing a soldier's uniform. To make eyes at loose girls! To spend money on them. And I must scrape along here living like a pig, and an ill-fed one at that."

They listened in silence until her tirade ceased, then Marco said, "Listen, Mama, if we don't go—they'll come for us. We ought both to have done military service before, but—well, it was arranged somehow. There won't be much walking about big cities; anyway, the uniforms that I have seen wouldn't attract any girl."

"No, that is true," Franco agreed. "And as for spending money . . ." He laughed. "Italian private soldiers aren't millionaires or anything like them! It's no use raving or crying, Mama, just help us to get our things together. Antonia, give us a hand. Is my clean shirt ironed?"

When their father returned from work they told him. It

was evident that he had been celebrating Italy's—at the
moment non-existent—victories.

Pietro embraced both his sons, his eyes streaming with
tears. He, too, would stand side by side with them fighting
Italy's battles; together they would carry through a new
Risorgimento. Neither Franco nor Marco appeared visibly
elated at the prospect. Pietro indulged in a great flow of
rhetoric; he waved his arms; he took Maria in his arms and
told her that she was the wife of a hero and the mother of two
others. He caught Antonia—who was ironing Franco's clean
shirt—to him, almost causing her to scorch it, and kissed her soft
hair, murmuring that with her father and two noble brothers
fighting in her defence she was safe from the invading German
and Austrian hordes.

Franco and Marco stood by, watching and listening
stolidly, their faces immovable, until their father turned to
them and announced his intention of going to the Town Hall
immediately.

"It's closed, Papa," Franco said, "you'll have to wait until
the morning."

"Wait!" his father exclaimed. "Wait! Does Italy wait for
her defenders to rally to her aid? Italy never sleeps, Italy waits
and watches. The Germans, the British, the French—what are
they, tell me? *L'Italià fara da sé*—by herself—with the strong
arms of her sons—this war will be won by Italy. *Avante!* To
the Town Hall, to the mayor, to all in authority, they shall
welcome with open arms Pietro Trolli and his gallant sons.
Avante!"

Unwillingly the two young men went with him. Later they
told Antonia that there had been a great scene. The mayor
was angry at being disturbed, and told Pietro smartly that first
he was too old, and secondly that persistent drunks were of no
use to the country. The sons returned home to put together
their small parcels of clothes, their father remained in the

osteria drinking, returning when the sky was already showing pale in the dawn, proclaiming himself to be Garibaldi, and announcing that the mayor was a traitor. He then fell into bed, and was still sound asleep when his sons crept quietly out into the light of early morning. Antonia watched them walk away, side by side, swinging their bundles, and felt for the first time that the war was a reality, something which was threatening them all.

They had a postcard from Franco saying that he and his brother were in Vicenza, and shortly leaving for Monfalcone. They were well and the life was not bad.

She went daily to the convent. Some of the nuns were growing old, and her help was invaluable although she was so young. Mother Anna Maria said, "This one has a head on her shoulders!" and Mother Lucia, sighing, told Reverend Mother that without the help of little Trolli she would never be able to complete all the mending which must be done.

So Antonia at thirteen worked in the kitchen, worked at the sewing, and helped with the milking; it was hard work, but she liked it far better than being at home, trying to persuade her mother to let her reduce the dirty, untidy kitchen to some kind of order.

Most of the younger men had gone to join the army, and the factory needed more girls to work there. Maria wished Antonia to get a place there; the pay wasn't good, but it was better than nothing, and without the contributions of Franco and Marco it was difficult to buy sufficient food. Years in the convent had made Antonia in many ways older than the average girl of her years, and in other ways singularly young and inexperienced. She had never made great friends with the village girls, and the thought of being in close proximity to a crowd of them terrified her. She had grown to speak as she heard the nuns speak, and this had come about unconsciously, and not because she wished to be "superior" or to "give herself airs". She had never enjoyed walking about the village in the evening, arm in arm with girls who giggled and whispered and made strange confidences to each other. This for the simple reason that she enjoyed other things so much more. To be entrusted with Mother Anna Maria's precious cookery book, to copy the methods of preparing various dishes and to copy out the recipes in her careful, round, childish hand was one of her greatest joys. Carefully too she made lists of the words which she could not understand— *D'Uxelles, faire revenir, chaudfroid, boudin, ramequin, pirepoix* and the like—and these she would take to Mother Anna Maria who would expound their meaning, and when it was possible within the limitations of the convent cuisine, give Antonia a demonstration as to how to prepare these things or use these methods.

When her mother's insistence grew, so that Antonia felt that she never entered the house without the word "factory" being flung at her, she tried to make her mother realize that she cost nothing for food, which she had in the convent, that she was allowed to do her washing and ironing there, that Mother Lucia found her pieces of material with which to patch her clothes, and that sometimes the nuns would give her vegetables and fruit.

"I don't cost anything, Mama," Antonia protested. "I work hard, and one day I shall be able to earn far more than the girls in the factory."

"One day," her mother repeated. "Ah, this one day—it is the day which never comes, we all know that."

At last in desperation Antonia went to the Reverend Mother, and told her that she was afraid she must leave the convent and take some work in the factory.

"You won't like that, will you, Antonia?"

"Not very much, Reverend Mother. But my mother insists

that I must earn money, for now my brothers are away she finds it difficult to provide all we need."

The nun watched her anxious little face. She had grown very fond of this child, who had blossomed so bravely under their care. She had never been lazy or dilatory, she appeared to long for knowledge, and to be quick and intelligent. The Reverend Mother knew her home, a dirty, untidy place, with a mother who had no method, no orderliness, and a father who was perpetually drinking too much. She remembered what had happened to Carolina, and frowned when she thought how easy it might be for this child to go the same way. Antonia was pretty, she had a fine, smooth skin, her hair—hidden now under her print working-cap—was always beautifully clean. No, it was terrible to think of banishing this child to such a home and such surroundings.

"How much do they get at the factory, Antonia?" she asked.

"As much as seventy-five lire a week, Reverend Mother."

"As a beginner you would not get so much, no?"

"Perhaps thirty-eight, Reverend Mother."

The older woman nodded, made some notes on a slip of paper before she spoke. Then she said, "My child, this is a poor Order, but we can—and will—give you thirty-five lire a week. You will have your food, and you can continue to do your own washing here. Your food—of course. You will help Mother Anna Maria and Mother Lucia——"

She saw the flush rise in the child's cheeks, saw how her blue eyes sparkled, heard the sudden catch of her breath, and noticed how she had clasped her hands very tightly. Antonia said, "Reverend Mother, I do the milking too; may I go on doing it?"

"Yes, my child, the milking too. Antonia, you have never felt that you were drawn to the religious life, have you?"

The blue eyes met hers very steadily, instinctively she knew that this child would speak the truth, and never attempt to temporize.

"No, Reverend Mother. I love going to Mass, I know that it is all quite real, real and true; I love Our Lady, and the Blessed Saints, and—oh, everything we are taught here. I have often thought that it would be wonderful to be—well, to be inside, so safe, to know that you were helping people in the outside world by your prayers, but—I can't quite explain, Reverend Mother. I think that I was made like Saint Martha, not like Saint Mary."

The nun smiled. "Are you then 'troubled about many things'?"

"I don't know, Reverend Mother. Not *troubled*, but I may be too interested in many things. If you're a nun, you have to be only really interested in one thing, haven't you?"

"*One* thing, dear child, must be the primary thought, the first interest, but—you may have others in a lesser degree. There, run along to Mother Lucia. I think that I understand what you mean. God bless you."

The war dragged on, news filtered through to the village, often incorrect, frequently distorted, of the armies. Neither Marco nor Franco were good at letter-writing, and their communications were of the most brief. Antonia wrote to them at the dictation of her mother, letters which were filled with pious sentiments, and grumbles concerning the difficulty of making both ends meet. Sometimes Antonia protested gently, saying that it would be nice to tell them of pleasant things.

Her mother eyed her sourly. "Pleasant things! Tell me what are the pleasant things, please? Papa was drunk last night, the rent is not paid, the tax collector says that he cannot wait any longer, we owe money to the butcher—are these the pleasant things we shall tell them?"

Maria accepted the lire which Antonia brought home each week, though she grumbled that the girl could have earned more at the factory. Pietro took Antonia's side. "Let the girl alone; she's only a child. Thirty-five lire is better than a smack in the face with a dirty stick. Leave her alone, Maria."

News came of Caporetto, and hung like a dark cloud over everything. Antonia felt that the sun itself was darkened, that the air held an additional chill. She thought that even the chirping of the birds was muted, as if they mourned for the men who had died, and were ashamed for those who had been found wanting. All her life, the very sound of the word— Caporetto—caused her to shudder.

Pietro drank steadily for several days after the news came, and on the fourth day returned to the quarry, heavy-eyed and sullen. About two in the afternoon Antonia, who had been hanging out some washing in the courtyard of the convent, heard her name called.

She ran back to the kitchen. Reverend Mother was there, speaking rapidly and quietly to Mother Anna Maria.

"Yes, Reverend Mother, you called me?"

"My child, you must go home at once, your poor father has been hurt, they are bringing him home. Do all that you can to help your mother."

"Is Papa dead, Reverend Mother?"

"No, my child, but gravely, terribly injured. Go quickly."

As Antonia ran home she caught up with the men who were carrying her father on a hurdle. She scarcely dared look at him, but when she summoned up sufficient courage to do so she saw that his face was covered with blood, his eyes were closed, his mouth hung open and from time to time he uttered a muffled roar, a sound which reminded her of Farmer Vicini's bull. It was a dreadful sound, it seemed impossible that it came from a human being, there was something so primitive, so innately furious in the sound.

One man said, "If we get him home alive that's all we shall do."

"Is he very badly hurt?" she asked.

"Seems that his back's broken—listen to him," as Pietro uttered another furious roar. "Makes your blood curdle."

She ran on to prepare her mother, but the room was already filled with people, all talking at once, all the men explaining how the accident had happened, the women voicing ejaculatory prayers and invocations to the Saints. Antonia's eyes went to the bed, where the sheet was turned back and the pillows arranged ready for Pietro. How dirty it looked! How she wished that all these people had not seen the grubby sheets and the dingy blankets! She felt ashamed and shy that the state of her home should be plain to everyone. The men carried Pietro in, still uttering his dreadful stifled roars. Maria wailed and called his name, but he did not seem to know her. Antonia shrank back against the wall, hoping passionately that no one would call her over to the bed. A discussion began about sending for the doctor; voices were raised, and for the time the injured man seemed to be forgotten.

"The doctor!" cried a man with a black beard. "Of what use is this doctor, tell me? Wiser to send for the priest."

Another man who was known to be an unbeliever sniffed scornfully. "And of what use is the priest? Can he cure broken bones! Pah!"

"Send for both," suggested another man, "then at least all has been done that can be done."

"Neither will do him any good," asserted one of the men who had helped to carry the hurdle. "In my opinion his back is broken—no man lives long with a broken back."

"How did it happen, Beppi?"

Again the torrent of voices began, everyone talking at once. Antonia heard the words—detonator, dynamite, blasting— then Beppi's voice rose above the others, telling how the

warning had been given that everyone must take cover as the
explosion was about to take place.

"Pietro was not quite himself, you understand. Last night
he was very drunk; in fact he has been drinking for days. He
stumbled and fell, the explosion happened, and there he was
lying with a great rock on top of him." From the bed came
Pietro's strange roar, as if he wished to take part in the discussion and to draw attention to himself as the chief actor in
the tragedy.

The priest came, and almost on his heels the village doctor
in whom no one had the least faith. He was inept, casual, and
his observance of elementary hygiene was of the slightest.
Again the story of the accident was told, punctuated by the
dreadful bellowings from the injured man.

Beppi said, "He grows weaker, at first the noise was twice
as loud."

The doctor made his examination; roughly and cursorily
it was done. He said to two of the men who were assisting
him, "Turn him on to his back, he's dying. Now, Father, it's
your turn."

The men pulled off their hats, the women cried, although
few of them had liked Pietro, regarding him as a bad influence
on their own husbands. The priest put his stole round his
shoulders, and his voice, though low-pitched, seemed to fill
the whole room. Only the avowed unbeliever remained apart,
leaning against the wall, his eyes scornful.

"*Omnipotens et misericors Deum. . . .*"

Antonia knelt down and prayed that her father might have
a good death. The low voice of the priest continued, gently
rising and falling; there were murmurs from the men and
women as they associated themselves with the prayers which
were to ease Pietro Trolli's passing, and help to cleanse his
soul before it fled to his Maker.

Antonia opened her eyes and looked towards the bed, the

priest was bending over her father, speaking to him in a whisper; once Pietro voiced his terrible bellow, and then a new sound filled the room, the strange, rattling noise which heralds death. She closed her eyes and prayed for her father.

Later women came and washed the dead man, arranged his hands, passive now, on his breast, and two of the nuns came bringing candles which they lit at the corners of the bed. Antonia watched and listened. She was not conscious of any great grief, but the sight of her father's still face frightened her. She thought that there was a new presence in the room, something strange, inexplicable; something which filled you with dread and forced your eyes back again and again to where the dead man lay.

Her mother sat rocking backwards and forwards, moaning. "What will become of us? We shall starve—my child and I. How shall we even be able to buy bread! God has laid His hand heavily on us."

Women kept coming in and out, the carpenter came to measure Pietro for his coffin, the owner of the quarry came and said that he and his partners were ready to pay for a first-class funeral. He was a small, paunchy man, who seemed frightened to death of the still figure on the bed. The news that the owners would pay for the funeral seemed to bring great comfort to Maria, and she told each succeeding visitor with pride that the owners were paying because Pietro had been such a fine and honest workman. Don Dominic returned and said that he had made all the arrangements, and Maria asked anxiously if the driver of the hearse would wear his traditional white wig. The fact that he was instructed to do so appeared to afford her great satisfaction.

Antonia watched and listened; the whole thing seemed strange and unreal to her. It was like what she imagined a play might be on the stage, although she had never entered a theatre in her life. Everyone seemed to be acting a part assuming a character. No, not Don Dominic, who was as he had always been—kindly, quiet and gentle; but the others who came and shed tears, who stood by the bed where Pietro lay, murmuring prayers, wiping their eyes, and making the Sign of the Cross not once but ten times, bewildered her. She knew that her father had not been popular, he had been aggressive and quarrelsome; true, he had performed his religious duties with meticulous care, but even his religion had not prevented him from wasting money on *vino* or beating his wife when he grew angry under the influence of drink.

Did these people really believe that he was destined to find a place among the Saints, with gentle Saint Francis, with the Holy Saint Catherine, submissive Saint Lucia, and the wise Saint Benedict? Did God forgive everything, even when a man was unable to speak—to think—and only able to make dreadful noises like an animal? Or were these dolorous women relieved that Pietro Trolli was dead and so could no longer incite their husbands to drink, lead them into heated arguments and keep them out of their homes until such a late hour that even the patient keeper of the *osteria* intimated in no doubtful terms that he preferred their room to their company?

She asked her mother if she would like something to eat, and Maria cried that it was impossible to eat while her dear husband lay dead. That again was strange, for her mother had often railed against her father, said that he was a waster, and cared nothing if they were brought to want and extreme poverty.

Quietly Antonia made some coffee, and with some bread-and-butter placed it before her mother. Maria cried, "No, how can I eat when my heart is broken?" But she drank the coffee and ate a roll, and seemed better for it.

Late at night two women came to sit with the dead man. Antonia, who felt that she could drop asleep at any moment, left them and went up to her room. She had made up the bed in her brother's room for her mother and crept into her own bed, stretching out her limbs with relief; it seemed that she had been standing and kneeling for hours. In the room below she could hear the sound of voices rising and falling; they did not seem to be unduly depressed. She lay there, lying straight in her bed, and realized that from now life would be different. Her thirty-five lire could not possibly support herself and her mother, pay the rent, and buy clothes. She must find some work which would bring her more money. How? Where? She had no idea. She only knew that she had certain gifts—Mother Anna Maria had said so, Mother Lucia had said so; even Mother Angelica had admitted that, while she was no scholar, she worked hard and applied herself. Surely she could put such small gifts as she possessed to better use than by entering the hated factory?

She felt that once she entered the factory she was caught and would be forced to remain there, in an atmosphere she hated, until some man wished to have her for his wife. Then—perforce—she would marry, live in a house which with all the willingness in the world she could never keep in the sweet cleanliness which she loved. She would have children, grow old while still young, and slowly all the things she had learned —cooking, cleaning, exquisite laundry work—would be forgotten and she would grow old and untidy, tired and dispirited and—just go on from day to day.

Her slim body stiffened, she clenched her hands, and whispered, "No, no, I won't. I want something more than that. There are things in the world I want to see, to know—this village isn't the world! Carolina may have done wrong but she is seeing things! I want to *know*, want to taste, want to experience. I'm a woman now, not a child."

Her thoughts were not set out in such an orderly fashion, they were rushing through her mind, tumbling one over the other; but she knew what was in this determination of hers.

There was no thought of gaining great wealth or a high position, but there was a set purpose that she must go forward and use such gifts as had been given her.

She fell asleep, the sound of the murmuring voices below still in her ears, and awoke in the morning conscious that something had happened. Then her mind cleared and the mists of sleep dissolved. She remembered; her father was dead, he was lying in the room below waiting to be laid in his coffin. She lay quite still for a moment thinking of him, not unkindly, but without any particular sense of grief at his loss. She remembered his breath laden with the fumes of *vino*, she saw again his hands with the black hairs on their backs, and that mutilated finger which had always made her shudder. She remembered the day when Carolina had run away, how he had caught her to him, and talked rapidly, his hot eyes staring at her. She could feel the clutch of his hands still, the smell of dust and sweat which emanated from him.

She flung back the clothes, got out of bed and knelt praying for his soul. "Poor Papa, I hope that you'll be happy. I hope that God will forgive you all your sins, and be kind to you. Amen."

She admitted the men who had brought the coffin, the men from the village who brought the *tributo*, a great mass of flowers mounted on a stand like that which Mother Angelica used to hold the blackboard, only lighter, which had been subscribed for by the villagers.

Beppi said, "It was necessary to go by bicycle to Treponte to get this. Phew! What a weight it was, but it is magnificent—no?"

The men were offered wine, and then Father Dominic came, and the hearse, with the driver wearing a curious coat of the style of the early 19th century and a grimy white wig which did not fit, and showed his dark hair underneath. He came in, holding his cocked hat with its tarnished gold braid in his hand, and accepted a glass of wine. The small boy who was to carry the Cross propped it against the wall of the house and came in, self-important in his cotta and cassock. Antonia remembered two *caramelli* which she had put in a tin box and gave them to him. He sucked them with loud appreciation.

The procession formed, Maria held Antonia by the hand, they walked immediately after the coffin and the great tribute of flowers. First the men, in rows of three, then the women, all carrying lighted candles, while Don Dominic recited in his clear, gentle voice the Litany of the Saints.

As the sound reached Antonia, she thought how nice it was that all these important and holy people should be asked to interest themselves in Pietro Trolli.

"Omnes sancti Discipuli Domine," and the murmured response, *"Ora pro nobis*; then later, *"A subitanea et improvisa morte,"* and again the response, *"Libera nos Domine."*

The whole Litany gave her a sense of satisfaction, it provided for everything. The Saints, doctors of the Church, the Apostles, even Our Lord Himself and His Holy Mother were asked to be interested in Pietro Trolli, and then the prayers which followed, the prayer against sudden and unexpected death, against lightning and tempest and—*"A morte perpetua"* —everlasting death. Yes, surely her father should be well cared for and his future assured.

With a sense of great assurance and confidence Antonia entered the church holding her mother's hand.

CHAPTER THREE

THE day after the funeral Maria told Antonia, not without a certain bitter satisfaction, that she was going to apply for work at the factory.

"Since you are only prepared to work at the convent, doing tasks which do not mean that you soil your hands, it is necessary that your bereaved mother goes out to work! I shall be pitied by all the village, but it is necessary that we keep a roof over our heads and your thirty-five lire—what do they mean?—nothing."

So Maria went out early each morning, and returned in the evening, while Antonia cleaned the house as it had never been cleaned before and then went to the convent. She had never worked so hard in her life. She rose before her mother, prepared coffee, and rushed to the baker's to buy rolls. She put her mother's lunch into a tin box, and the moment she had left began her cleaning. On the way to the convent she bought something for their supper, and then hurried on to do the work which she loved and enjoyed.

The work in the factory appeared to suit her mother, for Antonia had never known her so cheerful, so talkative, so ready to laugh, as she recounted small incidents which had happened at her work. Maria Trolli had hated her life for years; she had loathed housework and cooking, and had reduced both to a minimum. In her heart she had envied Carolina working at the factory, with plenty of people to talk to, with the cheerful noise of machines, the voices of the women as they sang at their work, the sudden bursts of laughter, and the weekly pay packet which held money which she had earned, and for the spending of which she was responsible to no one.

All through her married life she had been forced to wring

money out of Pietro, who, while he was always ready to pay for drinks in the *osteria*, grudged every *soldi* which had to be spent on the barest necessities for the house, for food and clothes. Matters had improved somewhat when Franco and Marco began to work, but even so, every week Maria had to face a scene with Pietro when she asked for money for the rent, the taxes, and even to pay the cobbler for mending Pietro's boots.

Now with her own seventy-five lire, and Antonia's thirty-five each week, she felt both rich and independent. She scarcely noticed the change in the house, for the lack of cleanliness there had never bothered Maria Trolli. She enjoyed the food which Antonia prepared, and realized that the girl was a far better cook than she was herself. Although there were times when she sighed gustily, and spoke with emotion of "my poor Pietro, God rest his dear soul", she was happier than she had ever been. She took more pains with her appearance, keeping her hair well brushed, and indulging in more washing of her person than she had ever practised before.

The war dragged on. It seemed to be a long way off, Antonia thought, and wondered what the country was like where Franco and Marco were fighting. She heard stories of the bravery of the Alpini, of the Bersaglieri; listened to Father Dominic recounting the exploits of the gallant Brescia Division, and pictured her brothers as taking part in every engagement which was spoken of.

Then came the news of Monte Grappa, when Italians held their heads high and felt that their fighting men had wiped out the disaster of Caporetto. Monte Grappa meant the vindication of the army, it meant also that Franco and Marco Trolli lay dead, riddled with Austrian bullets.

Antonia felt stunned. Her father had seemed to her to be old, but Marco and Franco had been young, with life stretching before them. Franco had fallen in love, perhaps he had dreamed

of the time when he would marry his Giselda and have a home
and children. Antonia remembered how she had watched
them both walking away, carrying their bundles when they
left to join the army. She remembered how at the turn in the
road they had stopped and waved to her, and how she had
waved back, and shouted, "Go with God!"

Now they were dead. Never again would they see the
Spring come to the valley, watch the haze of heat which hung
over it in the Summer, watch the leaves change from green to
red and gold, or feel the keen, sharp wind which blew from
the mountains in Winter. And they were only two among so
many of Italy's young men, of England's youth, and the rising
generation of France.

Father Dominic read from the pulpit an account of the
division composed entirely of young men, they had fought like
tigers, showing no trace of fear, united against their common
foe, the hated Austrians. He read how their commanding
officer, seeing that their position was hopeless, ordered them to
retreat, and how they had cried, as with one voice, "*Avanti!
Viva Italia!*" and continued to hold the position until the great
majority of them fell dead or dying.

The women, and many of the men, in the congregation
cried, many sobbed audibly. Antonia squared her shoulders
and held her head erect. She fancied that she could hear
Franco's deep strong voice and Marco's lighter tones crying,
"*Avanti! Viva Italia!*" She felt proud, almost arrogant, as if
she longed to do something which should make her the peer
of her brothers.

During the afternoon people came crowding to the house,
women sobbed and condoled with Maria, calling her "the
afflicted one", and eyeing Antonia with disapproval because
she remained calm, her eyes dry and still holding their
expression of pride.

"How strange it is," said Sabina Zoppa, "that a girl can

remain without tears on hearing of the death of her two brothers!"

Maria said, "She is hard-hearted, Sabina, this one never sheds tears. When her beloved father—may his soul rest in peace—died, did she weep as I did——"

"As we all did," added Carlotta Finzi, who never missed a funeral, and visited every house where death had been to view the corpse. "How I cried for this poor, good man! I shall never forget."

"Not so his daughter," Maria assured them, her voice charged with righteous complacency; "she only bothered about making coffee and getting out sheets to make up her poor brother's bed for me. On the night of her father's death, one might have imagined she would have wished to sleep with her mother, no?"

Antonia walked to the table where they were sitting. She stood there, very straight, slim, and composed. The women stared at her, she never seemed to belong to their life at all, she was "different", and all people who were "different" were suspect.

She said, in her clear, young voice, which lacked the accent which distorted the Italian which the village spoke, "I do not cry for my brothers because I am very proud of them. They were good boys, hard workers, but they went to fight for their country, to die, signore, so that we might live in peace. They might have obeyed their officer, and saved their lives, but they remembered what Garibaldi said, 'Rome or death'; they chose death, and the honour that went with it."

Sabina said, "Who mentioned Rome? Who mentioned Garibaldi? Not me!"

Maria said peevishly, "She learns to talk like that at the convent."

The other nodded. "Ah, nuns' talk! What do they know of the loss of sons, never having borne any?"

Antonia left the table, and opening the door went out into the fresh air. The kitchen had felt suffocating. She had hated the women's talk, feeling that it was false, emotional and self-indulgent—all this talk of death, deprivation, and affliction. Things that really mattered were too deep, too private, to chatter about. She did not want to talk about her brothers, she wanted to remember them, as she had seen them last, young, strong and eager for life.

ii

The war ended, and everywhere Antonia saw changes. Father Dominic had died during the last Winter of the war, many people were ill, the ground was soaked with rain, there were biting winds, and his boots were long past their first youth. He had gone tramping over the muddy roads, his clothes hanging heavily on his thin body because they were drenched, his feet cold and damp.

Antonia remembered one day when the rain was pouring down. She had met him, and had been struck by the pallor of his face and the heaviness of his eyes. He had spoken to her as he always did, asking how she was, and if she were well.

"I am very well, Father, very happy in my work." Then, greatly daring, she added, "Father, can't you go home and get your cassock dried? It is wringing wet."

He shook his head. "I have a sick call, 'Tonia. You'd not have me stay at home drying my clothes, would you? No, no, you—the sister of two soldiers—know that I am a soldier too." His eyes twinkled. "I have to obey orders. God bless you, 'Tonia."

He contracted pneumonia, the nuns nursed him, but his frame was too weak to fight the fierce flame of the disease. Antonia felt that the grief of the villagers was genuine, that the tears shed were not merely demonstrations of a passing emotion, but for the loss of one who had been not only their spiritual director but their friend.

A new priest was appointed, a young man filled with energy and zeal. Until then there had been no authorized school; the nuns had taught the village girls, and Father Dominic had added to his multitudinous tasks by teaching the boys. Recently the Bishop had set plans on foot to build a new school and at the time of Father Dominic's death it was practically finished. The question of providing staff had not yet been settled. Father Dominic held that it was possible and advisable for the nuns to continue to teach there—after all, there were not very many children, and Mother Angelica was quite capable of giving them the necessary instruction.

The Bishop had laid his fine fingers together, and had listened patiently to the old priest who, he felt, privately, might be the most holy of men but was undoubtedly terribly slow and utterly incapable of marshalling his facts.

"Your lordship, Mother Angelica has taught the village girls for many years, and they are as well taught as any girls you could wish to find. I have given lessons to the boys, and the boys in our village, while perhaps lacking in some of the modern subjects . . ." the old, gentle voice droned on; the Bishop longed to yawn quite openly.

He held up his well-kept hand. "Quite, quite, Father. I am sure that you and Mother Angelina——"

"Angelica, Your Grace."

"Of course, Mother Angelica, have done admirably. I shall give the whole matter my most earnest thought. I shall pray that we may be guided wisely. Good-bye, Father."

Now Father Dominic was dead, and Father Paulo reigned in his stead. Father Paulo was sent for by the Bishop. He was a good-looking young man, well shaved, his hair properly cut, his clothes well kept and brushed. The Bishop felt a sense of relief, the other man—Dominic—holy, no doubt, he had most certainly worked himself to death—yes, the old-fashioned type of parish priest—and yet surely the dignity of the Church demanded that her priests should be decently groomed, possessing the ability not only to minister to the peasants but to meet the more educated of their parishioners on an equal footing. True, Morano was not a particularly important parish, but it might be a stepping-stone for a young priest of ability.

The Bishop greeted the young priest warmly. "Ah, Father Paulo, I shall be interested to hear what you find in Morano. Be seated."

Father Paulo gave his report with considerable insight and touches of humour which pleased His Lordship; he liked to be amused even when matters of his various parishes were under discussion. The new school, it appeared, was admirable; the Government were ready to make a grant—not as large as Father Paulo could have wished—but still quite good. There remained the question of the teachers.

The Bishop said, "Mother Angelica, Father?"

"My Lord, she is an old lady; her methods are out of date. She has taught the village girls merely the most elementary subjects. Another nun has taught them sewing and embroidery. I submit to you, my Lord, that in these days our young people must be equipped better than by a very limited knowledge of reading, writing, and the most simple arithmetic. Their knowledge of history, for example, is—so far as I can discover —confined to the lives of the Saints. Very right, very meritorious, but——"

The Bishop nodded. "Quite, quite."

"The boys were taught by Father Dominic——"

"God rest his soul," the Bishop murmured, and Father Paulo hastily muttered his agreement with the pious wish.

"But it is a scattered parish, m'Lord, and if I am to do my

duty by it and to you, I shall have no time to be giving lessons to the village boys. Added to that I am not a qualified teacher, and that is what is needed."

"Quite, quite. Teaching is a specialized work. Highly specialized."

The Bishop picked up an ivory paper-knife and balanced it with great care on his fingers. He frowned; once he cleared his throat gently. At last he raised his eyes and met those of the young priest.

"How many nuns are there at Morano, Father?"

"In all, m'Lord, fifteen."

"Ah! Now at Cormia we have a small convent, a teaching Order. The Reverend Mother is a most admirable woman, energetic and capable. The school at Cormia has been closed. It was old, out of date, and the number of scholars was small. The majority of the people have moved to Peronella on account of the new engineering works there. Such children as remain with their families can go into Peronella, it is only a matter of five kilometri. The nuns from Morano—they are not actually a teaching Order, you know—can be transferred to Cormia; the nuns from Cormia can go to Morano. There are only ten of them, and they will staff our new school admirably. Now for the boys . . ."

It appeared that Father Paulo knew of a man who had fought in the recent war, and who had been a teacher at Foggia, by name Enrico Mazotti. His credentials were excellent and he had lost a leg in the war which—Father Paulo suggested respectfully—surely entitled him to consideration. Mazotti had a younger brother, also a teacher, who lived with him and his wife.

"It seems providential," the Bishop said. "Well, leave the address of Signor Mazotti with my secretary, a letter will go to him this evening. I shall also apply for permission to make the exchange between Morano and Cormia. I hope, Father, that your cure at Morano may be filled with fine work and the greater glory of God."

The interview was at an end, the fate of the nuns at Morano had been sealed. Father Paulo bowed over the Bishop's hand and took his respectful leave. The Bishop rang for his secretary.

"You saw Father Paulo? I think that we have in him an energetic and zealous priest. He mentioned to me that the priest's house is in a deplorably dirty state. Give orders that the rooms are to be repainted; let the painter submit an estimate to you. By the way, I have Canon Vitterbi dining with me, and Father Bonetti. Kindly tell the cook not to reduce the veal to rags, and to use rather more white wine in the sauce. The last was practically tasteless. Also, as we are not Englishmen," he laughed softly, "there is no necessity to serve the vegetables in a bath of green water. They must be *dry*! I abominate vegetables which are soaking in water! Now, I wish to dictate some letters. You have your notebook, Father? Good."

When Antonia, some weeks later, was told by Mother Angelica of the Bishop's decision, she felt that the end of her small world had come. She could not imagine life without the convent, life without the gentle presence of the nuns, life without the regular tasks which she had always loved to perform.

The old nuns' eyes were filled with tears. "No doubt the Bishop, and even those more exalted than the Bishop, are right. We are a small community, and no doubt teachers are necessary to the new school. None of us—except perhaps Mother Anna Maria—are highly trained, and children must be given a good education if they are to make their way in the world. It is a sad blow to us, Antonia, dear child. Like uprooting a plant which has its roots firmly embedded in the earth. We have got our roots firmly into the earth of Morano. In Cormia we shall have to put out new roots, and when one is old, dear child, it is not easy."

Antonia felt the tears gather in her eyes and roll down her cheeks.

"Mother, what shall I do without you all? I shall feel like a lost child. The convent has been my home for so long. I was so young when I first came here, and now I am past sixteen. I have loved it all so much, so very much."

She said good-bye to all of them. Reverend Mother—white-faced and tight-lipped—bade her be a good child, and told her that they would all pray for her. Mother Lucia enfolded her in her arms and shed tears over her. Mother Anna Maria pressed into her hand the precious cookery book, saying, "I have asked Reverend Mother as a special favour to be allowed to give you this. Remember, dear child, in frying always wait for the blue smoke, in making salad dressings—no matter of what kind—to be a miser with the vinegar and a spendthrift with the oil. Use herbs as I have taught you, carefully, with discrimination, and never try to make pastry if your hands are hot. God bless you, dear child."

Antonia watched them go, their treasures, their beautifully embroidered altar cloths which she had helped to make, their bundles, cooking utensils, and all the other homely things which had been in daily use and almost part of her life. She stood there, blinking her eyes to keep away the tears. The little procession of nuns walked to the waiting motor-bus and climbed in. Antonia realized for the first time how old many of them were. She had never thought of Reverend Mother as old, had never noticed how bent Mother Angelica had grown, or how Mother Anna Maria wheezed as she walked. Father Paulo was there to bid them "Good-bye"; his hearty voice rang out with great cheerfulness. He assured them that they would find Cormio delightful, a much nicer convent than this at Morano, more convenient, more modern, warmer in Winter.

Reverend Mother, standing ready to enter the bus, said quietly, "Yes, Father, we know all the defects in the convent here, but it has been our home for so many years, perhaps we have grown blind to its shortcomings. Good-bye, Father."

Maria said, when Antonia came home, "Ah, your nuns have gone! Now what are you going to do? I can't afford to keep you idling about."

"I shall go and see the new Reverend Mother. I have a note which recommends me."

"At the same wage! Are you going to be content with thirty lire a week all your life?"

Three days later she went to see the Reverend Mother. She was a tall, well-made woman, with a high colour, and very bright eyes. Antonia asked if there would be any place for her.

"My child, I don't imagine so for one moment." The voice was kindly but almost unbearably brisk. "We cannot afford servants to wait on us."

"I can cook quite well, Reverend Mother."

"But Sister Mary Joseph—our Irish sister—does all the cooking."

"I can sew and embroider."

"But so can Mother Caterina." The nun laughed.

"I can clean, bottle fruit for the Winter, make jams and pickles."

"Mother Eleanore does all these things, my child."

"I can do laundry work, iron, I can milk and make butter, Reverend Mother."

"Dear child, so can several of our good nuns. No, I am afraid that there is no place for you here."

"I see, Reverend Mother. Thank you."

She walked slowly home, her feet felt heavy, and her heart heavier still. The colour seemed to have gone from everything, the grass looked dull and almost grey, the trees seemed to stretch out long unfriendly arms, even the mountains in the distance looked cold and forbidding.

She was not afraid of work, she enjoyed it—liked to clean and polish, and had a real sense of pleasure when she contemplated some piece of laundry which she had ironed perfectly so that not the smallest crease remained. She liked handling the butter, making it up into smooth yellow pats on the top of each of which she imprinted a design from a wooden stamp. More than all she had loved the orderliness, the consciousness that everyone was busy about their particular tasks, and yet there was never a sense that anyone hurried unduly; no one ever rushed about breathlessly, exclaiming that they could not find this, or had mislaid that.

True she had attained complete cleanliness in her own home, though it had needed months of work and considerable tact, but Antonia felt that it was a cleanliness which had very little in common with that of the convent, almost as if in her own home orderliness and well-kept furniture—such as there was—were there under protest.

She walked home slowly, the shadow of the factory seemed to loom before her; she clenched her hands in sudden determination.

"I won't go into the factory! I will find some work that I can do, do well; something where I can be learning, not just going on week after week doing the same things, turning myself into a machine."

iii

She had prepared a dish of well-cooked tripe for her mother's supper, the pleasant smell filled the kitchen, the table was laid, and Antonia admitted to herself that the whole place looked comfortable and welcoming. Maria was a little late, and when she entered Antonia noticed that her face was flushed, not unpleasantly so, but with a colour which made her look younger, happier. Maria laughed when her daughter exclaimed, "Mama, how nice you look!" and sat down at the table still smiling. When supper was finished she pushed back her chair and folded her arms on the edge of the table.

"I want to talk to you, Antonia," she said, and her voice sounded more gentle and kindly than Antonia had heard it for a long time. "I've not had a very easy life," Maria continued, "it's been a hard road—your father was a difficult man, then losing the boys—may their souls rest in peace—and having to go back to work. Though mind," with a sudden burst of frankness, "I'd rather be working at the factory than messing about at home. I'm going to get married again." She watched her daughter intently, there was something almost pathetically anxious in her gaze.

Antonia said, "Mama, married again! When, who to?"

"He's a good fellow, not very young, one of the overseers at the factory—Luigi Ferrari. You've seen him, he's short— shorter than I am, and getting a bit fat. He's always lodged with the widow Lisini, but when we are married—next month —he will come and live here. I have spoken to him about you, 'Tonia, and he says, 'Let the little one stay. We shall be out working all day, and she will be a great help in the house.' You have not found work yet, 'Tonia?"

"No, Mama, but I shall; but it is kind of Signor Ferrari to let me stay here. I am grateful."

With a hint of her old acidity Maria retorted, "Tut, after all it is my house, my furniture, and you are my daughter! This time, 'Tonia, I earn money. No more will I go and beg for a few *soldi* from my husband to buy bread! No, this time shall be different. Luigi earns good money, we shall do very well I believe." She smiled again, and Antonia thought how much younger she looked, how her eyes shone, and her mouth softened. "I shall have a new dress for my wedding, and we shall go for a honeymoon—*la luna di miele*—imagine it! To the lake of Garda, which I have always longed to see—yes, Luigi insists. We are to stay at a hotel! He has saved money, and says, 'At the beginning of a journey always start off on the proper foot.'"

For perhaps the first time since she was a very little girl, Antonia put her arms round her mother and kissed her. For the next week Antonia spent every possible moment making clothes for her mother. She had been taught to sew rapidly and beautifully, and the underclothes which she made so swiftly and carefully seemed to Maria Trolli to be miracles of elegance.

During the wedding ceremony Antonia watched her mother standing and kneeling beside her husband. He was a short, stout man, with a round cheerful face and a wide smile. He was growing rather bald, and his teeth were poor, but there was something very kindly about him, and Antonia felt that her mother would be secure in his care.

When, after the wedding feast, the bride and bridegroom departed by the autobus which was to carry them to Lake Garda, Antonia washed dishes and set the disordered room to rights. She did not feel lonely at the prospect of spending a few days alone, she enjoyed being alone, and as she worked she sang softly. If only some work might be offered to her during the next few days, how happy she would be.

"Oh, dear Saint Antonio," she prayed, "please send me some work, and with my first wages you shall have something for your poor. Please think of me, dear Saint Antonio."

Next morning when the sun shone, and the house was set in order, Antonia went down the village street to buy a bone and some vegetables for soup. She disliked the village street, there were smells which offended her, the gutters were often filled with decaying cabbage stalks and fruit stones, to say nothing of less reasonable things. She disliked the slovenly women who stood gossiping at their cottage doors, while their children played, squabbled, and fought, unwashed, their hair tangled and uncombed. At the public fountain some women were washing. Their voices rose high and shrill, some of them greeted her as she passed; one woman laughed, making a bawdy joke about her mother's marriage. An older woman rebuked her, saying, "For shame, Liza, is that the way to talk to a girl of her mother!"

Antonia, her face still flushed, bought the vegetables, a few *soldi's* worth of each, and went on to the butcher's. He was a big, stout man with a scarlet face and small twinkling eyes; he came from Tyrol and his hair was very fair, and always looked clean. His name was Andreas Innerhoffer. He greeted Antonia warmly, for he admired her for the way she bought carefully and with discretion. She might not spend much, but she always looked tidy and neat, and he deplored the untidiness of the general run of women in the village.

"Little Signorina 'Tonia! You come in a good hour. Now the good nuns have left us, you are without work, no? Ah, listen to what Andreas will tell you. I have work for you—nice work—work that is fit for a girl who knows how to keep herself nice. You know my little cottage on the road to Cormia —one kilometre outside Morano. Not too far, eh? It is rented to—this is a surprise for you—an English lord. For amusement he paints pictures, imagine it! He has money, so much that you would never believe. He is sending furniture from Mezzolombardo in carts. The cottage is to be like the King's palace in Roma. He wants someone to clean and cook." He paused, and drew a deep breath. "I despair, who can I send? Rosetta, never! She can neither cook nor clean; Elena"—he wagged his head—"I have my reasons for not sending Elena. True there is Francesca, but she has her sick mother to nurse and there are the children of her dead sister for her to look after. My wife said, 'Dumbhead! There is the little Antonia

Trolli, where need you look further?' Then you walk into the shop to buy a veal bone!"

Antonia said gravely, "I asked Saint Antonio to find me some work; he has listened. Thank you, Signor Innerhoffer. I am very grateful. Where is this lord, please?"

"He stays with Conte Zevio, and there I go soon in my cart to deliver some splendid veal. He speaks Italian, this lord, not well but sufficiently. I shall occupy myself with this matter. Remember that he is rich and can pay better than the nuns, little signorina. There, here is your bone, and what a bone too! See how filled with marrow. How much? No, today I make presents because I have found a cook for the lord. Remember, signorina, you will buy the meat from Innerhoffer, when you are installed, no?"

She hurried home, smiling happily. True the thought of working for a lord was somewhat frightening, but surely Saint Antonio, having interested himself already in her welfare, would give her help. How different everything looked today. Even the women standing at their open doors looked less untidy, the children not so uncared for. As she stood looking down into the valley, she saw the mists of the morning swirling, opalescent in the pale sunshine; the mountains with their snow-covered peaks had ceased to look austere, rather they seemed protective and strong, as if they wished you to know that you could rely on them. The busy little stream which hurried down to the valley was singing, Antonia thought; congratulating her that she had found work. She tried to catch the words of its song, and then threw back her head and laughed at her own childishness.

She entered her house, and set about preparing the soup, good *minestrone*, filled with vegetables, tiny bits of macaroni, a few beans—but not too many as they induced wind—a little carrot, and a sliced onion. The splendid veal bone was already simmering gently. She sat down for a moment and thought of the cottage which the lord had taken. She knew it very well. It was, she thought, a rather large place to be called a cottage; there were two sitting-rooms and a kitchen, upstairs there must be at least three bedrooms. Many of the villagers had laughed at the foolishness of Innerhoffer because he had put in a bath with a great copper cistern which supplied hot water. Innerhoffer had blown out his chest and said in a superior manner, "I come from Tyrol!"

Beppi had sniggered. "Are you then so dirty in Tyrol that you must have a bath in the house?"

Innerhoffer replied with dignity, "We have baths in our houses so that we never *get* dirty."

The cottage had a little garden and an old well head, but there was water in the house which came from the big pipes which ran under the road, and which came originally from the mountains—clear as crystal, cold and sparkling. She sighed happily. If only, when the lord saw her, he didn't think her too young for such a position.

"I am cook to a lord," she would say to people, "an English lord."

As she worked she imagined all the wonderful dishes she would prepare for him. She might even write to Reverend Mother and tell her, asking her to assure Mother Anna Maria that the lord was pleased with her cooking.

At midday she made some *polenta*, but she was too excited to eat, and when she looked at her plate where there was still some *polenta* left, she thought, "Perhaps the lord would let me have a little cat. It would eat up all the *polenta* that was left."

Part Two

CHAPTER ONE

FRANCIS WINNERTON had loathed the war and everything that went with it. He had fought, he had made a reasonably good officer, his men had liked him, and he had made no grave mistakes, but all the time he had resented the fact that he was forced to be a soldier when all he wanted to do was to paint.

Again and again he had stared from the trenches to the desolate "No Man's Land" and thought how he could reproduce it in terms of paint. He had been sent to Italy, and there he had studied the blue shadows in the snow, the effects of cloud, of rarefied air, of the tumbling rivers. These things he could paint, and yet he was forced to be a soldier. True he had contrived to make odd sketches, they had accumulated until he had managed to send them back to his friend Conte Zevio to store for him. He had been rather pleased with those sketches, and had summoned up sufficient courage to show some of them to his fellow officers. They had stared at them and said, "I say, jolly good, old man, damned jolly good!" But he knew by the tones in their voices that what they actually wanted to say was, "I say, old chap, what is it supposed to be?"

One man had said exactly those words, and Francis had answered that it was what he felt, that it was what "No Man's Land" looked like to him, and that he was trying to get the "feel" of it.

The other had stared, and stared again at the sketch, saying, "But, I mean, you don't feel that, do you? What does it make you feel?" Not that he really cared, his master in Paris had praised his work, had urged him to continue to paint, and had told him that one day men and women would accept it as something precious.

He didn't know if he really believed that, he only knew that he had this urge to paint, and that nothing must be allowed to prevent him. He had been ill while he was serving in Venezia Giulia, and in hospital for a long time; when he was better the war was over and he came back to England.

His father, the Earl of Maudesley, congratulated himself every day of his life that his elder son, Mostyn, had been spared to come home, because Mostyn would know how to handle the estates, and would probably stand for Maudesley—on the right side of course—and generally comport himself as befitted a country gentleman. Francis—well, ever since Francis wanted to go to Paris his father had felt uneasy. If he had felt that Francis wanted to have a gay time, that was only natural, but to go to Paris and live in some god-forsaken attic, and paint incomprehensible pictures, shook the Earl profoundly.

The war had come and Francis had behaved decently, he had taken a commission and gone overseas, so had Mostyn; but where Mostyn had returned covered with honours and glory, declaring that the war had been a "jolly good show", Francis had ended his military career in a hospital at some place with an unpronounceable name.

Francis came home looking as thin as a rail, inclined to be listless and uncertain. His father had talked to him—sound common sense.

"And now, my boy, what are your plans? The Bar. How d'you feel about the Bar, eh?"

"I don't think so, Father."

"But you've got to do something with your life!"

"I want to paint, Father."

"What, Paris again?" So possibly there had been a woman at the back of it all!

"No, Italy. It won't cost much. I have a friend, Zevio, a good chap, who can find me some place to live, someone to cook for me, and the doctors seem to think that it—well, that it might be good for me. The air and simple food and all the rest of it."

His father stared at him. Certainly the boy didn't look well; far too thin, fine drawn, chest too narrow. "You're not ill, are you?"

Francis laughed. "Apparently not too—robust, Father."

"What's the trouble? Chest?" Pity the boy's mother wasn't alive, she could have tackled this job better. "Better go to Davos, or one of those—er—accredited places. Italy is a dirty kind of country. I went with your poor mother to Naples years ago. Shocking people! Place absolutely filthy. We were disgusted. Glad to get away."

Francis had stuck to his point; and when the Earl took him up to London to see Sir Malcolm Fallory, he had upheld him. He said that the trouble was slight, that the air of the place where Francis proposed to go was excellent, and that it would in all probability do him far more good to go to a place he liked than to a place he didn't like.

He added, "There's a lot in the psychology of these things, you see." Lord Maudesley didn't see. Privately he thought it a lot of rubbish, but he said that possibly Fallory was right, and that he hoped Francis would come to England from time to time for a vetting.

Mostyn came home and filled the house at Maudesley with his friends; fine, upstanding fellows, who rode hard, and generally enjoyed life. The kind of fellows that a man liked his son and heir to have for friends; men who had a stake in the country, who voted as straight as they rode, held the right opinions, and appreciated a sound port.

Francis appeared to have few or no friends; while he was at Maudesley he only invited one man there—old Rivermead's son, John Trevor.

The Earl was disappointed in young Trevor. He had been born with a silver spoon in his mouth, and one day he would own estates which were fantastically large, and which brought in an immense income. Added to that he was an only child, and his mother was a fabulously rich American, reputed to be a millionairess in her own right.

Trevor was strikingly handsome; it was rumoured that women broke their hearts for him. He was tall, his figure was magnificent, and he talked amusingly. He was one of the most envied young men in England, and yet when he came to Maudesley he seemed to the Earl to hold most extraordinary opinions.

True he said all the right things about the house, he admired the gardens, showed proper interest in the orchid houses; he rode well, and said pleasant things about the mounts which were provided for him. He appreciated the wine, the food—he appeared to have a great knowledge of food—and stated that the piano was one of the finest he had ever played on.

"Its tone, sir, is superb. It is a masterpiece."

The Earl said, "I believe that it's a nice enough instrument."

Young Trevor said gravely, "Believe me, it is far more than that." They talked of Francis, of Mostyn. The Earl said what a fine fellow his elder son was, how certain he felt that he would do an excellent job of work, make his mark in life—"in whatever career he finally decides upon. Yes, a fine chap my elder son."

Trevor said, "I'm certain of it, but Francis is a genius."

"Genius! That's a big word!"

"I use it advisedly, sir. You've seen his paintings?"

The Earl sat bolt upright, he stared at the young man, then said, "Are you joking?"

"Nothing was further from my mind." He leaned forward and spoke with gravity and a certain weight. "Believe me, sir, in another twenty years' time those paintings of your son's will be world famous. Admittedly he is in advance of his time. In England at least. His master in Paris already saw something of what he was capable. He has not reached his zenith, he is still—fumbling a little, but it is all there!"

"And might I ask, my boy, what you know about painting? I mean, you don't paint, do you?"

Trevor shook his head. "I have no executive ability, but I have an appreciation of painting. I have studied. I have studied a good many things, sir."

"What d'you actually do?" The words were rapped out. The Earl began to suspect that this handsome young man was a poseur and nothing more. Trevor remained unmoved.

"Do, sir? Try to learn how to live. There are so many people who are *doing* things, they are so busy, and usually very tiresome. I want to cultivate appreciation. By the time I am forty I trust that I may have achieved that, if nothing else."

That was when Maudesley exploded. "Sounds to me like a lot of damn' rubbish! Men should set out to do a job and to do it to the best of their ability. Appreciation! Why, I appreciate fine paintings. I've got some pictures that would surprise you. Have you seen the gallery? I don't mean the old pictures—I mean some of the new ones I bought just before the war. Magnificent. But Heaven forbid that I should go about the world burbling about—learning to appreciate this and that."

Later when he sat with Mostyn in the library, which was always slightly stuffy and smelt, in addition, of old leather, he opened the question of Trevor.

"Seems to think a lot of Francis. I—er—I suppose it's—well, all right? No sentimental rot about it, eh? I'd kick the fellow out if I thought that."

Mostyn, his face scarlet, said, "Great Heavens, Father, don't even hint at such a thing! Trevor's a first-rate athlete, one of the best welter-weights I've ever seen, he's got a punch like the kick of a mule. Won the quarter mile at Rugby, and again when he was at Oxford. Got his blue for footer. He'd have rowed for Oxford but he went down with an appendix at the last minute. Mentioned three times in despatches, and got the M.C. with bar."

"Ugh, then he's damned affected, that's all I can say."

Francis and Trevor walked together on the long, broad terrace, where the great slabs of stone showed tiny plants between their joins. The huge trees threw the dark shadows of approaching evening, dense and heavy, and the splendid parklands stretched away to where the river wound like a silver ribbon. An old dog rose and followed them, then as they turned at the end of the terrace decided that their walk was a purposeless one, and lay down again, its dark nose between its paws, sighing regretfully.

"Then it's all decided, Francis?"

"I think so. I've written to Zevio, he will look around for a place for me. You see, I believe that I shall find all kinds of new things there, new shadows, new shapes, new impressions."

Trevor said, "You won't be lonely?"

"I don't think so. I'm still abominably tired; that must sound silly when you did so much and I only managed to get myself into hospital, but it's a fact. Zevio's a good chap, he thinks my pictures quite mad, but then so do most people. Anyway, it's the only way I can express what I want to say, mad or not."

"To hell with what anyone says—English or Italian," Trevor said warmly. "You go, Francis, and get busy. I'm off to see what Tibet offers. Might be amusing, eh? I'll come and look you up in your Italian retreat when I get back—if some infuriated lamas don't bump me off. I say, that sherry of your father's is remarkable, but—forgive me—the sauces are deplorable. Let's hope that I find some new and quite original dishes in Tibet."

So Francis left for Italy, and Trevor went on his way to Tibet, where he was to remain for nearly three years. They wrote very seldom, for Trevor's address was always uncertain, and Francis hated writing letters. His father grumbled a little at his going, and again pressed the claims of Davos and Arosa, but when he left both his father and brother saw him go with a certain sense of relief.

His friend Conte Zevio welcomed him warmly, and stated that he had discovered a cottage which, if not ideal, was as nearly approaching the ideal as was possible in an imperfect world. He pressed Francis to stay with him, "for a week, a month—for ever if you wish", but Francis was aching to begin painting again, and impatient to see the cottage.

He loved the country immediately; he saw possibilities everywhere for pictures; he watched the lights, the shadows, the early mists and the strange—almost violet—light of the evening. The cottage itself was, he thought, ugly, but it was clean and it possessed a bath. The view from the windows was superb; it faced North, and he visualized himself being able to paint even when the weather was inclement. Before him stretched the valley, and on the further side the hills rose, fold upon fold, until they merged into the mountains; those mountains which towered up until they seemed to reach the sky.

He remembered that Zevio had given him a piece of paper on which was written the name and address of the woman who might be a suitable servant for him. He found it, and read the directions. Antonia Trolli. He wondered if she'd be anything like the old Frenchwoman who had cooked for him in Paris, and who was supposed to clean his studio and never did. Gaunt, with wispy grey hair, and sharp, keen eyes. He didn't regret leaving Paris. He had been happy there, but he wanted to find new scenes, to try new methods; above all he wanted to breathe good air, which might result in his tiresome lungs becoming sound again.

He peered at the number on the wall of a cottage, then crossed the road and examined the place more carefully. It was an old cottage, but it looked clean, and the window-panes shone with polishing. There were crisp-looking curtains, and the doorstep was washed and whitened. He knocked on the door. "Here it is! Now for Signorina Antonia Trolli."

The door opened and a girl wearing a blue cotton frock and a white apron stood there. Her hair was a bright brown which delighted Francis—not red, not even auburn, but brown which seemed to have been burnished. Her eyes almost matched her dress, they were an intense blue, wide, and very clear. He thought, "I'd like to paint her, in that dress, with her eyes the same colour. I *will* paint her!"

He said, in his careful Italian, "May I speak with the Signorina Trolli, if you please?"

She drew a deep breath, and laid one hand over her heart, then said, her voice awestruck but very pleasant, "Ah, you are the lord?"

He stared back at her, repeating, "The lord?" then laughed. "No, my name is Francis Winnerton. I have been told to speak with the Signorina Trolli."

She nodded. "I am Antonia Trolli. I was told about you —that you were a lord in search of a cook, and someone to clean your little house. Will you please come in? My mother is away, or she would tell you that I am a good cook, lord."

Again he laughed, and her grave, pointed face broke into a smile.

"You mustn't call me lord," he said. "It sounds—well, it sounds so biblical, doesn't it? What a delicious smell! If you have been preparing something you must be a good cook to make it smell so wonderful."

"It is some *minestrone*. It was when I was buying the bone this morning that Signor Innerhoffer told me about you." She hesitated, then said, "You would not take some of this soup, perhaps? As a kind of—trial—to see if I can cook?"

"Indeed I will. I shall be delighted." He felt happy, young, and strong. He had forgotten his cough, his horrible sweats at night; he felt that this interlude was something delightful, almost fantastic in its simplicity and charm. The girl motioned him to a chair, and began to lay the table. A coarse linen cloth, but it was smooth and white as snow, the wooden platter on which she placed the bread—rather rough-looking brownish bread—was scrubbed milk-white. The knife had a black horn handle, the spoon was of metal, but it shone with cleaning.

Her movements were quick and deft. Francis watched her, and noted the contents and arrangement of the room. A large room, with a low ceiling, the walls whitewashed. In the far corner stood a large bed, covered with a white quilt, and near it was a ladder which probably led to other rooms. From a shelf came the glint of burnished copper pans; there was a wide-open hearth where a small fire of sticks burnt under the hanging pan. The whole place was simple to the point of poverty, but he noticed a jar on the table which held bunches of green leaves and scarlet berries, and a row of plant pots which stood on the further window-sill, in which were growing what he took to be herbs.

The girl herself he thought enchanting; she moved so easily, her hands never fumbled, and she was so delightfully "paintable". Not that Francis Winnerton wished to paint conventional likenesses of anything or anyone. He had embraced wholeheartedly the modernistic school of painting, and readily accepted its dictum that all contemporary painting was bad. It mattered very little to him that people stared at his pictures and asked, "What is it meant to be?" As he watched Antonia moving about, he smiled, wondering what she would think of the portrait he might paint of her. He was not a self-opinionated young man, his general attitude towards life was modest and retiring; only when it came to a question of his work did he venture to express his opinions dogmatically.

His master in Paris had praised his painting, he had gone so far as to bring the great Furiasco to the studio and the celebrated artist had been delighted. He had clapped Francis on the shoulder, exhorted him to continue to work hard. "Paint, paint, always paint," he had said.

"Today," he said, "people laugh; they laugh because they are still hidebound by convention, they are like small kittens who creep about with their eyes closed. One day they will see —and then you will tell them, when they hail you as a great success, 'Ah, my friends, when you all laughed, Furiasco and my master Jean de Bachelet both believed in me!' You will see, my friend."

Only those two men and John Trevor had encouraged him. John had looked at his work, admitted that much of it was incomprehensible to him, but that "something tells me it's— all right, something tells me that you're going to do things and go places, Francis."

He was roused from his thoughts by Antonia setting down a bowl of steaming *minestrone* before him. A pleasant bowl, white with three broad blue rings round it. Francis touched it with his finger-tips. "I like that. I could make a picture of that bowl, the wooden platter, and those red berries in the jar."

She smiled at him. "Take it while it is hot," she said.

"I'd call it—'The Feast'," he continued.

"Signor, it is no feast, just a bowl of soup."

He tasted it. It was excellent. He said, "I've had *minestrone* before, many times. How is it that this is so different? There are new flavours in this, ones I don't recognize."

"Because, signor, I was taught to use many herbs which are not in general use. Onions, parsley, cabbage, beans and pepper and salt are not sufficient. There, on that window-sill, I grow herbs——"

"I noticed them. Oh, this is excellent. Where did you learn to cook, signorina?"

She told him, and told him too that the nuns had taught her to speak without using dialect, without distorting words. "Though," she laughed, "I can speak *dialetto* if I wish. Signor, will you have me to look after your house? I work very hard, I would keep it beautifully. At half past seven every morning I should be there to light the fire and prepare your coffee."

"But aren't you very young to work so hard?" Francis asked.

"I am seventeen, signor. I am very strong; I am never ill."

"And wages? At the convent, for example, what wages did they pay you?"

"Thirty-five lire a week, signor." Then, seeing his face of astonishment and incredulity, she added hastily, "It was a very poor Order, signor. They could not afford any more; they gave me thirty-five lire out of the kindness of their hearts, because—otherwise I should have had to work in the factory."

"I'll give you"—he made rapid mental calculations—"a hundred lire a week. When can you begin? The furniture will arrive tomorrow, they say at seven in the morning——"

Antonia said, "Possibly they will arrive at ten o'clock. I shall be there long before ten. If you will trouble yourself to come at ten, that will be early enough. I shall bring food; and perhaps you will take your meal at midday there?"

He thought, "When she speaks about the house, her work, she seems to grow older. She's not only attractive, she's capable. What astonishing good luck!" He said, "Money, you'll want money." He pulled out his wallet and gave her some notes; she counted them carefully.

"This is far too much, signor. I shall not need a quarter of this."

"Then make it last for two or three days, then come and ask me for some more. Signorina——"

"If I am to work for you, signor, to be your servant, you should not call me 'signorina'. You should call me 'Antonia', please."

"Then—Antonia—it's a pretty name—in the morning. Look, here's the key of the cottage. Now you can let yourself in. Thank you for the soup—how I enjoyed it! Feed me like that and I shall get so strong I shan't ever visit a doctor again. Good night, Antonia."

She gave him an odd little curtsey. "Good night, signor, and thank you."

That night she washed her aprons and darned stockings. Her heart was singing, not only because she was to earn good wages, but because she was to work for someone who was— her mind halted and sought for a word—fine. He was fine. His hands were beautiful, his clothes, those strange, rough clothes which smelt like a smoky wood fire, were fine, however rough they might be. "*Prima qualita.*" He must have thought their table-cloth and the small fringed napkin she offered him very coarse, yet he had not shown any sign of it. He had drunk her soup as if he really enjoyed it. Ah, what delicious meals she would give him; she would write to Mother Anna Maria and tell her some of the difficult dishes she had prepared.

He had said that with such food he would grow strong. Was he ill then, this tall, fair lord—who said that he wasn't a lord after all? She looked at the little bundle of notes which he had given her. Five hundred lire, as if it had been nothing. He must be very rich; with a little uplift of her chin, she decided that in spite of this fact she would shop as she had always done, buying the best but never wasting anything. Naturally she would not eat the same meals that he did, she would prepare the expensive things for him, and for herself the simple food to which she was accustomed.

She went to bed that night happy and excited. Life at the convent had been wonderful, but now she was embarking on a life of her own. She would be responsible. It would be her duty to see that the linen was exquisitely washed and ironed, the silver polished, every room smelling sweetly of the herbs which she would scatter in drawers and on shelves. Mother Anna Maria had taught her how to make pomanders. How to dry the oranges stuck with cloves, and suspend them by tapes from hooks in the wardrobes, where they not only gave out a smell which was delicious and delicately astringent, but kept away moths.

Antonia rose very early, the light was still dim when she cleaned the living-room, and hurried out to buy what was necessary for the day. Fortunately the people of Morano rose early, and she was able to return to the little house with newly-baked rolls, butter, fruit, and small, thin pieces of veal which she planned to cook in marsala. How exciting to think of the carts rolling up from Mezzolombardo, to see beautiful furniture unloaded, and—while keeping a sharp eye on the men who would carry it into the house—still contrive to prepare a simple but excellent lunch for the signor.

She put the key in the door, her heart swelling with pride. She was trusted; the signor had realized that she would watch his interests as she would watch her own—more, because she was his servant, and she owed him a duty.

He came to the house about nine o'clock, and he was as excited as she was over everything. Together they visited every room, and they inspected the bathroom, where he stared with astonishment at the great copper cylinder.

"It is dirty now, signor," Antonia said. "Soon it will shine like the purest gold."

"Do you know how to work the thing?" Francis asked. "I don't."

"Indeed yes, it is the most modern method," she told him with great seriousness, not realizing that the system of heating bath water by means of a wood fire had long been

superseded. "They always longed for one at the convent, but"—
she shook her head—"they cost so much. Signor, you have
had coffee?"

He laughed. "I was too excited to eat or even drink much.
This is the first time in my life I have had a house of my own.
I am longing to see the furniture arrive, to get things into place.
Perhaps," his voice sounded suddenly shy, "we might hang
some of my pictures in the rooms."

"But certainly, signor. What else should hang there? If you
could wait I shall run to the village and bring back coffee and
milk. I too was in such a hurry this morning I forgot many
things. I shall be very quick, in no time at all I shall be back."

Impulsively he said, "I'll walk with you, shall I? I can help
to carry the parcels, eh?"

Antonia knew that she would be filled with pride to walk
through the village with him, to show everyone that she was
the servant of the English lord—even though he denied being
a lord. Then her discretion asserted itself, and she said rather
primly, "Perhaps it would be better if you remained here,
signor. The men might arrive while I was away. I shall not be
long."

Francis was disappointed and showed it. The morning was
fine and dry and he would have enjoyed walking to the village,
watching and listening while Antonia made her purchases.
After all, he was going to live here, this was going to be his
village, and he wanted to see it.

Rather sulkily he said, "Very well. Shall I light the fire?"

"Tut, tut, where is my mind this morning? No, signor, I
will light it in one moment, there are plenty of sticks outside.
How could I forget!"

Still rather sulky, he said, "I can light fires with anyone. I
learnt how to do it during the war."

She flashed a smile at him. "Now, however, the war is
over." She ran out, returned with sticks, and in a few moments

had a fire burning, crackling bravely. "There! Signor, I must buy a pan, perhaps two pans, unless things for cooking are coming with the furniture."

He rumpled his fair hair, a trick she was to find habitual when he was uncertain. " 'Pon my word, I forget. Did I order pans? I know that the Contessa Zevio bought all kinds of useful things, but—I forget what they were. We shall have to buy you a bicycle, that will save so much time when you go on these shopping expeditions."

How easily he spoke, as if bicycles grew on trees and were there for the picking! She felt so much older than he, as if she were his elder sister as well as his servant.

"I think I know of one for sale—*seconda mano*."

"Oh, we don't want some bone-shaker of a thing! We'll have a new one, brand new. There, off you go."

She bought, she felt, spending wildly—pans, real coffee, milk, a cup and saucer in case the men had not arrived. In her own home they always drank coffee out of bowls, but you could not expect that an English signor would tolerate that kind of thing. Sugar, butter, all kinds of extravagant things. She seemed to have spent a great deal of money, and hoped that he would not shake his head and say, "Ah, I am afraid that you will waste my money, Antonia. Perhaps it might be better if I found an older woman, a woman with greater experience." How dreadful that would be!

Innerhoffer greeted her warmly. "So you have the job! This is a fine thing. Be sure and buy your meat from me, 'Tonia. Yes, I know that you bought escallops of veal this morning, but continue to do so. Be sure that the English lord shall have only the best. See, I am driving to Castello Zevio. I shall give you a ride; I go past the house of the lord. Jump in."

She told him gravely, "The signor says that he is not a lord. He would not allow me to call him so. He wishes to buy a bicycle so that I shall be able to get quickly into the village. I know that Baptista wishes to sell her bicycle, but the signor wishes it to be a new one. He says the *secondo mano* shake the bones."

The jovial butcher laughed. "Shake the bones, eh? But your bones are young, 'Tonia, and well covered! As mine are!"

He insisted on getting out at the cottage, and while Antonia made coffee said that he should interest himself in the purchase of the new bicycle. It appeared that his wife's brother, Massimo, sold bicycles at Cormia which were superior to any in Italy. By great good chance he was driving to Cormia after his call at Castello Zevio.

Francis said, "Then, signor, please buy one. Mind, I want a good one."

"It will be of the best," Innerhoffer assured him. "The tyres will be pneumatic, the lamp of the latest *modello*, the saddle of pure leather. The frame—ah, it will be magnificent. It will be of great lightness, but of a strength not to be believed. It's name is—a fine name, signor—'Gloria'."

He went. And Francis, sipping his beautiful coffee, and eating his roll with unexpected appetite, grinned at Antonia.

"Old windbag, eh? He and his bicycle! Well, we'll see what this vaunted Gloria is like!" He laughed. "Just like any other bicycle."

The van arrived with the furniture; the time was twenty minutes past ten. Antonia rated them soundly. They had promised to be there at seven; was this how they kept their word to the English lord? He had spent immense sums with them, buying their furniture—which all the valley knew to be indifferent stuff—and this was how they repaid him. It had been necessary to go out and spend a small fortune on a cup from which he might drink his coffee, because they had not arrived with the beautiful porcelain which he had bought. It was shameful! How they could ever hold up their heads again passed her comprehension. If they worked like slaves they might do something to lessen his displeasure, his disgust, his disappointment in the Italian people. They expressed their willingness to work like a hundred slaves.

They began to unload, while Antonia explained to Francis that they were from Mezzolombardo, and that all people living there were of a vastly inferior quality to those living in Morano. She assumed her mature expression, which had already begun to amuse him, and said, "One must thank God that the house is clean, though not as clean as it will be at this time next week. Innerhoffer may talk too much, but he had the sense to employ Maddelena to clean everything, and she is well known to be honest and capable. Now, we shall see to everything!"

It was difficult to wash china on which to serve the dinner, and to prevent your eyes wandering to the splendid furniture. There were carpets which would cover the whole of the floors, the beds—there were actually three of them—were unbelievably soft, the chairs were large and covered with rich material. The china and glass were of a quality which Antonia had never seen before. She felt almost giddy. There were quantities of pans—for boiling, for frying, for baking. There was a fine stove—an *economica* which was painted white where the parts were not plated with silver. Already one of the men was fitting it into the pleasant little kitchen; Antonia felt proud to be giving him orders as to exactly where she wished it to stand.

Tolerantly, she admitted that the signor was not a great deal of use; he seemed incapable of sticking to one piece of work, and was continually coming to her with questions.

"Antonia, come and tell them which carpet should go down in the bedroom at the back," or, "Antonia, what is this for? I've never seen—whatever it is—before." "Oh, these two chairs, little ones, will they be for a bedroom?" She felt that it was like having a child over which she must keep watch.

At midday the men intimated that they were exhausted, and

must have their food. Antonia eyed them scornfully and
expressed the opinion that it was strange their firm should
send out men who were so obviously weak and almost too old
to work.

Francis said, "Give the poor devils some money, Antonia,
and let them go down to the village and get something hot to
eat. I expect they can do with it."

He felt that her eyes were scornful, but she answered
obediently, "*Sì*, signor, as you wish."

Later he asked what she gave them; she replied that at the
trattoria they would get soup, perhaps stewed veal and bread
and some red wine for fifteen lire each. "It is a great deal," she
admitted, "but I must respect your wishes. Now, signor, your
meal will be ready in a few moments. The fire is lit in the
bathroom, the water may not be very hot but it will perhaps
serve for today. Tomorrow I shall do better."

When he came down he stopped and looked at the table
with real pleasure. The cloth was clean, the glass polished,
there was a carafe of white wine, the cutlery and silver gleamed
brightly. He smiled and rubbed his hands.

"It looks perfect. But why only one place? Aren't you
having any luncheon?"

"In the kitchen, signor."

"But eat here, my good girl."

"I should prefer not to, signor. It would not be correct."

"Oh, what rubbish, Antonia!"

"Excuse me, signor. We say here that a good beginning
makes a good ending. I wish to begin properly."

He sat down alone. He drank his strong soup, and ate his
veal stewed as he had never tasted it before. She bought him a
small cup of black coffee, set an ash-tray and matches beside
him and disappeared, he presumed, to eat her own meal.

That evening when dinner was over, when she had washed
up and left the kitchen in order, she told him that while he was

out in the afternoon searching for dresser-hooks in the village she had aired his bed and the bed linen.

"Everything is not completely in order, signor, but with a little patience it will be."

He looked round the room. "It's all very simple stuff, Antonia, but I didn't want anything elaborate. I like simple things, and they are easier to keep clean. Do you think that you'll like working here?"

"Signor, it is the most beautiful house I have ever seen. I can never be sufficiently grateful to you for allowing me to work in such—such a—palace."

"If there is anything you want, you'll tell me, won't you?"

She hesitated, her cheeks flushing a little, then raised her eyes to his. "Signor, forgive me, but could I have a small cat, or do you dislike them?"

He snapped his fingers as if she had solved a problem for him.

"I knew that there was something missing! Of course; now would you rather have a little cat or a little dog? Conte Zevio's wife has a little dog which has had five puppies. By the time the house is all in order the dog might be able to leave its mother."

"For dogs one must pay a tax, signor. For a dog which is a luxury dog, it is heavy. Also they cost more to feed." She sighed. "Imagine it, a small dog!"

"The dog is yours, or will be very soon."

"Signor, I am overcome," and indeed he saw tears in her eyes. "Good night, signor, and may all the colours of the heavens be in your dreams."

CHAPTER TWO

For the first time since the war Francis Winnerton knew what real enjoyment meant. He thought that his life had never been so full, never so well ordered. Not even in Paris had he been conscious of such a sense of well-being. There he had been excited and stimulated by the knowledge that he had a gift for painting, that he not only had the ability but the imagination to pin his ideas and impressions down on to canvas, but here at Morano there was so much more.

His Paris studio had been a huge room, grillingly hot in Summer and arctic in Winter; the old woman who "did for him" was perfectly content to sweep the dust under the various rugs and leave it there. She had been kind enough, but she was terribly untidy and, he suspected, not particularly clean. Her cooking had varied, true, her omelettes were excellent, there were various stews which she had made to perfection, but she had what Francis had called her "off days" when the food was greasy and almost uneatable.

Now he had a house of his own, furnished simply but with everything that he needed. His clothes were pressed, his linen beautifully washed and ironed, h/s meals perfectly cooked and served. Antonia made no attempt to conceal her pride in the house, in the new bicycle, in the small dog which was rapidly making itself master of the house.

Francis rarely saw her flustered or hurried, she was always quietly, unobtrusively busy; she deferred to him without ever growing subservient. Each week she insisted that he went through her accounts, and initialled them as being correct; at first he spent hours adding up the unfamiliar lire and centesimi, later he would say, "Ah, the accounts, that's right. Leave them and I'll go over them." Once she was out of the room he would hastily open the black-covered account book, scrawl his initials, and when she returned assume an expression of conscious virtue—for he hated anything to do with figures—and assure her that he found them perfectly correct.

Soon after the furniture was installed Antonia reminded him that he wished to have some of his pictures hanging on the walls. He was pleased at her remembering and Innerhoffer was ordered to bring the canvases from Conte Zevio's. Special hooks were sent for to Cormia, with very fine nails which would not injure the walls. The pictures arrived in big packing-cases, and Francis was like a boy, running his fingers through his fair hair, his eyes shining, his hands busy but ineffective, attempting to open the cases.

"It is like meeting old friends," he told Antonia. "I have not seen them for so long."

She smiled her kind, half-indulgent smile. "It must be, signor." He began to take them out, holding them at arm's length, and telling her about them. This was painted in the early manner of Renoir, then de Bachelet insisted that he ceased to paint in "the manner" of anyone, however great—"and Renoir, mark you, was great!"—and paint in his own style and no other.

"This was the first thing I did, the Luxembourg Gardens in Spring. It's pretty dreadful, but I'm fond of it because it was my first attempt to—be myself. That is an impression, only an impression, of 'No Man's Land' above Monfalcone. Ugh, how ugly it all was, but I had to paint it. Venice, of course, I had to paint when I got there. See the Santa Maria della Salute, and the reflection of the gondolas in the water? It was a wet day, and the rain was making little dents in the water. I tried to paint that. I think that we'll hang that one first, eh?"

He turned to her, and at the sight of her face his expression of excitement vanished. He said, "Ah, you don't like them?"

"Signor, I know nothing of pictures. I have never seen any good pictures—I have only seen reproductions of some in books at the Convent—Morone, Romanino, Veronese, Leonardo. That little one," she pointed to a small canvas, "that makes me feel happy, it is so gay, I like the colour."

Francis nodded. "It's a wheat-field with poppies, it's not very good, too photographic. We'll hang it, if you like it."

His spirits revived a little when they had hung several of the paintings; after all, he *did* know that de Bachelet had praised them, he knew too that he had painted honestly, literally as he had felt the subject.

Antonia grew to have quite an affection for them, though she never understood them. When he was out, if anyone came with a message or to deliver goods, she would see their puzzled faces and say with a slightly overdone superiority, "No doubt to you they seem strange, but this is the new manner of painting. Not what you *see*, you understand, but what you *feel*. These have been praised by the greatest artists in France, I assure you."

Privately she thought that all artists must be slightly mad, for how could they think these strange splashes of colour beautiful? There was one which her signor really liked, and said, "I shall never paint anything better than that, Antonia." It depicted an ordinary green earthenware jar, and leaning against it, an old cotton umbrella. Not even a good umbrella, but one in which the cotton had faded to a dingy grey, with a common wooden handle. Even the jar was not quite right; one side bulged and looked as if it had been distorted while the clay was still moist. There was also, standing near the jar, a saucer which contained something she judged to be the cat's dinner, but it might as easily have been earth or *polenta*. It was all very puzzling, but so long as it kept her signor happy and contented—what matter?

The little dog, called "Aramis" for some reason she did

not know, was small, very fat, and fluffy. He was the joy of her heart; she brushed and combed him, and sought carefully for non-existent fleas, for she believed that all dogs inevitably had fleas, and Aramis was to be the grand exception to the rule.

One day Francis was sulky and irritable. He had wanted to paint out of doors, and it was raining hard. He mooned about the sitting-room, kept wandering into the kitchen, asking idle questions about this and that, then wandering back again to stand and stare resentfully at the rain as it splashed down the window-panes.

"Antonia . . ." he called.

"*Si, signor.*"

"Does it rain a great deal here?"

"Not more than in other places, signor. Tomorrow the sun will be shining again."

"I wanted to finish that picture of the women washing at the fountain in the market-place. Oh, damn the rain!"

"Signor, why not paint the little Aramis? Look how he plays with that piece of paper screwed into a ball!"

His face cleared. "You're clever, Antonia; it's an idea. I'll call it 'Youth'." He was completely changed; he got paints, brushes and a small piece of prepared board. Antonia went back to her kitchen; she sighed with satisfaction. Her signor was himself again.

Later, when she carried in his tea, which she served in the English manner, with tiny hot cakes of her own making, and what she called "Ploom Kak", he showed the picture to her.

"Look! It had to be done quickly, because Aramis got tired of his playing and went to sleep. Now, tell me!" Francis cried.

She clasped her hands. Here at last was something she could understand, though she could not tell why. If you looked too closely, it seemed that the signor had merely made a number of white marks, like marks of interrogation. And yet, it *was* Aramis.

She said, "Ah, but it is the small dog! He moves, I can see him jumping after the paper ball. Oh, signor, how is this achieved? I see his paws, I can see his bright eyes, and a very small piece of red tongue, but—the fact remains it is Aramis."

Francis threw back his head and laughed. "So, you are learning, eh? It is what I have always told you. You get the sense, the feeling of a little dog playing. There is movement; that there is no form does not matter. It's no masterpiece, but it was great fun to do."

When Conte and Contessa Zevio came to dinner one evening, when Antonia was more nervous than she had ever been in her life, they saw the picture and were delighted with it. They praised the dinner, and the Contessa asked her where she had learnt to make such dishes.

"Francesco, I shall have her kidnapped! My cook at the Castello is incapable of making a dinner such as this."

Zevio, a sallow-faced man with a long, melancholy nose, known to be the greatest joker in the district and yet looking as if he never smiled, said, "At least, Francesco, when we have a dinner-party, be generous. Permit this wonderful cook of yours to come and make the sauces. Would you come, signorina?"

"If the signor permitted, excellenza."

"Only on condition that I am invited, Bruno!" Francis warned him.

"It is arranged. I will even invite that enchanting dog of yours, the dog immortalized in paint."

Antonia had been working for Francis Winnerton for over a year. She often told herself that such happiness could not last. At home she recounted the day's doings to her mother and stepfather. How her mother had changed since her marriage to Ferrari! She still worked at the factory and liked housework no better than she had ever done, but she smiled easily, she was growing rather stout and heavy, and her increasing weight made her look good-tempered and jovial. True, Antonia still cleaned the cottage, and in some way contrived to keep it spotlessly clean. It was hard work, for she never left the little house before half past eight, and later still if Francis had people to dinner. She was always back at work by half past seven, and yet the work was done, and done well.

Ferrari loved to hear of everything she had done during the day; it seemed to him to be a door opening and showing him a different world. A world of luxury and ease.

"A clean shirt every day! Imagine it! And when people come to have dinner he puts on a clean shirt with a stiff front, and only wears it for a few hours! Even the dog has fresh meat bought for it every day. And baths! A bath each morning and sometimes one again at night. He shaves sometimes also twice a day; shaves himself. This is strange; one would imagine that a man so rich would visit the barber each morning, eh? And soap—listen, Maria, his soap is sent by post from Paris, and smells like a bean-field—it is so beautiful. Ah, there is much to be said for such a life!"

Maria would smile at the plain, elderly little man and say, "We do very well, *caro mio*."

There were times when Antonia feared that she might be growing proud and vainglorious. She had so much to be thankful for, so many privileges, opportunities. She confessed this fear to the priest. She had a bicycle, a dog, she ate well, and was trusted with vast sums of money; she was afraid that she might grow to look down on people less well off than herself. The priest reminded her that humility was a great virtue, and that she must keep on praying for it to be granted to her.

In the Spring when the crocuses were covering the fields with carpets of purple, white and yellow, when the "flowers of the snow" were lifting their lovely delicate heads, and the birds were returning from their Winter overseas, Francis told her that he must go to England. For a moment she felt the blood drain from her heart, and had to rest her hands on the back of a chair to steady herself.

In a very small voice she said, "For—always, signor?"

"Always?" He laughed. "Can you see me leaving my home—for always? To say nothing of leaving my superb housekeeper and my dear little Aramis. No, no, only for two or three weeks. There are business matters which must be attended to. I am taking my pictures with me—yes, that will be a relief to you, Antonia, eh? Because at last I am to have an exhibition, in Bond Street. Only a small gallery, but it is a *good* gallery, and people will come—and perhaps be puzzled, perhaps laugh, but they will see what I have done. It is all arranged; they wait only for me and my pictures. I'll tell you something else; I shall come back in a car—yes, a motor-car. It is foolish not to have one. True, you lend me Gloria, but I want to be able to go further afield. I'll take you and Aramis with me, shall I? I'll show you places where there are lovely pictures—Verona—we might even get as far as Venice—oh, it's going to be wonderful fun!"

She watched him. His face was a little flushed, but he looked well, a different person from the man who had come to Morano over a year ago. His skin was tanned by the heat of Summer and the clear, cold sunny air of Winter. His hair seemed to have taken on a brighter shade of colour, his eyes were shining; they seemed to dance when he grew excited.

He was going away for two or three weeks—twenty-one days, she thought how interminable they would seem, how she would miss his questions, "Antonia, explain this to me, my Italian isn't good enough yet"—his comments—"Antonia, what is this? Veal? It is quite marvellous!" or "Has Aramis had his dinner? He seems hungry." "Oh, I saw Innerhoffer in the village. He has some—what did he call them?—*animelle*, sweetbreads we call them in England. He is sending them up; I adore sweetbreads!" "Bruno has caught some river trout; I bought them. You won't send them to the table with the heads on, will you? I hate their eyes—they make you understand what a 'fishy eye' means."

His paintings she would never understand, and when she did understand some of them, they seemed to her to be inexpressibly dull—old umbrellas, a kitchen bowl with a wooden spoon lying beside it, and some eggs on a plate. Even the eggs were not the shape of real eggs! He had painted old Tomaso, and when Tomaso came wearing his best suit, the one he wore to attend Mass, the Signor sent him home to put on the one he wore every day, which was all faded by the sun, and unbelievably patched. True, the picture did bear some resemblance to Tomaso, who was an ugly old man, but not very much.

When Tomaso saw the portrait he asked Antonia to tell the signor that there was a man in Peronella who gave drawing lessons, he was very good and under his tuition no doubt the signor would improve tremendously.

Antonia said proudly, "You do not understand, Tomaso. The signor is a great artist; he paints not what he sees, but what he feels."

Now he was going to have an exhibition of his paintings in that great town, London. She hoped that no one would laugh at his pictures, that they would not ask questions which might hurt him. The thought of him being hurt was intolerable to her.

"While you are away"—and even the thought of him being away was painful—"would you mind if I slept here? I should not like the little house left alone. May I sleep in the little room, signor?"

"What, all alone? Won't you be frightened?" Francis asked.

"With Aramis! Never. He is so brave, this dog, and would be so fierce if anyone should try to enter the place."

"If you're certain that you'd be all right, why, of course. You'd better ask your mother if she objects, though."

Antonia smiled. "The idea would never enter my mother's head. So long as I prepare supper for her and my stepfather—she is content."

So Francis Winnerton left for England, with a number of beautifully made packing-cases which held his pictures, and Antonia watched the big car, hired from the garage in Cormia, drive away. He leaned from the window and waved. She called, "Go with God, signor," and then turned back into the house—the house which felt suddenly so sad, deserted, abandoned.

She sat at the table and laid her shining head on her arms; she knew now that she loved him, perhaps she had always loved him, from the very first moment he had come to her mother's cottage. She cried softly, her sobs shaking her, her grief taking possession of her completely. Then she felt that the small white paws of Aramis were resting on her knee, and heard his gentle whimper as he begged her to remember that she still had him. She laid her hand on his smooth head, then lifted him into her arms, so that he licked her face as if he wished to wipe away the tears on her cheeks.

She talked to him, taking herself to task.

"How foolish I am," she whispered, "and how presumptuous. I am a village girl, with a little education given to me by the nuns, and some small knowledge of housework and cooking. He is—not a lord, but he is the son of a lord, and lives in a palace compared with which the Castello Zevio is a hovel. How dare I say that I love the signor! It is true, I have become proud and puffed up with my own importance. How could such a man, an aristocrat, ever feel anything for a girl like me? He is kind, because it is his nature to be kind; he is generous because he does not know what meanness is; he is considerate because he is good and gentle. I am his servant, and it is only those people who have money but no fineness who are rude to their servants. When he has brought me little presents from Cormia, or Mezzolombardo—he has not brought them from any sense of—affection. How could one even imagine this! He has thought, 'Poor little Antonia, so poor, she has so few pretty things. I shall get her a pair of warm gloves to protect her hands when she rides Gloria to the village.' Or an umbrella; true, it was an expensive one, but that is because he is used to the best and to buy cheaply would never enter his mind. Handkerchiefs—it is possible that my coarse handkerchiefs offended his eyes. 'Oh, let me get her some that won't look so dreadful!' Stockings, 'She wears such terribly thick ugly stockings, and her legs are not bad; it is a pity; she shall have some finer ones!' These, Aramis, were his thoughts. If men love you I think they don't give you useful presents. They give you flowers they have gathered, red and purple berries, they give you looks which are very tender—which say more than words could ever do. They forget to call you by your name and answer, saying, 'Yes, cara mia?' or 'Si, tesoro', and do not know that they have said these things."

She put the little dog down very gently, then rose and squared her shoulders. "Now, we have three weeks in which to make this house really clean, in which to polish everything that will take a polish. No use, Aramis, my dear little boy, telling me that it is clean already—just see what it will look like when we have finished! Soon the wild strawberries will be ready and I shall make that jam—a French jam—called Fraises du bois. How the signor will enjoy eating it with a good fresh cream cheese! In front of the house there is a small piece of ground—we shall make a garden; think of it, a garden filled with flowers. Ah, ha, my boy, the two little servants of the signor will be very busy, as busy as bees."

Yet all the time she "swept and garnished", worked at the little garden she made, and went searching for the earliest wild strawberries, she knew that she was doing it all for one reason—she could do nothing for Francis but work for him, and that work should be the best possible. All her energies must be directed towards that end. She could not help loving him, but—she prayed earnestly and sincerely—that he might never know it, and so make a barrier between them.

ii

Francis looked forward excitedly to being in London again. All his life he had loved change, new scenes and new experiences, in fact he had often been surprised to find that he was so happy, so content to remain for over a year living in a small cottage in an out-of-the-way village in Italy. He had been happy, he would go back and be happy there again, and his thoughts began to imagine his return.

He would buy presents for everyone! He loved buying presents, and he had lived cheaply, and had plenty of money to spare. The fat Innerhoffer should have an English pipe, very large and elaborate if he could find one; naturally Zevio and his wife—but that would be easy—expensive ties, equally expensive scent, the finest silk stockings, and large, exquisitely fine handkerchiefs. The stepfather and mother of Antonia should have presents too, sensible presents, and—for a moment his thoughts halted—what should he buy for Antonia? He would go down Bond Street and look in shop windows for things to take back to her—a gold wrist-watch, a beautiful brooch, silk nightgowns, silk underclothes. He laughed. What nonsense! The village would raise its virtuous hands in horror and suspect the worst. No, he must be very careful over his presents to Antonia.

He wondered what she was doing at that moment. Of one thing he could be certain—she was working. He could visualize her shining hair, as she bent over one of her bowls mixing some elaborate sauce, or when she worked at her beloved copper pans until they shone like gold. He imagined how she raised her eyes when he entered the kitchen, those expressive, gentian blue eyes of hers, with their well-drawn eyebrows, and the long eyelashes which when she looked down threw a shadow on her cheek. Her skin looked so smooth that he had often longed to say, "Antonia, let me just touch your cheek with the tip of my finger; it looks so smooth and soft."

Sometimes, when he had grown sulky—for Francis knew his faults and saw them clearly—she had answered him calmly, kindly, and slowly he had come to feel ashamed of his bad temper. She seemed to have an additional sense, to understand exactly how he felt if his painting had not pleased him, or if some particularly necessary tubes of paint had not arrived exactly at the moment when he wanted them. She never said, briskly, "I expect that it will be here tomorrow." She realized that the all-important thing was that it should be there today, at the moment when Francis Winnerton wanted it!

He knew that she spoiled him, but he had enjoyed being spoilt. So often he had felt that she was older and wiser than he, that she was lenient with him because she felt that he was young, and must be humoured—but cleverly humoured—like a rather naughty but much-loved child.

"Much-loved . . ." The words seemed to stand out in huge letters! Francis moved restlessly in his corner of the railway carriage; he turned impatiently and looked out of the window at the flying landscape, seeking something to attract and hold his attention. He concentrated on every passing farm building, church, followed the course of every stream and river as long as it was possible, trying fiercely to drive away that phrase which had come unbidden to his mind.

He heard the ringing of the attendant's bell announcing luncheon, and wished that he had taken his ticket for the first instead of the second service, only that made the afternoon so long. The meal would be quite good, for usually they fed you better on the Continental trains than on the English ones. Again he moved restlessly, conscious that he was forcing himself to think of things which held not the slightest real interest for him. Why not face up to the truth? Here he was alone in this carriage, and here he would remain until they reached Calais. Surely he might try to understand himself during that period of solitude, try to come to conclusions, even permit himself the luxury of allowing himself to think, remember and make mental pictures of Antonia. He had been seeing her every day for over a year, except when he had gone to Milan for two days to buy paints and canvas; she had become woven into the pattern of his life; he had not attempted to analyse his feelings for her, he had just accepted her. Perhaps when she was with him, when at least he knew that she was under the same roof, or would return to the house after one of her brief shopping expeditions, he only saw her, felt his admiration for her, and his love for her subconsciously. Now, with every moment putting more and more miles between them, he had realized that not only did he love her but that he had loved her for months. This was no sudden rush of devotion, it was merely the clarification of something which had existed for a long time, which had only needed separation, distance between them, to become clear and definite.

He had been standing too close to a beautiful, intricate pattern, so close that except for the general impression of colour and design he had been unable to see all the delicate spirals, twists, and forms. Now, standing back, looking at this wonderful piece of tapestry, he saw it all clearly for what it was. As he might have been watching one of Monticelli's pictures, standing within two feet of it, blinking and attempting to find out—what it all meant. Then, moving back, the movement, the glorious colours and the delicate hues had become apparently clear and defined, and you blinked your eyes again and wondered how you could have been so foolish as not to have understood it all from the first.

He asked himself when he had first begun to love her; like all lovers, he felt that such a passion as he knew that he felt for her must have begun at some given and stupendous moment. Was it when she voiced her delight at the little picture he had painted one wet afternoon of Aramis, or was it perhaps that first evening, when she had asked if she might have "a small cat", and when he had suggested a dog she had reminded him that keeping a dog meant paying a tax? Did she love him, he wondered, or did her character and her determination to be "correct" preclude her from even thinking of such a possibility? If that were so, he would have to break down her rigid ideas about masters and servants, peasant girls and people who were "almost lords", as Innerhoffer told him she had stated Francis to be.

The first thing he would do on returning home would be to paint her. Yes, he would paint her in that blue frock which was just a shade lighter than her eyes; she should sit in the big wooden arm-chair with a piece of bright brocade flung over the back. He would not paint the brocade slavishly; he had seen too many portraits where the artist had depicted some curtain, piece of china, so accurately that it threw the whole balance of the picture wrong. A portrait of Antonia should be —just that; her portrait, as he, Francis, saw her.

She might have Aramis on her knee; that would please

her. How she loved that small, fluffy dog! Renoir had painted "The Girl with a Cat"; he would paint "A Girl with Aramis" —that would puzzle them. "Who is Aramis?" they'd ask. It should be the best picture he had ever painted. He remembered hearing a Frenchman say, "Artists are fortunate. If they cannot decide whether they love a woman or not, they can paint her portrait. By the time it is finished they will know whether they love her to distraction or hate her violently."

Now he laughed softly. "That's all right for the silly fools who are not sure," he thought. "I am sure—gloriously, perfectly, unshakably sure."

He would paint her a picture especially for herself. Again the thought made him smile. Not one of his usual paintings, which she tried so hard to understand and to admire, but something she would feel was a real picture, over which he had taken great pains. What should it be? A saint painted in the completely conventional manner? The idea did not please him; he believed that one must feel whatever you painted— no matter if you painted well or ill—and he had no particular feeling about the saints. A picture of the house—no, he had too much feeling about that, and his own method of painting would assert itself. A bowl of wild flowers, every petal painted lovingly, painfully exact, photographically correct. That was it! A bowl of wild flowers.

iii

The superintending of the arrangement of his pictures was exciting, the gallery was charming, well lit and attractive. He flung himself wholeheartedly into all the details of the exhibition—programmes, catalogues, invitation cards, the private view—nothing was too small or unimportant for

Francis. There were over thirty paintings, some of them very small, things done as he had painted "the small dog" in an afternoon, others larger and more ambitious. One section was given to his sketches made while he was serving in the army; the sight of them brought memories rushing back to him; he could almost feel the cold of the trenches, the greasy smell of the food, and the constant itch of the lice.

The owner of the gallery, a man of great taste, who frequently lost money over his gallery, but derived the utmost pleasure from it, said, "I've not forgotten the red tickets, Mr. Winnerton," and smiled.

"I don't suppose we shall need any of them, unless my father buys one with a view to encouraging me to do better," Francis told him.

Glassier shook his head. "I think you're wrong. I believe this is going to be a great success. To put it at its very lowest level, you are the son of an Earl—that excites a certain type of buyer, they judge that you must either be very good or you'd prefer to be living a life of ease and luxury, or that you must be very bad, and only your father's influence has made this exhibition possible. In that case the paintings may be interesting, or amusing by reason of their ugliness.

"There are several other reasons—it's a good time of year, painting is popular at the moment; 'the old order changeth' and people are looking for 'new men'. In addition to all that, if I may say so, you happen to be a remarkably fine painter, Mr. Winnerton."

Pleasant to see the young man flush so readily, as if he wasn't used to appreciation, and enjoyed it. A nice young man, Glassier judged him, unassuming, ready to listen to reason, to take the advice of people older and—where the hanging of pictures was concerned—wiser than himself. He'd go a long way if he took care of himself. He didn't look too strong, probably one of those youngsters who had felt the strain of the war too much. London wasn't much use to him, he wanted good air, possibly "coddling" a bit.

"You're not taking a studio in London, are you?" Glassier asked.

"No, no, rather not! Once this is over, I'm going back to Italy. I've got a little house there, among the mountains, miles from anywhere. Our nearest town is Mezzolombardo, and the inhabitants of my village regard it as the hub of the universe—it's a dull market town as a matter of fact. I've got a cottage, and—a small dog."

"Ah, the one in the painting there—it's very clever."

"I don't want that sold—not that anyone is likely to buy it —but I promised it to a friend of mine who admired it. A very stern critic, and usually averse from my kind of painting."

His voice sounded so happy and even excited that Glassier felt that there must be someone else who shared the cottage, some Italian girl perhaps. Well, he hoped that she was good to young Winnerton, and that she gave him something more nourishing than huge plates of *pasta*.

"I shall see that it is marked 'sold'. Good night, and good luck for the private view tomorrow. I've a little surprise up my sleeve for you. Good night."

CHAPTER THREE

THE morning of his private view came. Francis knew that he was nervous, that he hated the idea of wearing formal clothes, making him look as if he were going to a wedding or to Ascot. He felt sulky and irritable, but here in this huge London hotel there was no one to play David to his Saul, and he told himself that he had better "snap out of it". He sent a short letter to Antonia, written in his careful and rather stiff Italian. He longed to write that he was missing her dreadfully, that he loved her and longed to get back to her; instead he said that the gallery was very nice, the weather very bad, the food not as good as he got at Morano, and ended by asking her to give his love to Aramis.

In his anxiety not to arrive at the gallery too early, he dawdled over his luncheon, forcing himself to eat, and drinking a small bottle of champagne to wish himself good luck. As a result he arrived at the gallery rather late and found his father and Mostyn both there.

His father said, "Hello, glad to see you looking so fit." Then with a movement of his hand which took in the gallery, "You've been pretty busy, eh?"

Mostyn shook his hand warmly. "You're jolly tanned, aren't you? Winter sports? Lots of pictures you've got here. I like the one of the little dog best. It's sold, I see."

Francis grinned. "I bought it as a present to myself. It's my dog; he's called Aramis."

"I know a man who has some first-rate brindle bull pups if you'd like one to take back."

Francis thought that he had never spoken to his brother without hearing that he knew of "a man" who had something for sale which was absolutely first-rate.

"Thanks, but I don't feel that Aramis would take kindly to a brindle bull pup, Mostyn. He's used to being cock of the walk."

"That's all right; he'd learn. You want more than one dog, don't you? I mean, one dog, well . . ."

That again was typical of Mostyn, typical of all the people who were his friends; it was necessary to have several dogs. You never groomed them yourself; if they were sick you told the groom that he'd "better send for the vet". If the dog got better, you told your friends that the vet was "a sound feller"; if it died you said it was a shame, and that you'd have to get another.

"You've seen the pictures, Father?" he asked.

"Yes, oh yes, we'd been here ten minutes when you came in. I'm not the kind who can stand gaping at pictures for an hour. I hope you'll sell some, m'boy. Hope so, I'm sure." His tone implied that he doubted if there were many people sufficiently foolish to spend money on such daubs. "Going back to—wherever it is you live?"

"Yes, of course. I want to get a car so that I can go further afield. I want to have a shot at some mountain scenes."

"A car, eh? Ask Mostyn, he's certain to know of someone who has a car to sell, and it will be a good 'un too. Sound feller, your brother. Works hard; may stand for Maudesley at the next election. Well, I must be off, I've an appointment with my dentist; lucky the appointment coincided with this exhibition of yours. I rarely come to town. You'll spend a week-end at Maudesley before you go, eh?"

"Thanks, I'd like to. Good-bye, Father, nice of you to look in. I hope the dentist doesn't hurt too much."

The gallery was growing fuller; Francis saw no sign of Mostyn, and reflected that he had probably gone to meet a man with something to sell. He walked over to where Glassier stood greeting the arrivals. He whispered to Francis, "The

stout man leaning on the stick is Lane, the dealer. Good
afternoon, Sir Jacob, delighted to see you. May I introduce
the artist, Francis Winnerton?"

Lane stared at him. "You're ferry young, no? Chust
amusin' yourself, yes? Vell, let's hev a look at it all." His
small, sharp eyes twinkled. "Deffacing goot canvas, perhaps!
Dot's my leetle joke."

"I recognized it as one," Francis said, smiling.

A tall, exceedingly handsome man entered, and with him a
woman whose beauty made Francis feel that he longed to
keep on staring at her. Glassier whispered again. "That's the
man who can make or break a young artist—or practically.
Leon Hast."

"And the woman with him?"

"Juliet Forbes, the singer. One of the few singers who can
make me endure an evening at the Albert Hall."

Hast strolled over to where they stood; he greeted Glassier
with sufficient civility but with a certain arrogance which
made Francis dislike him instinctively.

"Really got something this time?" Hast said. "I've seen
some of this man's work; in fact, I bought a sketch of his—
some war study—from a man who'd been with him in the
army. He looks to me as if he really had something. Young,
is he?"

"Here he is, Mr. Hast. Judge for yourself."

Hast stared at Francis, as if he were trying to assess his
value.

"You *are* young, Mr. Winnerton. Where did you study?
Ah, Paris. Under de Bachelet. That's a good man; I trust his
judgement as I trust very few people's. I'm looking forward
to seeing your work. Where are you working now? Italy—
a good place to study. Oh, Morano—almost in Tyrol. You're
not going to give us another 'Spring in the Austrian Tyrol',
are you? England's suffered sufficiently."

"Not quite in my line, Mr. Hast."

"Well, let me go and see what your line is. Then, if I may, I'll come back and have a few words with you."

He walked away and Francis saw the lovely woman join him. She did not appear to mind having been kept waiting; her smile was charming.

"Now here is my little surprise," Glassier said in excited tones. "See that big car outside? Watch! The great man and his daughter-in-law. Here he comes."

A very tall man, wearing a heavy coat with an astrakhan collar, and carrying a cane with a very large ivory top, entered with a woman. She was not so beautiful as the woman with Leon Hast, but her smile was so unforced as she greeted Glassier, and her whole manner so delightful, that Francis felt this was a woman he would like to have as his friend. The elderly man was speaking to Glassier. He was clean-shaven, with very keen eyes, and a rather wide, generous mouth. The aquiline nose was masterful and yet sensitive; his hair was beautifully white. Francis judged him to be about sixty.

"Und hev you somet'ing r-really good, Glassier? You t'ink so. Ah, t'en I must go und make certain, eh? Don't esk me to come again to see t'ose dr-readful t'ings of Seyres. I can buy coloured photographs vhich please me better!" He looked at Francis, raising a gold-rimmed eyeglass to his eye. "Ah, here is the artist! I r-recognize you, you are Fr-rancis Vinnerton, yes? Your fadder is a patron of the arts? Indeed, I have sold him pictures. Enchela, my dear, forgive me, and permit t'at I pr-resent to you Francis Vinnerton, the cleffer boy who hes giffen birth—may I use such an expression?—to this exhibition. Yes, Mr. Vinnerton, I do not tell tales vhen ve are no longer in school, but not long ago I sold to your fadder," he paused and his eyes danced with amusement, "an Alma-Tadema. It was in the best manner, all pink ladies and marble baths—very large. The fr-rame was very expensive. I was very

heppy to sell t'is picture. I had it in my gallery for many
years; I once offered it to people who make soap, I forget
their names. Your fadder came to my gallery to puy a vedding
present; he was goot enough to say t'at my sherry was
excellent. He fell so in love vith the Tadema. I esk very little,
und even so I tr-remble t'at it is too much. He said, 'You
only esk . . .' vhatever it was. 'Are you med, Gollantz? It is
vorth more!' I said t'at he was such a goot client—vhich indeed
he is—and the price was a pleasure to me—vhich it was indeed!
How heppy I was to see the end of t'ose rose-pink ladies!"

The pretty woman with him laid her hand on his arm.
"Emmanuel, you talk too much." But she smiled as she said it,
and the old man looked down from his great height and
smiled in return.

"Vot you mean, Enchela, is t'at old age is making me
garrulous, no? Very vell, I am ready, let us go and find fault
vith Mr. Vinnerton's pictures."

Glassier chuckled as they walked away. "Didn't I tell you
that I had a surprise for you? He's the greatest figure in the
art and antique world today. He's a Jew—they're most of
them Jews—but what I say is that when you find an honest
Jew—well, he's the most honest man alive. You've done
pretty well, Winnerton, you've got some big fish in your net—
Hast, who is a millionaire and the world's greatest collector,
it's my belief that he does a little dealing as a side-line. Jacob
Lane—though he's nothing nearly so good as Gollantz—he's
the prince of the lot of them. No, I'm very satisfied."

Francis said, "And I am very grateful to you for all you've
done."

The gallery was growing less crowded. Leon Hast came
strolling back with Juliet Forbes. He stopped to speak to
Francis, and this time introduced him to her.

He said, "I've enjoyed coming here. Unfortunately old
Gollantz bought the Venice picture before I reached it. I

don't often enthuse—do I, Juliet?—but that is a very lovely
thing. I wanted it very much indeed. Leave poppies growing
in ripe corn alone." He smiled and slid his dark eyes round to
Miss Forbes again. "Anyone can paint that kind of thing."

Francis thought that she flushed faintly, and wondered
why. She didn't paint, surely?

Hast continued. "The little dog is clever. I should have
liked that. Is it really not for sale?" Francis shook his head.
"Pity. Well, my congratulations, Winnerton. Don't let them
persuade you to repeat successes; for example, no more
cotton umbrellas, no more plates of eggs. Oh, they're good,
but if you satisfy the taste of your public, nine times out of
ten you satiate them. Would you care to come and dine one
evening? You might be interested in some of my pictures;
no, no, not painted by me. I don't aspire, not even to be
a successful painter. Let me see—is Friday possible for you?
Splendid! There's the address, and perhaps you'll come,
Juliet, and"—his voice was soft and persuasive—"possibly
sing for us, eh?"

Francis watched them go, and thought what a handsome
couple they made. He wondered concerning them; somehow
he felt that Hast was like a splendid black panther. You would
always have to be careful of his claws no matter how loudly
he purred.

He felt that when Emmanuel Gollantz and his daughter-
in-law came back they brought a different atmosphere with
them. Fresh tea had just been brought, and he saw Gollantz
glance at the tea-pot with a certain expression of disappointment. Glassier laughed.

"No, Mr. Gollantz, I have coffee here for you. I remember
your tastes, you see. It is freshly made by my secretary."

The old man sat down, murmuring to his companion,
"Excuse me, my dear Enchela. Looking at pictures is always
a little tiring, even," with his small ceremonious bow t

Francis, "vhen t'ey are goot pictures." Glassier stood at his
elbow with a tiny pot of coffee and a fine cup and saucer on a
salver. "Ah, t'is is kindness. How he remembers my devotion
to coffee! A nice little pot, Glassier—French, yes. The cup
and saucer—unless I am mistaken—Meissen."

Glassier smiled. "You are never mistaken."

As he sipped his coffee with obvious enjoyment, he turned
to Francis. "Vell, young man, you hev made a goot start,
eh? Leon Hast has bought your old man and the cotton
umbrella. He vanted the Venice, but I vas too qvick for him.
Dot is a fine piece of vork. If you can do that—there is ver-ry
leetle t'at you cannot do, giffen industry, healt' and—yes,
heppiness. My dear old friend, Jacob Lane, he buys a corn-
field mit poppies. How I vish for his own sake Jacob vould
not buy pictures. It is the vorst of all in the gallery, my boy,
und yet it is not a bed picture. *Nu*—yes, Enchela, t'at vas my
second cup of Stanley's admirable coffee. Ve must—like
beggars vhen t'ey hev got all they vish for, they wave the
hand, no? Kom and see me von morning, young men, at
Bond Street. I shell see if you hev your fadder's goot taste in
sherry, but I hope not his bed taste in pictures. Stanley, you
hev done ver-ry vell."

He moved away, Francis thought the epitome of dignity,
offering his arm to his daughter, and, walking down the steps
which led to the street, erect and splendid.

Glassier sank down on a sofa. "Whew! Gollantz, one of
the first to come and the last to go! Pictures sold to him, to
Hast and to Lane! Miss Mollison, how many have been
sold?"

"In all, Mr. Glassier, fifteen pictures and seven drawings."

"Splendid!"

Francis said, "He's delightful, isn't he?"

"Emmanuel Gollantz? He's as I told you, a prince. Years
ago, when I was a very young man, and like most young

men, very hard up, I bought a picture. It was sold to me as being of the school of Carlo Dolci. I took it to Gollantz because I thought that it was very much better than the average run of Dolcis, and felt that it was an original. He examined it; I can see him now peering at it through his magnifying-glass. He said, 'Tell me what is your name—as well as Glassier?' I won't attempt to imitate his accent. I told him, 'Stanley Mawson.' He chuckled. 'Stanley, hey. Then,' tapping the picture, 'this is Doctor Livingstone! You have found him, no?' He went on to tell me that though I might be a 'goot boy' I was not a very clever one. He explained how I should have known immediately that the picture was no Carlo Dolci but a Bellini. Did I wish to sell it? I said that I did, but that I had come to sell it as a speculative Dolci, and that I was content to stick to the price I had in mind when I came. He looked at me in a kind of pained astonishment, then said that he did not profit by the ignorance of other people. He laughed. 'I only advise them to learn more—to learn as much as Emmanuel Gollantz.' It wasn't even a very good Bellini, but he paid me a price for it which set me on my feet. Since then he has always, when he is in a jocular mood—oh, he can be very stern, believe me—called me 'Stanley'. He said today to me, 'Stanley, I like your new Doctor Livingstone!' Winnerton, you're in on the ground floor!"

That night Francis longed to be able to talk to Antonia, to tell her all that had happened, of the people he had met and the pictures he had sold. Instead he wrote to her in his halting Italian, saying,

Dear Antonia,

Today I believe I have had great success. Many pictures are sold but never the small dog, your Aramis. Tell Tomaso that his portrait is sold to a very clever man who knows all concerning painting. I shall return as soon as possible.

He added greetings and compliments, and read the letter through again, wishing that he were able to express himself easily. Juliet Forbes might be, indeed was, beautiful, Mrs. Gollantz was completely charming, but Antonia was set apart. There was some quality in her which other women did not possess. During the Summer he would teach her English and she must help to improve his Italian. He would buy a car and teach her to drive; he would take her to Milan, to Venice, to "the peach-blossom city" of Verona.

Someone had said that love knows no conventionalities. They were right. She might be a peasant, but she was the woman he loved and he was going to marry her. He wasn't the eldest son. Mostyn would marry some eminently satisfactory young woman, and have eminently satisfactory children. Francis would go back to Tyrol, and spend his life with Antonia.

He stared round his impersonal, comfortable hotel bedroom, and thought of his room at Morano. Much smaller, smelling sweetly of herbs, a window which looked out on to a wide stretch of fields and vineyards, then the land rising slowly, growing more and more rugged. Finally it was merged into the mountains themselves, still mounting up and up until they ended in the jagged, needle-like spurs which were typical of the Dolomites. He remembered the sunsets, when in early Autumn the rocks had changed from grey to a dull, warm pink, and later in the year when the snow fell to a bright rosy colour—almost carmine.

His mind went back to the flowers, growing in such lavish profusion; the crocuses, the roses of the snow, and later the cyclamen with their enchanting scent. The dog violets, and the astringent smell of herbs as you trod them underfoot—the thyme, rosemary, wild parsley, and garlic. The sounds which he had grown to love—the tinkle of the cow-bells, the lighter sound of those which hung round the necks of the goats;

the sudden barking of a fox, the bleating of sheep, and the distant barking of alert dogs. The voice of Antonia when she arrived in the morning, speaking to Aramis; so light, so clear, that even as he lay half awake in his room upstairs he could hear, if not the words, at least the tones and cadences. The heavy rolling voice of Innerhoffer when he came bringing some meat, or something which he had been asked to bring from the town, the querulous tones of old Tomaso who always had a grievance, the more youthful voice of the priest, very hearty and always, Francis felt, slightly overdone. He recalled the chatter of the women as they washed their clothes at the public fountain, high and reedy like the chirping of birds, the deeper voices of the men who sat outside the *osteria*, the yelping of dogs, the cries of carters to their horses or their oxen.

Here, in the middle of London, he heard the dull roar of the traffic, felt the very slight deposit of grime on whatever he touched, and smelt the odour of petrol in his nostrils whenever he went out. He was an Englishman, he loved England, he had suffered when she suffered, and he had rejoiced at her ultimate victory, but he did not feel that he "belonged" to London.

That afternoon had started half a dozen trains of thought in his mind. Who was Hast, and who was that exquisite Juliet Forbes? How had Emmanuel Gollantz begun his splendid business, gained his knowledge and won his stainless reputation? Old fat Jacob Lane—who had bought his worst painting —who was he, and where did he come from? Stanley Glassier, what was his history?

He didn't want to bother about people's beginnings, their histories, not even about their present positions. He didn't really care if Hast were a millionaire twice over. He only knew that he wanted to get all his work, his social duties, and his buying of presents over and drive back to Morano and

Antonia. He felt that, driving back, conscious that every mile brought her nearer, his thoughts regarding the future would clarify. He felt that it would be easier to write to his father from Morano announcing that he was going to marry Antonia. He could imagine his father's fury and Mostyn's disgust. Not that either of them wanted Francis at home; he knew that they had no patience with him, but the thought that "it might leak out" that he had married a peasant—that would anger them.

Morning brought a letter from Antonia. He turned it over and over before he opened it. Her writing was good; not particularly formed, but clear and distinct. He felt that his hands shook a little as he slit the envelope carefully with a paper-knife. The letter was short, obviously the letter of someone to whom letter-writing was a rare thing. She called him "Dear Signor", told him that Aramis was well, that she had made a little garden, and that the weather was not good. She hoped that he was in the best of health, sent her respectful compliments, and remained his "faithful servant, Antonia".

Francis could imagine her seated at the table writing slowly, carefully, while Aramis watched her with adoring eyes. A wave of tenderness swept over him, and he felt his eyes sting with tears, his throat ached; the nostalgic desire to see her again was almost unbearable.

He put the letter away in his wallet. "My first letter from her," he said softly. "My faithful servant—that's what I'll try to be to you, my dear."

London felt stuffy in spite of the chill air. Francis knew that it tired him, while in Morano he had walked for miles with no sense of weariness. Here, Bond Street seemed to stretch for miles; in addition the noise of the traffic worried him. It seemed like the roaring of some great beast, menacing and unfriendly. He went to the gallery, where Glassier made him read various notices in the morning papers.

"Didn't you get them at your hotel?" he asked.

Francis shook his head. "I didn't know they'd have written anything about it. They're mostly quite kind, eh?"

"Miss Mollison, get on to one of the press-cuttings agencies and arrange for them to send everything dealing with his exhibition to Mr. Winnerton, will you? You haven't learnt the ropes yet," he told Francis.

The day dragged on; in the evening he went to a theatre. The next day he bought a car, and lunched with his old Aunt Honoria in Portland Place; she was nearly eighty and very deaf. He wrote to Antonia, he slept for a little, then went to a theatre again. The following day he bought a meerschaum pipe for Innerhoffer; it was completely hideous. A bulldog's head, complete with a massively carved collar. In the evening, by which time he was almost ill from boredom, he went to dine with Leon Hast.

Portland Place again; Francis prayed that the dinner might be better than the luncheon at Aunt Honoria's. The flat was immense, he was used to the splendid rooms at Maudesley, but he had never seen rooms so filled with treasures as these of Hast's. Wherever he looked something caught his eye and held it—yet there was no suggestion that the place was a private museum. It was all exquisitely arranged and utterly lacking in ostentation. Hast came in, smiling and cordial, yet for the life of him Francis could not feel drawn to the man.

"I didn't make it a dinner-party," Hast said, "because I thought you might like to look at some of my pictures, and also Miss Forbes is coming in after a concert—I forget where it is at the moment—and bringing her accompanist, Gilbert. I dislike having a mob of people here when she promises to sing. Let them pay to go and hear her, she's worth paying for."

He talked of painting, and Francis listened, realizing that he was listening to an expert. He finished dinner and wandered about, cigar in hand, pointing out his treasures to the young

man. He spoke with contempt of modern Italian art. "It may
be that this new man, Mussolini, will awake in Italians some
spirit that—at the moment—appears to be very sound asleep.
They seem to concentrate only on their music, some of the
loveliest in the world, their singers are admirable, their
painters—Heaven preserve me! Induno, Fracassini with his
horrors—Morelli; some of the present 'fashionable' painters.
If these new Fascists had them drawn and quartered I, for one,
would join them tomorrow. The French," he said, "at least
attempt to evolve something; they are not slavish imitators;
they think. We may not like what they produce, but at least
they succeed in startling us. Only so many painters who were
regarded as 'modern' are now becoming almost classics, then
everyone feels that they have earned the right to be admired.
Degas was regarded as modern, but he was painting in the
1870's. People have seen his pictures so often, they believe
that they appreciate them, whereas it is only that they enjoy
the sense of familiarity. Monet, Manet, Sisley, Van Gogh,
Cézanne, Picasso are moderns, but they are accepted because
they have been reproduced by this and that society by 'special
colour processes'." He laughed. "Never let them reproduce
your pictures, Winnerton."

There were moments when he spoke gently, almost
tenderly, as a man might have spoken of some woman he
loved. "Crivelli—you know him? No, not a great artist, but a
charming one. His nice little self-conscious Madonna, showing
off her child—not a very pleasant-looking child either—is
delightful. The actual painting is wonderful. And Bellini,
his most lovely picture is in Venice, the most touching face,
without any attempt to make it reflect 'the shape of things to
come'. Pisanello, his Madonna of the Quails, it is in Verona.
One day I am going to hide in the Castello and steal it in the
dead of night. There are moments when I feel that I cannot
live without her."

Then Juliet Forbes arrived, breathtakingly beautiful, and with her a small, fair man who looked like a nervous rabbit. Hast asked eagerly about her concert; she smiled her lovely serene smile and said that it had gone very well. Hast demanded a programme, and scanned it rapidly, murmuring names which conveyed nothing to Francis.

"Yes, yes—splendid. It went well, Gillie?"

"Supremely well. The audience—I thought that they would never stop applauding."

Hast's lips parted in his sardonic smile. "Of that applause, Juliet, fifty per cent was for you, thirty for that excellent dress you are wearing—Paris, eh? I thought so—and twenty per cent came from people who actually know something about music and voices."

She said, "It is possible, Leon; let me speak to Mr. Winnerton, we're being terribly rude. How are you? What a success your exhibition is; I've read some remarkable criticisms. Leon, give me something to eat, I'm starving. Singing is a hungry business. Oh, yes, I will sing, but two of those tiny sandwiches won't hurt me—and poor Gillie is eyeing them with a longing that is positively pathetic."

She ate with evident enjoyment, while Hast watched her, his expression inscrutable. Francis thought, "I don't know their relationship, I don't want to, but that man is never going to make her happy."

Then Juliet walked to the piano, the little fair man trotted after her and sat down, whisking his coat-tails out of the way of the stool in a way which made Francis feel that he did it habitually. He played what seemed to be the introduction to a song, and Juliet said, "Yes, very well, Gillie."

She began to sing. Francis was not a particularly musical young man, and he did not understand what the song was about for she sang in French, and his French was limited to the ordering of a meal in a restaurant, but the lovely sounds reached him, seeming to present, mysteriously, a solution to all his problems. He must go back to Morano, as quickly as was compatible with decency and expediency; he must see Antonia, perhaps paint her portrait—just to get himself orientated as it were—and then ask her to marry him and to marry him soon. Nothing else mattered. She was good through and through; she might be a peasant but all her thoughts, her actions, were kind, generous, and essentially gentle. He had sufficient money to keep her, well and comfortably; he had made a success, he could paint, make more money if it were needed, but, what mattered most—what was the only thing that really mattered—was that he and Antonia should be together, happily content.

The sound of the voice died away. Hast, lounging in a big chair, his legs crossed, showing a slim ankle covered in a very fine silk sock, said, "Excellent, Juliet. Voice is admirable, eh, Gillie? I never heard it better. I should take that last phrase just a *little* quicker, I think." Then, turning to Francis, he asked, "Did you enjoy that?"

Almost breathlessly, Francis said, "It was quite wonderful. I didn't know that there was—singing—like that."

Hast laughed. "There isn't, my friend. Could you manage one more?"

She smiled. "Of course. What shall it be, Gillie?"

Again that little tinkle of notes, and again she said, "Yes, very well," and the magic began once more.

This time Francis listened. He had dealt with his own problems, and now he could listen to the music completely. The round, golden notes rose and fell, he was able to understand what complete mastery she had over her voice, such mastery that it all seemed entirely effortless. Hast lay back with his eyes closed, and as the song ended he opened them and Francis saw Juliet turn to him almost instinctively. "It is his approbation she wants," he thought. "Whatever she means to him, he means to her—what Antonia means to me."

Again Hast thanked her almost formally, again he passed his opinion—tentatively and with complete courtesy—on the rendering of the song. She listened, and then said to Gillie, "I think he's right."

Gillie nodded. "We'll try it that way tomorrow. It may be that it is the better rendering. I'm open to conviction."

Soon afterwards he left. He walked down Portland Place feeling better, more confident than he had done since he came to England. Juliet's voice still rang in his ears. He could not have whistled or even hummed either of the songs she had sung, but the impression remained as a scent might linger on the air.

The next day he went down to Maudesley, not because the prospect of a week-end with his father, Mostyn or Mostyn's friends attracted him, but because he wanted to see if the daffodils were out in Borret Wood, and the violets and celandine on the banks of the little river Swathe. He packed his rucksack with paints, brushes and a couple of small canvases and drove down. It was a fine, gusty morning, and Francis was glad that the car was not "run in" and that he was forced to drive moderately slowly. His head and his lungs felt clearer, his heart lighter, and he was able to look with appreciation at the little Norman churches, the small tidy villages, and the splendid trees. The roads must have looked more attractive when they were still "white roads" that poets used to write about, but these dark surfaced roads lent themselves to wonderful shadows and reflections after rain. The first sight of Maudesley impressed him as it had never failed to do, the immense façade, the long windows and the wide terrace, all mellowed by time, built when men used the best materials and only the finest workmanship. He loved the long yew hedge, clipped into the shape of eagles, peacocks and other strange birds, the names of which he could not even guess at. The big cedar in the centre of the lawn might, as Mostyn grumbled, ruin the turf, but its blue-green foliage, the wide spread of its branches, made a pattern which he longed to paint. "Big yew tree at Maudesley"—and Mostyn would stare at it and say, "But, damn it, you've painted it blue, old man!" No, better not paint it, not while he was here at least. He'd make a quick sketch, and try to memorize the colour and paint it from memory when he got home again.

He drove his car into the yard, and looked in at the loose-boxes to see the horses that he knew, patted the old dog who lived in the saddle-room, and felt the stable cat rub against his legs. There was a nice friendly feeling; he liked animals, he decided, better, in the main, than people. Old Collins came over to him, touching his cap.

"Nice ter see yew, Mr. Francis. I did y'eard as you'd had some piksures i' Lunnon, and folks had gorne proper crazy over 'em."

"Who told you that, Collins?"

"I forget who it weer, now. Someone who'd read about it i' the Sunder papers, or maybe the daily papers, I'd not be certain. Is it trew, Mr. Francis?"

"Moderately, at least. People have been very kind about them."

Collins nodded. "Aye, no doubt, they'd know as you was his lordship's son, everyone has a gert respect fer his lordship. You staying, sir?"

Francis told him, "Yes, until Monday morning."

"Daffys is out in Borret, aye, an' vilets is out b't' river. I mind as you like 'em, doan't you? I'll see to the car, sir."

Francis walked into the house, his father was coming out of the library and greeted him.

"Hello, Francis, nice to see you. How's the show going, eh? I read something about it in *The Times*. B'Jove, I was surprised that *The Times* mentioned it; quite a long notice. Praised some of the pictures. Sold many?"

"All except half a dozen and a few of the sketches. I've been lucky, Father."

"B'God, I should think you have! Tell me, Francis, who *buys* pictures like that? Reasonable people, or just—well, rather cranky folks?"

"Jacob Lane bought one, and Leon Hast bought two."

His father shook his head. "Never heard of either of 'em. Who are they—dealers, speculating, eh?"

Francis disregarded the question. "And Emmanuel Gollantz came himself; he bought two. He's asked me to go and see him one morning next week." He saw his father's expression of astonishment with some amusement.

"Good Gad! Gollantz of Bond Street? Old feller with—well, with an air about him. I've heard that he was an Austrian nobleman, don't know if it's true. He's the big noise in antique business. He sold me a picture once, and sold it cheap too. Lovely thing; you may recall it, the 'Alma-Tadema', eh?"

"I remember it quite plainly, Father."

"And he's asked you to go and see him! If he offers you sherry, take it. Served with some special dry biscuits. It's as good as my own; that's saying something. Well, you can find your way to your room, eh? See you later."

Francis climbed the wide staircase, with its carved banister and low treads, and made his way along the corridor to his own room. There, seated on the wide window-seat, he took out his sketch-book and made several drawings of the big cedar tree on the lawn.

CHAPTER FOUR

THE wood was very quiet. In the tree-tops Francis could hear the wind rioting about, but here among the daffodils he barely felt it. The golden flowers scarcely moved, but grew there serene and lovely, their clear colour catching the light and, he thought, intensifying it. It was inevitable that as he set up his easel and canvas he should glance at them affectionately and murmur, ". . . that come before the swallow dares, now let me get down to it!" He whistled softly, because the flowers, the knowledge that he was going to paint, the consciousness that he was alone and undisturbed, that no-one could ask him if he didn't want to ride, or walk, play bridge or billiards gave him great satisfaction. Here alone in this little wood he could immerse himself in his work—that work which was such a joy and which at once presented problems and gave him happiness—and allow his thoughts to fly over Europe and speculate as to what Antonia was doing.

He squeezed out his colours, speaking softly as he did so.

"Clear colour—nothing dingy about daffodils—clear, young, yellow. Now that I'm going to ask her to marry me—of course I always knew that I was going to do that, but Juliet Forbes' song somehow clarified it all; I can take her back as many presents as I like. That grass hasn't quite lost the hint of winter grey, *grigio verde* they call it in Italy—green-grey." His voice rose a little, and he painted with great intensity. "I've got it! That faint movement, and the sturdiness of the flowers. It's coming all right!"

He forgot all about time, until a voice at his shoulder said, "That's good, Francis, damned good!" and he turned to find John Trevor standing at his side. John looking tremendously tall, rather gaunt, and smiling down at him.

"John! I thought you were in Tibet!"

"I was; somehow the lamas didn't greet me as a blood brother, in fact they were quite remarkably unfriendly. I was barely allowed to stay over the week-end; most inhospitable people. Then I returned to London, saw your name on a poster, rushed round to the gallery, saw Glassier—nice bloke, isn't he?—and he told me that you'd come down here. I walked over, asked for you, was precipitated into a crowd of Mostyn's friends, and then remembered that it was Spring, that daffodils grew in this wood, and deduced—that's a good word—that I should find you here." He pointed to the picture. "That's delightful, really delightful."

"You really think so?"

"If I didn't, I shouldn't say so. You've made the success I predicted for you, eh? Glassier told me about it. Congratulations."

Francis turned back to his painting. If there had been one thing needed to complete his happiness it was John's presence. Here was someone to whom he could talk, really talk, not skim along the surface of everyday affairs and trivialities.

John sat down on the grass beside him, lit a pipe very carefully, and watched the development of the little picture.

"I like small pictures," he said at last. "Great big canvases nine times out of ten give you too much to take in. This, it's amazing how much colour, movement, atmosphere can be packed into—what is it—twelve by eighteen?"

Francis, a brush held between his teeth, did not speak.

"I saw a Veronese in the Louvre the other day. Possibly you don't care for him; I revel in him. Only I didn't know how to look at it *all*. There was a lovely girl in a dull yellow dress, a very handsome middle-aged woman who looked like a duchess—or as duchesses ought to look and so rarely do— there were several good-looking men, and a charming page about fifteen with a dog. The dog was a strange breed, but perhaps they went in for strange breeds in those days. There were golden goblets, and dishes of fruit, some flowers—it was all too much for one picture. This," he pointed with the stem of his pipe to Francis's painting, "is concentrated. It fills your heart—yes, and your mind—with daffodils and what they stand for, and leaves you rested and content."

Francis laid his palette down on the grass and took out his cigarette-case. "Perhaps because I am happy and content," he said.

"Eh? D'you mean with your exhibition?"

"Other things, far more important things. John, I'm going to ask a girl to marry me when I get back home again. I'm not telling anyone about it, because my father and Mostyn will disapprove, but I'm aching," he laughed, "simply aching, to tell you about her. Will it bore you?"

"My dear fellow, drive ahead."

Slowly Francis told the whole story, told it simply and without embellishments; he did not try to depict Antonia as anything but what she was—a peasant who had received some education from the nuns, a person of innate uprightness and essential kindness, a restful person, simple and yet possessed of discernment.

"Pretty?" John asked.

"Charming, her eyes are very blue and her skin looks so soft and smooth that I have been on the point of asking her twenty times if I might touch it with the tip of my finger. Her hair is brown, not dead, heavy brown, but with a burnish on it which is gold when the light catches it."

John had ceased lounging; he sat upright, his keen eyes watching the expression of Francis's face. The fellow was in love, there was no mistaking it. She was a peasant; that would mean all kinds of complications, arguments with old Maudesley, protests from Mostyn.

"You'd come to live in England?" he asked abruptly.

"Heavens, no! I'm the younger son, I've enough money to live on, and live in decent comfort; I have made money by this exhibition, and apparently I can make more. I've a little house; while I've been away Antonia's made a garden, she tells me in her letter—what on earth should I come to England for!" He laughed. "Oh, and I have a dog."

"You don't mind the prospect of being, virtually, an exile? I've heard that, apart from everything else, these people—who really belong to the soil—don't transplant well."

The look on Francis's face surprised him. John Trevor had been in love, still more often he had imagined himself to be in love, but he had never seen a man's face so transfigured as Winnerton's was at that moment.

"I should only be an exile when I was away from Antonia."

"Then, apparently, there are no insurmountable obstacles," John said, and Francis turned back to his painting.

"Tell me about this—little house," John said after a short silence.

"Stone, facing north-north-west, looking over a valley towards the mountains. The house stands rather high, clear of the morning mists. There is a large living-room with an open fire where logs are burnt; I gather fir-cones because I like to see the flames leap and hear them crackle. The furniture is very simple. There is a kitchen, larger than you would expect—with an electric stove, and another called a *stufa economica*. There is even a refrigerator of the most modern type. The china, just country pottery, is blue and white, white with beautiful blue rings round it. The kitchen is like the rest of the house—very clean and shining, and just a little austere. There are three bedrooms and a bathroom. Only three people have bathrooms in the village—Conte Zevio, Innerhoffer, the butcher, and myself. It is inclined to set us apart somewhat from ordinary folk—from 'lesser breeds' without a bathroom.

"The air is very clear. There is a factory, but it is miles away beyond Cormio. In the morning it is fresh and clean, and slowly as the sun climbs the earth gets warmed and everything seems to glow. As it sinks in the west, the shadows grow very dark; they look almost like something that you could handle and feel. The nights are very dark and mysterious; the sky is a deep, almost impossible blue, studded with millions of stars. When there is a moon, and she sails through the sky, aloof, cold and slightly superior, the whole valley lies tranquil and quiet as if it were waiting for something to happen. It feels easier when the moon hides behind a cloud, and animals stir, and birds rustle, then she appears again, and everything is still.

"When the snow falls it is a magic carpet, a carpet which glitters as the sun rests on it. It is cold, but dry, and though your fingers and toes may tingle, it is delightful because you take great deep breaths of the air, and know that there is a fire in the open hearth waiting to greet you. Sometimes it rains, and how it can rain too! Everyone is philosophic about the rain but me. I grumble because I can't go out and paint. Then Antonia thinks of something which I can paint indoors— flowers in a bowl, eggs on a plate, the little dog—my bad temper goes and I am content. In the morning the sun is shining again."

John said tentatively, "Antonia suggests . . .?"

"Yes, she is always there. She's my housekeeper."

"How old is she?"

"Eighteen, I think—either almost eighteen or just past eighteen. She cooks, cleans, irons, mends—if it wasn't too much trouble I'd take off my boot and show you a darn in my sock. It's perfect."

John stood up and shook the creases out of his immaculate trousers. "I must be moving. Francis, let me drive back with you. I can send my car on to the South of France. Yes, for a month or two I am going to lead a life of complete civilization—indulge in ultra-civilization. I'm going to change my clothes at least three times a day, play tennis, do some mild motor-boat racing, gamble—I hope—considerably, and dance a great deal. It's an antidote to the lamas.

"I am seriously contemplating sponsoring a society for the introduction of scented soap and heavy perfumes among the lamas. Only they would never use the soap and probably drink the scent. Can I come and stay with you for a few days—literally a few days?"

"John, I'd be delighted. You're the only person I know who I want—really want—Antonia to meet."

His face was radiant, and his eyes shining. There was no mistaking his sincerity. John nodded; to a young man already grown slightly disillusioned and even bored through always having too much money and no specific ambitions, the sight of Winnerton, with his tumbled fair hair, his air of eagerness, and his wide, delighted smile was almost touching.

"Right!" he said. "I'm at home; you can get in touch with me there. Let me know four days before you want to start, and I'll meet you in Town. Good luck—and congratulations."

He turned and began to stride away through the wood. Suddenly he halted, turned, and called, "Francis!"

"Yes?"

"The picture in the gallery of Venice is superb, and the old man, grand! Good-bye."

ii

Francis stood on the steps of his hotel and watched the luggage being stored away in the car. The pictures—not that there were many to take back, except the painting of Aramis and two or three he had made while at Maudesley and an impression or two of London—were in John's car. He felt free, expectant, and happy. He had fulfilled all his social duties, and had called to see Emmanuel Gollantz at his gallery in Bond Street. He had been ushered into "the presence" —for that was how he felt—by a stout, unprepossessing Jewess, and the old man had greeted him warmly. He had talked, easily and wisely, about painting, he had given advice which was so kindly phrased that it did not sound like advice at all, and he had offered Francis sherry and dry biscuits.

"Und now," he said, "you are almost r-ready to r-return to your loved Tir-rol, no?" His eyes twinkled. "Only to Tir-rol?"

From anyone else Francis would have resented the question; from this man it only brought a sense of warmth that he was sufficiently interested to ask the question.

"No, sir. I hope to be married soon."

"Ach! Is this public pr-roperty?"

"I'd be grateful if you'd regard it as confidential, sir."

Emmanuel bowed, his little formal movement. "I em flattered."

"I don't think that my family will be very much pleased, but," his very boyish smile widened, "but—well, it's all I want, sir. That and to paint decently."

The old man laid the tips of his well-kept fingers together, and began to talk gently and quietly. As he spoke, Francis thought sometimes that he talked to himself rather than to a listener.

"Es a young man I was impulsive. I said to someone who was engry vith me, 'I shell be married in a mont'.' I was fortunate, I was able to keep my pr-romise. I met a lady who became my vife in less than a mont'. I r-remember t'at I took her to see the Tower of London." He chuckled gently. "V'en she esked me to take her t'ere, I did not efen know v'ere it was. But—v'at is the phrase?—but I put up a goot performance.

"She was incr-redible, so charming, so alive, so attr-ractive. Now, it was not alvays easy, Francis; t'ere vere times v'en I was ter-ribly unhappy, v'en I t'ought t'at I could not continue. Dark times, cold times—t'en the sun burst out from behind clouds und scattered t'em. Sometimes it is necessary to make v'at ve call—in our stupidity—sacr-rifices. T'is v'at I wish to say to you—und I say it because I like you—t'ere are no sacrifices v'en t'ese matters touch the person ve love. Sacr-rifices do not exist, v'at ve call by that name are only small gifts, small pr-resents, small pr-roofs t'at ve love the person for whom t'ey are made. Ve learn to lift the shoulders —so!—to say, 'T'is is not'ing, t'is is somet'ing so small, so tr-rivial, it is not'ing to t'ink about, a vort'less t'ing'—but v'at is most important is—that ve learn to mean it! So ve forget the silly gnat t'at hes bitten us, the nettle t'at hes raised a small blister on our hand; ve laugh and say, 'Nossing! Gnats, nettles, v'at are they? I am sufficiently big to t'ink only of essential t'ings.' "

He turned to meet Francis's eyes and smiled. "I am a Jew, an Eastern, r-really. Ve are all Easterns, and so I talk in parables, stories, but I believe t'at you understand, no? T'ere, Francis, go back to Tirol, and—r-realize happiness. Maybe ve meet again, maybe ve don't, v'at does it matter? V'at does matter is t'at ve *have* met.

"T'ere—paint vell, and above all paint—honestly. *Mazaltov.*"

The porter said, "Everything is in, sir. All ready."

"Is his lordship here?"

John's voice said, "Indeed he is, waiting, cooling his heels while you were dreaming, staring into Piccadilly as if it were the Promised Land."

They slid out of London, the car was almost run in, and

soon Francis would be able really to let her out. He had felt tired, slack, but with every mile his spirits rose, and he felt filled with energy. They spoke very little; with John you could always keep silent without feeling that he was growing bored. He lay back in his seat, watching everything, and, Francis felt, storing away whatever he saw as some piece of additional information. John's brain was like that; like some perfectly kept card index. You mentioned some subject, some name, and immediately out came the proper card, and on it were exactly the facts which you wanted, to which might be added some original thought of John's own.

They stood on the quayside and watched the car slung into the hold.

Francis said, "I hate to watch that. The poor car looks so helpless, I'm always certain that they'll drop her."

"I believe that you endow everything inanimate with a definite personality, don't you?"

Francis nodded. "I believe that I do. It gives them a sense of importance, and they try to live up to it. Whew, that wind's cold."

The flat German plain was dull. Francis saw with delight that the car had done the necessary mileage, and he was able to show her qualities off to John. To John she was probably rather small beer, when you compared her with his Rolls-Bentley, but she pleased Francis. He didn't want to drive about Italy in a super-car; this would do very nicely for him—and Antonia.

They spent the night at an inn, where everything was shining and clean and impersonal. John said that he liked the Germans when they suppressed their own personality and character; it was when they became intimate, too close, that they were insufferable.

The next day they were in Austria.

John sighed his satisfaction. "Ah, this is better. I like the Austrians."

"But they fought against us as Germany did. They even asked for an armistice before the Germans did."

"Come, don't quibble, my lad; not much difference between October the twenty-eighth and November the eleventh."

John's card index was at work, Francis thought. He said, "Everyone makes excuses for the Austrians except the Italians. I suppose it is because they have pleasant manners and . . ."

John said, "And charm. How many people have got away with the most astonishing things because they had that? Then, of course, they have always Strauss and the Viennese waltz which endears them to all hearts. All hearts, at least, as sentimental as the English."

They reached Innsbruck too late to go further. Francis was restless, his cheeks looked flushed and his eyes too bright. John asked him if he had seen the town, the house with the Gold Roof.

"No, what is it?"

"A house with a gold roof—and there are magnificent suits of armour in the museum. Worth seeing."

"You go; honestly, I don't feel like it."

The next morning he looked better, and as they drove over the Brenner Pass, through the Italian customs, and slowly down to Bolzano, he was humming a little song, something about, "Tiroler land . . ."

At Bolzano, John said, "Luncheon here, I think, at the Greyhound. It's run by an old lady like a milder edition of Madame Schaffer in Vienna, and a little less mild than the two old ladies at the Frau Emma at Merano. There is not one of them can come up to our own Rosa Lewis at the Cavendish for sheer character, though."

"I don't mind lunching here," Francis said. "Now that I'm almost within sight of home, I'm content. I had a feeling that, somehow while I've been away, the whole of Tyrol might have vanished." He sent the porter off with a telegram. John remembered that he had sent a telegram every day since they left England, and wondered vaguely what kind of messages he sent.

What a strange fellow he was, brought up in a completely conventional atmosphere, a father who believed that all English gentlemen should be cut to a pattern, and a brother who knew exactly what was demanded from him and his position in the world. The war had scarcely touched them, life had gone on in almost the same strain; at one time servants had been absorbed into the army or munition factories, but everything had settled down again. Mostyn said frankly that it had been "a jolly good war, taken by and large", and his father had voiced the opinion again and again that, "They needed a lesson; b'Gad, we've given it to them. They'll think twice before they begin anything again. On the whole it's been a blessing to the world, and the Empire stands more firmly than it has ever done!"

Francis had been "different". He had resented the war because it interrupted his work in Paris. He had done his duty to the best of his ability, but he wasn't the type to enjoy—even vaguely—being in a herd. John couldn't imagine him planning "binges" or week-end visits to Paris, or later to Verona.

He said suddenly, "Ever been tight, Francis?"

"Me? Never since I was a kid, and the rum sauce on the Christmas pudding made me abominably sick. Why?"

"I just wondered, that's all."

You couldn't stigmatize him as a milksop, or pansy, or anything of that kind. He was manly enough; only he knew what he liked, what he enjoyed, and he was determined to follow his star. He had admitted to John that he loved Maudesley, but that he hated "all that goes with it". He'd taken a great deal more punishment during the war than Mostyn had done, he had been frightfully ill, and even now John wasn't certain that he looked awfully well. Perhaps he was giving

himself the best chance by staying out here, and—the thought
came with a little shock—marrying this girl. Strange to think
of the Earl of Maudesley's daughter-in-law being a peasant
girl from some small-sized village hidden away in the mountains. It would be fatal to try to transport her—he could
imagine how the family would inspect her, and form their
conclusions to her detriment. They would all decide that
Francis had lived with her, assume that she was pregnant
and that he had done "the decent thing". He could imagine
their cold, appraising eyes, old Maudesley, Mostyn, Lady
Honoria Swainton, Lady Blasford and the rest, to say nothing
of innumerable cousins and first cousins who would all come
and stare and probably smile behind their hands, thinking
what a fool Francis had made of himself.

"And yet," John thought, "they're practically all a set of
nitwits. Francis has more brains than the lot of them put
together. At least he can create something. None of them has
ever had an original idea or done an original thing in their
lives. The very thought of doing so would shock them
unutterably."

They were mounting slowly and, turning to Francis, John
saw that his face looked strained; there were drops of sweat
on his forehead.

He said abruptly, "I'll take over, you can direct me."

Francis said, "Thanks, that's good of you," and stopped
the car. Higher and higher they went; Francis was talking now,
talking rather quickly and excitedly.

"This isn't a very good road, but we shall soon be off it.
Look, there are the Dolomites; I'm going to paint them this
Winter. I believe that I can make something of them. This is
Mezzolombardo. It's our—metropolis. We're very proud of
it. They have been known to have an opera company here
for three nights. Look, the snow hasn't quite gone in the
hollows, but it's beginning to look grubby, eh. This is Cormia.

I like Cormia." He said it almost defiantly. "Now I've got the
car I shall be able to bring Antonia over to see her beloved
nuns. They were moved from Morano by the Bishop—we
don't like the Bishop much. He comes from Genoa. Now!"
suddenly, and with a voice filled with excitement, "the next
turn and we shall see the cottage. Gosh, I'm home again!
John, you've been wonderful. I know that I've been a dull
kind of companion, but I'll make up for it, I swear that I
will. Look! There, with those pines in front of it."

John looked and saw what seemed to him to be a cottage
like those which had been either described or pictured in fairy
stories which he had read in childhood. Not particularly
attractive, separated only from the road by a narrow strip of
garden. It was built of grey stone, it looked unpretentious,
homely, weather-tight and friendly.

The blood was pounding in Francis's ears; he felt trem-
ulous, and at the same time wildly excited. Maudesley had
never stirred him as did this little house. Almost before
John brought the car to a standstill he sprang out and rushed
round the front of the car, giving the bonnet a pat as he
passed as he might have patted a well-behaved dog. The door
opened, and Antonia stood framed in the opening, her eyes
alight, her lovely hair shining, her hands outstretched.

She cried ,"Ah, *caro signor*, you have returned!" and dropped
him one of her quaint little curtsies. Aramis rushed out and
began to leap round his master's feet; Antonia reproved him.
"Aramis, be careful, the signor is tired. Quiet now, quiet."
But Aramis had no intention of being quiet, and rushed out to
discover who his master had brought with him.

Francis said, "Oh, how nice it is to see you! I have brought
you a real lord this time, and a new car. I have brought—oh,
so many things. You've missed me, missed my sulky tempers
and tiresome ways?"

"Tut, tut!" She reproved him softly. "Such things to say!"

E

John climbed out of the car and came towards the house. Antonia saw a very tall man, with a handsome, aristocratic face, a high-bridged nose, kind, quizzical eyes and a mouth that smiled.

"John, here is Antonia; Antonia, this is John Trevor, Marquis of Rivermead. Yes, a real, genuine lord."

Again Antonia curtsied. "And the other signor in a long blue coat and a cap like Innerhoffer wears; is he—a lord?"

"He's my chauffeur," John told her. "Has he brought in the things? Good! Please, signorina, where is the *albergo*? I must go with him to garage the car and get him a room for the night." He spoke very rapidly; he wanted to get away to give these two a chance to be alone if only for a few moments. How charming the girl was; she had poise and dignity; she was neither familiar nor subservient.

She answered, "The *albergo*, lord, it is down there in the village. I myself would take Gloria and ride down to show you, but the signor is—I know—longing for his tea—*Té Inglese*—and the kettle is about to boil."

Francis said, "Oh, I can wait. You'd like tea too, John, eh?"

"Above all things, but let me get Mills settled. I'll drive your bus down and he can follow. You'll have to build a garage. I shan't be five minutes."

Francis was wandering about the room, smiling with satisfaction. How nice it all looked, how sweetly it smelt, and how good it was to be home again.

Antonia had the table laid, the checked cloth he liked, and the blue-ringed china; the brown tea-pot which he had sent for to England was standing on the hearthstone growing warm from the brightly burning fire. He sniffed with appreciation. Fir-cones! Delicious.

"You're glad to have me home, Antonia?"

"Very glad, signor. I did not expect you to return so soon."

He laughed. "To tell you the truth, I couldn't bear to stay away any longer."

"You find everything—in order here?" she asked.

"In order! It is all—perfection perfected. Antonia, you have that blue dress you wore the first day I came? I want to paint you in it; yes, with Aramis on your knee. It is to be my best picture!"

"I have a nicer dress, signor—that blue is old."

"But it goes so well with the colour of your eyes; your eyes are like gentians." She flushed a little. Imagine the signor even noticing the colour of her eyes! Francis went on, "I hoped to find some gentians when we stopped at Bolzano, but I saw none in the flower shops. I wanted to bring some with me. Antonia, my pictures have had a great success; nearly all were sold, and for prices which I thought were quite good. People—art dealers, critics and so forth—think that they are good, that I have a future, a career. Oh, there is so much I have to tell you. You like John? Yes, he's a splendid fellow, a good friend to me."

She said gravely, "Then if he is a good friend to you I shall of course like him very much, signor." She filled the tea-pot and set it on the table. Then went into the kitchen, returning with a covered dish, saying, "The little hot cakes which you like."

She turned as if to return to the kitchen. Francis cried, "Oh, don't go! I've just come home! For once, please, stay and have a cup of tea with me."

She hesitated. "But the lord will be back at any minute. What will he think?"

"He'll think how lucky we both are to have anyone so charming to take tea with us. Yes, you pour out. Oh, this is pleasant."

She poured out his tea and half a cup for herself. She didn't really like tea, it wasn't actually unpleasant but it was not really worth drinking. Francis had it sent from London; it didn't look like the tea they sold at Pietra's shop. Didn't smell the same either. This was tea made for an Earl, it said so on the packet. She thought that perhaps the Earl Grey was some relation of Francis's. If so, it was meritorious to show respect to your family. No one could really enjoy drinking such stuff.

Francis sipped it with satisfaction. "That's good, and the cups I like with the blue rings on them. I saw no cups as nice in England. See, here is John!" The tall young man entered and Antonia rose.

"Sit down, please, signorina, sit down. I found the *albergo* —no, no sugar, thank you—and settled Mills in. The proprietor sent his *complimenti* to you, Francis, and hoped that England had not been too foggy." Antonia noticed that he spoke Italian much more fluently than Francis; he spoke it almost like an Italian, she thought.

"Ah, these fogs," she said in tones of commiseration, "how terrible they must be. The signor says that they do not arrive *every* day, but I think almost every day, no, lord?"

He returned gravely, "Shall we say that they come far too often, that they are most unpleasant, and bad for the health. Signorina, I shall be here for a few days, and I cannot allow this deification—this reference to me as lord. It verges perilously on blasphemy! If you must give me a handle to my name why not call me—*conte*?"

"Is it the same?" she asked Francis anxiously.

He nodded. "Practically. Both mean almost nothing!"

She didn't feel completely happy about it, but there were so many other things to be happy about. She had longed for Francis to return, she had laid his letters away as treasures, scarcely daring to re-read them for fear she might wear out the paper. As the time for his arrival had grown nearer, she had been filled with forebodings. Suppose that he decided not to come back after all, suppose that he had an accident in this new car, suppose—suppose—suppose? Then he had, it seemed so suddenly, been standing at the door, not changed, except, she thought, that he looked thinner. That would be the bad food and the terrible fogs, to say nothing of late hours and lack of good fresh air. It was well known that if the windows of a London autobus were scraped, the deposit on them could be used to kill rabbits!

He wanted to paint her portrait. She knew that it was a compliment, but she doubted, with a kind of tenderness, if anyone would recognize it. But it was the wish to do it that pleased her so! He had thought of bringing back gentians, because they were the colour of her eyes. In her kitchen, preparing a dinner which she had planned for days before, she peered into the little mirror trying to decide if her eyes were really the colour of gentians.

She could hear the two men talking as she worked, the conte's voice deeper and fuller than the signor's; his was higher and, to her ears, more melodious. There in that pan was her own special soup, which took at least three days to prepare. How delicious it smelt! A Poitrine de Veau with green peas. Admittedly, the peas were from a tin but she had prepared them with great care. The book which Mother Anna Maria had given her advised the use of sherry, and she had been forced to use marsala because there was no sherry in the village; Pietra said that she had never heard of it. A "Ribbon Jelly" because the signor loved a sweet, and then—and she viewed the dish with satisfaction—a Chaudfroid of Sweetbreads, decorated with asparagus tips.

Francis came to the kitchen door, and she cried, "Ah, signor, no! Please, I make a surprise for you and the lord— I mean the count."

He stood smiling at her; they must have been talking seriously about something or other, Antonia decided, for his fair hair was ruffled, and one lock fell over his forehead.

"You're a treasure," he said, "dear Antonia. I won't look, I won't even try to *smell* out your secret. Can we have baths, that's what I came to ask?"

There was a good deal of dignity in her tone when she answered.

"But, signor, naturally. In your own house you can always have a bath, two baths if you wish. The water is hot, it has been hot since before tea-time. Will Orvieto be right to drink at dinner?"

"Splendid. I'll come down and mix some cocktails. There is some ice, eh?"

"In our refrigerator there is always ice, signor. Oh, what a wonder machine it is, and how thankful I am to have it. Imagine to yourself, only the Count Zevio and you have such a thing, and the chef at the Castello says that he would rather have an ice-box! How are we to progress when people are so stupid?"

Her little air of self-sufficiency made Francis smile. "What a funny little soul she is," he thought. A year ago she'd barely heard of an ice-box, now she regards a refrigerator as a necessity in any decent kitchen. He longed to put his arms round her, kiss her soft cheek, and whisper that he loved her completely, and wanted to marry her. "How do I love thee, let me count the ways," he said softly as he climbed the stairs and entered his immaculate bedroom. How did he love her? In every way, for everything she said and did and—was. Nothing mattered—except perhaps his work—except Antonia. Maudesley, much as he loved it, could go; he might never see it again. London and the "bright lights" had never interested him a great deal; Paris—yes, he loved Paris, and he would take her there, show her the places he loved, the bridges and the lights on the river. His friends—most of the men of his own age, and none of them had been very close friends—had died in the war. There was only John. He never wanted to lose John—Antonia, John, and in a queer way, that wonderful old man, with his noble face and his excellent sherry.

He called, "I say, John! I've no sherry; it will have to be cocktails."

John shouted back, "Sheer poison, but I'm willing to martyrize myself to save my host embarrassment. I've finished my bath; shall I run yours?"

CHAPTER FIVE

THE door closed behind Antonia, the time was half past nine, the night was bright with moonlight. She had stood for a moment in the doorway to bid them "Good night."

John said, "If I may say so—a perfect dinner, signorina."

"The count is too good."

Francis sat there, leaning back in his chair, smiling at her.

"It was a beautiful dinner," he said, and she read into his words the fact that he was happy and glad to be home again. They had wanted her to sit down with them at dinner; she had been flattered and pleased but had explained that she preferred to be in her kitchen while dinner was in progress.

Francis had said, "Antonia, you're a little snob."

The count added gravely, "An inverted snob, which is much more culpable."

She didn't know what they meant so she laughed, and said, "*Si, si,*" and hurried back to her kitchen.

"Good night, signor," she said, and hoped that he could hear all that she meant in her heart. Such lovely things she would have liked to say to him, wishing that God might guard him all through the night, that his dreams might be filled with all the colours of the Heavens, that the most glorious saints would stand at the corners of his bed.

He said, "Good night, Antonia," and suddenly got out of his big chair and came to open the door for her, saying, "I have forgotten my manners in England; forgive me. Again —good night."

As he closed the door, he turned and said to John "Well . . .?"

"Charming, oh charming, and—what a cook! The sauce on the sweetbreads, what is it? I've never tasted it before.

know how it's made, but there was something additional in it that I couldn't place."

Francis came back to his chair. "Oh, damn her cooking, it's Antonia herself that interests me. Do you wonder that I'm in love with her?"

"In your shoes I should probably be in love with her myself."

"Thank God you're not in my shoes!"

"Mind, Francis, I'm not going to say that I don't question the wisdom of it all. I don't say that there won't be difficulties. But, after all, difficulties are only there to be overcome, and wisdom is a monopoly of old men. Very few of them acquire it anyway. 'Gather ye rosebuds . . .' because even when the roses fade you can always keep the petals in a Chinese jar and they smell delicious. Anyway, the scent reminds you that at one time you did have the roses themselves."

They went to bed in the little quiet house, and Antonia returned to her mother's cottage. Ferrari greeted her, smiling. To him she was as good as any newspaper, bringing him, he felt, news of the great world.

"Ah, the lord is home, no?" he cried.

Antonia nodded. "And he has brought with him another lord. This one is not almost a lord, but completely one. They have two cars and a man wearing a long blue coat to drive one. My signor has bought a car, it is the colour of old wine. Its name is 'Umbaire. The signor is going to build a garage near the house. He has sold hundreds of pictures at immense prices; he has made a great fortune. He is said to be the greatest painter in the world."

She was busy while she talked, stacking the supper dishes in the sink, pouring hot water on to them and washing them busily. Her mother watched her closely. Maria might be slow, indolent when it came to housework, but she was sufficiently observant. Antonia had been quiet, talking little while the

signor was in England; now she came in with her eyes
sparkling, her cheeks like roses. She moved about lightly,
her washing-up was accomplished very quickly.

Maria thought, "She's happy because he has come home.
She's in love with him. I hope that she won't do anything
stupid as did the daughter of Bronzini."

Antonia slept soundly, tired out with happiness and
excitement. The morning sunshine slanting into her room
woke her, and she sprang from her bed, for she was one of
those people who are fully awake the moment they open
their eyes. She hurried downstairs—where at her suggestion,
and with the approval of her stepfather, a curtain had been
hung round the big bed—and lit the fire. While it burnt into a
flame she went outside to the shed, and washed in water which
was so icy cold that it made her set her teeth. She imagined it
coming down from the highest of the Dolomites, where the
snow never melted, and it brought the tang of snow with it.
Glowing after rubbing her body on a rough towel, she
hurried back to the house. The room was swept. As she began
to dust, there was a knock at the door. This was the baker's
son, Enso, with the rolls. The darker, cheaper bread for her
mother's house, finer, white rolls for her to carry up to the
English. The small boy unwrapped the clean cloth and sniffed
with appreciation.

"They smell good, no?" he said. Then added, "The English
signor is back, he brings with him a new car and a lord; the
lord has a man in a long blue coat to drive his car, the Englishman drives his own. That is because the lord is so important."

Antonia said, a little haughtily, "The English signor
prefers to drive his car. He is a true sportsman."

"It may be so," the lad agreed, and ran off back to the
village.

Antonia woke her mother; Maria yawned and stretched,
and rubbed her eyes. Ferrari waved his arms as if trying to

fight his way through the mists of sleep. Antonia went back to make the coffee and lay the table. Her stepfather hurried through the kitchen, wearing his shirt and trousers. He did not spend long in the shed over the ceremony of washing; later he would go to the barber's and have a luxurious shave. He came back, sniffed the coffee, and smiled at Antonia.

Her mother came through, still yawning and making strange noises, "U-ugh—a-aah!" indicating that sleep was not yet completely vanquished. Presently they were both seated at the table, with bowls of steaming coffee, breaking their bread into small pieces which they soaked and then ate, making small sucking noises.

The warning hooter from the factory sounded; in fifteen minutes they must be at the factory gates ready to stamp their work cards on the machine. Ferrari finished the last drops of his coffee.

He jerked his head in the direction of the factory, saying, "Wage slaves, that is what we are! Workers of the world unite, you have nothing to lose but your chains, and when you have lost them, some new party will provide fresh ones!"

He liked to say things of that kind, always as if he spoke in a jocular way, but actually there was an element of truth in his words. Antonia knew that he hated the Communists, but that he hated as much, and possibly distrusted even more, the new party. He asked if Italy, the Italy of the Risorgimento, of Garibaldi, of—history—were to be led by the nose by an agitator, an ex-Bersaglieri—some people said not even a sergeant. "One does not rule a country by editing newspapers," Ferrari said. "A country is ruled by the man who controls the hearts of the people."

"He would be one of the *onorevole*—ah! He and his pen-pushing friends would direct Italy's foreign policy." Ferrari had very little idea what a "foreign policy" meant.

Now he repeated, "Ah, yes, wage slaves, but we have the spending of our own wage after all!" Maria was pulling on her black woollen shawl. "Come, Maria, let us go back to our treadmill!" He laughed, for he had the reputation of being a humorist and he enjoyed his own jokes. "*Ciao*, 'Tonia."

They went out; Antonia finished the cleaning of the room, then, snatching up her own shawl, ran out to get the wonderful bicycle to ride to her own work. It was a beautiful morning, the promise of Spring was on the highway to being fulfilled. The air was full of that sweetness which comes with the rising of sap, the growth of new grass and tender young herbs. Down in the valley she could hear the noise of the great circular saw at the wood-mill, and looking down could see the sawdust flying, the grains catching the early sunlight.

Aramis met her, welcoming her with wild joy. She caressed him, and he followed her into the shining kitchen. She put the rolls, carefully wrapped, in a clean cloth to keep warm, put on the kettle, and began to hurry about her work in her usual calm and efficient way. She lit the fire under the bathroom boiler, and, glancing at the door of Francis's bedroom felt an additional sense of joy that he was back sleeping in h own house, under his own roof.

Beppi came with the milk; it was still warm, for he ha only just finished milking.

He wished her good morning, adding, "So the English one is back?"

Antonia nodded; she was too busy to waste time gossiping with Beppi; anyway, she didn't like him much. She didn't believe that his milk was very good; his cows looked poor. She always strained the milk through muslin and then scalded it.

"Has he made more pictures?" He grinned, and she felt a sudden longing to smack his face with its cheeks covered with stubble.

"Not as many as he took away," she said coldly. "Most of them have been sold for immense sums of money in London. I may be wrong, but I believe the King of England bought one. The signor has—arrived. He is now a famous painter."

"*Dio mio! Ma, Ciao,* 'Tonia."

Two small trays, each with a cup and saucer and one biscuit. She made the tea. How strange and inexplicable were the ways of these grand English people. There was the lord, who the signor had told her was a great traveller, able to climb mountains, and walk over sandy deserts, yet he, like the signor, had to drink a cup of this nauseating *té* before he could get out of bed. She wondered what was its attraction. It was certainly not a tonic, that she could have understood had it been a small cup of black coffee for example, but this straw-coloured, straw-scented stuff. She wrinkled her nose. "Pah!"

She knocked on Francis's door, and heard his voice, still heavy with sleep, call "*Avanti!*" She opened the door and went in. He was lying there, wearing the bright-coloured silk pyjamas which he affected and which she admired, his hands clasped behind his head, blinking his eyes at the morning sunlight. When he saw her, he stared at her—a queer, fixed expression, she thought—then said in what was almost a whisper, "God! It's Antonia. I'm really home!"

She smiled at him, but his expression had disturbed her, had set her heart beating heavily. She could not interpret its meaning; indeed she did not know that she wished even to attempt to do so, but she felt that it marked a change, a new phase, a difference in their relationship. She set down the little tray, and, going to the window, drew the curtains further back. With her back towards him, she spoke.

"Good morning, signor. I hope that you slept well. Ah, here is the small Aramis to see you!"

Francis said, and she felt that the words came with something of an effort, "Yes, thank you, I slept beautifully. Come, Aramis—there, don't upset my tea."

She carried the other tray to John Trevor; he was wide awake and greeted her cheerfully. There was nothing strange or unusual in his tone.

Back in her kitchen she told herself not to be foolish. Why did she imagine such things? The signor had been half asleep, his exclamation meant exactly what he said, surprised to find himself at home and his tea brought to him by the familiar Antonia instead of a strange servant. She rebuked herself for being imaginative and idiotic. "What could he have meant," she asked herself indignantly, "other than what he said?"

The count was the first to come down. He wore a tweed suit which looked rough like a dog's coat, and a tie which looked bright and soft. He came to the kitchen door, and said, "For the second time, good morning, signorina. Something smells very nice."

She smiled at him, and John thought what a pleasant smile it was, what good teeth she had, and how bright and clear were her eyes.

She said, "When first the signor came here, he wished to have the same breakfast—*colazione*—as people eat here. I slowly began to persuade him to take more, at first an egg, very fresh you understand, then perhaps a small trout from the river, grilled, and now—*ecco!*—he eats breakfast as the English, so he tells me, eat it. Kidneys, a small piece of fried ham, and sometimes a banana fried." She laughed. "This pleases me very much."

"Well, it smells delicious. And you, what do you have?"

"What I have always had—coffee and a fresh roll, *conte*."

He stayed for three days, during which time Francis drove him—or he drove Francis—to places in the district. John was enchanted by the beauty and peace of the place. Francis said that he ought to buy a house and stay there.

He shook his head. "No, old chap, not for me. I love this, but for how long? Then I want to wander about, or seek out the fleshpots of Egypt; I want the bright lights, pretty women in pretty clothes, music—one place could never hold me for long. I sometimes wish that it could.

"I can tell you one thing, that delightful Antonia is not only a superb cook, she is a natural cook. She has all that it needs to rise to the top of her profession. She has inventiveness; she has courage in her cooking. She is forever longing to try out the effect of new things. Have you ever asked her to show you her collection of herbs? Whew!" He whistled softly, "I doubt if any chef in London, though possibly in Paris, has such a collection."

Francis looked at him, his expression quizzical. "I'm not in love with her for her cooking, John."

"My good lad, I realize that. You give yourself away twenty times a day. A more sophisticated woman would have known that you were in love with her the moment you came back." He laid his hand on his friend's shoulder. "Go in and win, and by Gad, you'll win someone worth winning. She's pure gold all through."

The morning he left, while Francis was watching Mills store the baggage and giving him directions as to the best route to take, John came into the kitchen. He stood looking down at Antonia from his great height, his eyes very kind.

"If I were a gypsy," he said, "I should ask you to cross my palm with silver so that I might tell your fortune. I'm not, but I shall tell you just the same. You will see great changes, there will be times which will be like the morning sunrise on a clear day; there may be difficult, puzzling times, but you will face them all and—win, because God has given you a brave and loving heart. Never be afraid, never allow yourself to grow despondent—even if there is night, remember that the morning always dawns. If ever you should need me, if I could ever be of help, this address," he gave her a small card, "will always find me. It may not find me very quickly, for I am a rolling stone, but it will—eventually. I am very fond of Francis. Except that it is not customary for Englishmen to say that they love anyone—except their wives, when often they don't mean it—I should say that I loved him. Take great care of him; he is a genius, he is making a great name. He depends almost completely on you."

He took her hand and held it in his own strong brown ones. Antonia felt her eyes fill with tears. She answered in a small, almost childish voice. "Excellency, be sure that I will. I regard him with great admiration."

Suddenly John laughed. "He wants more than admiration, my dear. See that he gets it. Good-bye, and we shall meet again."

ii

The next morning Francis got out his canvas and set it up. He was almost feverish to begin his portrait of Antonia. He said that they would begin immediately after breakfast. Her face showed dismay.

"But the house, signor. The food. These things must be done and prepared."

"Can't you send down to the shop and get some cooked ham? Cooked ham, *salame*, *mortadella* and a salad. What more do we want?"

"Signor, I have been here for a year and a half, I have never yet given you cold ham and salad, and, excuse me, but I do not wish to begin now. I will ride down to the village, and if you wish, as this is your work, I will get Maddelena to come and do the housework. I will prepare something very simple for your meals."

He shrugged his shoulders. "When I was in Paris, I often——"

She nodded. "It is possible that you did many strange things in Paris. It may be that is why when you were in the war you became so ill. Then you had a dirty old woman to look after you. No doubt she robbed you and fed you on cold ham" (with great scorn). "Now you have Antonia."

The sulky expression left his face; he smiled. "Dear, wonderful, splendid Antonia. There, go, and come back quickly, and remember Maddelena is to come every single day! Remember."

She was back very quickly. She whisked into the kitchen and he heard her moving about, humming gently to herself. He had called her "Dear, wonderful, splendid Antonia"! No wonder, she thought, that her heart was singing. Her fingers, her brain, worked rapidly. She must not keep him waiting a moment longer than was absolutely necessary. There was his luncheon to stew very gently, and there were the bones for stock for the soup. She ran upstairs and put on her blue dress. She thought it was a pity that the signor did not want her to wear her new brown cashmere which she wore for Mass. Still, he had these strange ideas, it was his picture. She ran downstairs again.

He was making sketches of Aramis in a big sketch-book. He looked up as she entered, and laughed.

"How nice you look! What a good blue that is. There, I have moved the big chair. I thought that I'd have some brocade to throw over the back. I was wrong; it is better left quite simple. Now, sit in a position which is quite comfortable, and sit as if Aramis was sitting on your knee. See, hold this big china dog, and try to believe that it is Aramis." He stepped back. "Oh, excellent. Just your head a little more . . . yes, yes, perfect."

Francis painted very rapidly, working with great free

strokes, his face intent and serious. Sometimes, Antonia
thought, when anything pleased him, he smiled, but didn't
speak. The clock on the mantelpiece struck ten, eleven, and
then twelve. Her whole body was aching; she felt that at any
moment she would have to beg him to let her move. Maddelena was no longer moving about upstairs; Antonia thought
that she must have gone. Then Aramis whined and Francis
said, "What is it, little boy?"

Antonia said, moistening her dry lips, "Perhaps he is
hungry."

He stared at her, then laid down his palette, and came
towards her. He caught her hands; they were very cold and
he leaned forward anxiously.

"My angel, what a brute I am! You're exhausted. Antonia,
forgive me; it was so wonderful to be painting you, I forgot.
Don't move for a moment, darling, let me get you a little
cognac. Yes, I insist. Oh, my sweetheart, what a brute I've
been!"

He hurried away and she laid her head against the back of
the chair, thinking, "I must have fainted. I've never done such
a thing. Or have I been asleep, and did I dream that he said
those things to me? Darling—sweetheart! It is impossible!"

He was back, slipping his arm round her shoulders, and
holding the little glass to her lips. "Sip it," he told her. "Gently,
poor little sweet. There! Does that make you feel better?
Can you forgive me?"

Francis had slipped to his knees, and had taken her hands
in his, holding them against his cheek. Once or twice he kissed
them gently.

She said, "Signor, I am quite all right. The dinner . . ."

He looked up and his eyes met hers. "Dinner!" he said
and laughed. "What does dinner matter? Nothing, not a
thing! Not even a dinner which you have prepared. Antonia,
I knew that I loved you when I was in London; oh, long before

I reached London. I made up my mind to tell you so when I had finished your portrait. Then, the sight of your tired face, and the knowledge that I had kept you there, sitting so still for me, made it all too much. I had to tell you. Darling, you don't know how much I love you; I scarcely know myself. Antonia, do you love me at all?"

"Do I love you?" she said. "I didn't know that anyone could love anyone as I love you. It's bigger—bigger than the whole world."

He put his arms round her and drew her face down to his; he held her close and she made no resistance. She smelt, he thought, of fresh, clean water, of some kind of simple soap, of sunshine, fresh air, of health and energy, and withal a warmth emanated from her.

Once she whispered, "Signor, it can't be true."

He kissed her mouth, it was soft and tender beneath his lips.

"You mustn't call me that," he reproved gently. "Call me by my name, please."

Very softly she said, "Francesco, *caro mio*."

He said, "John knew, you know."

"The lord? What did he say?"

"He is very pleased; he told me that if I hadn't fallen in love with you first, in all probability he would have done so."

She laughed softly. "How foolish. *Carissimo—tesoro—*my dinner."

She pushed him gently away, and he followed her into the kitchen, the dog Aramis expressing its satisfaction that dinner was at last appearing on the horizon. Francis, leaning against the door-jamb, watched her moving so swiftly, first to glance at the simmering meat, then to take the little dog's plate from the dresser and get his food from her beloved refrigerator. He felt a sense of excited tenderness that even at this moment she did not forget the dog.

"There, *piccolino*, eat well," she said, as she set down the plate.

She began to serve the dinner, the delicious smell reached him, and he realized that he was hungry.

"It is very simple," she warned him, "but you were in such a hurry, I had no time. I shall do better tonight. I feel rather ashamed. In my happiness I forgot my duty."

"How nice to sit and talk over dinner. I've always hated the way you shut yourself out here while I eat in solitary state," he said.

Antonia glanced up from dishing up the elaborate stew which she had prepared. She looked startled, almost dismayed.

"But I don't think that it would be correct," she said. "If people saw us through the window, what would they think?"

"In the first place, angel, who the hell cares what they think? Let them think what they like! If you imagine that I'm going to bother about what Signora This and Signorina That think —you're making a mistake. I'm engaged to the loveliest girl in the world, and if I can't sit down to a meal with her, on this day of all days, well, it's a damned pity."

"Engaged?" she repeated, for he had used the word "*fidanzato*". "You mean—*a promessa di Matrimonio*, like Marco and Bianca?"

It was Francis's turn to stare at her. "My God, what did you imagine I meant?" He completely forgot that when he first knew that he loved her, his ideas regarding marriage had not been so clearly defined as they were at this moment. He felt outraged that she should have imagined that he could possibly have meant anything but marriage.

She turned to him, and flung herself into his arms. "I am a wicked girl," she sobbed. "I was so happy that nothing mattered except my happiness in knowing that you loved me. I thought—I thought . . . Oh, Francesco *mio*, I cannot tell you what I thought!" She tore herself from his arms, drying her eyes and exclaiming, "Oh, my dinner! It will be cold."

They ate their dinner together, at first talking gaily, Antonia delighted because Francis seemed to be enjoying his meal and eating with such a good appetite. It was while they drank their coffee that they spoke of marriage again.

"When can we be married, 'Tonia?" he asked.

"Ah! It all seems so wonderful. But, *caro mio*, you are not a Christian? I mean a—Catholic. That is difficult. You would find it difficult to change your religion, no?"

Francis Winnerton's religion was a thing which had never troubled him a great deal. He knew that he had been christened, that at school he had been prepared, by the Head, for Confirmation, and given certain words of advice regarding the general behaviour of Christian gentlemen which had made him feel hot under his collar. When he stayed at Maudesley he usually went with his father and Mostyn to the church where the huge family pew was situated and where the walls were covered with tablets recording the merits and splendid attributes of dead and gone Maudesleys; where there were ancient monuments where past knights and baronets and the first earl lay, their effigies above them, sometimes with their wives, sometimes alone.

He had rather enjoyed the service, for the Rector, conscious that his patron's eye was on his gold hunter, which he removed from its chain and laid on the velvet cushion before him as the clergyman entered the pulpit, never preached for more than ten minutes. He used to enjoy those ten minutes; the smooth cadences of the Rector's voice, the quiet atmosphere and the light slanting through the ugly, vividly coloured stained glass, flinging patches of red, purple, blue and gold on to the old tombs. In Summer the scent of the newly cut hay and the distant bleating of sheep came in through the open windows, the drowsy buzzing of a bee, clumsily, foolishly trying to find a way out, all contributed to his sense of peace and well-being.

He had gone to Notre Dame and the Madeleine in Paris when he heard that there was some particularly good music or noted singer at the High Mass; he had been to various churches in England, because he had been told that the singing was good, or the architecture was splendid, but religion—he was vague about it all.

He frowned, then remembered that he had heard something about Mixed Marriages. Yes, Lilian Fancourt—all the Fancourts were Catholics—had married Tommie Lessways, and his uncle was a Bishop in the Protestant Church. That was it! A Mixed Marriage.

He imparted this piece of information to Antonia, who looked dubious and said, "We shall have to speak with the priest, possibly even the Bishop. If we," she hesitated, flushing, "if we were blessed with children, would you mind if they were Catholics?"

"Mind, no! Of course I shouldn't mind."

"And your father, the Earl, would he be very angry?"

"About our children being Catholics? Probably, he easily gets angry. Oh, you mean about us being married?" He nodded. "Certain to be. Only as I'm the second son, and am never likely to inherit, it doesn't matter. He believes that I am living with someone at the moment, I'm certain of that."

"Living with someone?" Her voice held unbelief and distress. "And who, please, does he believe it is? Oh!" She was indignant.

"You, my adorable goose," Francis told her. "He imagines you, no doubt, as some dark-eyed, bold-looking Italian wench, with a large bust and swinging hips, smelling strongly of garlic, and sharing my bed and board. Don't look so shocked, my sweet. What on earth does it matter what he thinks? He doesn't like me, and I can't say that I'm bubbling over with affection for him. Now, let's get back to work. No, no, you mustn't look at it. When it's finished, not before. I had an old Scottish nurse once who used to say 'fules an' bairns should never see things 'hauf din'."

"I don't understand; this Scottish—what language is this?"

"It means," he said, with his arm round her, "that idiots —that's you, darling, and bairns—that's children—and you're a child too—should never see anything when it is half finished."

"Then, sit by the fire for ten minutes, while I wash these dishes; at least the idiot can do that! No, Francesco, I will not leave the table in this disorder, not even to please you. There, put another log on the fire; not that it is cold, but a fire is a friendly thing."

iii

That evening when she walked home Francis went with her. He was determined that there should be no chatter, no gossiping. He would "start off on the right foot" from the beginning. He would talk to her mother and stepfather, make his position clear, give them the presents which he had brought from England, and in their presence put the ring which he had bought in Bond Street on Antonia's finger.

He had painted all day, as long as the light lasted, and he was delighted with the progress which he had made. The likeness was, he felt, emerging more rapidly than he dared to hope. He felt that he was painting some of his own happiness into the picture, that some of the joy which made his heart feel as if it were singing was actually appearing in the brush-strokes.

When the light began to fade, he laid down his brushes with a sigh of content.

"There, darling, that's all for today. But I did remember to give you little rests this time, didn't I? I was so ashamed this morning, so selfish, so self-centred. You have forgiven me? Antonia, this is the happiest day in my life!"

"And in mine, *caro mio*."

After dinner they walked down to her mother's cottage, Aramis skipping beside them. Francis said that he believed that the little dog knew, and Antonia assured him that he had said so to her.

"He told me, while I was preparing your mid-day dinner, that he had always known that I loved you, but that he had doubted if you felt anything about me—except that I was a good cook."

Francis caught her by the arms, swung her round and faced her. His eyes were very bright, and the heavy lock of fair hair which tumbled over his forehead always gave her a feeling of additional tenderness for him.

"The lying little hound," he said. "Tomorrow I shall send him to England, and during the six months' quarantine he'll learn to regret saying such things. 'Tonia, kiss me!"

"Here in the road!"

"It's partly our road, we pay taxes for it!"

She lifted her face and kissed him; Francis Winnerton felt a wave of affection sweep over him. What did he care if he never saw Maudesley again? Nothing. He loved England. Some day he would wish to take Antonia there, to drive slowly through the Dorset villages, to see the ruins of Corfe, the lovely hamlets of the Cotswolds, Warwickshire, Shropshire, and further north to Lancashire and Yorkshire to the Dales where life seemed to flow so easily and tranquilly, and slowly on to Scotland, hills and valleys, mountains and the islands of the Hebrides.

He held her to him. "Oh, there's so much I have to show you! Such lovely places, so much music to hear, and so many wonderful pictures to see. Isn't it splendid that we are young, that we've got so much time to spend together?"

She nodded, whispering, "Touch iron!" to avert bad luck. Then as they continued their walk, she said, "Francesco, you know that my home is very poor, my mother and step-father are just simple people."

He cried almost indignantly, "And what am I? Aren't I a simple person? Don't be silly! I shall get on very well with them both. I have brought with me, yes, in the pocket of my coat, a bottle of very good brandy. Oh, don't be afraid."

When he had told her that he wished to speak with her mother and Ferrari, she had sent a note down by the boy who brought the meat for evening dinner. She had written:

Dear Mama,

This evening the signor wishes to come and speak with you and Signor Ferrari. It is about me. Do not be disturbed.—A.

But Maria, when she read the note, had been disturbed. She had flung it from her as though it were red hot, slumped down in her chair, and had beaten her hands on the table. Her husband, busy putting on the meal which Antonia had left prepared for them, turned and said, "What is it? Is the house on fire then?"

Without speaking she had indicated Antonia's note. "Read that!"

He read it, his face grave, but Maria broke in on his speculations.

"Am I cursed then, that both my daughters should behave in this way and disgrace me? First Carolina, of whom we have never heard since she left, and now Antonia. Rest assured that he comes, this Englishman, to tell us that she is with child by him. He is rich, he eats only special bread baked for him; he baths every day, changes his clothes more often than ordinary people do; there is no doubt——"

Her stout little husband silenced her. "Peace, Maria. We know nothing. For myself—I wait. It is a good thing that the Englishman comes to see us, he might have run away to England and have left her. This seems to mean that he will, at least, provide for her. For myself," and he rubbed the hard palm of his hand across his forehead, "I find this hard to believe. I know our Antonia, she is good. But I am what they call a 'man of the world' and young people have blood which is hot, they long to take, to know—everything. Is it for us, the old ones, who have blood which begins to run thin, to blame them? I don't know. What I do know is that I am about to put on my best suit and hurry down to Primo to have a shave. I shall meet the Englishman in perfect condition. And you, Maria *cara*, will put on the dress which I bought for you last November. I shall bring back a bottle of good wine. Have glasses laid out ready. I shall also bring some sweet biscuits. What is money at this moment?"

Maria started to her feet, her face flaming. "I should put on my best clothes! Huh! You should buy wine and sweet biscuits! Why? To greet the man who is the seducer of my daughter! *Santa Maria!*"

He stared at her, his face grave and only faintly disturbed, for he knew in his heart that she would do as he ordered.

"Tch, tch! These words—seducer! Cursing! Let us wait. I tell you, Maria, to change your dress."

With that he disappeared behind the curtains, and she heard him taking down his Sunday clothes and putting on a clean shirt. Unwillingly, she put a clean cloth on the table, set out glasses, and a plate for the sweet biscuits. Sweet biscuits indeed!

Ferrari passed through the room calling, "*Ciao*, Maria." She shrugged her shoulders. First Carolina and now Antonia.

Her two sons dead at Monte Grappa. What a life! Reluctantly she took her best dress from the big *armadio*—which had belonged to her first husband's mother—and first smoothing her hair, with a comb which had lost a number of teeth, she pulled it on.

She went back to the living-room, threw some small logs on the fire, and sat down heavily to wait. If this Englishman were to take Antonia away, what would she do? There would be meals to prepare, cleaning and mending, washing and ironing. How she hated them all!

She sighed heavily. No, if Antonia were pregnant, she must come home, and then she could keep the house clean and cook the meals. Ferrari enjoyed his meals. Maria doubted if he would enjoy those which she cooked!

CHAPTER SIX

FERRARI returned. "They have not arrived?" he demanded.

Maria shook her head, and her husband pursed his lips. It was evident that he was deciding what course he should pursue. He had a great affection for Antonia, but if this Englishman had been amusing himself at her expense, then he should pay, and pay heavily. He sat down and evolved some very telling phrases which he would deliver with marked effect, he did not doubt. The words "driven snow", "pure as the lily", the "light of her bereaved mother's heart", and so on.

When the door opened and Antonia came in, his ideas took flight. He stared at her, and said at last, "Has—he—the signor come with you?"

"He is here, waiting for permission to enter," she said, smiling.

"Permission to enter." Ferrari decided that his worst fears were well founded, otherwise surely the Englishman would have come in and greeted them in a friendly manner. Maria uttered a long-drawn-out "A-a-ah", folded her arms and began to rock backwards and forwards gently.

Ferrari said grandly, "He has permission to enter. I wish to speak with him."

She held the door open, calling, "Francesco, *prego*!"

Francis came in. Ferrari saw him catch Antonia's hand as he passed her and give it a little affectionate squeeze. He beamed at them all. It was evident that he wished to put a bold face on things.

Ferrari twirled his moustache, he held himself very erect, looking both judicial and stern.

"Signor, please admit your faults, whether we—my good

156

wife and I—can ever forgive them is doubtful. This is a sad day for us all."

Francis threw back his head and laughed. He turned to Antonia and said, "Didn't I tell you! They think the worst!" He turned back to Ferrari, saying, "Patience, Signor Ferrari. For me this is not a sad day, neither, I hope, is it for Antonia. I have come to ask your permission to marry her. I love her with all my heart, and she tells me that she returns that love. Antonia, excuse me one moment, that is Aramis scratching the paint off your good mother's door. Ah, come in, Aramis, my friend, to share our joy!"

Ferrari and his wife stared at them both blankly, while the small dog rushed about sniffing for imaginary rats.

"To marry? You wish to marry Antonia, signor?"

"It is the great wish of my life—and as soon as possible."

Ferrari felt that he had been robbed of his great moment, when he might have denounced the seducer; not that he wished Antonia to have been seduced, but he felt that he could have acquitted himself magnificently.

"Antonia's mother and I give our consent, but tell me— is there a reason for this haste, signor?"

Again Francis laughed. "Why, yes. We are young, we want to live in our own home, to visit places together, to be happy."

Antonia laid her hand on his arm. "S-sh, *caro mio*, let me speak. Mama, and you, Signor Ferrari, remember that you speak to an English signor, also that you speak to me, Antonia Trolli. I know what is in your minds. I know that you think we wish to marry soon because I am going to have a baby! I am angry, very angry, not only because you have it in your hearts to think ill of me, but because you have not the proper respect—not to say understanding—of Signor Winnerton."

The name was difficult to say, but she made a brave attempt. "If perhaps I did what is right, I should leave this house and refuse to enter it again until you had asked pardon of the signor and of me!"

Ferrari, flushing and twisting his moustache furiously, said, "Ah, it is possible to make mistakes. I am sorry for that mistake; I was only trying to—to——"

"Say no more about it," Francis said. "Both Antonia and I are too happy to remember it. You consent, that is splendid. Now I must talk to the priest about this—what is it, sweet?—mixed marriage. I suppose, Signor Ferrari, it will be easy to arrange?"

Ferrari had recovered his composure. He had made a mistake, but now he would step back into the good graces of the Englishman.

"Naturally, naturally. I shall occupy myself with this matter. Do not disturb yourself, I beg. It may be necessary to visit the Lord Bishop, but—that I can arrange with ease. Now, I have here some wine——"

"But so have I! Let us drink mine first."

The cloud was dispelled. Antonia brought glasses, having rubbed them carefully on a clean, soft cloth—how was it that her mother was incapable of polishing glasses? They drank the health of the young couple. Maria emerged from her fit of gloom and even laughed once or twice at things which Francis said. He brought out the presents for them, and they exclaimed at their beauty and costliness in the usual Italian fashion.

Finally Francis produced the ring which he had brought for Antonia. He had spent a great deal of time over that ring. It was inevitable that she would continue to cook, and the big diamond ring which he had wanted would have been both unsuitable and inconvenient. He had bought two, one of plain gold with the single diamond sunk into the metal, the other a ring that she could wear when work was over and she was ready to sit and talk to him.

Unlike her mother and stepfather, she said very little. Francis slipped both rings on to her finger and then, raising her hand to his lips, kissed them. He looked up to see her eyes filled with tears.

"You like them?" he asked anxiously.

"I like them so much that I have no words. I like them for themselves, because they are beautiful. I like them because of what they—mean, and I like them, also, because of your thoughtfulness in getting two, so that I may never be without one of your dear rings."

Her mother asked questions. Would they return to England? Francis shook his head. Not likely. Here they had a dear little house. He was going to build a garage, and Maddelena was to come every day, yes, every single day! Also, Innerhoffer had told him of a woman who had lived in France and was a splendid laundress.

"That will be Hortense Mor; Mor was in France for many years. Yes, she is good. You might do worse then submit your clothes to her."

"I would far rather do it myself," Antonia protested. "I know that she will not rinse the clothes sufficiently. She will scorch them, perhaps wrench off the buttons."

"Then let her," Francis said. "Let her tear them in small pieces, but you will not do the washing. Here," he turned to Ferrari, "is the first time I demand obedience, and you see that she argues with me. I am going to have a difficult life, no doubt."

"Perhaps her excellent cooking will make life bearable."

The time passed very pleasantly; they were friendly and the warmth of Francis's evident affection for Antonia made itself apparent. He was an essentially kindly person; he liked to smile; he liked to feel himself in company which was sympathetic. Maria, watching him, noting his well-kept hands, his good clothes, and shoes which were neither paper-thin nor heavy as lead, thought that Antonia was doing very well for herself. Her mind reverted, as it sometimes did, to her elder daughter, Carolina, who had gone to Milan, and from whom they had never heard since. At first her disappearance had been a genuine grief to Maria, but now, with the passing of the years, the grief had almost died and instead there remained only a dull anger that her daughter should have disgraced her. It was a relief to know that now Antonia was settled; she would live near and could no doubt come in often to help her mother in keeping the place clean and tidy.

Francis was talking eagerly about the portrait which he was painting of Antonia. His cheeks were flushed, his eyes were very bright; and he gesticulated, trying to show Ferrari his method of painting.

"It is to be my best painting—my masterpiece. It will be simple, and yet it will convey everything. And now, signora, I must say good night. It grows late, and I have spent a very happy evening."

He shook hands with them, reminding Ferrari to speak with the priest, then Antonia went with him to the door, and they went out together. In the quiet darkness, with the sky lit by thousands of stars, they stood side by side. Francis put his arms round her and drew her close. He felt that his heart was almost too filled with happiness; it was unbearable. Her little show of dignity, when she had reproved Ferrari and even her mother, had touched him deeply. She was a peasant girl, but she had inherent poise and judgement. As he held her in his arms, his mind raced forward to the time when he would not have to leave her, when together they would walk home in the quiet of the evening. The thought of the little house, so warm, so well ordered, was very pleasant. He felt a sense of security which would be his when he shared that house with Antonia. He sighed.

She said, "Francesco, you are tired, *caro mio*."

"No, no, only almost too happy. Filled with content at what lies before us. The thought of the years which are before us: I shall grow old, have furrows in my cheeks, perhaps be stiff with rheumatism. Other people may think that you have changed, they may see silver in your hair, they may imagine that your eyes have lost something of their gentian blue. To me—there will be no change, and to you, I shall still be the same as I am tonight—because we shall have grown old together. Ah, Antonia, dearest Antonia, please love me half as much as I love you."

She said softly, "I think that I love you more, because I don't think that anyone in the world can imagine what you mean to me. There, you must go. Look, little Aramis is growing impatient. Good night, my loved one, go with God."

ii

Father Dominic insisted that it would be well to visit the Bishop. Francis thought privately that he stressed the necessity because it made him feel important to put on his best cassock and biretta and to visit the Palace, being driven there by Francis. Francis didn't really care a great deal for Father Dominic; he was noisy, too hearty, and talked too much.

He said, "I am glad that you are wearing ceremonial clothes, signor. To have appeared before His Lordship in rough clothes would have been a mistake. He, like yourself, comes from an exalted family."

Francis growled, "Glad I'm dressed for the part."

They were shown into the Bishop's study, where they waited for His Lordship. Francis was restless, inclined to be irritable, when the priest pointed out to him various paintings which hung on the walls.

F

"Here is a Piazza, and this—this is by the great Maffei. Ah, the Bishop has some splendid paintings, no?"

"They're both very poor paintings; if that's the Bishop's taste I don't admire it. I wish he'd hurry; we don't want to wait all day."

"It is possible," Father Dominic said, "that he may offer us a glass of his admirable wine—as a mark of his favour."

Sulkily Francis retorted, "I don't want his wine."

The door swung open and the Bishop entered, handsome, urbane, with a smile which was polite without being anything more. He offered his hand to the priest, who made his genuflection, then turned to Francis.

"I am pleased to see you, signor," he said. "I have heard about you." He walked to his desk and sat down in the great carved chair. "The son of the Earl of Maudesley, yes?"

"The younger son, Your Grace."

"And you are a painter of distinction, I hear. One day I must come to Morano and ask you to show me your pictures. I am devoted to art. You may have noticed some of my pictures here on the walls. Shall I commission you to paint me—what?—let me see—a Madonna and Child? Or the draught of fishes! After the style of Mantegna, eh?"

"Your Grace, I have never attempted a religious painting, and I am not good at painting—fish. Might I speak of the question of my marriage with Signorina Antonia Trolli? It will be possible to get a dispensation for a mixed marriage?"

The Bishop leaned back in his huge chair and laid the tips of his fingers together. He nodded graciously. "Be seated—yes, and you too, Father. I shall ring for some wine. You will take a glass of wine, Signor Winnerton?"

"Thank you, Your Grace."

He began to explain the question of mixed marriages. He spoke quietly and temperately. He stated the whole case very carefully and logically. Francis began to realize that while he might not be particularly drawn to this prelate, yet he was undeniably a man of brains, education, and great tact. A servant, wearing a discreet livery, brought the wine; the Bishop with a movement of his hand indicated that he should pour out three glasses. Each glass was finely cut; it stood on a tiny silver salver, and with it was handed a very fine, small napkin.

The Bishop sipped his wine reflectively. "A pleasant wine, I think?"

Father Dominic said, "Excellent, oh, excellent."

Francis nodded. "A very fine wine, sir."

The Bishop returned to his subject. He stated the obligations which were laid upon the non-Catholic partner in the contract. He even elaborated the difficulties and possible dangers.

"I have considered these things, sir," Francis said.

"Quite, but when one is—in love, the judgement is not always at its most sound. I wish you to realize fully the importance of this step which you are taking. You are a man of education, of good birth, you are accustomed to travel, to meet important people, to visit splendid houses. Tell me—not as a Bishop, but as one man speaking to another—how would little Signorina Trolli comport herself if you were to introduce her to your family, your friends?"

Francis flushed with annoyance. "Signorina Trolli would comport herself with dignity and distinction wherever she found herself. I have, however, not the slightest intention of taking her to England. She is happy here—in Tyrol—so am I. I beg that Your Grace will have no apprehensions regarding Signorina Trolli."

Thoughtfully the Bishop poured out another glass of wine. He sipped it, then spoke again.

"I have made enquiries. Her mother works in a mill—a factory—her father was a quarryman. She has received some education from the good nuns who are now at Cormia. I am told that her mother's house is of the most simple. Is this correct, my son?"

"Perfectly, Your Grace. Her handwriting is far better than mine; she is far more useful and efficient than any of my cousins, who could not boil an egg if they were asked to. My father gobbles his food and belches when he finishes a meal; my brother has an illegitimate son by a barmaid at Cambridge, since then he has kept a girl as his mistress in a flat in London. The Signorina Trolli is a most completely virtuous girl, her manners are charming. My friend, Lord John Trevor, who stayed at my house for a few days, found her enchanting. So do I, m'lord, and I am going to marry her."

"And if you are blessed with children——"

"My wife can bring them up in her own Church, m'lord."

The Bishop leaned forward and pressed a bell on his desk. His fine, full lips were curved into a smile, his eyes were bright. After all, he might be a Bishop, but he was an Italian, and this young man's determination, his pride in this village sweetheart of his, was, to say the least of it, romantic. He said to his secretary, when he entered, "Bring the documents relating to the marriage of the Signor Francis Winnerton."

He added his signature, a fine, impressive one, and handed the documents to Francis. "There, my son, and allow me to wish you great happiness, and go with my blessing. Who knows, one day I may hear that your wife has—converted you." He laughed. "I suppose you would say—perverted, eh?"

"Your Grace, if I ever embraced your faith, through Antonia's influence, it would be conversion. May I hope that one day we may have the honour of asking you to luncheon with us? She is a miraculous cook, and I may say that I have some wine which is not unworthy of your appreciation."

They bowed themselves out. The Bishop had been gracious,

indeed almost informal. Father Dominic was murmuring about his affability, his kindness, and his great wisdom.

As they drove back to Morano, Francis said, "Now there is nothing to stop us being married, eh, Father? Can we get a special licence? Will you arrange it? I don't care what it costs."

iii

Francis felt, alternately, that the days flew past, or that they dragged interminably. He insisted that the first thing of importance was the picture. No matter what was left undone, that must be finished. He was excited over it, and was conscious that his power, his facility of execution, was growing and developing.

He heard from his father in reply to his letter stating that he was going to marry Antonia. The reply was what he expected, violent in its abuse, imputing that he had been living with her, and that the marriage was one of necessity.

I use the word "necessity" foolishly. Apparently these people are poor and a lump sum would have satisfied them. She would have been able to marry some Italian lout of her own class, once it was known that she had some money behind her. Italians are completely mercenary. All I beg is that you will not consider it necessary to bring this dago woman to Maudesley, because I should refuse to see her. The whole thing is disgraceful, and my only comment is that— I am not surprised. You have always been self-centred and a damned fool into the bargain. You have your mother's money, which is lucky for you. You won't get a penny of mine.

Mostyn wrote in the same strain. He reminded Francis that it was one thing to keep a mistress and another to be fool enough to marry her. "We've all been guilty of indiscretions at some time or another, but we're not bound to hang them round our necks for life!"

Francis threw the letters into the fire, and laughed as he watched them burn. What fools they were, his father and his brother! Couldn't they see that he had never fitted into the life at Maudesley, that he knew so well what he wanted, and was going to make all his dreams and ideas, his hopes and ambitions, into realities? He turned from the fire and looked at the picture on its easel. It was finished. It was good; strong without coarseness, vigorous without losing anything of the fineness which he had longed to put into it.

When he allowed Antonia to see it she had stood silent, and then had turned to him smiling. "Yes, *caro*, it is very fine. I don't understand your painting, but I can understand sufficiently to know that this is very, very good."

"Do you think that it is like you?"

"*Tesoro*, how do any of us know what we are like? I see a girl—yes, she is a nice girl. I should like to know her. She looks grave, but I think that she can smile and laugh when she is with her sweetheart. And Aramis for the second time you have painted him—as in life. I think that I must call you— Leonardo. Because people are going to admire your paintings as they do his, no?"

He placed some money in the bank for her and explained to her how to use a cheque-book. At first she cried a little at the thought of what seemed to her to be an immense sum being placed to her credit. Then, having dried her tears, she told him, with that queer touch of dignity which he loved, that she had already some money; she kept it in a box under the mattress of her bed.

"I should wish to spend money which I have earned, *tesoro*, on my wedding dress. It will be a quiet wedding, being a mixed marriage; there will be no music or flowers, and so my dress must be simple. You will not need to wear your beautiful London clothes, or that shining hat which lives in a box all by itself. If you could perhaps—now the picture is

finished and your mind is at rest—drive me to Mezzolombardo, I can buy very quickly."

So Francis drove her to buy her wedding dress. She refused
to allow him to go into the shops with her, saying that it
made her nervous. He sat in the car waiting, thinking about
her, which he realized was his chief occupation in these days.
He had no doubts, no apprehensions, he was content and
happy, and yet she presented many problems. In fact, he
smiled. "She is a very charming problem altogether."

She had dignity, she had poise—though he doubted if she
would have known what the word meant—and she had a
firmness of will and a determination which surprised him. He
had insisted that Maddelena came every day, that she was to
be paid a regular wage for working regular hours. Antonia
had protested that it was not necessary.

"Have I ever left your house uncleaned? Have you ever
found dust or dirt?" she demanded.

"Never, and no doubt we shall find both with Maddelena.
I don't care. It's impossible for me to have my wife—washing
the kitchen floor! Impossible that she should spoil her hands
peeling potatoes. 'Tonia, you must see that!"

"I peeled potatoes while I was—and still am—Antonia
Trolli. It wasn't impossible then. I admit that my hands
are not very soft, not very smooth, but I would rather
have rough hands than potatoes with all the eyes left in
them."

He remembered how they had argued, and how—in
common justice—he had to admit that her arguments were
sound, but he persisted.

"All right, let's say that I am foolish, that I am an idiot,
that I am anything you like——"

Antonia laughed softly. "I will say it with all my heart.
You are foolish, my Francesco, not completely an idiot—but
sometimes a little weak in the head, and as for being—anything

I like—well, you are exactly the thing that I do like, best and most in all the world. Continue, Signor Vinnaireton."

He persisted and in the end had won his battle. She might cook, she might sew—he was going to buy her a splendid sewing machine, a "veritable Seengair", but she was not to do housework. She was not to wash and she was not to iron.

He knew that many things were strange to her; she was the most fastidious person imaginable, but she disliked waste in any form, and would "Tut, tut" in annoyance if a mark appeared on the table-cloth. Once he complained, "This glass has a chip out of it. Break it."

She examined the glass closely, and said, "It is a very small one, the glass is quite good, one can drink from the other side. It would be a pity to break it. Glasses get broken soon enough, God knows."

When she said that her shoes were letting in water, Francis suggested that they should go into Cormia and buy new ones. She was positively shocked. "Indeed no. Toni can resole them."

He had looked more closely at the shoes. "They've been soled once already."

"They have been soled four times, my dear, and they will have to be soled several times again. The uppers are still very good."

She bought eggs from a farmer's wife, bought them by the dozen, for Francis liked eggs in any form, and the farmer's wife was charged to deliver them three times a week. Francis came into the kitchen one afternoon and found Corina Mancini there, asking if Antonia could let her have three eggs. With a slight air of reluctance, Antonia consented, saying, "Eggs are a dreadful price now. Three for five lire." Signora Mancini produced five lire, and they both agreed that the price was terrible.

"What can one do?" Antonia demanded. "No doubt the farmers make a great profit, no?"

"Be certain," Signora Mancini assured her, "that always someone makes a profit out of people like ourselves!"

"Undoubtedly the poor always pay the most heavily."

"It is the way of the world. Good-day, signorina."

Francis said in surprise, "Did you let her pay for the eggs?"

"But certainly. Why should you, *caro*, make a present of eggs to Corina Mancini? She is not poor."

"She doesn't look very rich."

Antonia shrugged her shoulders. "Oh, rich! Who in this village is rich, except Innerhoffer, the Count and perhaps you?"

Yet, when some old woman, ragged and more than a little dirty, came begging, she was all kindness. She kept all the stale bread, she gave them soup—the beggars—and carefully emptied all the ash-trays, stripping the paper off the stubs and keeping the tobacco in a tin to give to old men, the *Poveri*.

If she heard of a sick child, she would make meat jelly, strong soup or milk puddings. Once when Francis saw her starting off with a basket covered with a clean cloth, he asked where she was going.

"The son of Beppi is gravely ill. That mother of his cannot cook *polenta*, I am taking down some proper food for the boy. No doubt Beppi and his lazy wife will share it!"

"You don't pay for these things yourself, Antonia, do you?"

She flushed. "Innerhoffer lets me have pieces of meat for a few *soldi*. He is grateful because you spend so much money with him."

"But—oh, damn it, darling, I should like to pay for these things!"

She shook her smooth, shining head. "*Caro*, then where

would there be any merit left for me? You are so generous, you would give away the teeth from your head, but—no, please let me do this small thing."

Then, as he thought of all these things, he realized that she had been away for what seemed a long time, as he always did if she was absent for long. A kind of panic seized him that she might have left by another door, she might be looking for him, she might be distressed or worried. He got out of the car and entered the shop. There she was, standing at the cash desk, her shabby old leather purse in her hand. The sight of that purse touched him! She had always lacked pretty things. Before they drove home he would buy her a new purse.

She turned and smiled at him, that lovely, wide, friendly smile, which he said always warmed his heart.

"I told you not to come in," she said. "Women's shops are no place for men." Then to the woman in the cash desk, who appeared to be an old friend, "Signorina Antonietta, may I present my future husband to you? Signor Winnerton."

"I wish you all happiness, signor. In Antonia Trolli you find a jewel, a pearl."

Francis bowed, conscious that Antonietta eyed him with approval.

"That I have discovered, signorina. I am no Christopher Columbus but it was easy to discover this—treasure."

Antonia laughed. "Tut, tut, Francesco *mio*. Still, it was clever to find me, for I am not so big as America."

The woman in the cash desk rocked with laughter. The owner of the shop came up and demanded to know the cause of their mirth; he too was overcome at the brilliance of Antonia's joke, in which even Francis shared, for had not he declined any right to be called Columbus?

They went back to the car, Francis carrying the parcels which Antonia assured him contained material of a beauty not to be surpassed in Milano itself.

"But oh, the cost! It is wicked that such prices should exist. Imagine it, *caro*, thirty lire a metre. But it is good. It will last for years, with care."

Very shyly she told him that she had bought some "fine white lawn" and asked if he considered that it would be either wasteful or wicked to take it to her dear nuns to be made into —she hesitated—and Francis laughed and said that she must find the words, he wasn't going to tell her.

"Underclothing," she said, blushing furiously. "It will be most beautifully made, and it will help my dear nuns."

They stopped at the convent at Cormia. Francis thought how cold and poor it looked, but Antonia was in the highest spirits. The nuns embraced her, she presented Francis, who bowed in his best manner, and finally was taken to the Reverend Mother herself, who sat and talked to him while Antonia was taken off to discuss the making of her trousseau.

"And you are to marry our little Antonia, signor. A good child, and clever. She has intelligence and heart, she has energy and ability. I am very happy about this, it is—admittedly—a pity that you are not of the Faith, but—one never knows what mercies may be shown to you in the future."

Impulsively Francis said, "Reverend Mother, Antonia wished to have underclothes made by your nuns. I am speaking frankly. I do not know what material, what lace, what—whatever is needed she has bought. She is so modest in her ideas, so economical. May I ask of you a great favour? If other material, trimmings and so forth, are needed, will you instruct your nuns to buy them? I want her to have the best, the finest—and the best and finest only. May I write a cheque for you? I have an account at Mezzolombardo." He took out a pen and wrote the cheque, handing it over to the Reverend Mother.

She took it, he saw her fine eyebrows raised. "Signor, we shall not require half this!"

"The rest is Antonia's small present to the convent, Reverend Mother."

"Ah!" her eyes twinkled. "You ask me to connive at a small deception, signor, but I have no doubt that I shall be forgiven. She shall have beautiful things, that I promise. And the remainder of your gift will keep us warm throughout the whole winter. I am very grateful. Signor, you are doing a brave thing to marry this little girl. We know that she is not born in the same class as yourself, but she is essentially good, she is true and sincere. You may have to be very patient, for she will have much to learn; if she is taught with kindness she will learn quickly. Do not force her to live at once in a life to which she is not accustomed; travel slowly. I do not know if you propose to take her to England——"

"No, no," Francis said, "unless we go there—without taking her to see my family. They would frighten her, and I don't want her to be frightened. I will take her wherever she wishes to go, but not anywhere where she might be patronized or humiliated."

"I am relieved. I take it that your family do not approve of this marriage? Well, that is something on which I express no opinion. All I hope is that this dear child may be happy, and that she may add to your happiness, that always . . ." There was a knock at the door, she stopped and called, "*Avanti!*"

Antonia, flushed and smiling, came in, made her small curtsey, and stood like a child waiting to be spoken to.

"Everything has arranged itself, my child?" the Reverend Mother asked.

"Everything, thank you, Reverend Mother."

"We shall all think of you, and pray for you on your wedding day. But you will visit us again, in order to collect your things?"

"They will be ready, Reverend Mother, in ten days' time. May I come back then?"

"Indeed, yes." She kissed Antonia gently on both cheeks, gave her hand to Francis and said, "Go with God."

iv

The morning dawned bright and crisp and clear. Maddelena was already bustling about downstairs when Francis woke. He felt hideously nervous and wildly excited. This was his wedding day. In a few hours Antonia and he would begin their life together. First they must go to the Town Hall and before the *podesta* have the civil ceremony. Then to the church, and once that was over, there was a *festa* arranged, to be held in the big dining-room of the local *albergo*. His own cottage was too small, and Antonia had disliked the idea of leaving the house filled with people when they drove off on their honeymoon.

"Added to that, they might put lighted cigarettes on the tables, ash on the carpet, and bring in a great deal of dust and dirt on to the polished floor. No, a room at the Albergo Morano will be much better."

He met her at the Town Hall. She was wearing her new blue dress, very quiet, with very neat, fine cuffs and collar. Her face was grave but her eyes shone when she saw him. Ferrari and her mother, both looking supremely uncomfortable in their best clothes, Innerhoffer, large, red and important, the Count and his wife, both slim and elegant, were all there too.

The ceremony was over very quickly. The *podesta* shook them warmly by the hand and wished them good luck. He was coming to the *festa*, and hurried away to the barber to be meticulously shaved and heavily scented.

Francis, with Antonia's arm in his, whispered as they walked out into the street, "And they were married and lived happily ever after."

She looked up at him and shook her head. "Not until we

have been to church, then I shall feel that—we are married. Francesco, I am so happy."

The church looked dark and rather gloomy. There was no music, no candles on the altar, only the sanctuary lamp burnt like a star. No flowers, and only Father Dominic to officiate. Francis looked round the big church, which always seemed so much too large for such a small village. It was not a particularly beautiful church, having been built at a bad period, and there had never been sufficient money to beautify it in any way. The smell of incense hung in the air; the scent of flowers lingered in spite of their absence.

The atmosphere was chilly; he shivered and wished that it was over. Father Dominic bustled in with his usual air of all being right with the world, and began the service. Francis glanced at Antonia kneeling beside him, her face intent as if— in spite of the ceremony being robbed of all pomp and elaboration—she still found in the words which the priest spoke something which comforted and reassured her. The rings were exchanged, she had insisted upon buying his with her own money as her wedding gift to him. He looked at it, that symbol, his eyes misted suddenly.

> "... *vivit et Regnat Deus*
> *per omnia saecula saeculorum. Amen.*"

It was over, Antonia was his wife, nothing could separate them now; Maudesley, his father, Mostyn, all his disapproving relations receded into the background. Only Antonia remained, standing at his side, smiling at him, while Father Dominic wished them well, and then hurried away because he, too, was invited to the *festa*.

The room was large, but it soon grew very hot, faces grew moist, and the air heavy. Francis did not remember that he knew so many people, but he had instructed Ferrari to invite everyone possible, and Ferrari announced with pride that there had been no refusals.

The Count made a speech, carefully delivered, beautifully spoken, then he and his wife excused themselves. Ferrari made a speech, which was long, and involved, and accompanied by much applause and the banging of knife handles on the table. Father Dominic spoke, and at considerable length, his mild jokes were greeted as pearls of wit.

Francis rose, and in his rather slow, precise Italian thanked them all in the name of himself and his wife. Then, explaining that they were driving to Verona, he begged that they might be forgiven if they left. The company, he begged, would remain as long as it pleased them.

In the car he drew a deep breath, saying, "Whew, I'm glad that's over! Antonia, we're really married. When we turn the corner on the Cormia road we'll stop. I want to put my arms round my very own wife."

She leaned her head against his shoulder. "And your very own wife wants your arms round her."

Part Three

CHAPTER ONE

To Francis their honeymoon was a revelation. He had imagined that he understood Antonia, yet with each day she did something which astonished him. She never forgot—true she might have looked with some apprehension at the impressive array of knives and forks, the multiplicity of wine-glasses of various sizes—but Francis noted with a kind of tender amusement that she never showed the slightest confusion. She waited, watching him, and followed his lead almost immediately. If there was any hesitating it was so brief as to be unnoticeable.

In the big hotel where they stayed in Venice, he watched her composure when she gave orders to any of the hotel servants. She was never in the least arrogant, never even faintly subservient; her manner was polite, kindly, and yet full of dignity.

As his servant she had been perfect in her manner; her respect had been complete and never in the least over-stressed. Now, as his wife, he knew that he could take her anywhere and introduce her into any society without the slightest qualm. Sometimes he wondered how she came to understand the fine shades of behaviour which appeared to come so naturally to her.

He took her to see pictures, statuary, splendid buildings; she listened to all he had to tell her, scarcely speaking, gravely attentive. Modern art was beyond her comprehension, but Francis found that when they saw the works of the great masters her taste was admirable. He came to the conclusion that her good taste was something innate, that she relied on her own judgement, and that her opinions were her own, not those superimposed by other people.

179

She was modest without being *gauche*, she was passionate because she loved him, not because she was particularly sensual. She was ready to show her affection, but she never grew cloying or sentimental. She seemed to grow more attractive every day.

"You're like a flower coming into bloom," he told her.

"Because I'm so happy. I never knew that anyone could be so happy."

"You don't get bored with pictures and palaces?"

"I'm only afraid sometimes that you may find me so ignorant, *caro*."

"I've never known anyone who absorbed knowledge as you do, 'Tonia."

"That's because I have such a good master to teach me!"

Only once did he find her shy with him, and that was one morning when he planned to sit at the window of their sitting-room and paint. He loved looking over the lagoon, trying to put into execution his ideas, and his theories into practice.

"And what will you do while I am defacing good, clean canvas?" he asked.

He saw her flush. When she answered she spoke in a low, subdued tone.

"I think that I must get some more clothes, Francesco. My wedding dress is very nice. The cloth is splendid. But perhaps if we are to stay in this very fine hotel I ought to wear something—well, something smarter in the evening."

He sprang to his feet, the painting which he had planned forgotten.

"Darling, what a fool you must think me! Of course you must buy clothes, heaps and heaps of clothes, the loveliest you can find in Venice. Let's go out together. The lagoon will still be there tomorrow, and the next day. First we'll go to the bank and get stacks of lire!"

She looked at him, he saw that her eyes were swimming with tears and that her mouth trembled a little.

"I have some money, Francesco, but I have looked at the shops, and the prices, and"—the tears overflowed and rolled down her cheeks—"and I shall not have enough—not enough to buy even two of those beautiful handkerchiefs with lace round the edges. Oh, I am so ashamed to have to ask you for money!"

"But, my sweet, what are husbands for?" He took her in his arms and kissed her very tenderly. "I feel ashamed—terribly ashamed that I have not thought of it before. Of course you must have money, plenty of money to carry about with you. Antonia, if you cry I shall go mad and fling myself out of the window! Ever since I first met you, you've given me so much, you've made life a different business for me, you've shown me how to be happy, really happy. Come, dry those lovely eyes and we'll go out and despoil Venice. We'll show them what the beautiful Mrs. Winnerton can look like! We'll have every woman in Venice hating you! Then when we get to Florence, you shall buy their wonderful embroidery—I think the finest in the world. And in Rome, oh, we'll find really smart things in Rome. There—that's better! A bride to cry on her honeymoon! It's a scandal!"

He found that her taste in clothes was good. She rejected anything which was too elaborate, too stylized. Only when she saw the wad of notes with which he paid for two dresses did he hear her catch her breath suddenly.

"You're pleased?" he asked, smiling. "My dear, you're quite pale. It's this hot room, the smell of materials. Let's get out into the air."

"Francesco," she whispered, "to spend so much. It seems wrong."

"Wrong? Why is it wrong?"

"When you think of so many poor people, only able to afford *pasta* and *polenta*."

He pulled her arm through his. "Silly 'Tonia! Listen. The woman who keeps that shop must live, she must pay her assistants, she must buy silk and lace, velvet and satin. The making of those things keeps factories going, where hundreds of people are employed. Now—forget about everything, except that your husband wants to atone for his stupidity, his mutton-headedness——"

She laughed, that soft laugh which was almost a chuckle. "This word—mutton'eadedness? I don't know it. What does it mean?"

"It means the kind of head your husband was evidently born with."

They drove on to Florence, and Francis insisted that she must have the finest embroidery, the most exquisite materials. Again he showed her the glories of Florence, and marvelled at her memory, her quickness and her appreciation. He painted there, several of those small, beautiful pictures which seemed to capture the actual spirit of the city.

"I'm improving!" he told Antonia. "I'm really beginning to understand something about it all. I'll make you proud of me yet!"

She answered gravely, "I could not be prouder than I am now."

On to Rome, she sat with her hands clasped tightly when he pointed out the Holy City in the distance.

"What do you want to see most in Rome?" he asked.

"Two things—His Holiness and Saint Peter's."

"Are you religious, 'Tonia?"

"I don't think so, caro. I love—goodness. I believe that God and all His saints wish us to be good, because that is for our happiness. I don't believe that you will go to hell because you are not of my faith, because I don't like even to try to imagine anything which—it seems to me—put limits to the goodness and lovingness of God. I never wish to hurt anyone, never wish to hurt any animal. I want to be honest and"—she laid her hand on his arm—"be a good wife to you."

They wandered about Rome, staring at everything, like two children, astonished and amazed. Again Francis was delighted at Antonia's appreciation of what was good. She never rushed headlong into paeans of praise concerning what was obvious and second-rate.

Then one morning she stood beside him at their window and slipped her hand into his. He turned and looked down at her, smiling.

"Yes?" he queried.

"It's all wonderful," she said. "I never thought to see such places, pictures, statues—I shall remember the Moses all my life, and the lovely *pieta* in Saint Peter's. The food has been wonderful too." She laughed. "It has been like moving from a lower class in school to a higher one—exciting and making you want to learn. Perhaps one day to be the top of the class."

"Yes," Francis said again, "and what else?"

"It will be nice to get home again, won't it? To see Aramis, and the nice furniture, and—everything."

"I believe that you're a little homesick—suffering from nostalgia for your little house, eh?"

She nodded. "Perhaps—not too badly, but enough to make me want to see it all. This honeymoon has been a miracle. I have been so happy, so excited, I feel that now I'd like to go home and—think about it all. Almost as if I had eaten too much and wanted to have time to digest it."

Two days later they were driving back to Morano. Francis had asked what she wanted as a souvenir from Rome, and she replied promptly that she wanted books on cookery, ". . . a great many, please, so that all through the year I may never tire you with the same food day after day. This winter I want you to teach me English, for there is, I have heard, a famous book written by a married lady all about cooking. I should like to be able to read that."

Back home, Antonia admitted—a little grudgingly—that Maddelena had kept the house reasonably clean. Not perfect, she assured Francis, but better than she had dared to expect. Aramis, too, had been well fed, and his coat brushed almost as well as Antonia did it herself.

"She does her best, the poor Maddelena," she told Francis, who found her small housewifely airs delightful. Maddelena was at least ten years her senior, a rather gaunt woman, who attacked whatever work was on hand as though she had an active and personal grudge against dirt.

The new garage was finished, though there also Antonia rubbed the cement doubtfully and said that no doubt the builders, in the absence of the master of the house, had used more sand than cement!

"The wood of the doors, Francesco, is not the best quality. See, here and there are knotholes! It is not too bad, but it is far from being perfect."

For several days she worked furiously, until finally she sat down and sighed happily.

"The house is itself once again," she said. "No doubt in a few days many things will have become dirty again, but—for the moment it will do."

"And so Alexander, at the moment, has no more worlds to conquer!"

ii

The Summer passed peacefully for them both. Francis was painting every day, happy in the consciousness that his work was gaining strength and maturity. He was planning another exhibition, this time in Paris, where, Emmanuel Gollantz

wrote, he could arrange everything through his connection
with the Laras.

From time to time they heard rumours of political events,
of the clash between the new Fascists and the Communists.
The stocky young man who had fought as a Bersaglieri, who
had turned journalist, and was now the accepted leader of the
Fascist Party made speeches in the big towns—in Verona,
Milan and Bologna, but it seemed that only the distant and
faint echoes reached Morano. The local politics of the district
—the matter of installing running water in all the houses, of
re-roofing the Town Hall, the choosing of a new mayor at
Cormia—these things loomed larger and more importantly in
their lives than what Benito Mussolini and his adherents were
planning.

When the days became shorter, Antonia began to study
English with Francis each evening. He sent to England for
books and taught her as a child would be taught. She was very
quick and eager to learn. He found it a pleasure to teach her,
and took an enormous pride in her progress.

"I improve, Francesco?"

"With every lesson, darling."

"I have a fine teacher," she said in English, and laughed
with delight. "It is necessary that a wife speaks the language of
her husband, eh? Soon I shall be able to read the masterpiece
of the great Mrs. Beeton."

"I shouldn't wonder if you wrote a masterpiece yourself
one day," Francis told her.

"One day," she said gravely, "I shall be a really great cook.
It is my ambition, as it is yours to paint wonderful pictures.
When you go to Paris for this exhibition, will you take me?
Then I can study French cooking."

"I can't imagine myself going to Paris or anywhere else
without you. I don't believe you realize that I love you more
and more every day. It is almost frightening, you fill my life

completely, you make the colours of everything brighter, the
skies more clear, and—oh, my sweet, you permeate everything!"

The days seemed to Antonia to rush past, she was always
busy, always happy. Whenever Francis wished her to sit for
him, she put her work aside and took up her pose, holding it
carefully, but never with the least sign of rigidity. He swore
that she was the ideal model.

Then came Paris, and she was intoxicated by the beauty of
the city, the gaiety, the wonderful clothes, and enchanted with
the courtesy of Emmanuel Gollantz, who came over himself
to superintend the hanging of the pictures which Francis had
brought with him.

"Of your age," he said, "I can pr-romise you that you are
what Fr-red Walker was of his. You have yout', and t'is
appears in your work." He smiled, sending a quick glance
towards Antonia. "You hev, I t'ink, gr-reat happiness, t'is too
is apparent in your work."

The first picture which he had painted of Antonia, Francis
refused to sell, as also the little picture of the dog Aramis.

"Both," he told Gollantz, "are part of my home. The one
of the little dog is my mascot! The other is a picture of my
Good Angel. These I will show, but I must keep them—
always."

His pictures fired the imagination of the Parisians; they
bought. The prices were sufficiently high, for Emmanuel
Gollantz and Lara both knew their markets, and could assess
the value of a picture with complete exactitude. Francis was in
the highest spirits, it seemed that as a painter he had really
arrived. He delighted in his success, he was gay, longing to
take Antonia everywhere, to spend money on her, to take her
to the restaurants where she could—as he said—continue her
education.

Then to his surprise and pleasure John Trevor came to

Paris. Tall, immaculate, bringing with him a subtle air of worldliness and sophistication which made Francis feel very young and inexperienced.

He visited the gallery, he was critical, discriminating, but withal he was ready to give unstinted praise where it was due. He refused to acclaim all the pictures as masterpieces; he told Francis that he was inclined to be "greedy", to imagine that he could make a good picture out of subjects which were trivial.

"The treatment is admirable, but sometimes it is so evident that you have been faced with a wet day, you have had to paint indoors, and you have clapped your hands and declared that this and that will make a fine study. Or it has been a beautiful day, and you have rushed out, almost intoxicated with the desire to paint—to paint at all costs! You need more discrimination. It is almost—yes, almost impossible for you to have more talent, but—discriminate."

For many of the pictures his praise was unstinted, the first portrait which Francis had painted of Antonia roused him to complete enthusiasm. He could scarcely find words in which to praise it sufficiently.

"Classical in its simplicity, realistic in its modernity. It is as nearly the perfect portrait as either you or I are likely to find."

Francis said, "I like it, I have given it to Antonia."

"Then," John said, "you have given her something which is unique in its beauty."

It was to John that Antonia confided that she had ambitions to become a great cook. She told him that what painting was to Francis, cooking was to her. She talked confidingly, without conceit, merely stating her hopes and asking for his help to find restaurants where she might, as she said, "study very hard".

The idea attracted him. He had tastes which were those of a sybarite, and his knowledge of Parisian restaurants was

extensive and exact. He constituted himself her guide, together
the three of them visited the historic restaurants—Voison,
Paillard, Larue. John discussed the meals with the proprietors,
they listened and offered suggestions with obvious respect for
his knowledge.

So Antonia learned the flavour of perfectly cooked *cote de
veau, cochon de lait, poulet au sang, timbale de gueues d' ecrevisses
Mantua,* and *caneton à la rouennaise.* John explained to her the
various merits of wines which were suitable to drink with each
dish. He persuaded proprietors to bring out their precious
Chambertin '78, and their Laffitte '75.

Francis said, "I didn't realize that you were such an
epicure."

"In everything, I hope," John replied. "Heaven knows
that I have spent enough time and money cultivating my
taste."

"In everything?"

"I hope so. I have finished rushing about the world in
search of new ideas. I have sufficient ideas. I have seen all that
I wish to see; there are very few places I want to see again
outside Europe. 'Better fifty years of Europe . . .' You know
the rest. I'm over thirty; one day I shall have to—do what is
regarded as my duty—marry, settle down, provide an heir, but
until then . . . Signora, tell me if you like this *caille.* Let me
recommend you to specialize—in sauces. I won't bore Francis
with talking about English sauces—not that it would take
long, for there are very few. One is brown and thick, the other
is white and thick. There may be brave spirits to attempt
others, but they are almost invariably variations of those two."

She smiled at him, and he thought how charming she
looked, and how she had developed during the last year. Since
her marriage with Francis she had gained in every way—in
poise, dignity (though he reflected she always had that!), and
her whole character had become formed and defined. Francis

had found the wife who suited him exactly, possessing intelligence, full of appreciation, with taste and discrimination. He thought of some of the girls of Antonia's age who had been suggested as suitable brides for him—girls on whose education vast sums of money had been spent, who were trained and groomed for the marriage market as fillies were trained for the racecourse. Many of them had been lovely, very few particularly intelligent, and still fewer capable of having a definite ambition, and working towards its attainment.

Their ambition had been—in most cases—to make a successful marriage, to wear beautifully made clothes, and to do the right thing in the right way at the right time.

Their stay in Paris was a fortnight of enchantment to Antonia. She was inordinately proud of Francis and his success; she loved to see him happy, laughing, showing a zest for everything, and yet retaining a certain simplicity in everything which added to his charm.

She told him once, "You are my master, my husband, and my little boy all at the same time, and I scarcely know which one I love best. As my master—you appreciate all that I try to do for your comfort, as my husband you are kind and very tender, and as my little boy—oh, you are adorable! I love Paris as I loved Venice, Rome, Florence, and I love them all the more because I know that our little house is waiting for us."

They returned to Morano. Francis said, "With a pocketful of money," and Antonia added, "And with laurels hanging round you, Francesco."

The late Spring was exquisite in Tyrol. Francis painted every day, making pictures which Antonia began to understand—the fields of white, yellow, and purple crocus, the sudden patches of gentian, the vivid blue of the hellebore, the soft, clear yellow of primroses. He would go down to the big sawmill and make pictures of the huge electrically-driven saw, the pale clean wood, the men pushing forward the trunks of trees which would be sawn into planks. He painted the shop of Innerhoffer. Antonia never liked it, no matter how clever it might be. The depicting of raw meat, carcasses, and the like made no appeal to her. He obtained permission from the priest to paint the interior of the church; dim, mysterious, with only the sanctuary lamp throwing the altar into prominence. On the Feast of Corpus Domini he painted the procession—she stared at it, and slowly the full meaning of it reached her—the vague figures took shape, there were the darkly-clothed men and women with their candles making little points of light, the children in their white clothes, the huge cross with the figure of the suffering Christ, and the vested priest, and with him a suggestion of colour, light and gold.

Emmanuel Gollantz had said that Francis was like someone called "Fred Valker". Who was this man? She asked Francis. He had painted very well, it appeared, had been charming, and had died while still quite young. She shivered. Did all men of genius die young? She thought of poets, of other brilliant people, then remembered that Leonardo had been quite old, so had Michael Angelo, and felt relieved. Perhaps this "Fred Valker" was an exception.

The Spring slid into Summer, and even though the village stood high, and the air of the mountains was fresh and clear, the heat was considerable. Antonia did everything possible to keep the little house cool. From early morning until the real heat of the sun was gone she kept blinds lowered, and opened doors to allow a current of air to pass through the house. Even so the days were terribly hot, and the nights airless and heavy. Francis seemed to have lost his appetite, and not even her most delicious dishes tempted him to eat. She racked her brains and sought through her cookery books to find cold dishes which would give him little trouble to eat and still provide the nourishment which he needed.

She confided her worry to her mother and Ferrari when she

went down to see them and to do the dozens of small tasks which always seemed to escape her mother's notice.

"It may be," Maria said, "that the signor needs cooler air."

"Where shall I find cooler air, Mama?"

"Go higher into the mountains. There are actually places where the snow remains all the year. Get a map and find some names."

Ferrari nodded. "That is wise advice, 'Tonia. There are plenty of places where rich people go for Winter sports— where they go ski-ing and skating. I shall occupy myself and find suitable names for you."

He gave her a list a few days later. She showed it to Francis, and suggested that it might be pleasant to go somewhere where the days were cooler and the nights less oppressive.

He exclaimed, "You're not feeling well! What a fool I am not to have noticed that you're looking pale. It's this cooking you do; working at a hot stove in this infernal heat. We'll go immediately."

She protested that she felt perfectly well, that she was used to the heat. Had not she lived in Morano all her life? But a cooler place would be nice and it might improve his appetite. They drove to the mountains, and immediately Francis became excited at the thought of painting new scenes. The air was cooler, and the nights less heavy, but the food was poor, the service rough, and the beds not particularly comfortable.

"You don't like it very much, Francesco?" she asked anxiously.

"You've spoilt me for anything short of perfect comfort, and cooking to match, 'Tonia."

"But you like the good air?"

"You know the old saying." He laughed. "A man can't live on air."

She fancied that he was better; and when he told her that he was sick and tired of mountains, and that he longed for their own home, she fell in with his wishes and they returned to Morano. There at least he was content, even though he still looked thin, and had developed a cough which worried her. She bought linctus which the village chemist swore to be little short of miraculous. Francis took it obediently enough, but the cough remained.

She met Count Zevio in the village one morning and asked him if he thought Francis looked ill. He looked at her intently, his eyes very grave and kind.

"I am glad that you have asked me, signora. Both my wife and I are troubled about him. Has he seen a doctor? No, not here. I don't mean the man here, but a specialist?"

He saw the sudden terror in her eyes. To Antonia the idea of seeing a doctor at all meant that you were seriously ill, while a specialist seemed to imply that you were almost past mortal aid.

"A specialist!" she almost whispered the word. "Does he seem so terribly ill then to you?"

"My dear signora, going to see a specialist is only—what shall I say—a precaution. These little village doctors are so stupid, it is waste of time and money to visit them. I go regularly to see specialists. So does my wife—why, only a few weeks ago we both went to Milan to visit a famous specialist who prevents us developing rheumatism. Don't look so worried, I beg you."

"Could you give me his name? I could perhaps take Francesco to see him. Milano—he could make a painting of the Duomo."

The Count smiled. He had heard Francis Winnerton's opinion of Milan Cathedral. "I doubt if he would do that," he told her. "No, go first to a good doctor—let me see—in Bolzano there is an excellent doctor. Mario Bandello. If you permit, I shall write to him to expect you—no necessity to state a day."

"Dottore Mario Bandello," she repeated. "I thank you from the bottom of my heart."

Francis was difficult. He protested that he was not ill; once he could get rid of this annoying cough, which was certainly much better thanks to the linctus which his clever Antonia had bought for him, he would be completely well. Anyway, he asked, what did she know of this Dottore Bandello?

"One told me that he is considered very clever."

"One?" Francis demanded irritably. "Who is this—one? Some old woman in the village. She thinks that he is clever because he cured her of something trivial years ago. In all probability this Bandello——"

"It was no old woman!" She knew that her voice shook and that tears were very near. For Francis to speak to her like that—her beloved Francis who was never short-tempered! "It was your friend, Count Zevio. He recommends him."

"Zevio!" he exclaimed. "So you've been discussing me with him, eh? What the devil has it got to do with Zevio—he and his wife are crazy about doctors, they always have been. Let Zevio mind his own business."

Antonia by a great effort regained her composure.

"No doubt he will do so, but I shall also mind *my* own business. My business is to get you well, see you looking better. Is it nice for me to know that the Count and his wife think that I neglect you? That they say, 'Poor Francesco, this is what comes of marrying a peasant girl!' She probably imagines that I feed you on weak soup and *polenta*!"

"Don't talk such rubbish; they both know that you cook superbly, that I am pampered and petted abominably. Antonia, don't let us quarrel; we've never quarrelled, my sweet."

"You tell me that you love me——"

"I do," he cried. "You know that I do—wildly, completely, absolutely."

"And yet you allow me to be unhappy, because you refuse to visit a doctor. Francesco, it's not kind."

He began to laugh, protesting that women—clever women like his Antonia—turned everything round to suit themselves. They were all Jesuits, all the direct descendents of Machiavelli —then suddenly he began to cough. She saw him fighting it down, saw his handkerchief held to his mouth, and saw that it was stained with scarlet.

She screamed, "Francesco!"

The attack was over, he sat down heavily, and smiled up at her.

"That's nothing. I think that I perhaps have a little ulcer in my throat. It may be that."

"Don't move!" she ordered. "Don't dare to move."

She remembered one of the nuns—Mother Philomena— had coughed and that her handkerchief was stained when she took it from her lips. Reverend Mother had said to Antonia, "Quick, child, quick! Thank God it is Winter! Bring an icicle from the pump. Run, run!"

Now Antonia rushed into the kitchen—how well she remembered rushing across the yard at the convent, breaking off an icicle from the pump spout, and running back to Reverend Mother, who broke off a small piece, putting it into the mouth of Mother Philomena, and saying, "There, suck it as you might a sweet—slowly, slowly."

She snatched out the tray of ice cubes from the refrigerator, tipped several of them on to a plate and carried them back to Francis. He was leaning back in his chair. His face was very pale; she thought that he looked frightened. She pushed one of the little bits of ice into his mouth, saying, "There, suck it as you might a sweet—slowly, slowly."

She sat beside him, holding his hand. Slowly he relaxed, opened his eyes and smiled at her.

"You always know exactly what to do, sweet."

"But you will go and see the doctor? You promise, Francesco?"

"I promise, but it's nothing—I think an ulcer in my throat."

"You said that before," she responded drily. "Now you are going to bed, as soon as I have put hot-water bottles in it. Then I shall arrange for us to go to Bolzano in the morning, if you have slept well. Now, close your eyes until I come to take you to bed."

While the kettle boiled, she stood, her hands pressed against her breast, praying, "O God, not the same as Mother Philomena—please not that."

CHAPTER TWO

ONCE Francis was safely in bed, Antonia wrote a note in her round, careful hand to Count Zevio. Would he, of his great kindness, make a telephone call to Dottore Bandello, and say that in all probability they would call on him in the morning? Maddelena was sent off with the note, full of importance and delighted to think that she would be able to give the news of the signor's illness to the village. Not that she wished him to be ill, far from it; he was a good gentleman and a considerate master. She wished him nothing but what was good—but there was a satisfaction in knowing that she could impart news of the man who had married little Antonia Trolli, who was a great painter—even if his pictures were almost incomprehensible—and was obviously very rich. More, the fact that he made no secret of his love for Antonia added to the romance of it all.

Francis slept well. The night was cooler than usual and from time to time Antonia, raising herself on her elbow, looked down at his peaceful face, and noticed that a little colour had returned to his cheeks. Her heart was full, she felt what almost amounted to a physical pain when she thought how dear he was to her. As she had told him, he was—everything.

They had talked of the possibility of having children, and Francis had said, "Plenty of time, darling. At the moment I am so crazily in love with you that I should be jealous of a child, even if it were yours and mine. I don't mean that I shall ever love you less, that's impossible, but one day I may have attained something like sanity about you. Then if you were going to have a child I should be so frightened for you. I couldn't bear to see your lovely body distorted, it would hurt me. To think of you being in pain—even in acute discomfort, and to know that, in a way, it was my fault—oh, darling, wait, let's wait. We're both young, we've all our lives before us."

She watched him sleeping, and so many things came flashing through her mind. The first day she had seen him, the day they had come to the house, when she had been so busy, so anxious to get everything in order, he had been like a tiresome small boy. "Antonia, what is this?" or "Antonia, where shall I put that?" She thought of walks they had taken together, when he had stopped suddenly at intervals and said, "I could make a picture of that," or, "What a perfect setting for that queer little cottage!" She remembered her disappointment when she saw his pictures for the first time, and thought them quite hideous. She didn't like all of them now, though each one had a value to her because it was something which had emanated from Francesco's brain.

Their honeymoon, his tenderness and gentleness, her own surprise and almost dismay when she realized that she loved him not only with her heart and mind but with her body as well. Their visit to Rome, when she had stood beside him in Saint Peter's and watched the Pope being carried past, his beautiful hand upraised in blessing.

Francis said, "All these people kneeling as he passes, they're like a field of corn when the wind passes over it. What's that phrase in the Bible—about a 'rushing mighty wind'. Sometimes, 'Tonia, I wish that I belonged to your religion—there's something so big and firm and lasting about it. An anchorage."

She had held his hand in hers and said, "If God wills, *caro*— one day you may perhaps join the Church."

"It doesn't make you unhappy that I'm not of your faith?" he asked.

"Not unhappy, no. I know that you're good, and except that you might be happier, I don't think even the Faith could make you better."

She remembered his pleasure at the small things she did for him, even holding his newly-darned socks at arm's length and declaring that her darns were works of art.

And now he was ill! That dreadful red stain, that strangling cough. He had grown thinner too—sometimes she fancied that the colour in his cheeks was due to fever. Tomorrow they would see Bandello, and hear what he said. On one thing she was determined, that if he were ill she—Antonia—would nurse him, and no other living soul.

He seemed better when he woke, and teased her that she had been frightened, assuring her that the whole thing was nothing at all. "If this Bandello says to me, 'Francis Winnerton, you're a fool to come wasting my time, there's nothing wrong with you. You're thin—well, so are plenty of people. You have a cough? Stop smoking cigarettes. You've not got much appetite? Then that is probably due to the fact that your wife can't cook food decently. Go home and beat her until she learns how to feed a great, hearty, strapping brute like yourself!' If he speaks to me in this way, I shall admit that you can't cook well, that I am badly fed, and that in future I will go down to the *albergo* in the village for my meals."

"In which case—while you are eating veal like leather, and beef like brown paper or cardboard—I shall hire myself out to Contessa Zevio, and tell her that you insist that I work for my living," she assured him.

They drove into Bolzano, that pleasant town with the church with the green tiles, which Francis said looked like a huge lizard in the sunshine. Dottore Bandello proved to be young, he spoke quickly, with the accent of an Austrian grafted on to his fluent Italian.

He asked a great many questions, he made a great many notes, and finally suggested that Antonia should go into the waiting-room. She smiled at him calmly. "I thank you, I prefer to stay here."

Francis said, "*Dottore*, my wife is an obstinate woman, and short of picking her up and carrying her there, I don't see what you can do."

She asked, "You don't mind my staying, Francesco?"

"Not unless it offends the doctor, my sweet."

She folded her hands, smiled at them both and said, "I shall stay then." He was, she felt, very thorough, this doctor. He looked at Francis through a glass screen; he tapped, listened, made Francis say "*Trentetre*" a number of times, asked him to cough and take deep breaths immediately after coughing.

At last he stopped, laid down his stethoscope and nodding said, "Please put on your shirt and coat again." He sighed; he was a sensitive man and he had never become used to giving his patients bad news. It still hurt him to watch the colour fade from their cheeks, the light dim in their eyes. This pretty girl, and the young man who was so obviously in love with her! He wished that he could shelve the responsibility and say that they had better go into Brescia, Verona, or even Milano and see some other doctor who would, later, talk the matter over with him. He couldn't; the young man seemed contented enough, the girl smiled, but Bandello saw that the smile did not come easily, and when she achieved it, it remained too long. As if having made the great effort to smile she was unwilling to relinquish it.

Francis Winnerton said, "Now the verdict, please, *Dottore*!"

The doctor laid the tips of his blunt, meticulously clean fingers together, and peered at the notes which he had made. He thought that he could sense Antonia's impatience.

"I am glad that you came to me—as soon as there were evidences that something was wrong. No, signor, there is no ulceration of the throat, the colour came from your lung—the apex of the left lung. Also I must tell you that there is a slight infection apparent in the right lung. It is for you to clear this up! Yes, of course," in reply to Francis's exclamation, "much of the cure will rest with you. I shall ask you to go to Brescia, where a doctor—whose name I shall give you, has all the very latest machinery for making X-ray photographs. He will, in a few days, send them to me, and I shall know exactly the amount of the—the trouble. Then, we shall see. It may be necessary for you to go to a great specialist in Milano. Until then, I shall tell you exactly what you must do." He looked at Francis, his eyes twinkling suddenly. "There is a man of whom you may have heard, Mussolini. I am no Fascist, but this is what he tells the men who are his supporters. 'Obey, believe, fight.' This is what I say to you, signor."

Antonia listened. So this was the dreaded tuberculosis. She must make a note of every word, and she would obey, believe, and fight. Dear God, how she would fight for Francesco! She would fight every one of the hours of the day. Food—yes, that was easy, she could do all the doctor asked with regard to that. Rest—he must rest, that was not so easy, but she could find ways and means of making him do that. Fresh air—she had alway insisted upon open windows. She knew that many Italians of her own class definitely feared the fresh air—she had always feared rather the smell of "used-up" air, of cooking which hung about, of anything that was stale.

"And now, when can you go to Brescia?" Bandello asked.

Antonia answered, "Tomorrow, *Dottore*. We shall start early. Will you make the appointment with the specialist, please?"

He took a card and wrote the name and address of the doctor, and gave it to her.

"Tell me," she said, "is the village where we live, Morano, a good place for my husband? It stands high, the mists never reach it. In Winter it is cold, very cold, but our house is well warmed, and gets sun. The house is dry, there is no damp anywhere."

He answered, "For Winter, for Spring, it is good. When Summer comes it will be necessary for your husband to go higher into the mountains."

Francis laughed. "To the uncomfortable hotels, and the unpleasant food! Tell me, *Dottore*, is this illness—serious?"

"All illness is serious—from tuberculosis to the slight cold. All must be arrested whenever possible. You are young, you live quietly, you can rest—regular rest is necessary, as necessary as anything else that I can prescribe."

"I shall get better?" The question came abruptly.

"I see no reason why you should not. You are in a happy position; you can work when you wish to, and rest when you do not wish to work. You have a wife who will take care of you, encourage you, uphold you. I am not a prophet, but I repeat—there is no reason why you should not get better."

Antonia rose. Bandello was astonished at her poise and dignity. Zevio had told him that she was a peasant, but now she stood erect and completely mistress of herself.

"Francesco," she said, "please leave me to speak with the *dottore* for a few moments. I shall not be long."

Bandello saw a kind of sulky cloud come over his face.

"What is there that I cannot hear? Surely it is——"

She said, firmly but very gently, "Francesco, please——"

His face cleared. "Oh, very well. You love secrets, don't you?"

Bandello asked her to sit down. She shook her head.

"I would rather stand. I find difficult things more easy to speak when I stand on my feet. *Dottore*, we have been married —not very long, about a year. We are still—very much in love. I mean——"

He said, "I understand, signora. I might tell you that it would be better if you had your own room——"

She interrupted him. "Do you mean that it might be bad for me or for Francesco if we continued to share a room?"

"It might, conceivably, be bad for you."

"That is all right—that does not matter. And"—for the first time her cheeks flushed—"to make love, is this bad for him? We are so much in love."

He talked to her wisely, frankly, and kindly; she listened, her charming face grave and intent. When he ended—and he told her many things about disinfecting, precautions regarding plates, dishes, cups—he advised her to make him rest before meals, and much more, she held out her hand.

"You have helped me very much. I am very grateful. Is he—very ill?"

He met her eyes, watching him very steadily and directly. He wanted to make light of everything, but there was something in the expression of those intensely blue eyes which forced the truth from him.

"He will need very great care. He has a weakness, begun I imagine when he was a soldier. He was very ill then, you remember, he told me. That weakness is there, and it has taken an ally, you understand. Together they will be difficult to fight."

She nodded. "Again—thank you. Believe me I shall fight with him and for him."

ii

For weeks Antonia felt they visited doctors. Francis was X-rayed, specialists sent their reports to Bandello. Bandello came out to see their cottage and pronounced it ideal for Francis.

The specialist in Milano, a tall, gaunt man with an irritable manner, said bluntly, "I recommend a sanatorium. Davos,

Arosa, somewhere high, in Switzerland, even in the Italian mountains."

Francis listened, then smiled. "Nothing will induce me to go. Could I have my wife with me? Very well then, then I repeat—I will not go to a sanatorium. I could not face being separated, seeing her perhaps for an hour a day. No, Morano is as good a place as any."

"Perhaps if we took a house in one of these places, when it gets too hot at Morano——" Antonia suggested.

"Pshaw! *Perbacco*, a house! He wants the regularity of a sanatorium, medical attention there, on the spot. Medical discipline. A time-table, rules, a regularized diet."

This time Francis laughed, and the tall specialist frowned.

"Discipline! *Dottore*, no doctor could exercise such discipline as my wife does. I live to a time-table. 'Get up', 'Go out', 'Lie down', 'Now come and eat'. I am regimented."

The weeks passed. Sometimes Antonia felt that it was impossible that Francis could be ill, she had never known him so gay, never known him so anxious to paint, to enjoy everything to the full. He was right; she did discipline him, and he took it all beautifully. He was obedient, and appreciative of everything she did for him. Once a month they went to see Bandello, who applied his tests, asked questions, and told Antonia, "At least he is no worse—thanks to you, signora."

John Trevor came to stay with them at Christmas time, and, for the first time since Francis's illness had been apparent, Antonia had someone to whom she could talk. While Francis was resting, she plied him with questions.

"Please tell me exactly what is in your heart, John. Do you think that he looks very ill? The truth, please," she insisted.

"He looks very thin, he's browned by the sun, and he is in good spirits, but—dear Antonia, he's a sick man."

"Do you think that it would be wise to persuade him to go into one of these sanatoria?"

He shook his head. "I think that it would kill him. He'd never stand the separation from you. His whole life revolves round you."

"And mine round him."

Francis too talked to John Trevor when they went walking together. The lovely clear air, with its pleasant tang, the crisp snow underfoot, the beauty of the distant snow-covered mountains, the clear blue skies were, it seemed to John Trevor, a tonic in themselves.

"You like living here?" he asked.

"I don't feel that I ever lived before, John. Here I *savour* everything, there is a meaning in everything. Sometimes, just at first, the quiet used to oppress me; now—when we come back from Bolzano, and that is not a particularly noisy place, I feel that the quietness welcomes me back. There is something so personal in it all—everything now is so absorbingly interesting. Even a new load of logs, smelling of resin and cold air, excites me. To watch the load drawn up, the horses' flanks steaming after coming up the hill, to watch the men unload and stack the logs so neatly in the shed, to see Antonia hovering round to make certain that everything is done correctly. I painted a picture for her—her Christmas present. I showed it to her and then put it away so that Santa Claus might bring it on Christmas Eve. It's the only picture of mine that she has really liked. Yes, she likes the one of Aramis and she is rather pleased with the portrait of herself—though she couldn't tell you why. This is a bunch of rowan berries and some 'flowers of the snow'; it is painted with the most slavish fidelity. Every petal, every vein, most meticulously done. I honestly believe that there is something in—that style of painting! I don't admire it, but I swear to you that it's a devil of a sweat to do it!" He laughed, that queer laugh which always sounded rather hoarse. "The Pre-Raphaelites had nothing up on me in that picture!"

Tentatively John asked about his health. Francis grinned, almost impudently.

"I feel magnificently well some days—other days not so good. Those are the difficult days, because I have to prevent Antonia guessing. On those days I don't want to eat, I hate the sight of food—even the food which she prepares for me. Honestly, I don't think that I'm much worse, even if I'm not much better. Only one thing frightens me, John—not dying, not what's in the hereafter—it might be astonishingly interesting. It's leaving Antonia. It seems to me," he continued, "that I have sloughed off the skin that I used to wear at Maudesley, and have become a different person. I never want to go back, though the place is beautiful, but I couldn't live that life again. I suppose that my father and brother imagine me as living in squalor, wearing dreadful clothes, not bothering to bath much, and spending my time alternating between painting and hobnobbing with the peasants drinking *vino*.

"They'd never realize that since I married I have read more, thought more, achieved more, in the sense of development than I did in the rest of my life. There's very little chance of anyone degenerating with a woman like 'Tonia. Her mind is the most active thing imaginable. I don't say that she wants to delve into science, politics—for that matter neither do I, politics mean nothing to me—or even art and literature—but she is *curious* about everything, and once her curiosity is roused it must be satisfied.

"She decided that she would learn English, that it was a bad thing for a woman not to be able to speak her husband's language—well, look at the progress she has made, it's amazing. She's improved my Italian out of all knowledge. Now she talks of learning French. She's got tremendous tenacity of purpose, that girl. She has real and great appreciation of art—not my pictures"—he laughed—"but of the masters—the classical painters. Imagine the average girl, living in a village all her life, finding Giorgione's La Tempesta the most wonderful thing in a gallery filled with wonderful pictures! No, I shan't go back to Maudesley, not even for a visit. To take Antonia would be to make her nervous, shy— and she would not be as we know her here, she'd possibly even be a little *gauche*, though I can scarcely imagine it. The place would oppress her, she'd be conscious that people, servants, were 'watching her', that they knew she was the foreign wife of that strange painter son of the Earl's.

"For once in my life I've been completely sensible, and let me tell you, very businesslike. I've made a will; I've left everything to her. I've got my mother's money, about seven hundred a year. Until I married I had an allowance from my father. I've done pretty well, my pictures have sold. Living here doesn't cost a great deal, y'know. I've left everything in the house to her too, including the pictures." Again he laughed. "If she sells them, which I hope she will do, that detailed bit of painting of the flowers and berries is going to puzzle the critics and the dealers!"

John listened and found it impossible to grow depressed. Francis might be a sick man, might never recover from this wretched illness, but he was cramming concentrated enjoyment of everything with which he came in contact into his life. He was deeply in love, he was watching the development of Antonia with a passionate interest, with love and with admiration. There would most certainly be "no moaning at the bar" when Francis put out to sea, John reflected, and then frowned irritably because he had found such a very obvious quotation, and in addition he disliked Tennyson.

He stayed at Morano for three weeks, and watched both Francis and Antonia carefully. John was an astute young man in spite of his general air of boredom and inefficiency. He had long ago adopted the rôle of a complete dilettante very carefully. He was something of a *poseur*, except where his affections were engaged, and he felt a warm affection for Winnerton and his wife, his feelings for them were strangely simple and uncomplicated.

He enjoyed being with them, and their courage in the face of this possible tragedy called for his admiration. Illness was never mentioned, the whole atmosphere was cheerful, they were both able to laugh at simple things without the laughter being either forced or over-hearty. Even the necessity for Francis to rest was treated lightly.

"It is necessary, John. Ot'erwise I have heem—what do you say?—under my feet all the time. So it is better that he go to his room and leave me in peace to do my work. Also, the rest improves his temper!"

"Did you know that I was bad-tempered, John?" Francis asked.

"I've known you fairly irritable at times, yes."

"Listen to Antonia's picture of me!"

"No, no," she protested, "but he is—w'at you say of small babies—he is *tiresome*. It is always, 'Show me this', 'May I have that?' 'What is it you are doing?' 'Why not come and sit down and read?' I suppose that it is I who am really bad-tempered, but—oh, dear, this Francesco, he can be—a tedious boy!"

The night before John left, he met Antonia walking back from her mother's, the roads were too slippery for her to use Gloria. He fell into step beside her, thinking how well she walked, her shoulders back, her head held high, and her back straight as a Guardsman's.

"I shall be sorry to go tomorrow," John said. "I've enjoyed being here."

"We also shall be sorry. It has been pleasant. When will you come again to see us?"

"I should try to come whenever you wanted me. I go to America with my mother. She is an American and she has come to dislike living in England. I think perhaps she and my father do not get on very well. I may stay six months. By then you will be in the mountains, eh?"

He heard her catch her breath. "Yes, we shall be in the mountains. Francesco will not wish to go; he hates the mountains, he says that at a distance they are splendid, but—not to sit down to breakfast with them! He says such funny things, this boy. He would like to go to the sea, but the doctors do not think that the sea is very good for him. Ah, John, sometimes I am very frightened. Sometimes I wish that I did not love him so much, then I could be—what do you say—stern? I could say, 'You must go! I insist!' He would look unhappy. In the mountains he is always unhappy—he loves his home, his small dog, so much. I have been given too much, I think sometimes 'all kingdoms of the world', too much happiness, too much laughter and smiles, and now I am so frightened that I may lose it. When you live for a long time —for before we were married I was so happy too, as his servant I was happy—in the bright sunshine, to move into a small piece of shadow makes you shiver."

John looked down at her. "Do you think Francis will get better?"

She stopped, then met his eyes. He felt that hers were immeasurably sad, yet her face was calm as she spoke.

"No," she said, "no, I don't think that he will get better. But so long as he remains with me, he shall have every happiness that I can give him."

"And then?"

"Then? Nothing will matter very much to me. I shall go on, because life is given to us, and we must take care of it—reasonably—as a gift from God, but everything would be different. I should want to go away, to live somewhere quite, quite different. You may think, John, that I am taking it with calmness, that is because I must never allow Francesco to see what I am feeling. Sometimes, when I am alone, in the kitchen perhaps, preparing something that will make him eat, there is a pain in my heart. I have known when sweat—cold sweat—has run off my face because I was in agony. I have to press my hands against my chest—so!—so that I shall not cry out with the pain of it.

"I shall never lose hope—never. I shall never stop *trying*, for miracles can and do happen. But I do not think one will happen for him. He is like a bright candle burning to the end. His painting—he says—is better than it has ever been——"

John nodded. "That's true, it is. The man's a marvel."

"Sometimes I think that his work—and his love—are consuming him."

"Yet he would not be happy without either."

"No, that is true. There, we must go back and be very happy for your last evening. You will leave me your address, and if it is possible you will come—if Francesco wants you."

He took her hands and held them in his, he was terribly moved, more deeply than he would have believed possible. The sight of her lovely face, her clear, brave eyes, the sense of youth which hung about her, and yet her readiness to take responsibilities and face the possible end of her happiness with steadfast courage made him long to put his arms round her and swear that he would stay at Morano—so long as she needed him.

He said, "Antonia, dear, brave Antonia, I'd come for you, for Francis, for both of you—for either of you if you needed me."

iii

John sailed with his mother for America, and often the picture of Antonia, her hands held in his, came back to his mind. He wrote to Francis very often, short, amusing letters, telling him that he must come to America and paint, "The Great White Way", the skyscrapers, and the "L" as it rushed past. Francis replied, often illustrating his letters with sketches of the village people, Antonia talking to Aramis, Maddelena sweeping the front door-step. He said very little about his health, only that he had promised Antonia to go with her to the mountains at the end of May. *I shall hate it,* he wrote, *and in her heart so will she, but it will make her more content because she has some almost superstitious belief in the healing power of snow and general discomfort.*

Then in March Antonia wrote that Francis was ill. He had contracted bronchitis. *This early sunshine is not really warming. It makes you believe that it warms you, but it is only just that the outside of you becomes heated. Bronchitis is not very serious for strong people, but for my dear love—I tremble.*

A few days later a scrawl in pencil from Francis. *I've managed to get pneumonia like the fool I am. Ever had it? It's simply beastly. If anything happens, be kind to Antonia. I'm afraid she'll hate it all terribly. What a mess it all is. But how good the last years have been. Good Luck, John. Glad I've known you.*

John sat staring at the unsteady writing; he could imagine it all so well. Francis trying to make light of his illness, Antonia remaining calm while despair filled her heart. The little house where they had been so gay, where they had laughed and talked, was now filled with the sense of fear and apprehension. If Francis died, what would his father and brother do? Descend upon her, patronize her, suggest that Francis had died because he was living in unsuitable surroundings?

He went to his mother's sitting-room. She was a fine-looking woman, all her life accustomed to giving orders, and knowing that unlimited money was always at her disposal. She had been a Miss van der Heyden, her father had owned immense canning factories, and his great ambition had been that his beautiful daughter, Cécile, should marry an English peer. She had met Rivermead and he had proposed. Old van der Heyden was enchanted. He had hoped for a title, but for his daughter to become a duchess had been beyond his wildest hopes.

Rivermead and his "stately homes" had bored Cécile. She had never cared for the country, and the continual talk of sport, of the prospects of the year being a good one for "the birds", Scotland and deer-stalking—how she hated venison!— had become intolerable. She did her duty, she provided an heir, and on him she lavished all her love and devotion. She had watched him carefully through his school days, had read his reports with avidity, and felt that he had a great future before him. Learning came easily to John; later, she was to realize, it came too easily. His career at his public school was meteoric; he won prizes, his cricket and football were both excellent. He went up to Oxford with a reputation for being a coming man. Then his interest evaporated. He got his football blue, then rested on his laurels and gave up the game. He spent a great deal of money, was not always in the good graces of the authorities, and contrived to enjoy himself immensely.

Now he was thirty-three; he had travelled widely, he had experienced adventure, even hardship, but he had come home, shrugged his shoulders and decided that he must learn "appreciation of life".

John was handsome, possessing a beautiful figure. Women found him attractive, and for a time he had taken a mistress and installed her in an *appartement* in Paris. At the end of six months, Cécile, who had no inhibitions about such matters, asked him bluntly what had become of her.

John said, "Ah, yes, you saw her once or twice, didn't you? Charming, but at the end of three months—darling, I was so delighted when she decided that she really loved Armand Bommé. He is in love with her, they are to be married. I gave them a very handsome wedding present. I hope they'll be very happy. Yes, she was charming—but a bore."

Now he stood before her, his handsome face very grave. She looked up.

"What is it, John?"

"Would you mind if I went to Europe at once, Mama?"

"In all probability I should mind very much indeed. Why are you going?"

He noticed that she did not protest. She might not wish him to go, but she never argued with him.

"You remember Francis Winnerton, the painter?"

"Very well. How he ever came to be Maudesley's son I don't know."

"I'm afraid that he is dying, in North Italy."

She raised her eyebrows. "That nice boy! How dreadful. Consumption, I suppose. I believe that his mother died of it. You'll come back—I mean as soon as you know that—that he is out of danger? I shall miss you."

He stooped and kissed her. "Thank you. You always understand."

"If I don't, I pretend to, which does just as well."

John cabled to Antonia that he was leaving New York at once. Francis died two days before John reached Genoa.

Count Zevio telegraphed to Maudesley, and three days later Mostyn arrived in Morano. He had driven from Mezzo-lombardo, and thought that he must be arriving in the wilds of Italy. He eyed the towering mountains with distaste, compared the little villages through which he passed unfavourably with the ones he knew on his father's estate. Dirty, untidy-looking places, probably no decent sanitation, no wonder people contracted consumption in such holes. How different from the English villages, with their neat gardens, thatched roofs, compact little grey churches—here all the churches looked far too big! Catholic ostentation, of course. He had heard that the priests wrung money from the poor, no doubt to pay for the upkeep of these great edifices!

The driver said, "Morano, signor."

Mostyn spoke no Italian, he therefore answered very loudly and firmly in English.

"I," he pointed to his own chest, "wish the house of Mr. Winnerton."

"Ah! Signor Vinnerton! *Poverino!*"

A neat, small house, scarcely more than a cottage. It looked clean enough. Terrible ordeal to face this peasant girl, who probably spoke no English. He was distressed at his brother's death, but they had never been particularly friendly, and it was difficult to feel much affection for a brother who had cut loose and married some slut of an Italian peasant.

He got out and said, "Wait!" to the driver.

He knocked and the door was opened to him by a young woman. A young woman whose face was devoid of any colour, even her lips looked pale as if all life and energy had been drained out of her. She was dressed in a simple black dress, her hair was very smooth and shone in the light. Mostyn thought, "By God, if she had some colour she'd be a beauty. This can't be—no, this isn't a peasant!"

He said, "I am the brother of——"

She answered him in English; true she had an accent, but she spoke correctly, and her voice was very pleasant.

"Yes, I know. Please enter, signor. The funeral was this morning."

CHAPTER THREE

MOSTYN followed her into the cottage. He stared round the simply furnished room, thinking, "And Francis left Maudesley for this! He must have been crazy!" The room was spotlessly clean, a small bright fire was burning in the open hearth, the furniture was simple but he had to admit that there was nothing offensive about it. Over the long bookcase hung a picture of the girl who had admitted him—Francis's widow. The idea was fantastic. One of his brother's queer paintings. The public seemed to like them; he had been acclaimed as a great painter.

The girl said, "May I give you some coffee, or wine, signor?"

He nodded. "Thanks, I should like some coffee—if it's no trouble."

"Please seat yourself. I shall be very soon here with the coffee." He sat down and continued staring about him. So this was where his brother had lived; this was where, probably only a few hours before, his coffin had been carried on its way to the hearse or whatever they had in these outlandish places. Damn it, they'd hurried the funeral on! Poor chap only dead for three days—at the most four. They might have waited for his arrival.

The telegram had been signed "Zevio". Who the devil was he? They had been drinking sherry before dinner—his father disliked what he called "the cocktail habit". Morrison, the butler, had brought the telegram in on a silver salver, and his father had said irritably, "Now, what's this? What's this?" He had ripped open the orange envelope and read it.

"Good God! Francis is dead! Here, read it for yourself."

He had read, *Deep sympathy your son died last night. Zevio.*

He said, "I say, that's pretty awful, poor chap. Will you go out, Father?"

"Me? Me go out? How can I go with this wretched gout! Might bring on the damned thing. No, you'll have to go, you'll have to go. Most upsetting. Remember I'm making no promises to the widow, none at all. Probably she'll expect to be kept in luxury for the rest of her life. Have no hanky-panky, Mostyn. Be firm about it."

"Francis may have left her his money, the money he had from Mama."

His father stared at him. "And if he has, it will be a damned disgrace. Your poor mother's money going to some Italian slut! You'd better catch the last train to town and get off as quickly as possible. All most upsetting. Confound it, there's that twinge in my toe again! No, I most certainly daren't go."

Now here he was in the wilds of Italy, in some village of which he had never heard until Francis mentioned it in a letter. He was sitting in what had been his brother's house, waiting to be given coffee by the girl who was—presumably—Francis's widow.

She came back and set the coffee down on a small table beside his chair. The china, Mostyn noticed, was charming, the tiny coffee-pot shone with much polishing. The scent of the coffee was delightful.

"Thank you—er—I don't know your name, I'm afraid."

"I am *Signora* Vinnerton."

"My brother's widow! You're very young, surely."

"Time will remedy that, signor."

She had seated herself opposite to him, her hands lying loosely on her knee. She looked terribly tired, he thought. There were dark circles under her eyes, and her eyes themselves looked heavy. Marvellously coloured eyes, the brightest, clearest blue he had ever seen.

He sipped his coffee and said, "It's excellent coffee." Then, "I must say I think you might have refrained from hurrying the funeral on so. Scarcely decent! I mean—I got here as quickly as I could."

He saw her draw a deep breath before she spoke. "My husband died at ten o'clock, three days ago. No, four days ago. I have lost count of time. In Italy we do not—delay funerals."

"Umph!" He wished that she were not so completely mistress of herself, wished even that she would assert herself, make demands, anything but speak in that controlled voice, her face so calm and expressionless.

"My father wishes me to say that he cannot promise to provide for you in any lavish way. My father is a landowner and things are difficult for landowners in these days. Wages are very high, and so are prices. One is continually having to do expensive repairs . . ." He stopped short. Why on earth was he offering excuses to this girl?

"I am provided for; your brother attended to that. I shall not need to accept anything. Please excuse me, I hear Aramis." She rose and went to the door, and when she opened it a small white dog came in. She caught him in her arms and spoke to him. Her voice was low but very tender. "My dear Aramis, yes, you miss him. Poor little dog. There, you must eat your supper. Come." Again she turned to Mostyn and said, "Please excuse, I did not understand that you had a car here. I shall give the driver some wine."

Again she disappeared into the kitchen and he heard her talking to the little dog; presently she returned with a small flask of wine and a glass. There was something also on a plate, but Mostyn could not see what it was. He heard her call to the driver, and caught disjointed words as he spoke to her.

"You are very kind," he heard her reply, "I am grateful. All people loved him." Then she spoke in Italian, something which he could not hear. Possibly explaining what she had said first. She came back to her chair. "I forgot that he does not speak anything but Italian. Poor man, he is sad about your brother. All people are sad in the village also. He was very much loved."

"Did he leave a will?"

She nodded. "Yes, now I only wait for his friend to arrive, and he will do whatever is necessary. He is coming here now, on his way from Genoa. His ship was a little delayed, but he sent me a message by the air. He comes from America—New York. He will attend to everything. Francis trusted him above all people."

"Who is he—this friend?" Surely the right thing would have been to leave matters in his hands or his father's, not to delegate them to some wretched Italian.

"His name is John Trevor, he is a lord, but we never call him so."

Mostyn frowned. "John Trevor? You mean Rivermead's son? Why is he coming here? What has he got to do with it?"

"He is a good friend; he was the great friend of my husband. Many times he stayed here. I do not know anything about his father. I only know that Francis said that he was a lord. He is very good, very kind man."

"When he gets here he'd better get in touch with my father's solicitors. If you'll give me a piece of paper I'll write down the address for you. Have you any idea what my brother has left you, Mrs. Winnerton?"

She gave him paper and a pencil, then said, "He said the furniture and this house which he bought from Innerhoffer four months ago. There is some money in the house, also in the bank at Cormia. I have the right to sign cheques, he gave me that right when he grew so ill that to sign cheques made him tired. There is some other money, but I do not know how much that is. It is in England. It does not matter. I will give you something of his if you wish it for a *ricordo*, perhaps. There are no debts, we have never had debts.

"And, signor, if you could leave me I should be happy. This has been a terrible day. I should like to be alone. To-morrow I shall be more—more myself. I will tell you then anything you wish to know."

Mostyn stood up; it was astonishing to be virtually dismissed by this girl who was a peasant! She didn't seem to understand who he was, what was his position, and what might have been Francis's position if he hadn't been such a fool. She talked of John Trevor as if he were a nobody. "A very kind man," and apparently he had come over from America to see to Francis's affairs. The world seemed upside down. The future Duke of Rivermead!

He said, "Yes, must have been trying. I'm staying at a place with some fantastic name—Messo—something or other. I'll come over in the morning. About eleven. Hope you get a decent night."

"You are very kind." She opened the door, took the little tray from the driver, and wished him good night.

ii

Antonia had scarcely slept. She woke feeling that she was living through a dreadful dream, a nightmare. If only she could wake and find that Francis was still here in the house he had loved. Nothing was left except things which he would never want again. Down in the *camposanto* there was a heap of newly-turned earth, some flowers—dying already—and that was all.

She had hoped and prayed, she had held fast to the belief that even though he would never be well and strong again, he might at least be spared to her for a little longer. Even when Bandello had said that he had pneumonia, that she must have nurses to help her to nurse him, she had still hoped. She reminded him of what he had once said—"believe, obey, fight".

She said, "Now I have done both the first two, now I shall begin to fight!"

The nurses had been very kind; they had come from Milan, but Francis had wanted her all the time. He had been very patient, had given no trouble; and when she realized—as she felt he did too—that the end was drawing very near, he only wished to hold her hand and lift his heavy eyes to watch her face.

He whispered, "It's the finish, Antonia?"

By some superhuman effort she managed to say, "The beginning, *caro*."

"It's—all been wonderful."

His eyes had closed and he had not spoken again.

She dressed, and went down to the sitting-room which felt so empty without Francesco. There were still things there which reminded her of him. There was his cigarette-box, though he had not smoked cigarettes for a long time because they made him cough so much. There was a book which he had been reading, with the bookmarker which she had made for him. It was about Leonardo, and written by someone whose name looked as if he might have been a Russian. When she went into the little lobby by the kitchen there was his overcoat and scarf hanging on the pegs. She touched the scarf gently as she passed. How often when he was going out had she held it out to him!

"And this, *caro*, not only the overcoat," she had warned. "It is cold."

He had smiled, and said, "That's right, coddle me, wrap me up—am I salt or sugar that I shall melt?"

"More precious than either." Then she had thrown the scarf round his neck, wrapped it carefully over his chest and tucked it into his coat.

As she made coffee she talked to Aramis. The little dog sat and watched her with dark, soulful eyes.

"Today comes the brother of your master. I don't like him much. He has—hot eyes. He looks greedy. How unlike your master, eh? But also today John comes. That kind, nice John, who was Francesco's friend—yes, and mine. He and I will talk and I must make plans, Aramis. I am the widow of a great painter, and I must make something of my life, as he made something of his. I am nearly twenty-two; it is not very old, but I am not a child any longer. I must go into the world and make a road for myself. Don't be afraid, dear little dog, that I shall neglect you; you are far too precious. You were his friend, and I love you. There! Drink your *caffe latte* and bread. Don't be too sad, my dear; he did not like sadness. You remember how he laughed always, at so many things." The door opened and Maddelena entered. "Ah, good morning, Maddelena. You have finished at my mother's house?"

Maddelena sighed gustily. "Yes, in spite of my heavy heart. This is a day of sadness, everyone in the village speaks in low voices."

Antonia didn't believe it; down in the village the women were bawling to each other exactly as they always did. They might speak of Francis, of his funeral, of the sadness of it all, but most certainly they were not whispering about it.

She wished that Francis could have heard what Maddelena said, how he would have laughed, perhaps made Antonia imitate the women, for she was good at imitations he always said, then he would have laughed all the more!

She went down the village, Aramis at her heels. The people stared at her, many of them came and offered sympathy, and she thanked them calmly. She remembered that Francis had always told her not to "wear your heart on your sleeve". He had explained what it meant, and she had approved. Emotion, grief, desolation were private, sacred things, not to be displayed to everyone. Only to one's nearest and dearest might one wear one's heart where it could be seen by everyone.

Last night she had been restrained and cold with Mostyn, she had felt that he had not really loved Francis, that he had despised him for marrying a peasant in an Italian village. His manner had chilled her, repulsed her. How different it would be when John came. To him she would talk, say all that was in her heart, for he had loved Francis and admired him.

She visited the shops, and as usual made her purchases with care. If the brother of Francis were to stay for a mid-day meal, she must show him that his brother had been given food which was excellent, of the best quality and cooked in the best possible manner.

Innerhoffer was kind, saying only, "We are sorry, signora. All of us are sorry. Yes, a fine signor, respected by all of us." Then with a change of tone as if in spite of everything life must go on, "The veal is very fine, also here are sweetbreads. Look! Magnificent, no? Indeed, veal bones, nothing is better for making soup, as I do not need to tell you, signora. The beef steaks—ah, you have shown me how to cut them. Not too large, but *thick*, it is necessary this thickness. I shall send these to your house?"

Antonia shook her head. "No, I have my basket. Yes, and also a piece of liver for my small dog. Thank you."

They were all very kind, and helpful, but she felt that they thought she should have remained in seclusion and not gone about her daily tasks as usual. How strange, for surely she could remember—and regret—Francis as deeply and keenly when she was shopping as sitting by the fire and allowing her grief to overwhelm her. Then if his brother and his friend were coming, she wished to do credit to—not herself only—but to

Francis. He had loved to dispense hospitality, she remembered how he had watched the faces of their guests to see how her cooking surprised them. Again and again he had caught her eyes and smiled with satisfaction. Later with his arm round her shoulders he would assure her that she had "staggered" them.

She would "stagger" this brother who was a lord, who hadn't loved Francis and who despised her. She might even make him feel a little envious, for Francis had told her that although his father had numbers of servants, the cooking at Maudesley was shocking.

She called to Aramis and they walked up the hill, where the ground was less hard than it had been yesterday for a thaw had set in, filling the ditches with water which gurgled as if glad to be rid of the tyranny of the frost.

"So, Aramis," she said, "he will understand if I am busy in my kitchen. It is all being prepared, really, in his honour."

iii

Mostyn arrived at half past eleven. Antonia had worked at lightning speed, her hands had moved very swiftly and accurately; she had beaten eggs, and used herbs with great delicacy, she had mixed an elaborate sauce, had sent Maddelena for cream which had been whipped until it stood up like a pyramid. The tray with glasses was standing ready in the sitting-room, those glasses which she and Francis had bought in Venice on their honeymoon, and some of the pale dry sherry which he had liked, and which she privately thought dreadful, chilly stuff.

Mostyn entered rubbing his hands. "Good morning, signora. You see I'm learning Italian already. You look better this morning."

"Will you have a glass of sherry, please?" she asked. It was a difficult word to pronounce and Francis had always laughed at her and said, "Will I have a glass of cheri—yes, *chéri*." It had been one of their little jokes.

Mostyn looked at the bottle and whistled. "I say, this is good. Where did you get this? I didn't think you went in for dry sherry in Italy."

She replied calmly, "My husband used to send for it to a place which he knew. I hope that it is nice."

"It's first rate. Poor Francis! In fact, this is a remarkably nice place altogether. Cosy, isn't it?" She really was charming. Last night she had looked too pale, but this morning there was colour in her cheeks, and her lips were less compressed. "This wouldn't be a bad place to spend a holiday. If I brought my car, we could get about and you could show me the local beauty spots, eh? We might have quite a good time. After all—I'm your brother-in-law, that should make it all right."

Her eyes, which had been so blue, had grown suddenly very cold.

"I am very glad that you have remembered that—you are my brother-in-law." He thought, "Damn it, her voice might have come straight off the ice!" She touched the bottle of sherry again. "Will you have another glass, please?"

"I say, don't get cross." Mostyn laughed uneasily. "I didn't mean——"

"I don't think that I am very interested in what you meant." There was the sound of a car drawing up. She said, "Ah, excuse me, here is my other guest." She went to the door, and Mostyn wondered again how and where this girl learnt the expressions she used. "My other guest!"

He heard her voice, "John, I am so pleased to see you."

Then John Trevor's deeper tones, "And I to see you. My dear Antonia, forgive me. Everything went wrong with me.

We docked late, they missed a tide or something of the kind. I had difficulty in getting a car, we had a breakdown—everything went wrong for me."

"It does not matter—now that you are here. I have the brother of Francis waiting to greet you."

John followed her into the room. He looked very tall in his long travelling-coat; he brought with him an air of distinction, and yet when he spoke to Mostyn there was none of the warmth in his voice which had been so evident when he spoke to Antonia.

Mostyn said, "Hello, Trevor. Had a good run?"

"An exceptionally bad one, as I have been telling Signora Winnerton. I had hoped to get here yesterday morning. I'm sorry that we are both here on the same errand, though it is a privilege to offer sympathy and help to her." He stooped and patted the little dog which was circling round his feet. "Hello, Aramis, poor fellow."

"Yes, a bad show. Not that we were ever very—close, but Francis was young. I'm in a difficult position, as it were, representing my father, you understand. The whole thing is—difficult."

"Really?" John's tone expressed nothing, he was helping himself to sherry, for Antonia had disappeared into the kitchen. They drank in silence. Mostyn had always disliked John Trevor, always thought him superior and inclined to be patronizing. He had evidently made himself very much at home here—helping himself to sherry, taking off his coat and going to hang it up, Mostyn supposed, in some lobby.

He came back with Antonia, who said, "Luncheon is ready. I had not very much time, you understand, John—but you will be kind to what I can offer you, no?"

"I have never known the time when I had to—be kind." He smiled at her. "My trouble has always been to find sufficient superlatives to express my appreciation."

For the first time Mostyn heard her laugh, a low, bubbling sound which was almost a chuckle.

"You talk like many books!" she said. "Come, our meal is waiting."

The dining-room was small and very simple, but like the sitting-room everything was shining and polished. The table was meticulously laid, the cloth and the napkins glossy with ironing; they were exquisitely smooth, and stiffened to the correct degree.

The soup was served in cups with two handles. Mostyn tasted it with appreciation, for he loved good food. It was incredibly smooth, and the flavour was delicious. Small grilled river trout, served with a mushroom sauce. Antonia said, "They are very small, but they were only caught this morning in the river here."

John said, "Our old friend Beppi poaching again, eh?"

"I am afraid so. And also the mushrooms are not really what you call mushrooms, they are our own dried *fungi*."

She waited on them herself, eating very little, but merely toying with the food on her plate. Her movements were deft and she never fumbled. When she went out into the kitchen, Mostyn said, "By Jove, what a cook they have!"

"Signora Winnerton does all the cooking herself," John told him. Sweetbreads, brains, and small pieces of veal—with a sauce such as Mostyn had never tasted. John turned, smiling, to his hostess.

"Your own particular sauce! I shall never know how you make it, but I should recognize it anywhere. Again and again I have told myself that I have discovered the secret—yes, I can taste this, I can savour that—but always something evades me. This sauce would make the name of any great chef!"

She said, "I think that I have improved. I have at least five others quite as good as this one." She turned to Mostyn. "I am passionate about cooking. It was well, because my husband's

H

appetite was very—what do you say?—variable, one day good, the next day it did not exist. So I had to find new things to attract him. And now, truffles, you like them, I hope? It is a Lombardy dish; they are stewed in wine. Champagne it ought to be, but that is so extravagant, so I use a small bottle of *Asti*. It is inclined to be too sweet, so I must correct the sweetness by adding——"

John cried, "No, no, that must remain another secret! They are delicious. It all seems so simple, this cooking—what is this? Only truffles, some bacon, served on pieces of toast. But—it is the addition of this, of that, which makes the dish— perfect. Rather like life, Antonia, isn't it? Simple enough, but needing those additions to make it something more than ordinary."

"Perhaps—yes, it is the additions which matter." Her face was clouded suddenly, and John said quickly, "Now I only wait for your coffee!"

"It is ready, let us drink it in the sitting-room, please."

Liqueurs were there—drinks which Mostyn eyed with suspicion.

John said, "There is *aurum*, *cedro*, yes, even *grappa*, and cognac."

"I've never heard of them—I'll stick to cognac, thanks."

He was growing not only bored but rather sulky; he seemed so completely outside their circle of interests. They barely mentioned Francis, and when they did it was without the slightest emotion, but with affection, even with admiration. John had pointed to the picture of Antonia, and said in a voice which was almost hushed, "That's his masterpiece!"

They never dwelt on his death, and Antonia never recounted the manner of his passing.

A tall, gaunt woman entered and spoke to Antonia in Italian, a dialect, Mostyn presumed, for it was quite different

from the way in which Antonia spoke. Probably, after all, she
spoke dialect too, peasants did, surely. He kept impressing
upon himself that she was a peasant, and that this poise, this
control, this ability to say and do the right thing were all
things which she had acquired from his dead brother. He liked
to remember that; it made him feel superior, it soothed the
memory of the way in which she had snubbed him when, after
all, he had only made a perfectly feasible suggestion. She was
attractive, and attractive women—of her class—must expect
men to make advances to them. Damn it, he'd paid her a
compliment! He'd been perfectly discreet, had only offered a
vague suggestion, and she had stared at him with eyes like
chips of ice. She talked to John Trevor in a very different way
from that in which she spoke to him. To John her voice
sounded warm and kind, when she spoke to him it was cold
and formal. Nice thing, John Trevor hobnobbing with this
girl, and there he was shaking the gaunt servant by the hand
and pattering Italian to her. No dignity—that was what came
of living abroad and having an American mother whose father
had been a meat canner!

He rose and said, "Well, I think that I must be pushing
along. I have to catch the night train. I've work waiting for me
in England."

Antonia held up her hand. "Please, one moment. I have
some things of my husband's which I think you ought to
have." She went over to a bureau and opened it, taking out a
leather box. "Here is the watch which belonged, I think, to
your grandfather, and here is the gold cigarette-case which
was given to him when he was twenty-one by—I am not
sure—I think *fittoili*, no? People who live on your land? And
some *gemelli* for the shirtcuffs—they are very fine."

John held out his hand and she laid the links on his palm.
He looked down at them and smiled. They were platinum and
white gold set with diamonds and rubies.

"One of the indiscretions of his youth," he said. "I remember when we both wore things like that. We've outgrown them!" He handed them back, but the smile still lingered, making his handsome face look very gentle and tender.

"Thanks very much," Mostyn said as he took the box, "very thoughtful of you." He turned to John, "Are you the executor or something?"

"Only the executor."

"Then I suppose you're in communication with his solicitor?"

"I am. I shall not be able to see him in London. He is coming to see me in a few days."

"Here?" the tone was slightly offensive. "I mean are you staying here?"

Again that dangerously gentle voice. "I believe that the signora has invited me to stay here. I have done so whenever I came to Italy."

Mostyn flushed. So Trevor could stay here! Even now that Francis is dead. "Bit unconventional, isn't it?"

"Perhaps you find it so, but then you've always had such a very—middle-class mind, haven't you? You couldn't really trust yourself, so you imagine that everyone else is conscious of the same defect. Forgive me . . ." He turned to Antonia. "Would you prefer that I went down to the *albergo* tonight?"

She had scarcely understood what they were saying. She was longing to be alone with John so that they might talk intimately, lovingly, about Francis. She longed for this red-faced man to go, she disliked his voice, his sudden scowl and his general air of truculence.

"But no, John, you have always stayed here, your room is ready. Francis always said that this house was as much yours— or almost—as it was ours. To go to the *albergo* would seem so— unfriendly. I have so much to tell you, so much to ask . . ."

Her voice was shaking, and she turned away to hide her tears.

"I shall stay with great pleasure, and many, many thanks."

Antonia walked quickly from the room, and John faced Mostyn. "You hound!" he said. "Can't you see that she's lonely, heartbroken? She put up a great show for you—for us—but you probably imagined that meant she—didn't care. How little you know her, and how incapable you are of understanding her! Do you know, I think you'd better go. I don't really enjoy being in the same room with you. Your driver's had luncheon, you can depend on that; everyone is well treated here."

"Confound you, you take a lot upon yourself, don't you?"

"I do, but then I am capable of—dealing with things. Have you got your coat and hat? Good. No, I shouldn't wait to say good-bye to Antonia, she scarcely knows you, after all. Let me open the door, the latch is difficult sometimes. There! Good-bye."

Mostyn shouldered his way out, saying, "This will make a pretty story in England, won't it?"

Again John was smiling. "No doubt, but have you sufficient imagination to concoct a good story, let alone a pretty one?"

He closed the door, and staring at the window watched Mostyn fling himself into the hired car and drive away. John dusted the tips of his fingers together as if to dislodge something which might have soiled them, then walked to the foot of the stairs and called.

"Antonia, your unspeakable brother-in-law has departed. Come down, please."

She came down slowly; her eyes bore traces of tears, but she was no longer crying.

"He's gone? How does he come to be the brother of my dear Francis? I don't understand it." She shivered. "John, he suggested that he might come and spend a holiday here, and that we could drive about the country together!"

"I don't doubt it," he said, "and probably thought you you should have been flattered. Come and sit down, there are better things to talk about than Mostyn. I have always disliked him. There, look, Aramis feels that we have neglected him, he is hurt!"

CHAPTER FOUR

ANTONIA never forgot that evening. Years afterwards she could picture the scene as clearly as if it had happened yesterday. The quiet room, with the flames leaping and throwing shadows and lights alternately into distant corners of the room. Sometimes shining on John's intent, quiet face, making the gold of his big signet ring gleam more brightly as they touched it with their light. The little dog curled at her feet, asleep, then rousing himself, turning round and flinging himself down again with a heavy sigh. Maddelena came in with the tea-tray, and she remembered how something had prompted her to say that Maddelena was sleeping in the house so that she might bring the early tea, because Antonia felt so tired sometimes after a bad night.

He answered, "I'm glad that she stays here. Maddelena, you must take great care of the signora. I am sure that you will."

She told John many things, talked about Francis and his courage and fortitude during the last weeks, of how he had said, "It's all been wonderful . . ." His last words to her.

"And they meant so much," John told her; "meant that you had made them wonderful for him. He told me the last walk we took together. He said that for the first time in his life he was really—living. That you had made him appreciate everything more, in fact that you had given him complete happiness."

"He was too generous," she answered; "it was he who gave everything to me."

On the first evening he said nothing about the future, did

not ask what she intended to do. He was wise enough to realize that she must be allowed to talk freely, to share the burden which she had carried alone and which she need carry no longer. She was controlled; her voice only shook once or twice when she recounted some moment when Francis had said something which had touched her deeply.

Yet there was not the slightest suggestion that her control denoted lack of feeling, rather, John thought, as though her grief went too deep to rise easily to the surface and be demonstrated by tears. That night he lay awake a long time. His thoughts were chiefly of Antonia Winnerton. John was always honest with himself, and he had known for a considerable time that his feelings towards her were very tender. He often thought that Francis had realized that too. He had never shown any sign of what he felt, never allowed his attitude to be anything but that of a good friend. Now . . . He turned restlessly in his bed, conscious that he was almost afraid to be honest with himself.

In many ways he knew that he was selfish, self-centred and to a certain extent indolent. Possibly what people called his kindness of heart was merely the result of his being too lazy to do anything but take the easiest path, and the easiest path almost invariably led to giving people a helping hand in some way or another.

He doubted if he had ever really loved any woman; he had felt attraction, passion, desire, but he knew that he would find it almost disturbingly easy to love Antonia. He could never live as Francis had done, content in a small village, seeing very few people, hearing no music except such as could be provided by the radio or gramophone records. But then Francis had his work; even his love for Antonia had never been able to quell his devotion to his art.

John had always lived a cosmopolitan life, had always liked to associate with people who were amusing, intelligent and intellectual. He knew that he possessed an excellent brain, but had never troubled to apply his powers to any particular profession. He knew very little about the administration of an estate, though his love for Rivermead, Glenhuron in Scotland, for the big dignified house in Belgrave Square was profound. He enjoyed riding round the estate, talking to tenants, even inspecting improvements, and listening to suggestions, but after all, his father had an excellent agent—a distant cousin —who was capable, just and energetic. Why, then, should he concern himself unduly about roofs, barns, gates, and the like?

But—Antonia? He realized that it would be so easy to fall in love with her, and that, loving her, he would wish to marry her, as Francis had done. Francis, he reminded himself, was a second son. He was the heir; the only son. The next in succession was a wastrel cousin, who would assuredly play ducks and drakes with the estates. He'd fill the place with rowdy, second-rate people, bring his unpleasant friends up for the shooting, and generally drag Rivermead and all that went with the title down with a crash.

Even if she would consider him as a husband, would she transplant? It would be impossible for him, when he became duke, to live permanently out of England; it would be his duty to entertain, and entertain in considerable style. There was not the slightest doubt in his mind that she would face anything with dignity and equanimity, but what would it cost her to do so? It was inevitable that her life would be spent on guard, and might not that very fact come between them? He knew his own failings, he loved perfection and was apt to grow impatient with anything which fell below that standard. She was lovely, her voice was charming, her intelligence undoubted, her hands—he smiled as he lay there in the darkness when he remembered them. At first, when he met her, they had been well shaped, but coarsened by hard work, the first finger roughened by much sewing. Although they had always been meticulously clean they never quite lost their marks of cleaning and scrubbing. Now, with the advent of Maddelena, when she confined herself to cooking, and work which did not entail soiling her hands, they had become beautiful—soft and well kept, slightly browned by the Summer sun, but quite delightful. Good hands, efficient hands, practical hands and well shaped and kept.

He moved restlessly, the thing was impossible. Try as he would he could not see her as Duchess of Rivermead. She would be miserable in those great rooms, roaming along those long corridors, giving orders to a housekeeper who was probably better born than she was herself—and would, while remaining perfectly respectful, let her know it. He must return to New York, and as quickly as possible. Of course he would do everything to help Antonia—dear Antonia—but he must be firm with himself; must not behave like some romantic undergraduate. If only she were not so lovely, if only she did not enchant him so completely, if only . . . And thinking of her he fell asleep.

ii

During the days which followed they talked of her future. She told him that she would never remain indefinitely in Morano, there were too many memories.

"Also I want to have a career, John. I want to make a career for myself. Francis made one in spite of ill health. I have complete health. I shall sell this house. Indeed Innerhoffer has told me that if I wish to sell it he will buy it back. My furniture Count Zevio promises to store for me in his house, which is so big that there is plenty of room. He told me so."

John felt a sudden spurt of jealousy. "When did you see him?"

"This morning when I was shopping. We walked back together. He is very kind, so—also—is his wife. They both loved Francis."

"I see, and when you have sold the house and stored your furniture?"

"I shall go to Paris. I shall drive over—perhaps tomorrow you would drive me in the car, it is clean and in good order— to the convent at Cormia. Mother Anna Maria will tell me of a convent in Paris where I can stay, and go every day to a school to become a *cordon bleu*. That is my plan, John. Do you approve?"

He felt an almost overwhelming impulse to say, "No, I don't approve. Stay here, or if you wish travel about Europe until I can come back from America, then I shall ask you to marry me. That will give you time to think it over." Something stopped him—fear, lack of decision, uncertainty, he didn't know. He only knew that he loved her dearly, and would like to spend his life with her.

She repeated, "Do you approve, John?"

"Yes, oh yes. Only keep in touch with me, let me always know where I can find you. If you ever need help, advice— come to me." He made a great effort to be completely practical, to dismiss from his mind all dreams, all romantic desires. "You know what the *avvocato*, Grayson, said yesterday. You will have nearly seven hundred a year, and if you sell this house and the furniture, that will give you something in addition. Only, remember, the pictures which Francis painted are of real value; if ever you wished to sell them, there are dealers all over the world who would rush to buy them."

She nodded. "Yes, I know. I don't understand them, but I heard what people said when we were in Paris. Dear Francis, how pleased he was."

The next day he drove her over to Cormia, and she visited the convent. It was a small place, rather mean and cramped, but when John entered with her he understood where her passion for cleanliness had been engendered and fostered. The Reverend Mother received him graciously, the nuns smiled and talked of their dear Antonia, adding *poverina* when they remembered that their dear child was now a widow.

He whispered to Antonia, "It's all terribly uncomfortable. Can I send them carpets and blankets and—well, anything they need?"

She smiled at him, her nice wide smile which warmed his heart, and made him feel suddenly weak and dreadfully disturbed.

"Oh, what a kind thought! But you are always kind, dear John. There are so many things they need. Francis gave them quite a lot; he used to say as an attempt to pay off his debt for teaching me to cook and iron shirts! I shall not be long. I must get the address in Paris from Mother Anna Maria, and then together we will drive into Mezzolombardo and—oh, how happy they'll be."

They went to the town, and John, watching Antonia buy blankets, linen, rugs and a great bolt of flannel, tried to imagine that she was choosing them for a house where they would live together. He noticed with tender amusement that although he had assured her she was not to have the slightest preoccupation as to what she spent, she bought carefully. She examined the flannel closely, she rubbed the linen between her thumb and finger; again, when a price was quoted to her he heard her exclamation, "Tut, tut, *troppo caro—per la prima qualita, bene; ma—questo!*" Finally she had finished and the goods were stacked in the back of the car. They drove back to the convent. They stood before the Reverend Mother, who looked up from her writing and said, "Yes, dear child?"

Antonia said, and John thought that she spoke as she might have done when she was a small girl, "Reverend Mother, here is John Trevor, who was the great friend of my dear Francis."

The nun bowed her head and murmured, "May his soul rest in peace."

"Thank you, Reverend Mother. He is—in England—a lord, and he wishes to make a present to the convent. May I go and help the nuns to bring it in?"

"It is very kind. We are most grateful. Yes, dear child, go."

John stood waiting, then asked if he might help them. The grave-faced nun smiled. "It must be a very large gift, signor. I trust that the dear child has not incited you to too lavish a generosity."

Later when the parcels were stacked on the floor, with the nuns uttering shrill cries of delight as Antonia told what the contents of each parcel was, the Reverend Mother turned to John.

"It is not possible for us to thank you. You must believe that we are grateful and that we shall offer for you—all nuns have to give—our prayers. We are glad to know that in her time of trial, of heavy affliction, our dear Antonia has a friend to help and guide her."

He felt shy, awkward and confused. He managed to say, "It is nothing, please."

"Good-bye, signor. And again, the thanks of all the nuns in this community. May God be with you, and with you, Antonia, dear child."

They hung round Antonia, embracing her, whispering comforting words to her, sometimes drying their eyes when their affection and emotion overcame them. John impulsively pulled out his wallet and took out a wad of notes. He pushed them into Antonia's hand, saying, "Give this to the Reverend

Mother, it's all I have with me, so if we run out of petrol on the way home you'll have to pay for it."

That evening he made her tell him about them all, of their work, and their lives. She spoke with warmth and affection, often with quiet humour.

"They are—good, John. True, when they are working or teaching it is possible that one of them may grow short-tempered, but it is only for a moment, because some child is rude or stupid, or because the snails have eaten the cabbages, or the hens laid away! The essential goodness is there all the time. They were so good to me, they taught me all that I know—except what I learned from Francis. To sew, to read and write, to milk, wash and iron, and to cook. It is nice to remember that tonight they will be praying for us all—for you, for Francis and for me. It brings us three friends even closer together—if that were possible."

The night before he left she opened her heart to him. They sat on either side of the fire and she spoke softly, while he watched her as if he wished to make a mental picture of her which neither time nor distance could eradicate.

"It has been so good to have you here, John. You have helped me so much. At first I thought that I should die of the pain of losing him. It was dreadful. Now—oh, it is still there, but it is just a pain, not an agony. At first before me I saw nothing but darkness, as if a great pit had opened in front of me, and there was nothing else—just a space filled with darkness.

"You have helped me to understand that I have had so much granted to me, so much joy, happiness and sunshine. What I have had no one can ever take from me. Memories of Francis, when he was happy, when he was excited, yes, even when he was sulky like a little boy. I had forgotten that I was so rich in these things, until you came and let me talk myself into sanity again.

"Perhaps I shall never know happiness like that again. He used to talk about—low tones in his painting, and perhaps my life will be painted in those—low tones. But he explained to me that they can be, and are, very beautiful, very satisfactory. Not, he used to say, all scarlet and veridian green—he never liked veridian green—but rose madder and olive green." She smiled. "Perhaps just sometimes, a small patch of very bright colour, a high light, eh?"

He answered a little heavily, "You're very brave, a gallant soul."

"If I am brave it is because you came to give me courage. When that brother of Francis's came, I was wretched, hopeless. Perhaps I was wrong, but I felt that he was—greedy, and that I had no one to send him away, to prevent him—snatching at things. Now"—and this time she gave her soft, chuckling laugh—"I have sufficient strength to drive away a hundred greedy men!"

"I'm afraid that you may find a great many greedy men, my dear."

"I am not afraid. I shall go to live in this convent. I shall work very hard, and one day you will hear of me, it may be, cooking for the King of England."

He left early in the morning. He was going back to France and taking the liner at Cherbourg. His last few hours with Antonia tried him terribly. He was leaving the little house for, probably, the last time. There he had known such happiness, long talks with Francis, heated arguments about pictures and painters, discussions, and, at rare intervals, complete agreement. Now his feeling for Antonia had complicated everything. He considered telling her of his feelings for her, and rejected the idea as being impossible with Francis dead only for a brief week. He knew that he loved her, knew that she attracted him to an almost unbearable extent, and yet—for he understood her deep sense of loss, her grief and her sense of desolation however bravely she might hide them—to speak now would be to shock her unbearably. She would rank him, in a lesser degree, with Mostyn. She would feel that he had betrayed the trust which she had placed in him.

He sat waiting for the car, talking to her, his face tense with the control which he was forcing himself to exercise.

"I go first to New York. I have written my address there for you on this piece of paper. Write to me—write often, Antonia. Whenever you are worried, know that you can rely on me to help you. I think that my mother is happy in New York, and that we shall stay there for quite a long time. Here everything is in order. Innerhoffer has made his offer, and I think that it is fair and honest. His lawyer is Boccardi in Mezzolombardo. I have seen him. I think that he is trustworthy. Count Zevio has promised to go through all papers. He's a fine fellow, and has your interests at heart."

Antonia sat watching him, her eyes steady and her face calm. How she would miss him, miss their long talks, their drives, their walks. He was not—she could almost have smiled—Francis, but then no one could ever occupy that place in her heart.

She said, "Listen, there is your car. You must not risk losing your train, that would be a disaster."

Impulsively he answered, "I wish that I could stay here—for ever."

Antonia smiled. "Ah, there is a saying—if wishes were horses, no beggars need walk! You have work to do, a duty to your mother, and, dear John, you would soon tire of Morano. Come!"

He rose. She thought how tall and distinguished he looked. Francis had been so charming to look at with his fair hair—always untidy—and his fine skin and good eyes, but John was handsome, he had—she paused mentally for a word—quality. Yes, John was *la prima qualita*.

He held out his hands. "Dear Antonia, take great care of yourself. You are a precious person."

"To you," she said, "I can say exactly the same thing."

He held her hands in his, then lifted them both to his lips and kissed them lightly. As he turned to go through the door, she called, "Go with God!" She would not watch his car drive away it was unlucky. Better to say "Good-bye" here.

iii

John sailed for America, while Antonia busied herself with the affairs which must be settled. She sold some of the furniture. It was good, if simple, and commanded good prices. The rest went to Conte Zevio. The house was sold, and the car. She wrote to John that she had sufficient money to last for a long time, and so would not need any money from the lawyer.

The night before she left for Paris with Aramis she visited her mother. Maria greeted her with open arms, and Ferrari beamed at her, showing his bad teeth.

"We too have news for you," he said. "I have always been the favourite nephew of my uncle who lives at Malcesine on Lake Garda. Perhaps because of all his nephews I am the one who has never asked him for anything, no? He was old, poor man, and now he has died. You were busy with your lord, talking business. We heard that the lawyer came all the way from England to discuss your affairs. Ah, it is wonderful! Well, my uncle died and your good mama sends me to the funeral. Imagine to yourself my astonishment! My uncle—may his soul rest in peace—has left to me a small house, a vineyard, some olive trees—very old and good—and a sum of money.

"It is time that I leave the factory. I am no longer very young, nor is your mama. Together we shall live in the small house at Malcesine—it is a very beautiful place——"

Maria interpolated, "It is a paradise this place!"

"We have finished with the factory, I shall work in the vineyard, among the olives, and she will attend to the house. Is it not a dream come true?"

Antonia looked at them both. Ferrari's plain, kind face was shining with joy, and her mother looked excited. Antonia hoped that she would indeed attend to the house, cook him good meals, or if this were impossible—for she knew her mother—find some woman who would come in and do the work. At this late hour she could not see Maria Ferrari changing to an energetic housewife!

She smiled at them both, saying, "It is wonderful news. I am so glad for you."

Maria said, "And tomorrow you leave Morano, eh? What changes we have seen! First your poor papa taken from us—a good man indeed—then my daughter Carolina left us and for a bad reason. We have never heard from her since. Your two fine brothers, killed in saving their country, and then you married to a lord—or almost a lord—and now a widow. The ways of God are strange indeed."

"Do not talk of these sad things in the hour of happiness," her husband begged. "Things might have been worse—I might have been killed by a fall of rock, Antonia might have been a wicked girl and gone to Milano, you might—oh, there are so many things; you might have suffered from paralysis, for example. Now, we three are here, all well, all looking with our eyes to the future, eh?"

As Antonia walked back to her home that night, with Aramis at her heels, she felt an unbearable sadness. She was not afraid of the future, she was only afraid of loneliness. Life had been so wonderful, and now leaving her home, without

Francis, with John thousands of miles away, she had only a small white dog as her companion. True, life might hold excitement, novelty, variety, but she was finishing the last chapter of a book which had been written about her and her complete happiness.

The end of anything was sad, that was why sunsets for all their glory were sad. They marked the end of a day. It was sad when Summer faded and the flowers stood black, nipped by the first frosts. She squared her shoulders.

"Yes, but where there are many sunsets there are also many dawns. There are other Summers, other flowers. Perhaps not *quite* so lovely as those we once knew, but in comparing them with the dawns, the Summers, the flowers we once knew, they gain rather than lose their beauty. Memories can hurt, can be like knives turning in our hearts, but they can bring comfort."

One evening she remembered when she had walked back to their home with Francis, the sky had been one great sheet of colour—scarlet, orange, yellow, even apple green. He had stood with her to watch it, and sighed, saying, "'We turn to catch one fading ray of joy that's left behind us.'" She had held his arm more closely, for she knew of what he was thinking.

She said, "We turn to watch the sunset, and tomorrow we shall see the sunrise! Things go round and round, my dear. Today soon becomes—tomorrow. Then today has become yesterday."

He had looked down at her, his eyes filled with affection.

"You're right," he said. "It all comes round and round."

In the morning, she stood for the last time in the sitting-room. Her heart ached. She did not want to cry, her grief went too deep for tears to give her relief.

"I am not leaving you, my dearest one," she whispered. "You came into my heart. I carry my heart with me wherever

I go, and so always you are with me. Good-bye, little house. Come, Aramis."

For the last time she drove to Mezzolombardo, for the last time she passed the convent at Cormia and thought of the nuns she loved so much. She shook hands with Innerhoffer, who had driven her, and he assured her that she need have no preoccupation regarding her affairs. "You have the money for the house, for the car, for the other things—the stove, the refrigerator, the machine for extracting dust? Yes, that is good. I shall—with Conte Zevio—attend to everything on your behalf. Good luck, and God go with you."

She smiled. "I hope that I shall—go with God," she said.

vi

In New York John found his mother bored. She was tired of New York, she hated the noise, the quick tempo which life held there. She wished to visit her relations in Washington, in Boston; later she planned to go to Chicago. "If it is as horrible as one hears, it might be interesting," she said. San Francisco had always attracted her. Later they could make their way to California, they could find a wonderful climate, amusing people; Miami she had always wished to visit. She had the whole tour planned and was anxious to get away from New York, the bright lights, and the endless social obligations.

John was the obedient son. He made all arrangements, and every day he waited for a letter from Antonia. He had written to her from the boat, a letter which he had tried to make affectionate and yet to keep within conventional bounds. He told his mother about her, speaking with restraint. He wondered if she knew what was in his heart. She was very astute, very understanding.

"Poor girl," she said. "She must be a brave person to launch out like that. She's attractive, you say. That may—or may not—be a help to her. You must tell me how she gets on. A girl setting off with only a little dog for company. Yes, a very brave person."

They left New York; the Duchess was restless. She liked a town for a couple of days, then declared that she hated it, and must move on. The weather grew very hot. She said that they must find somewhere where she could breathe, the itinerary was changed, they visited unexpected places. John waited for letters. Each day he questioned the hotel office.

"Letters for me? Thank you," then glanced at the envelopes, and when he found that there was no letter from Antonia, stuffed them into his pocket and felt resentful.

They were in San Francisco when at last a letter reached him. He knew that his fingers shook as he tore open the envelope—John Trevor who hated ripping open envelopes except with a paper-knife. The letter had followed him from one place to another. It had been redirected many times.

I am on my way to Paris, and stay for one night here in Munich. Aramis is very good and a kind companion. Everyone is very kind to me. I have no German, but many speak English. In the morning I shall go on to Paris. From there I shall send you my address. Thank you, dear John, for your goodness. I think of you so much and our happy times. I look for the time when we meet again.

After that, he waited for letters in vain. He wrote to Zevio, asking for her address. Zevio replied that he did not know it and that he and his wife were on the point of taking a voyage to Australia where he had some property. Antonia's mother and stepfather had moved to another place, somewhere on Lake Garda. John wrote to the lawyer, Grayson. He answered that

Mrs. Winnerton had written to say that with the sale of the
house, the car and so forth, she was well supplied with money,
and that the income left to her was to remain in the bank. He
had not got her address. He would of course write if there was
any news of Mrs. Winnerton.

So John continued to travel with his mother, and slowly he
gave up asking for letters, and only worried and fretted over
Antonia's silence. He found his mind constantly going back to
her, remembering their walks together, the good times which
they had spent.

In California his mother was taken ill. He faced the
additional worry in his usual way; he was kind, solicitous, and
attentive. He loved her dearly and no son could have given
greater care to his mother. The doctors said that her heart was
weak, and that rushing about America had done nothing to
improve it. She had an apartment in a luxurious hotel, nurses
who were skilful and kind, a son who gave up his whole time
to his mother and her comfort.

She said one evening, "I shan't see England again, John. I
belong to America and she's going to have the last of me. I'm
glad that my son will be Duke of Rivermead, and that one day
my grandson will be the duke. I've always respected your
British aristocracy. I might dislike your father, personally, as a
man, but as a landowner he has always done his duty. When
are you going to marry, John?"

"I don't know. Perhaps—when I fall in love."

To his surprise she answered, "You've done that already.
The Italian girl. John, my dear, it wouldn't work. They don't
transplant well, these people; however lovely, however
intelligent. The atmosphere of Rivermead would stifle her—it
almost stifled me! Where is she?"

He knew that his voice sounded stiff and constrained. "I
haven't heard. Only once, weeks, months ago. I don't even
know where she is."

She held out her hand and took his. "Poor John. I'm sorry."

Two days later she died, quietly in her sleep. John cabled to his father, but arranged for her to be buried with her own family in Feyetville. He returned to England alone. The first visit he paid was to the lawyer, Grayson.

Part Four

CHAPTER ONE

ANTONIA was very tired, the journey from Munich to Paris
had been long and difficult. Aramis had grown as tired as she
was, and had been restless. It would never have occurred to
her to take a sleeper. On her honeymoon they had travelled
by day, and when they came to Paris for Francis's exhibition
they came by car. She travelled second class and was astonished
at the cost of the meals in the restaurant car; furious at the
limited opportunities for washing, and the lamentable state of
the lavatories.

Holding Aramis to her, she whispered, "Why are people so
dirty, my dear? They speak of dogs being dirty. If you were as
unclean in your habits as they are, I should be obliged to be
very angry with you."

At last, Paris! Her first resolution was that she must learn
to speak French. Otherwise she would be, doubtless, cheated
and robbed by these gesticulating porters who screamed at her,
who snatched her luggage and rushed away leaving her to
follow.

"Taxi?" the blue-bloused Frenchman demanded.

She nodded, and replied in English, "Yes, at once a taxi."

She gave the address of the very comfortable and admirably
select hotel where she had stayed with Francis. It was near the
Etoile. As she drove through the streets she looked out,
drawing deep breaths of the morning air. Paris at the end of
April looked very lovely. There were flowers on stalls at the
street corners, the girls who walked so briskly with milliners'
boxes slung on their arms looked so trim and neat. The trees
had lost the stark outlines of Winter and were showing bright
green leaves. Her heart rose. She felt her sense of depression
leave her. She was young, she was hopeful, and she had also

251

determination. Aramis nuzzled against her and she stroked his head. She had at least one friend in Paris.

Arriving at the hotel she found them slightly patronizing. They were exclusive, and this young woman, attractive though she might be, wore clothes which were palpably provincial.

She said, "I am Madame Winnerton. You may recall that I stayed here last year with my husband, the great painter."

Winnerton! The clerk remembered those blue eyes and that bright, shining hair. She had been here with her husband. Now, since she wore mourning, she had suffered a bereavement. There had been another man with them, a lord from England. They had paid very well, had engaged an expensive suite and had entertained lavishly.

He smiled and bowed. "Madame, I remember perfectly. It is an honour to have you visit us again."

Antonia nodded. "I wish for a room, but I will not pay extravagant prices. I shall be here for several days—with my dog."

He snapped his fingers at Aramis and made encouraging noises.

"We like dogs, they are welcome, but it is not permitted to take them into the dining-room, madame."

"I wish my meals served in my room. I am very tired. I wish for a bath, and in a short time *caffè latte* and rolls with butter. Please show me a room."

He bowed. Other people arrived. They too bowed. The manager, portly and so filled with courtesy that it seemed to exude from him like an essence, bowed over her hand and smiled—a trifle nervously—at Aramis.

"Ah, a pretty dog!"

"He is good, quiet, and completely clean."

Again he smiled. "And are we to expect Monsieur Winnerton?"

"My husband is dead," Antonia told him. "Now, may I see my room?"

She saw several rooms, and noted their faults and their advantages. The management were not accustomed to ladies who were so efficient.

"No, this is far too noisy. Somewhere I can hear a cistern dripping. It would disturb me," and, "Here on the corner it will be very disturbed. I must have a quiet room, and plenty of air." At last: "This will do admirably. The water is hot, no? Please open the windows, I must have fresh air. And the price?"

The price, she thought, was excessive, but it was only for a few days, and she must have somewhere to collect her thoughts, to rest and enjoy quiet and tranquillity. She agreed, and asked for her luggage. Then, after fifteen minutes, she told them, coffee and rolls.

In her bath, feeling relief that the dirt of the journey was being washed away, and later when she drank her coffee and ate her rolls, she planned her campaign. First, the convent to which Mother Anna Maria had sent a letter of recommendation. After that, she would wait before making decisions; circumstances might dictate her actions.

She dressed carefully. She was a clever dressmaker and although her clothes might not have the chic of Paris, the materials were good, and her dresses well cut and carefully made.

Aramis drank his weak coffee with small pieces of roll broken into it. Antonia decided that later he should have a bath. His coat looked dusty from the journey.

She brushed him carefully, and felt that he appreciated the grooming.

"Come," she said, "we will go to seek our fortunes, dear little dog."

She walked for a short distance, and then hailed a taxi. It

was an extravagance, but the occasion demanded it. She directed the driver.

"The Convent of Our Lady of Perpetual Help."

He nodded, and proceeded to drive there, taking every turning on three wheels only. Antonia clutched Aramis and hoped that she might never have to ride in a Paris taxi again. This man was a devil in human shape; he drove like a madman. He drew up, the tyres screaming on the road, his brakes shrieking in protest.

"We are there!" he announced.

She paid him and said, "Do all drivers in Paris drive in this way?"

He grinned. "I spik Eengleesh. Why not? All Parisian drivers possess great courage. From place to place we go like wind."

Antonia said, "I should imagine the passenger had the courage."

She was shown into a parlour which struck her as being very grand and almost luxurious. There was a carpet on the floor, and a good one. The furniture looked old and was beautifully kept, there were great sprays of mimosa in a tall vase.

The doorkeeper went out and a moment later a nun entered. She was tall, and very handsome; her manner was composed and rather cold.

Antonia said, "I beg to speak with the Reverend Mother Superior, if you please, Mother. She has received a letter about me from the Reverend Mother at Cormia, also a recommendation from Mother Anna Maria."

"I shall see. Is this your dog? We do not have dogs in the convent."

Antonia smiled. "Then it will not be possible for me to remain. Where I go, so also goes my dog."

"Wait, please, for a moment."

When the nun returned she said, "Please come with me. For once, the dog may come with you."

They walked down long corridors, where everywhere Antonia saw signs of comfort, if not actual luxury. The room into which she was ushered was austere but filled with dignity. There were flowers, a carpet, some fine pictures, a great desk behind which sat the Reverend Mother Superior.

A handsome, dignified woman with a firm mouth and large, bright eyes. Antonia felt that here was someone who could take command, who would be able to deal with any complications and always remain completely mistress of herself, while imposing her will on others.

Antonia bowed, the nun inclined her head, then noticed Aramis.

"A dog!" she exclaimed. "Mother Anastasia, what is he doing here?"

Antonia spoke impulsively, "Please, Reverend Mother Superior, he is my dog. He is strange to Paris; I could not leave him. He is very good, and his manners are perfect."

She said, "He's a nice little dog. Let me see him. What is he—a Pomeranian?"

"A *volpino*, an Italian dog, Reverend Mother."

"His name?"

"Aramis."

She smiled. "If I remember correctly, the most religious of the Musketeers, eh? Yes, lie down, Aramis. Now, you are Madame Winnerton? Before your marriage—yes, I know of your husband as a fine painter. I offer you my sympathy on his loss. Poor man, he was thought highly of in Paris. As I say, before your marriage you were Antonia Trolli?"

"Yes, Reverend Mother."

"Mother Anastasia, please give me the two letters relating to Madame Winnerton. Now, madame, please tell me exactly what you wish."

Antonia explained, she wanted a room, a place where she could keep Aramis and from which she could continue her studies at a cookery school every day.

The Reverend Mother Superior listened and nodded.

"Listen, Madame Winnerton. Here in this convent we have—boarders. They are rather different from the usual boarders in a convent. In fact they are unique. Here we used to be a very rich order, but times have changed since the war, and our numbers have dwindled. There is a wing allocated to the boarders. There are—how many, Mother Anastasia?—ah, seven of them, all ladies of good birth, and considerable incomes. They demand good food, which is only right, for they pay high rents. We, the nuns, of course have our own kitchen."

"Mother Anna Maria told me something of this arrangement," Antonia said.

"Our dear Mother Lucia has cooked for them for many years; she is an experienced and wonderful cook. Now she has suffered a slight stroke. We hope, if it pleases God, that she may be restored to us, but in the meanwhile the cooking is in the hands of Mother Catherine, who is very willing, but who cannot completely satisfy the requirements of our— guests. Madame Winnerton, would you like to accept this position?"

"What would it entail, Reverend Mother Superior?"

"For breakfasts, Mother Catherine is quite capable. For luncheon, it would be necessary for you to visit the markets, to buy, and later to submit menus to the guests." She smiled. "I must warn you, madame, that they are not easy. There may be times when they wish to entertain—a luncheon for three, four, five people. Tea—that is simple, and can safely be left in Mother Catherine's hands; dinner is a light meal. Most of these ladies are old, they retire early, and their late meal must not be a heavy one. Omelettes, a little fish, a fricassee, and so

forth. Each afternoon you could visit this cookery school.
Here you could have a room, your food, laundry, and the
usual things—light and heat."

Antonia said, "And my small dog?"

"We have never had a dog in the convent, madame."

"Reverend Mother Superior, you have never had a cook
like me in the convent."

Her small chin was tilted, she was terribly afraid that the
nun might say that it was impossible to allow a dog in the
place, but she was ready to risk everything for Aramis.

To her surprise the nun threw back her handsome head
and laughed.

"Splendid!" she said. "How I like people who are sure of
themselves. The dog remains. He must not make a noise, you
must exercise him properly, he must not be allowed to grow
too fat by eating tit-bits at all hours. In short he must be kept a
healthy—and I hope—a happy dog. There, that is arranged! In
addition, madame, the community will offer you five hundred
francs a week. Is that satisfactory?"

"I am very happy."

"You speak French fairly well, for some of our guests are
French, also English—you speak English very well, madame."

Antonia smiled, her heart felt deliciously light, her smile
came easily. "Might I say, Reverend Mother Superior, how
well you speak English?"

Again the nun laughed. "But, madame, I am English—or
more correctly, I am Irish. Among our guests you will meet
my sister. She is delightful. She will—I may say—like Aramis
very much, and will probably make my life a misery because
she cannot introduce five or six dogs into the convent. When
can you begin your duties?"

"Tomorrow morning."

"Splendid! Mother Anastasia, the good Saint Jude must
have listened to our prayers, because this morning we were

I

wondering who could manage to cook for our—sometimes difficult—guests. Madame, *au revoir*."

Antonia dropped her little curtsey. "*Au revoir*, Reverend Mother Superior. *Au revoir*, Mother Anastasia."

ii

The work was not easy, there were times when the demands of the "guests" almost drove Antonia frantic. Each morning, with her alternative menus, and wearing her long white coat and chef's cap, she visited them all, notebook in hand.

They lived, these ladies, in rooms which had once been part of the convent, when it housed many more nuns than it did now. Fine rooms, they were filled with fine furniture which the ladies had brought with them. They all had their own personal maid, who slept outside the convent and arrived early each morning.

There was the Duchessa Molinet, who was very old, very dignified, and who addressed Antonia through the medium of her maid.

She lay there in her huge four-poster bed, with its splendid hangings, in a room which—to Antonia—was far too hot, and much too lacking in fresh air.

"Who is this?" she asked her maid.

"The new chef, Your Grace. She has brought the menus for the day."

"Read them to me."

The maid took the notebook from Antonia and read the items which she had arranged rather stumblingly. "Potato soup, *Oeufs pochés Grand Duc, Mousseline de Soles au vin du Rhin, tournedos Rossini, gigot de sept heures, crêpes Susette,* rice pudding *à l'anglais,* fruits and café."

The old lady sat upright in her huge bed. "Can you only make potato soup?"

Antonia smiled. "Madame, many others, but my potato soup is very good. I have twenty others."

The answer came very promptly. "Very well, this vaunted potato soup, *tournedos Rossini*—I like his music!—*crêpes Susette*. I eat very little, but it must be good. Remember!"

The Duchessa Massena was a handsome American, about sixty. Antonia discovered later that she was essentially warm-hearted, and ready to put aside all superiority, and be kind and friendly.

"What on earth are you doing here?" she asked. "You look like something out of a musical. Where did they find you? Oh, they're poppets, but—well, what do you know—a girl like you taking this on!"

"I like cooking, Your Grace."

"You'll have to like it quite a lot to satisfy these old women here. I think I'm the baby of the party. Maybe Miss Daly is about my age, but the rest! I never see them, but—I'll say I hear them! Now, don't bother to tell me what you've got on the menu; just see that I get something nice."

Madame d'Aurnigay, an old lady completely crippled by arthritis, was charming to her, praised her hair and good skin, and advised her always to wear flannel next to her skin in the Winter.

"Winters in Paris are positively dangerous." She smiled. "But you are young and can walk and keep your blood warm. You know many people in Paris? Companions who will go out with you, show you the lovely things in this lovely city?"

Antonia said, "I have only one companion, madame, a little dog called Aramis, and very graciously the Reverend Mother allows me to keep him with me."

The charming old face lit up. "A dog! This is delightful. I always had dogs, did I not, Germaine?"

The elderly maid nodded. "Always, many dogs, madame."

"You must bring him to see me. Yes, I insist, otherwise I shall be greatly offended and criticize adversely all your dishes!"

The rest—Madame Bourdon, Comtesse Boiselles, and Madame Dumont—were all stiff, elderly women, with their maids always in attendance, who addressed Antonia as "chef", and treated her as if she were a machine to turn out rich dishes for them, which Antonia felt certain were exceedingly bad for them.

There remained only the Honourable Miss Deidre Daly. She was a tall, rather gaunt Irishwoman, with short, curly hair, beautiful eyes and an infectious smile. Her accent was almost remarkably pronounced.

"I heard of you, from me sister the Reverend Mother— bless her. You're the first young t'ing I've set eyes on since I came to live here. I came because the damp of Oireland—and it's a lovely country—were likely to be the death av me. Now, d'you know Paris? It's a grand city. I must stop being lazy an' take you round, show you t'ings. 'Deed and it would give me great pleasure, m'dear. You must come in and take tea with me. I make it meself. I'd not care how good they are, French servants can't make tea, not as I like it, strong enough to trot a mouse on it! And didn't I hear you'd got a dog? That's a grand t'ing now. How I manage to live without dogs I'll never know. In me home—not so far from Killarney—the place was full of dogs, just shouldering each other out of the place. D'you think one day you might bring him in here? Now, I'll tell you what, come to tea and remember that I'm inviting the dog too."

So Antonia settled down in the convent. The work was not hard, though it was difficult to keep all her ladies satisfied. They might assure her that they were easy to please, ate any-thing, never troubled about food, but actually they were terribly jealous in case one should be shown more favour than another. True, the Duchess was out at least four days in the week, and Miss Daly scarcely looked at what she ate—Antonia wondered if she really knew what the dishes were; she was always absorbed in a book. She was very kind, and showed Antonia how to find her way around Paris, telling her the history of the places they visited, talking in her colourful way with the Irish accent which to Antonia was so musical, warm and friendly, and she taught the Italian girl more of the history of France than either of them realized at the time.

Four afternoons every week Antonia, with Aramis trotting at her heels, went to what the Reverend Mother Superior had assured her was the finest cookery school in France, possibly in the whole of Europe.

There she learnt new and elaborate dishes, delicate sauces, and exciting fillings for the exquisite pastry which her ladies liked so much. Madame d'Aurnigay, her eyes dancing, for she was always gay in spite of the arthritis which made her almost completely crippled, would say, "Ah, my child, I am so thankful that arthritis does not affect the taste! You provide me with what is almost my only pleasure in these days—those *lobster bouchées*! Positive poems."

Sometimes when the convent was quiet, and she knew that the chapel would be empty, Antonia would go there and sit, allowing her thoughts to go back to the days when she lived with Francis in Morano. It all seemed so long ago, as if she had lived a lifetime since then. Dear Francis, perhaps they had crammed sufficient happiness into their short married life to last her for ever. She received letters at long intervals from her mother and Ferrari. As a matter of fact, Antonia knew that although her mother might dictate them, Ferrari wrote them, for Maria was not a particularly good scholar and had always detested letter-writing.

She would wonder how everyone was. Was Innerhoffer

still as fat as ever? Did the one-legged schoolmaster still go plodding along—"Tip tap, tip, tap"—on his way to the priest's house where they indulged in long and often noisy arguments, and always remained the best of friends? What a noisy priest he was that Father Dominic! Did Count Zevio still look as melancholy as ever? And yet who played more jokes than he did, and how amusing he could be! And the Contessa, was she still slim and elegant and a little less friendly than her husband?

And John, where was he? She had written to him when she first came to be cook to the ladies, and he had not replied. She had written to a hotel in New York. After two months she wrote again, but still there had been no reply. It never occurred to her that she might have written asking for his address to Francis's lawyer, Grayson. True, she was not like her mother, unable to write easily, but she had never been accustomed to writing letters, and to receive letters had always been—in her life—something of an event. She had written to Mr. Grayson, told him that she wished the money which Francis had left her to remain in the bank until she needed it. He had replied, and when she moved to the convent she had lost the letter.

She was earning plenty of money, and her ladies were so kind, always giving her presents of charming things. Scarcely a week passed but the Duchess gave her something to wear, something which had come from America.

"Say what you like, Antonia, New York takes a lot of beating. Maybe Paris has greater chic, but some of the smart shops in New York—I'm not sure that they couldn't show Paris something. I'm told that Italian women dress very well. Someone at a luncheon-party—an Italian contessa—told me that the best-dressed women in Italy live in Turin. Is that so, d'you think?"

Antonia smiled. "I cannot say, madame. I have never been in Turin, and I have never been a judge of smart women."

She was happy enough in a quiet way, she had come to love Paris, the trees, the sudden bursts of colour at the street corners where flowers were for sale; she walked sometimes along the streets where incredibly luxurious things were offered for sale. She stared at the beautiful clothes, at the jewels, at the fine gloves and the elegant shoes, but she felt no great desire to possess any of them. She kept her clothes well, always looked neat and well turned out, but she had no sense of envy for the women she saw wearing clothes the cost of which would have kept Antonia Winnerton for a year.

She scarcely realized how lonely she was until she saw the children playing in the gardens, saw some young man come hurrying to a seat where a girl sat waiting for him, watched them clasp hands and smile at each other. Then she knew that life—except for Aramis—was very empty.

If she might sit on one of the wooden seats, perhaps with a little child playing near her, and see Francis—his fair hair a little tumbled—come hurrying towards her, to see him sit at her side, holding her hand and smiling into her eyes, saying—as he used to say so often, "You have the bluest eyes in the world, my 'Tonia."

She wondered sometimes what she was going to do with her life. When she first came to Paris she had been full of determination and ambition. She had been fortunate to find work at the convent; work which was pleasant, comfortable, and which allowed her time to continue her study of elaborate cooking. She had been there for nearly a year, and she had made no plans for the future. She couldn't stay at the convent for the rest of her life! She was nearly twenty-four, and surely it was time that she looked ahead, made—as she said—provision for herself.

She did not realize fully the shock which Francis's death had been to her. She had always been so busy, all her life, and after her period of working for Francis, and later her marriage, life had been very full and very beautiful. With his death had come the ending, so it seemed, of everything. The little house was her home no longer; without Francis life there would have been intolerable. Now, even John had disappeared from her life, the only living thing to whom she really mattered was Aramis. Other people might be kind, gentle, considerate, but she had literally no one in her life.

That fact, coupled with the shock that she had suffered when Francis died, had induced in her a sort of lethargy, what almost amounted to an inability to make plans for the future. Nothing at that time could have been better for her than the regular, tranquil life of the convent. The lack of hurry and bustle which brings with it a sense of fleeting time and impermanence was soothing to her, and imperceptibly she began to recover from that state of mental lassitude which had enveloped her.

Some of her ladies seemed to have sensed something of Antonia's uncertainty regarding the future. The Duchess said, "You're not going to bury yourself here, Antonia, are you? For the rest of your life to waste your talents on cooking for a lot of old women?"

Miss Daly told her, "Child, you ought to t'ink about spreadin' your wings. I'd not be overjoyed to see you go, but —there's other worlds for you to conquer." It was the frail Madame d'Aurnigay who offered a suggestion.

"Antonia, I have spoken to Reverend Mother Superior, and she will agree to what I wish—if you are willing. My doctors recommend me to go to Abano, near Padua. My son has taken a small apartment for me in Abano—I believe that it is quite a hateful place—but the apartment he says is charming. Will you come with me, as well as my own nurse, of course, and stay for two months? During that time will you cook for me, and possibly train someone to continue when you return to Paris? Reverend Mother Superior agrees with me that you must be given opportunities, that if you stay here very much longer you may possibly stay for ever. If, when you leave me, you decide not to return to Paris, my son has a wonderful *palazzo* in Verona and another in Venice. He also has an apartment here in Paris. He would welcome you as his chef if you care for the position. Now, what have you to say?"

Antonia felt her face flush. She flushed because she was surprised, because she was disturbed and a little frightened. Here had she been waiting, never making plans, and now plans for her future were suggested to her, presented to her, as it were, ready made.

She said, "It is a wonderful thing for you to offer me this, madame. I think that you are right. I should go out to—fight for myself, to learn more of the world, and to perhaps have wider practice in cooking. There is only one thing, madame—here I am allowed to have Aramis."

"The presence of Aramis is a condition, eh?" She smiled.

"Madame, I could not leave him. He is my friend—the only near friend I have."

The smile widened. "Aramis will be an honoured guest in my apartment. Now, you had better talk to Reverend Mother Superior."

"I am very grateful, madame," Antonia said, making her stiff little curtsey, and kissing the twisted hand which lay on the arm of the chair. "I shall always try to do my best, in every way which is agreeable to you. Please excuse me, madame."

Antonia had always liked and respected the Reverend Mother Superior, but never more so than after she had discussed the question of her making a change. The nun said, "Sit down, my child. Let me talk to you. I wish to make it quite clear that we here are not only satisfied but far more than satisfied. You have shown yourself to be hard working and diligent. You have never resented additional work—for example when the Duchess decides to give a luncheon party at very short notice. Oh, I know all of what goes on here, be sure!

"My sister tells me that you are a charming companion, and she is very particular. Your manners are beautiful. And as I say, your cooking is the admiration of all the ladies. But you are young, and as you have owed a duty to us, so we owe one to you. You need greater scope, and I believe that in the future which Madame d'Aurnigay has planned for you, you will find ample scope. Our prayers and blessings will go with you, dear child." She smiled that rare and delightful smile. "Also we shall remember with pleasure the little Aramis, he has behaved like the little gentleman he is all the time he has been here."

A week later Antonia left the convent with Madame d'Aurnigay, her nurse and Aramis to travel by car—the largest and most luxurious car Antonia had ever seen, with a smaller, more modest, car following with the luggage, for Abano. Monsieur d'Aurnigay came to see them start. He was very tall and elegant, with charming manners. For a moment he reminded Antonia of John Trevor.

"I commend my mama to your care—you and the good nurse," he said.

"I know that both will do our very best, monsieur."

"I shall look forward to eating a meal at my mama's apartment in Abano." He thought, "*Dieu!* She's the prettiest thing I've seen for a long time. I think there is no doubt that when she leaves Mama I shall be only too delighted to have her!"

They took over a week to make the journey, for madame could not stand the fatigue of a very long day's driving, and each evening Antonia found herself in a new town, which she could explore with Aramis.

France, Switzerland, and they came down into Italy.

Madame said, "You are back in your own country, Antonia."

"I lived many hundreds of kilometri from this part, madame."

They stayed for the night at Stressa, and Antonia leaned from her window to stare at the Borromean Islands, to marvel at the beauty of the lake, and to watch the stars come out in the velvet-like sky. Francis had always promised to bring her here, she remembered. It seemed that Italy was full of lakes, for they spent the following night at Desenzano, which was actually on Lake Garda. She looked at the map. Yes, there was Malcesine, and there too would be her mother and the kind Ferrari, neither of them dreaming that she was so close to them.

In the morning they drove on to Verona, and there Madame d'Aurnigay stayed in her son's *palazzo*, the largest house Antonia had ever seen, standing in a great flagged court-yard, where little trees stood in bright green pots, and you could hear the sound of pigeons cooing.

Madame asked her, "Do you like Verona, Antonia?"

"Indeed, madame, I came here on my honeymoon. My husband told me that someone—an artist, I think—called it 'the peach blossom city'. Such a pretty name."

Antonia left Verona very early in the small car. Not that it was a small car, but that was how they referred to it to distinguish it from the enormous Rolls. She found the apartment at Abano. It was large, commodious, and—Antonia thought—dirty. There were four women working there, all congregated in one room, all talking busily.

She entered and stared at them. "Please inform me why it is necessary for you all to work in one room? There are other rooms—all in need of cleaning. Kindly disperse yourselves, and I shall come round and instruct you."

One woman said, "Might one ask who are you, signorina?"

Antonia answered, not without a hint of superiority, "I am the chef, also the *governante* of the Madame d'Aurnigay. She will arrive in time for evening dinner, and by that time everything must shine. She is French, of a very aristocratic family. I am Italian, and I do not wish the French to speak together saying that Italians cannot keep apartments clean. That it is possible to bring this apartment to a state of perfect cleanliness in so few hours I am uncertain. But, if it is possible, it shall be done."

A woman said, "There is also a man, signorina. His name is Chico."

She disposed the women as a general might dispose his troops for a battle; she found Chico, who was cleaning his nails with a fork and chatting vivaciously to a friend who needed a shave very badly.

The friend explained, "I am on my way to the barber's, signorina."

She said, "I am glad. Hurry to him or your beard will be so long he will charge you double."

Chico, slightly sulky, was set to work polishing floors.

CHAPTER TWO

THE months slipped past. Madame d'Aurnigay said that she did not know if the treatment was doing her good or not; she only knew that it was disgusting to be plastered all over with hot mud and that the nurse who applied the mud had hands like flails.

Antonia, once Aramis had been exercised, never missed an opportunity of going into Padua. Very often she shopped there in the morning; the market delighted her. She wandered from stall to stall, buying small quantities of this and that as she liked to do—delicious salads, fresh vegetables, wonderful fruit, and fresh flowers. The stall-holders came to know her, and would chat to her about their homes, their children, and—if time permitted—their husbands. It appeared that most husbands were more or less unsatisfactory, and to recount one half of their failings and shortcomings took a long time.

Antonia found herself slipping into using all the old accustomed clichés which are such a considerable part of Italian conversation.

Praising the flowers she said, "Ah, a home without flowers is not furnished!" Listening to the beauties of the children— some of whom she had seen and found unprepossessing—she said, "They will be the comfort of your old age, signora. They are not only a great joy, but—if brought up to love their parents—they become an investment, eh?" Of unsatisfactory husbands, she would shake her head and affirm, "Each heart knows the bitterness of life, which it can share with no one."

Then, for madame made her take the "little car" when she went to the market, she would drive on to the great church of Saint Antonio—*Il Santo*—and there sit quietly to meditate, say her prayers very simply as a child might have done, saying always a special prayer for Francis, and asking Saint Rocco to "concern himself" about Aramis. Then, lighting candles, she would return to the car, to Abano, and immerse herself in her cooking.

She enjoyed devising special dishes for Madame d'Aurnigay, giving her small surprises which would tempt her somewhat difficult appetite. Gradually the old lady came to send for Antonia after dinner, and ask her what she had seen and done that morning in Padua. Antonia would recount her encounters in the market, tell stories of the women and their affairs, tell how she had refused to pay the price asked for a cauliflower, and imitate her conversation with the vendor. She would speak of the great church, of the crowds gathered there for every Mass held at the altar of the Saint, of the glory of the Treasury, and the beauty of the music.

Sometimes Maurice d'Aurnigay came over to see his mother. Antonia was always enjoined by madame to make special efforts; to buy whatever luxuries were in season.

"Remember," she would say, smiling, "when I return to Paris—and I do not think that I can stand this mud much longer, I prefer arthritis—Maurice is ready to employ you, and so you must make a good impression."

Antonia felt that she had made too good an impression, but not only as regards her cooking. Maurice was handsome, very elegant, but when he stared at her she felt uncomfortable and uneasy. Once he had stopped her in the long corridor and said, "Your dinner was delightful. I think because it was prepared by such a charming person, eh?"

Again, "When my mother returns to Paris, and she will, for she adores Paris, you'll come to me, won't you? Verona is a charming place, and although I am away a great deal—imagine to yourself how I should look forward to coming home—to you."

Something had warned her to lock her bedroom door, and

that night for the first time Aramis began to bark. Antonia, switching on the light, saw the handle of the door turn, heard too a muttered exclamation of annoyance, and saw Aramis, with his coat bristling, listening intently as careful footsteps died away.

She switched off the light again and said softly, "If the only work to be found was in the house of Maurice d'Aurnigay, I would not go there! To behave in this manner in his mother's house!"

The weather was growing very hot. Abano seemed to sizzle in the heat. Madame wilted, lost her appetite, and declared that she would return to Paris. Maurice would be in Verona for the opera season at the Arena. "Such a lover of music! He always gives magnificent banquets for the artists, and he will be happy to have you there to make them a greater success than ever."

"Madame, before I take up new work, I must go and visit my mother at Malcesine. I have not seen her for a long time. She is not very young."

"But Maurice would want you particularly for the opera season!"

Antonia thought, "Maurice can do without me for the opera season—and for everything else!" She said, "Madame, when do you wish to leave?"

"In a week or ten days. Could we be ready in that time? I might spend a few days with Maurice in Verona; surely you could go and see your mother then, Antonia?"

"May I think it over, madame? I am undecided. I might even go back to the convent. I am—uncertain."

"Very well." But the voice had lost its warmth. They were all alike, these rich aristocrats; everything must run as they wished, everyone must conform to their plans and ideas.

That morning in the market she felt a wave of loneliness and disillusionment sweep over her. If only she had someone to whom she could talk, someone who would advise her, who would consider her point of view and realize that the idea of being in the house of Maurice d'Auringay, to have to be continually repulsing his advances, would be impossible. She must make her own plans, and at the end of the week, when madame left Abano for Verona, she would look for another post. How one looked for such things Antonia had no very clear idea, but she would find out. She had all the sturdy determination of the north Italian, plenty of common sense, and—what possibly gave her added confidence—she had saved a considerable amount of money.

"Now," she thought, as she led Aramis to the various stalls where she examined fruit and vegetables with careful eyes, "one thing at a time. Now, I am Antonia the chef, in a week's time I shall be Antonia looking for work."

ii

A tall Englishman walked out of the Hotel Storione into the bustling main street of Padua, then, turning to the left, he went as far as the famous Café Pedrocchi and, turning again to the left, made his way along the narrow crowded streets which led to the market.

The morning was beautiful, but the day promised to be almost unbearably hot. Last night he had tossed about unable to sleep. He had tried the mosquito net, but one of the insects had got inside the net and he had flung it off with considerable force and irritation. He decided that he'd prefer being bitten to sleeping—if indeed he did sleep—under one of those foul nets.

He found himself standing in the market-place. There was the huge building—what was it? Town Hall, something of the kind, rather like the one in Vicenza. Perhaps this too was designed by Palladio. He had forgotten; it was years since he had been in Padua.

The market pleased him. Here at the entrance was a flower stall, blazing with colour, where a stout woman called to him to buy flowers for his signora. He hadn't got a signora! He smiled and shook his head, and the woman smiled back at him.

He stood for a moment surveying a fruit stall, and heard the owner talking, gesticulating wildly, acting the whole story she was telling.

". . . and behold, what had happened? The hen, this precious hen that must be brought all the way from Milano when my cousin comes to spend the week-end in Padova, because it might be lonely if left by itself—has laid an egg! Indeed yes, can you imagine in the autobus, the hen laying an egg, signora?"

The listener, who had her back towards him, laughed; the man started. He would have known that particular laugh anywhere—a little throaty, coming with a gurgling, bubbling sound yet conveying the impression of complete pleasure and amusement. He stared. She held a small white dog on a lead.

The Englishman whistled, then called, "Aramis!" The dog pricked up his ears, his bright eyes sought for the direction from which the voice had come. Again the man called, "Aramis!"

The woman turned, the little dog was straining at the lead, her eyes—so vividly blue—found where John stood. He did not move, only watched her, waiting silently for her to speak or move. She was thinner, her hair was as bright as ever— Francis used to say that it looked burnished—her eyes as clear. She was more smartly dressed than he remembered; almost elegant. Perhaps she had married again, some man who could afford to pay for good clothes; perhaps she was here shopping for him now. The thought almost frightened him. It seemed that in a flash the bright flowers, the fruits and the vegetables had lost some of their colour. Then she moved and came towards him, her face alight, her lips smiling.

"John! My dear John—at last," she said.

He drew a deep breath. She hadn't changed. Her voice had not altered. She was the same Antonia, perhaps with added poise and certainty, but the same.

He said, "I've found you at last! You vanished into thin air, no one could tell me anything. I went to Grayson, he showed me your last letter, after that he had heard nothing. I even went to Morano—there the fat butcher knew nothing; the Zevios were away. Why didn't you write to me?"

"But I did. I wrote twice, no—three times to a hotel in New York. Why did you not write to me?" She smiled.

"How could I write when I did not know where to write to?" he demanded. "Could I address a letter to Antonia, Paris? That was all I knew. Antonia, I've found you! This morning I cursed Padua, I hated it—yes, even the Giottos, and the two little Giorgiones—not very good ones either—now it is the most wonderful town in the world! Come and we'll have coffee at the Pedrocchi. I'll carry that basket for you, give it to me. And, Aramis, how is my friend?" He stooped to caress the little dog who leapt at his hand with delight.

"But I must get back to Abano," Antonia said, "I have luncheon to prepare; for this I have been buying vegetables."

John stopped. "You're not—not married?"

"My dear, no, but I am a cook. Chef to the aristocrat Madame d'Aurnigay. At the end of this week she returns to Paris, and my work is finished unless I care to become cook to her son. . . ."

He stared. They were standing in the middle of the narrow street, people were surging past them on either side, they were causing considerable inconvenience. Antonia gave a little tug at his hand.

"Come, we are in the way of everybody. Let us go to the

Pedrocchi. I shall have time for a cup of coffee. Yes, I have been offered to go to Monsieur d'Aurnigay——"

"I know the fellow, Maurice d'Aurnigay. If there is one thing certain in this uncertain world, my Antonia, it is that you are not going to cook for that fellow. The only women who should be employed by him—except in one capacity—should be over fifty, with bad false teeth, a squint and thin hair."

"I had already decided against it," she said. "I have met monsieur several times and did not find him—how do you say?—congenial or correct. His mother is not very pleased with me for refusing, I'm afraid."

Together they drank coffee in the historic Pedrocchi, and John, with his elbows on the table, stared at her, conscious that he was savouring every moment, watching every gesture; he was correcting all his mental pictures of her, and realizing that they had all been less delightful than the reality.

She finished her coffee. "I must go. The car is parked just across the road. I shall be late if I stay for another moment."

"Take me back with you, and I'll introduce myself as a friend of d'Aurnigay's—God forgive me for the lie—and I'll get invited to luncheon," he suggested.

"No, no. It would not do at all. Madame is rigid about matters of etiquette. Listen," for they had reached the car, and the chauffeur stood waiting, "this afternoon I shall be free. I will meet you at the Pedrocchi at three. Madame is driving into Verona to take tea with some friends of her son's, and she is remaining for the night. So I will meet you, and later we will have dinner somewhere, then you shall drive me back to Abano. So—*au revoir*, John." She laughed. "Oh, how very good it is to see you again."

He walked away, watching her car disappear down the long, busy street. He was more disturbed than he had imagined possible. For over a year, since he returned from America, he had tried to find where she was. Even in Morano, as he had told her, he could get no information. It was known that her mother and her stepfather had moved, but no one seemed particularly clear as to where they had gone. He had even visited Lake Garda because Innerhoffer said that he seemed to remember they had settled in one of the villages on the shore of the lake. He had wandered from one place to another, and then realized the futility of his search. He did not know the name of Antonia's stepfather, he had only seen her mother twice—brief glimpses—and how could he expect to find them? There appeared to be dozens of villages, and one seemed as possible as another. Now he had met her, found her standing laughing with a peasant woman at some story about an egg! One day he must ask her about that story.

She was to finish her work in a week. John paused, then entered a quiet *caffé* and sat down to think. He must try to face things squarely; to be honest with himself and with Antonia. Before he left for America, after Francis had died, he had known that she held a tremendous fascination for him, a fascination which, he knew now, had developed into love. If he had needed any proof, he had it when he remembered how something had clutched at his heart, leaving him with a sudden sense of what was almost physical sickness when he remembered that she might be married.

Francis Winnerton had married Antonia, but Francis had been a second son, also the estates of his father were nothing like so extensive and important as those of John's father. There were farms, there was a tremendous rent-roll, all kinds of matters regarding forestry and replanting. True, there were efficient agents for all these, but the Duke was the head of them when all was said and done. Times were difficult, many matters needed careful handling. They were not likely to grow easier as the years passed.

Then again, Francis had never loved Maudesley. He might

have liked bits of the estate which were paintable, but he had never had any intention of interesting himself in the running of the place. True, Mostyn was capable of doing that, and would no doubt do it admirably, and Francis would have been quite content never to see the place again. Even if he had been a second son, John doubted if he could have been content never to see his home again.

He knew that he loved Antonia; there was no doubt in his mind about that. No one experienced the joy which he had known when he saw her in the market unless they were truly and deeply in love. Life without her was unthinkable. He had searched for her, conscious that every fresh attempt to find her had grown more and more urgent. Now, what was he to offer her?

If he begged her to come and live with him, to share his life as a much-loved mistress, what would her reactions be? If he offered her marriage, throwing all caution, all restraint, to the winds, what would she answer? He doubted if, even if she loved him as he loved her, she would be ready to face a completely new environment, new surroundings and the whispers as to her origin and birth which would assuredly reach her.

He ordered a cognac, drank it, and squared his shoulders.

Damn it, if he loved her—and he did love her—the only thing to do was to offer her marriage. Nothing else was to be thought of. If she refused that, then he would—tentatively— make other proposals. She was the important person, she mattered supremely; and one thing was quite certain that, having found her, he was not going to lose her.

He paid his bill, walked back to his hotel, passing the medical school where, among the many coats of arms emblazoned there, was one of a John Trevor who had studied in Padua in 1478. John had often wondered what he had been like, that ancestor of his. Had he been studious or—like his descendant—given to indolence and lacking in continued application? Had he been quiet and well behaved, or had he rioted through the streets, under the *portici*, bawling songs, and ready to break heads or have his own broken?

He ate his luncheon, scarcely tasting what was offered to him. His mind was set on this momentous meeting with Antonia. She would meet him at the Pedrocchi, that *caffè* where students had gathered to talk and argue from time immemorial. It had been rebuilt and rebuilt, but it still retained certain obligations laid upon the management regarding the necessity of providing refreshment for students at any hour of the day or night.

He walked there. The place was almost empty, for the students had gone back to their lectures and the business men had returned home and were doubtless enjoying a *siesta*.

iii

Antonia prepared luncheon, served it as perfectly as usual. She fancied that there was still a slight coldness in Madame d'Aurnigay's manner. Doubtless she could not see why any young woman should not be willing and anxious to accept the position which her adored Maurice offered.

Madame said, "I shall be leaving for Verona, and I shall not be back until tomorrow. It may be that Monsieur Maurice may come with me, so will you arrange for us to have something which he likes particularly?"

"Of course, madame. It will probably be very hot again tomorrow. Monsieur likes food very cold, light and cold. I shall bear that in mind when I plan my menu."

The old face softened a little. "I know that I can rely on you."

"Madame, I met this morning in the market an old friend

of my late husband's. He asks me to dine; to meet him for tea and then stay and dine. Is that agreeable to you, madame?"

"But of course. How nice for you! And is he a painter also?"

"No, madame, he always says that he is a—it is an English expression—rolling stone."

Madame was all attention. Perhaps here was the reason why Antonia did not wish to go to cook for Maurice! It might be that she was in love and had been waiting for this "rolling stone". A friend of her husband's—madame knew all about Francis Winnerton, the son of an English earl. His friends must have been something more than merely successful merchants or business men.

"Is he—this gentleman—well off?" she asked.

Antonia said carelessly, "I believe so, madame. I have heard that he is very rich."

"That is good. Girls should marry using their good sense, not merely because they are romantic." It was a bow drawn at a venture, but the girl blushed.

"Madame," she protested, "there is no talk of marriage. We are—great friends only."

She returned to her kitchen, and the word "marry" kept running through her head as she worked. It was impossible that she should marry John. She had always refused to go to England, to be flung into a society which she would never understand, and where she would be acutely unhappy, and where everyone's critical attitude would have wounded Francis as well as herself. Francis had been "almost a lord", but John Trevor was a lord and would one day be one of the greatest lords in England. She knew that he was the only son, unlike Francis.

She realized that she loved him very dearly, that the thought that he had allowed her to slip out of his life had hurt her unbearably. She knew, too, that the sense of loneliness, of having no one who cared for her, had begun to weigh very heavily on her. She longed for companionship, even longed to live in a house of her own again, to give orders instead of receiving them. Despite all the kindness shown to her by her ladies, by the nuns, despite the beauty of Paris, its gaiety and charm, life there had been a cold affair. Everything was—unshared—that was the word which expressed it—unshared.

As she bathed, and brushed her hair until it shone, put on her nicest dress—very cool and attractive, made by a little dressmaker madame had told her of in Paris—she thought of John waiting for her.

In all probability he was not thinking of love, why should he? He had always been Francis's best friend. He had been a kind and good friend to her. No doubt he was glad to have met her that morning; he was glad to be able to ask her to meet him. They would talk and laugh, they would be gay, and when he brought her back to Abano this evening he would say, "Good-bye, Antonia, it has been so nice to see you again. Don't let me lose sight of you again for so long. Here is an address in London which will always find me. Write and tell me what you decide to do. Good-bye, my dear."

Then he would drive away, pleased that he had been kind to his friend's widow.

He was waiting for her, and as she entered he started to his feet. Antonia thought how handsome he was. His hair was going grey at the temples, but that, she thought, made him look distinguished. He had still the same air of easy indolence, still the same kind eyes with a certain laziness in their depths. His mouth was firmer, which pleased her.

When he spoke his voice held a note of excitement.

"I'm so glad that you've come. I've been here watching that door for what seemed to be hours. I wonder how many men have waited here, and watched that door as I've been doing, waiting—waiting for the one woman who matters."

She said, startled, "John! The one woman———"

"The one woman who matters," he said. "Listen, Antonia. I'm in love with you, wildly, completely in love. More than that, I love you. There is a difference, you know. I learned to love you when I first met you; then—I slipped into being in love. I was so afraid this morning that you might tell me you were married. If you had done, I should have abducted you quietly in my car. Antonia, dear Antonia, will you marry me, please?"

She raised her eyes and met his. "Marry you?" she said. "John, how can I marry you? It would be wrong. One day you'll be the duke, and you will have interests, responsibilities which I could never share. No, don't interrupt. I'm a cook, remember. One of my brothers was a carpenter, the other what you would call an agricultural labourer. My sister, so far as we know, is a prostitute in Milano."

He said with sudden irritation, "My father is a duke because one of my ancestresses slept with the King of England, and probably a good many other people. Antonia, darling, you'd fit into any society, no matter what. You have everything that half the women I meet haven't got—poise, *nous*, dignity—yes, and ability. Can't you understand that I love you, desperately? If the only thing that stands in our way is the title—damn it!— and the estates—damn them too!—then I'll give them up. Probably my father will marry again; he's sufficiently young to have other sons. I've argued this thing out, argued until I felt half silly with it all. I'll give the whole thing up if you'll marry me. I swear that I mean it."

She did not speak, but slid her hand across the table so that the tips of her fingers touched his. He said urgently, "Antonia—speak to me."

She looked up, her eyes swimming with tears. He had seen them so before, and had thought, "The gentians drenched in dew."

"You don't think that I would allow you to do that—for me, do you?"

He said, his voice thick, "You're worth it, darling."

"Listen. One day, when I was growing old, perhaps fat and heavy—for cooks do, you know—there might be the coronation of a new king. You'd read of the processions, the ceremonies, the state, and think, 'And I can't be there. Someone else is taking my place.' And you'd begin to wonder if it had been worth so much sacrifice. John, dear, I love you, far, far too much to risk ever seeing you look sorry, or disappointed. It's something I shall remember always—that you asked me to be your wife. It has made me feel very proud. Thank you, darling, *caro mio*."

He shook his head and said stubbornly, "It would never happen. I should never regret what I'd done if I had you."

"There is something else," Antonia went on, speaking very softly and evenly, "there is a duty that you owe to your land, and the people who live on it. My brothers were just two peasant boys, but they died at Monte Grappa, they—with many others—refused to retire even when they were told to do so. They went on fighting until they were killed. You can't run away, John *caro*, just because you're in love with me. It's taken hundreds of years to build up families such as yours, to make them responsible for the people who live on their lands. To make them—good overlords.

"I know how I feel about Italy; I know how happy I am when I hear of good landlords, men who do their duty to the country which is theirs. I know nothing about politics, but if this man Benito Mussolini can raise Italy, make her a great nation again—then I shall respect him, and have admiration for him."

As if he pushed the subject away from him almost violently, John said, "You've plenty of time. I've my car here. You remember how I love fast cars, eh? Let's drive to Venice, take a gondola, eat at the Taverna near the Fenice Opera House. I want to think. I must think. I can see happiness ahead, some-where—I just don't quite see how to reach it. Come, let's go, darling."

John drove as if it was imperative that he reached Venice in the shortest possible time. He scarcely spoke, and when he did it was in short sentences like the fire of a machine-gun.

"Going too fast? Good." And, "Flattish country round here, eh?"

She answered him quietly, but her heart was hammering wildly. She had made up her mind. She loved him; loved him too much to let him make the sacrifices he offered—so willingly —to make.

Only when they had parked the car, and were seated in a gondola slipping down the Grand Canal, did he seem to relax a little.

"How I love this place. They say that one day those old palaces will tumble into the water. Well, the world will be the poorer for their going. You love Venice?"

She nodded. Last time she had been here with Francis. She had cried because she had not sufficient money to buy nice clothes. Now she had plenty of money. Dear Francis, he had loved to see her looking nice, but he had never actually known what she wore. John, she felt, knew exactly.

She held out her hand. "This is a lovely day, *caro*. Thank you."

CHAPTER THREE

THEY landed at Saint Mark's and walked slowly past the Doge's Palace to Florian's. There they could see the full loveliness of the mosaics of Saint Mark's. The splendid, yet delicate, colours seemed to shine more brightly in the clear air.

"I never see it," John said, "without feeling that there is something so ethereal about it that I should never be surprised if the bronze horses developed wings and flew away, and all the mosaics dissolved into a rainbow mist. All lovers should come to Venice, not only for the beauty but because of the psychological effect it has. Think how many of the great lovers have come here, Antonia. For hundreds of years; and they will go on coming for hundreds of years in the future. It's the dream of all lovers to come to Venice—together, to use gondolas as a means of transport from one lovely place to another; to sit here in Saint Mark's Square and watch the pigeons rise in clouds as the clock strikes midday.

"Well, we're lovers, in that we love each other, even if you are not so deeply in love as I am. You'll have to be patient with me, and charitable. I want to explain—everything. I began by being a success; at school learning came easily to me, I was good at games. It was the same at the University—at Oxford. I might have really attained something, as it was I was already losing interest in learning, in games, but still I wanted to—make a good show. They thought that I worked hard and played hard; to a certain extent I suppose I did. In the war, which cut short my time at Oxford, I did fairly well, there was change, excitement, and—it was good to feel that men trusted you and were ready to follow you; obey you.

"When the war ended, I was tired. I wonder if older

people ever realized how the war tired—absolutely and completely—the really young men? Do you remember how utterly tired Francis was? He, poor chap, never recovered, but then he was physically tired. I was mentally exhausted. I suppose that if I'd been made of better stuff I should have thrown it off, flung myself into some work, profession, what will you. I felt that everything was so desperately futile.

"A civilization built up through the years, beauty, culture, could all be wiped out by this archaic thing called war. I wasn't concerned with the question of a just—or an unjust—war; it was the wastefulness of it all. I tried to dissociate myself from life as I saw it—stupid, boring, and generally tedious. I told myself that I would cultivate appreciation of beauty in all its forms.

"Antonia, did you ever hear such rubbish? What a young posturing idiot I was! Poor Francis listened and accepted it, while he—just as tired as I was—and more—worked and made beauty come to life by his art. Then I went to Tibet, really for no earthly reason except that it was difficult to get there. I had adventures. I was often dirty. I frequently was offensive, because I must have smelt. But as most Tibetans smell themselves, that didn't matter much. They didn't like me, and I didn't feel exactly drawn to them.

"I came home, wandered about, going here and there. I saw hundreds of pictures—I have some small understanding of those at least—and then came to see you and Francis. You'll never know how I envied him. To have a home, a woman you loved and who loved you with you all the time. I went back to Paris. I had a mistress—she was charming, Antonia, but, oh heavens, how she bored me!

"Now the war has been over—in so far as it ever will be over—for seven years. I've done nothing! I'm still tired, still have a sense of frustration and—am too indolent to do anything about it. More than that, I am lonely, desperately lonely."

He stopped and looked at her squarely. "As lonely as you are. I'm not sufficiently young to enjoy doing things which seem to me to be silly, and not sufficiently old to be able to say, 'I've grown too old for that!' I'm neither fish, flesh, fowl nor good red herring.

"While my mother was alive it was fun to go about with her. She was intelligent, amusing, mercurial. I don't like my father much, and although I love—yes, love—the old house, the land, the deer forest, the salmon river, he would resent it if I wanted to take an active part in the administration. He's still too young, too energetic, to want to have a son pottering about, reminding him that one day—everything will be mine."

He stopped and called to a waiter to bring more coffee.

"You'd like another cup of coffee? Now, at the risk of being an intolerable bore, let me finish my story—explanation, call it what you like. I must either make an effort, study something, possibly estate management or facts about agriculture—even some knowledge of coal mines might be useful—or else"—he paused—"drift.

"If, one day, I am to be the Duke of Rivermead, then I must equip myself, gather some knowledge which will help me to do my job decently. I'm in love, hopelessly, irretrievably, completely. For the last time, Antonia, will you marry me, will you imbue me with some of your own energy, your own determination, your own ambition?"

She watched him closely. There were beads of sweat on his forehead; his face had lost its colour and looked yellow under the tan. He had virtually admitted himself to be a failure, a man who had achieved nothing. That word "drift" had startled her. To drift, to admit oneself at the mercy of every wind that blew, every tide that swept in, to every storm and tempest, seemed to her to be tragic.

That he had ability she never doubted. Francis had spoken to her of his attainments, but always she had seen that indoience, that hint of laziness. He might be right. The war might have tired the young men too much for them to regain their energy easily.

He said, "Antonia, will you marry me? With you, I believe —and I swear that I am speaking honestly and sincerely—that with you to help me, I could achieve something." He laughed. "There's an admission! I need you to bolster me up! I'm not sufficiently strong to stand on my own feet. Again—dear, beloved Antonia—will you marry me?"

She drew a deep breath, their eyes met, then she turned away and stared out over the Square, where the pigeons strutted, where tourists posed before cameras, holding corn in their hands, laughing when the pigeons came and ate from their open palms. The ugly campanile, and the arch with the big clock where figures waited ready to spring into life at the striking of the hour. Saint Mark's with its riot of colour, shining in the sunshine, the fretted windows of the Doge's Palace. Opposite she saw the shops where glass of Murano, delicately embroidered linen and fine china were displayed. She saw all these things, while her mind seemed to work independently, trying to find a solution, striving to give him an answer. She longed to say "Yes," but her heart, her own good common sense, told her that—it was impossible. She loved him, she longed for a life spent with him, and most of all she longed to give him an answer which should never cause him regret or bring disillusionment.

He said urgently, "Antonia . . ."

She turned back from her survey of the great Square and smiled.

"John, I can't marry you."

His face changed, she tried to find a word, and only one came to her mind. He looked—stricken.

"Very well," he said, "then we must both go on being lonely, eh?"

Antonia moistened her lips, suddenly dry. She said very calmly and evenly, "There is no necessity, John—my dear John—for either of us to be lonely. Only when the time comes and your duty—remember that, your duty—calls for you, there must be no recriminations, it must be," she shrugged her shoulders, "accepted."

John stared at her. "You mean—you mean . . ." he stammered.

"You know quite well what I mean. I love you, you tell me that you love me. We shall be hurting no one. Only you will have to work, to study at these things which you have spoken of to me. The arrangements I leave to you."

There was a long silence, both of them sat quite still, and over Antonia came a sense of relief. She might be doing wrong—wrong in the eyes of the world—but she would be able to help this man, whom she loved, would be able to incite him to work, to study and to prepare himself for the position he must hold one day. For herself, she knew that the loneliness which had engulfed her was over, receding, presently to be lost in the distance. For how long? She refused to think of that. One day John would have to go and take up his work, and she must be sufficiently strong to send him away, to exercise her courage, and to call upon her fortitude.

John spoke first, very softly. "Antonia, you're wonderful. Have I any right to—let you do this?"

She laughed, the tension was too great, she must break it.

"Had you any right to make me fall in love with you? I know that you think you have the monopoly of—falling in love. Had you any right to realize how lonely I have been— which you must have done? I read in an English book—I forget its name, 'A fellow-feeling makes us wondrous kind.' Well, then, we are both lonely, we each know that of the other, we must be 'wondrous kind'. Look, my dear, the shadows are lengthening, growing more—solid. It is growing

late. We are both tired, emotionally tired. I ate no luncheon, I
suspect that you ate very little. Come—let us go and see what
the Taverna can offer us." Together, her arm through his, they
walked through the narrow streets, over the little hump-
backed bridge, and came to the little piazza in front of the
opera house.

John said, "Have you been there? The loveliest opera
house I have ever seen."

Antonia smiled up at him. "One day we'll go there."

ii

John had said, "Town or country, Antonia?"

"Don't you mind?"

"Not a bit, so long as you are there—you'll force me to
quote Omar Khayyhám in a minute! I shouldn't like to do that."

She shook her head. "I've never heard of him. John, the
country, or near the sea, but not somewhere like Rome or
Paris."

So when madame left Abano, Antonia joined John in the
South of France, and together they sought for a villa, and
finally found one which delighted them both. A garden which
commanded a view of the sea, and a long, low, two-storied
house, whitewashed, with bright yellow shutters. The rooms
were low and cool, the windows had striped awnings which
would keep out the sun but not the air. There was a study
which Antonia decided would be admirable for John, quiet,
and with a desk which gave him plenty of room. She remembered that he had once told her that no one could work
seriously at a small, inadequate desk.

The kitchen pleased her—sufficiently large to be old-
fashioned, but with all the modern improvements which made
such an appeal to her as a practical cook.

K

They were very happy together. Sometimes Antonia thought that John loved her with a greater intensity than she could give him. She tried to understand exactly what her love for him was. There was a certain element of protectiveness, a feeling that in spite of all his knowledge and experience, in spite of his position and his wealth, he had not found life either particularly kind or satisfactory. He had, she felt, found it difficult to make friends with people who did not place his position higher than they did his qualities. He had loved Francis, but Francis had been essentially simple. Position, money, great estates, meant nothing to Francis. Sometimes, when John spoke of people he had known, she detected a note of bitterness in his tone, as if they had disappointed him. The thought that he had been hurt roused in Antonia the determination that he should never be hurt again—through her.

She held the belief that no one could be really happy without work and consequent achievement. That laziness, that indolence of John's, disturbed her profoundly. He told her once when she found him sitting in the garden, merely staring out to the sea, half smiling and utterly content, that he had lost the habit of work.

She was shocked and showed it. "John, what a dreadful thing to say!"

"Does it strike you as dreadful? Might it not be just as good, as meritorious, to just—*be*, particularly to be content?"

"You're teasing me," she protested. "You know quite well that everyone ought to work—at something."

"Well, I am working—working terribly hard—at being happy!"

With that determined expression on her charming face, which never failed to amuse him, she persisted, "You'd be happier if you worked."

"How do you know? To begin with, you don't even know

that I am capable of being happier than I am here and now, do you?"

"Very well," with an air of resignation, "perhaps I don't, but I do know that it would make me happier."

"That puts an entirely different aspect on the matter. Come and sit down for five minutes and tell me what you want me to do." He smiled, caught her hand and drew her down beside him on the broad, stone seat. When John smiled at her, Antonia realized how dear he was to her. True, she resented his indolence, because she felt that he was allowing a fine brain to lie fallow, but his eyes when he smiled held such a light of affection and kindness that they disarmed her.

"I must get back to my kitchen," she said. "I have a great deal to do."

"Which that nice cook—what's her name, Hortense?—can do just as well!"

"Such nonsense!" she cried indignantly. "She is, I admit, a good cook, but she could no more prepare the dishes and sauces which I make for you than—than she could fly in the air."

"Surely the most important thing at the moment—I say at the moment—is to transform a lazy, idle, good-for-nothing into a horny-handed son of toil. Now, what work are you going to suggest for me?"

She frowned. It was all very difficult. He had promised that he would study matters appertaining to agriculture, but she knew him sufficiently well to realize that even if she succeeded in persuading him to remain in his study, she would go in to find him immersed in some book which had nothing to do with agriculture. It had happened so many times.

"Antonia, look, I found this book on the shelf there. It is about herbs, cures, and so on. Very old. Have you ever heard that if you wish your enemy to pine away and die, you find a toad and call it by the name of your enemy? Then you bury it

in a box in the earth, and as the 'toad shall perish, so shall the
enemy pine and eventually die'."

"I should think the person who did such wickedness would
die—and rightly. John, I thought that you were reading about
manures this morning." Her voice was reproachful.

"Darling, look at the morning; the sunshine, the scent of
the jasmine, can't you smell it? How can you ask me to read
about—manures—of all things, on such a morning?"

Now she tried very hard to think of some work which he
could do, and which would hold his interest.

"You might begin on this garden," she said. "If indeed
one can call it a garden! It is a wilderness. Hortense was telling
me of the garden her husband has made. It is small, but—what
it produces! He is, she says, a fine gardener, and perhaps he
would come and work with you, show you the best way to do
everything. They would be glad of a little extra money, I
believe."

John repeated, "A garden, yes, that would be pleasant. To
make something, to see results. Antonia, you are a wizard!
This very afternoon we will drive into Cannes and buy all
kinds of tools—for digging, cutting, pruning. We might even
have a little greenhouse, eh? Then I could grow immense
tomatoes, apricots, and take prizes at the local flower show, if
they have one. You've fired my imagination! I shall tie pieces
of string round my trousers, just below the knees. I've always
wondered why on earth people do that. We must write to the
best people in England for wonderful seeds, and you shall tell
me exactly what flowers you like best. I'll grow them—in
tremendous profusion. They'll be the envy of the Côte
d'Azur."

She laid her hands on his shoulders and kissed him.
"John, John, what a baby you are! There's a great deal to do
before you can expect flowers."

"I know, darling—the flowers will no doubt be the reward

that sweetens labour. Now, let us go and talk to the estimable
Hortense about her spouse."

Strangely enough the idea of a garden delighted him.
More, it absorbed him completely. He worked with Henri, the
husband of Hortense, regularly and energetically. He pored
over catalogues; he made plans for the formation of the
garden. These plans involved the delivery of several loads of
specially good earth, and the employment of a number of
blue-bloused Frenchmen, who, under the instructions of Henri
and John, did miracles in transforming the untidy, weed-
ridden ground into something which looked as if—one day—
it might be a garden.

Antonia thought that it must cost a great deal of money,
and wondered if the results would justify the reckless expendi-
ture. However, it gave John not only an interest, but provided him with exercise; she had never known him so happy,
so content.

During the Winter the garden seemed to her to take some
kind of shape. True it looked empty and rather desolate, but
John, rubbing his hands, said, "Wait for the Spring, angel,
then you'll see things."

Antonia was completely happy. It seemed to her that their
relationship was perfect. It irked her sometimes when she
remembered that she was "living in sin" and that the Church
would most certainly disapprove, and in all probability
Almighty God was at that very moment exceedingly angry
with her. Still, she told herself, she was making John happy;
more, she had saved him from drifting aimlessly about Europe,
looking for distraction, probably eating and drinking too
much, and as she expressed it to herself as summing-up
everything that was undesirable, "falling into mischief!"

She herself never found work lacking. The servants were
good, they worked hard and they appeared to take a pride in
their work, but she told herself that "without supervision,

they would doubtless be the same as all other servants". She cooked beautiful meals for John because she liked cooking, she wished to keep herself filled with knowledge, and whenever John wished to give her a present—which was very often because he was lavishly generous—it became a stock joke, "Now don't tell me that you want another cookery book!"

Their second year at the villa seemed to come round very quickly. The garden was paying for all the care which had been lavished upon it, the house was filled with flowers, and Antonia delighted in the fresh vegetables which John brought in with such pride.

To her surprise he was as enthusiastic as ever over his work, and one morning, when he brought in a basket filled with new peas, he announced as he sat on the edge of the table, drinking his midmorning cup of coffee, that he had bought the field behind the villa.

He made the announcement lightly, but Antonia knew him sufficiently well to understand that he was anxious to make her realize that he was taking his work seriously.

"I have been reading," he told her almost shyly, "more than you know, darling. Reading and talking to Henri. He thinks very well of the idea. We shall hire a tractor, plough up the field, and slowly reclaim it with patent manures and foods until we can really make a start at growing early vegetables—in quite a big way. It will be a long job, but," he laughed and smiled at her, "we've plenty of time."

Two years slid into three. Antonia was twenty-eight. John thought that she grew more attractive with each year. Her hair was as bright as ever, her eyes as clear, and her skin shone with perfect health. He was proud of her, and whenever he had to leave her for a few days to rush back to England on some business or other he felt his excitement rising the moment he left Victoria Station on his way home. She always contrived to have some small surprise for him—she had made new curtains, had recovered a chair which had grown shabby, had been into Cannes to her dressmaker and at the same time had bought him new bedroom slippers. "These which you wore were a disgrace. I was ashamed that the servants should see them."

To find her waiting for him, with little Aramis beside her when he returned home, was a joy which never failed to stir him, to make him think, as he did so often, what a lucky fellow he was to have such a wife. That was how John always thought of her, as his wife. He could not imagine life without her; their lives must be spent together. No matter what he was forced to give up, Antonia must remain with him, growing more precious, more beloved every day.

iii

He came into her shining kitchen one morning, excited and proud. Henri had pronounced that the field was going to produce marvellous results, that the soil had responded wonderfully to the treatment which had been given to it. John was like a schoolboy, drinking his coffee with gusto, and when Hortense left the kitchen for a moment, catching Antonia to him and whispering how much he loved her.

"Kiss me," he whispered, "quick, before she comes back."

"John—my dear!" she spoke half reprovingly. "There! No, that is enough. Go back to your work. Yes, of course I love you, more dearly with every day."

He grumbled. "You're parsimonious with your kisses!"

She laughed. "That's because I want you never to grow tired of them."

"Do you remember that it is more than three years since we came here? How quickly they've gone. How wonderful to think that there are other years—many, many of them. Be ready to bathe before luncheon, won't you?"

"You like me to bathe with you so that I can sit and watch how splendidly you swim! I, myself, shall never make a swimmer. Really I don't like it very much, this bathing. Say what you like, a comfortable bath is nicer. There, go! I'll be ready at twelve."

He went out, stooping to pat Aramis as he went. She watched his tall, slim figure striding through the garden on the way to his precious field. She smiled as she watched him. He was interested, really and absorbedly interested. Again and again, he would take Henri and go off to visit some farm, to investigate new methods, study new means of production. His study now was not merely a room where he went to pass the time, but where he worked, drawing up tables of comparison, reading reports, making countless notes. He had told Antonia that before long he would buy more land, he was ambitious— at last. She turned back to her cooking, well satisfied.

At twelve he returned and they went down to the strip of beach which belonged to the villa to bathe. John swam magnificently. Antonia, in spite of all the teaching he gave her, remained, as she said, "a fine swimmer while I still have one foot on the ground". She finished her daily ten or twelve strokes and sat on the beach, sun-warmed, watching him.

It struck her how satisfactory her life was to her. She was never lonely; she never regretted that they knew no one, that she never spoke to anyone except the servants and the trades-men. John was sufficient. Sometimes they drove into Cannes, several times they had been for a few days to Monte Carlo, and once as far as Marseilles. John had said that it was merely a business trip, that the only reason she wished to go there was to learn how to make *bouillabaisse*, and that she dragged him from one restaurant to another tasting the stuff made in every method known to the people of Marseilles.

"Not only the *bouillabaisse*," she told him, "many other things——"

"All particularly revolting!"

"You enjoyed the *coquille des Fruits de Mer*. The *sauce Poivrade* is a masterpiece."

"One more to add to your collection, eh?"

"I shall improve upon it," she assured him.

Yes, it was a good life, tranquil, filled with quiet happiness. She refused to look into the future. Time enough when the future became the present.

They walked back to the villa; Hortense was waiting for them.

"I was about to bring this to you, madame," she said. "It arrived a few minutes ago."

Antonia took the telegram and handed it to John. "For you," she said. "No one ever sends me telegrams."

He said indignantly, "I send you telegrams every day when I am not here!"

"Because you are too lazy to write to me! There, open it."

He opened the telegram, making a little sound of disgust because the gum was still damp. He read it, Antonia thought, very slowly, and she saw his face pale under the healthy tan. He looked suddenly older, thinner.

She laid her hand on his arm. "John—what is it?"

Without speaking he handed it to her. She read it. The Duke had died last night. John's presence was required immediately. The message was signed Coxton. She remembered that was the name of John's lawyer.

"Come and let me give you a drink," she said, and obediently he followed her into the *salon*. "Sit down, I will bring it to you."

He took it, and drank thirstily. "So—it's come," he said. "Well, remember what I said. I refuse to take up the—duties. Someone else must carry them through. I want to live my life here, with you. Oh, I must go home, that's inevitable. Remember, Antonia," he spoke gravely, forcefully, "either you marry me, become my duchess, or I remain here. No, don't argue. There is nothing more to be said."

He ate very little luncheon, then Antonia packed for him, neatly and efficiently as she did everything. When everything was finished, he turned and took her in his arms, looking down into her eyes, his own filled with tenderness.

"There is only you," he said. "You're everything. Never forget that. Nothing in the world could ever be so precious. Nothing! I shall be back again just as quickly as possible; until then—remember—I shall be thinking of you all the time. Don't come and see me off. Stay here."

From the window she watched his big car glide away. He was driving to Paris rather than wait for the night train, it would be quicker, he said. He did not look back, the car turned the corner and she saw him no more.

Antonia sat down on the bed, and covering her face with her hands cried as if her heart was broken. As once before, long ago, she felt the touch of a small paw on her knee, heard the whimper of a little dog, distressed and puzzled at what he saw and heard.

Antonia lowered her hands. "My dear small dog," she whispered, "I should have known that you would understand. Aramis, we are going away. We must go quickly and I must tell lies to the servants. If I stay here he will come back and refuse to let me go. I can't allow him to stay here, now when his great place is waiting for him. He must not be allowed to refuse to do his duty. Perhaps I have been very wrong to live with him when we were not married, but I have that on my conscience, and I will not burden it more.

"Oh, dear little Aramis, it breaks my heart to leave him. I can see how hurt his eyes will look; such kind eyes. Now, my dear, I must be brave, not sit here talking to you, watching me with your loving eyes, so sympathetic they make me begin to cry again."

She sat down at the desk in her bedroom and wrote to John. It took her a long time, for she wrote slowly, and sometimes she had to lay down her pen to wipe away the tears which would have splashed on to the paper.

My dear love, she wrote, *please do not try to find me. I am doing what I know is right. If before we have done wrong, now it is time that we do what is right. Three beautiful years, that is more than many people have in their lives. I shall not say—forget me. I do not think you can, as I shall not forget you. You must marry; have a son. I know that you will be a very good duke, kind to poor people. The jewels which you have given me are in your little safe, Hortense has the key. I have kept a few that I love more than the others—they remind me of wonderful days. Be kind, John dear, do not try to make me come back. Do not disturb yourself. I have sufficient money. I shall do very well. I send you all the love that I have. Go with God, beloved John. Your Antonia.*

She left the letter in a large envelope into which she pushed John's cheque book which he had forgotten, and some letters which he had left on his dressing-table when he changed. Carefully she packed her bags. She took none of the charming dresses which John had bought her, only the far more simple things which she had bought for herself. Then, putting her own cheque book, passport and various letters from Grayson into her bag, she called Aramis and went downstairs.

Hortense cried, "Madame, you go on a voyage?"

Antonia simulated surprise. "But naturally, I go to join the Duke. As you know, his father is dead. It was necessary for him to go away very quickly. He was always a very important person, as you know, but now he is second only to the King himself. It is possible that I may remain with my mother on Lake Garda on the way home again—for we shall doubtless retain this villa even though the Duke has many larger houses in England. I have left a letter—it contains some business papers, in case I remain with my mother and forget to mention them to him. He will have so much business to do, this poor man. Also, here is the key of the small safe. I can leave it safely with you, I know this."

"Nothing is more certain, madame."

"Then please telephone for a car. Yes, I wish to drive to Cannes. The big trains for long distances do not all stop here."

She did not look back. To have watched John's beautiful garden disappear into the distance would have been too much for her. She held Aramis in her arms, and leaning back let the tears run, unheeded, down her cheeks.

CHAPTER FOUR

THE Mayor, Thomas Whitegift, waited, and while waiting surveyed the room. He admired it wholeheartedly, and wished that he could persuade Mrs. Whitegift to furnish their own drawing-room in a similar way. There were few ornaments, but those that stood in the admirable glass-fronted cabinet were excellent. He peered more closely. Yes, Meissen figures, and two pairs of Chelsea figures which were perfect. There was also some Capo di Monte and some Bow. He stood back, admiring it, and whistled softly. That china alone was worth a mint of money!

He looked at the pictures—a fairly large one of an attractive girl with a small white dog seated on her knee. There was another smaller painting of the little dog alone—both those were, obviously, by her husband, Francis Winnerton, and the portrait was the finest Winnerton he had ever seen, a masterpiece. There was a third, a bunch of flowers in a jar. Beautifully painted, meticulously painted, every detail perfect. Surely that wasn't a Winnerton? Not his style at all.

The door opened, and he turned to greet the woman who entered.

"Ah, Mrs. Winnerton—I'm sorry to disturb you. I just came to make sure that everything was in train for to-morrow."

She smiled, and he thought what a pleasant "warming" smile it was too.

"Everything, Mr. Mayor. It will all go down to the Town Hall in my special containers. It will be as hot—where it is necessary for it to be hot—as when it leaves my kitchens. The sauces I shall make myself."

He nodded. "Your great speciality, eh?"

"Sauces? They say so. It's not really true. Perhaps I use a little more—originality than many people. The wines? You have ordered the wines I suggested? Splendid! I am sure that everything will go in a superb manner. Let me offer you something before you go? Yes, please. Whisky-and-soda, brandy—I have some really fine brandy."

Whitegift beamed. "If I might have a whisky-and-soda. No ice."

She turned to look at him over her shoulder, as she stood at the table where stood the tray with bottles and siphons.

"Never!" she said with considerable emphasis. "To ice whisky! Oh, I know that they do this in America, but," she laughed, "this is not America."

"It's a great day for Westbourne," the Mayor said. "A civic luncheon, the opening of the Victory Park, the presence of the Duke of Rivermead, and the luncheon organized by a Dame of the British Empire!"

"You pay me too much compliment," Mrs. Winnerton said. "It is as nothing! This organizing! After training cooks for the Army during the war. Ah, then one needed to understand organization."

"As you proved that you did!"

She sighed. "One had to do something. I am by birth an Italian. How could I sit there idle while I suffered the knowledge that my poor countrymen were fighting on the side of that terrible German—I cannot bear to speak his name—and being ruined by that inflated balloon—the Duce? Ah—the Duce—the Leader! Where did he lead them? Poor fools! I did not wish to make munitions, things with which my own countrymen might be killed, so I did what I could do—probably far better— trained women to cook properly for the English soldiers, and prayed for the day when Italy should come to her senses again. She did, Mr. Mayor, if you remember —on September the third, 1943. A surrender—but some surrenders are—more honourable than continuing to fight for a cause which was false, empty, and against the hearts of the people."

She broke off, and said, smiling, "Mr. Mayor, forgive me, I talk too much! I allow myself to grow excited. Now, for tomorrow, have no fears. All will go like a good clock, no?"

Urbane and pleased at her admissions, the Mayor thought how charming it was to see a woman lose restraint and speak feelingly—English women were of course admirable but they lacked the warmth and delightful impetuosity of these foreigners.

"Mrs. Winnerton, I regret that I have detained you. I look forward to tomorrow. I am sure that the Duke will be surprised at the luncheon which will be offered to him."

"Mr. Mayor, I believe that the Duke will be surprised. Good-bye, and it has been a pleasure to see you."

ii

Antonia Winnerton leaned back in her comfortable chair and smiled. Twenty-two years ago she had left John, had virtually run away, taking with her little Aramis, because she had felt that it was necessary for John to do—what she still believed to have been—his duty.

A year later she read that he had married. That did not disturb her. She possessed that strange philosophy which belongs to so many Italians, despite their apparent excitability and sudden bursts of grief or passion. It was all part of his work to marry, to provide an heir, and therefore she accepted the fact that another woman had taken her place. No, that she never admitted. Mentally now she corrected herself. No one, she knew, would ever take her place—the place which she had made for herself, the niche which she had filled.

He had written to her through her lawyers, but she had not replied to his letters. It was wiser to keep silent. Letters might have been followed by the desire to see her, talk with her, and she—loving him as she did—dared not completely trust herself.

She had read everything she could find concerning him in the newspapers. Had seen that a year after his marriage the Duchess had given him twin daughters, and eighteen months later the desired heir. Three years ago she had died and John had remained a widower.

Twenty-two years since she last saw him! He must be fifty-nine—Antonia tried to imagine how he looked, if his figure was still very spare and erect, if his eyes were as kind as ever. Well, tomorrow, at the luncheon which was to be given to the Duke of Rivermead after the public opening of the park which he had given to the town, she would see him. Would he, perhaps, taste the *filet sole en surprise* and wonder why it reminded him suddenly of the South of France? Would he find himself transported to a little house in an Italian village when he tasted the *chaudfroid of sweetbread*? Would the Mayor tell him who was responsible for the preparing of the luncheon?

"Mrs. Winnerton's school of cookery, Your Grace. Prepared of course under Mrs. Winnerton's personal supervision. Oh, the school is very well known and highly thought of in Westbourne."

Then what would happen, she wondered?

Twenty-two years ago she had gone to her mother's house in Malcesine. It had dismayed her considerably. True it was better kept than the cottage at Morano, but it was far from that state of perfect cleanliness which Antonia demanded. Her mother had grown very stout, she liked to sit on a chair outside the front door in the sunshine and talk to the neighbours who passed. The state of the house troubled her very little. True, a woman came in every day, and remained, it seemed to

Antonia, a surprisingly short time, accomplishing very little. She remained there for two months, cleaning, polishing, cooking as she had not done for three years. Ferrari beamed his satisfaction.

"Your mother is the best woman in the world," he told Antonia, "but she dislikes the work of a house. In a mill, ah, there she is a fine worker, now—there is no mill, and she cannot raise interest in the house."

"Do you like living in this disorder?" Antonia had demanded.

"My dear, I have learned not to *notice things*; I close the eyes and the heart does not grieve! My life is tranquil. This it would never be if I were constantly to be complaining, asking why these cups are not washed, or that knife polished. *Ecco!*"

Later Antonia had gone to one of the largest and most expensive hotels in Switzerland. She had written asking if there was a vacancy. The proprietor asked for testimonials. She went to Switzerland to speak with him personally.

"I have no testimonials," she told him, "but I always cooked for my husband—Francis Winnerton, the great painter, and his friends. Cooking is my passion. I suggest to you, monsieur, that for one week you allow me to work— without salary—in your kitchen. Instruct your chef to order me to prepare whatever dishes he wishes—no matter how difficult, how elaborate. These shall be my testimonial, no?"

She worked there for a year, and when war broke out returned to England. She went without Aramis, for he had died during the Winter in Switzerland, and had left a terrible blank in her life. Even now, as her eyes turned to his portrait, she felt the same contraction of the throat, the same sudden smarting of the eyes. Dear "small dog", so faithful, so affectionate, and so well mannered.

Everyone told her that war was coming, and she thought what she might do to help should this terrible catastrophe arrive. Francis and John had fought in the last war, they had fought on the same side as her two brothers, now she would do something to show that her heart was faithful, something that should make Francis proud of her.

She had long believed in the truth of the axiom first instilled into her by Mother Anna Maria, and later by the chef at the "Splendide" in Switzerland, that the British were unable to cook anything except underdone roast beef and over-cooked roast mutton.

"Figure to yourself," the chef had said, "these people have the best food in the world—food, madame, you understand. But they have no cooks! They have no taste, no discrimination. They know nothing of flavouring—except salt and pepper, and these they put on their food with automatic regularity before they even taste the dish! It has become a tradition to do this; the result of unflavoured food for many hundreds of years. If an Englishman were given larks' tongues—I speak figuratively, madame, he would say, 'Ah, larks' tongues—interesting. Pass the salt and pepper!' "

War was declared. Antonia, living in a small respectable hotel in Kensington, read the announcements with horror. So Mussolini had been fool enough to join hands with the German! He was allowing Italy to be led by the nose into this terrible war. Now, these poor soldiers! They must be fed if they were to defeat the German hordes; somehow she didn't think that the Italians would need a great effort to defeat them. The British were their traditional friends, the Germans their traditional enemies, their hearts would not be in this war. There would be more Caporettos and fewer Monte Grappas!

She talked with the elderly ladies in the hotel who twittered about the war in high nervous voices. They were in the main too old to take any active part; they told her that they were joining sewing parties, they were going to knit comforts for the troops, they were going to help to pack parcels.

"And you, Madame Winnerton?" they asked.

"I shall cook," Antonia announced. "I am by birth Italian, but I have a British passport for I married an Englishman, Francis Winnerton, and took his nationality."

"*The* Francis Winnerton, madame? The painter?"

"The same, madame."

"He was a son of the Earl of Maudesley—rather, of the late Earl, I should say, was he not?"

"He was, madame. Indeed yes."

She made enquiries, she went to the headquarters of one of the women's services, and was interviewed. They were charming to her; she was very attractive, her manners were delightful, and she spoke with firmness and decision. Finally she reached the head of the organization, and wondered how much time she spent in putting on that admirable make-up, in having her hair so exquisitely waved, and her nails so perfectly manicured.

"And now, Mrs. Winnerton, what is it you want to do?"

Antonia felt suddenly helpless. For over a week she had been telling these women what she wished to do; she had submitted a scheme, they had passed her on to someone else—now, she had reached the woman who was presumably the head, and she asked, "What is it you want to do?"

"Teach women to cook for the Army, madame."

"Quite," the pleasant voice had sharpened a little. "And you are a trained cook?"

"A *cordon bleu.* I can also cook most simple things, and cook them well."

"Yes, I see." Antonia thought, "That is exactly what you don't do, you haven't read my suggestions, and you're completely in the blackness." "And you have a concrete proposal to make?"

"I made it in my suggestions, madame. Take a hotel, many will be—what is it called—evacuated, perhaps on the coast? With a garden, for girls must learn to cook out of doors as

well as in a kitchen. I will engage to train them—and I give
you my assurance that they will be *trained*. There will be no
waste, no extravagance."

"Quite—oh yes, quite. And the waste, if the organization
is properly run," the tone had suddenly become brisk and
businesslike, "that can be sold to farmers, for their pigs, eh?"

"If the pigs, madame, rely upon the waste from any school
which I have under my charge, they will be poor, thin creatures.
I dislike any kind of waste."

Finally she had admitted, "The idea appeals to me very
much. I shall suggest it to," she smiled, "my superiors. Good-
bye, Mrs. Winnerton, you will hear from us."

Antonia felt herself dismissed. She remembered how she
had waited, at first patiently, then with growing impatience,
and finally, when she had almost given up hope, she had been
sent for. She was interviewed by three men, officers, one with
red tabs on his shoulders. They were charming to her, they
admitted that her scheme was good, they smiled and stated
that they wished it were possible for them to taste the results of
her cooking.

She said calmly, "Ah, I think that you would be happy,
no?"

Then things had begun to move. She was told to wear
uniform, which she had altered so that it fitted admirably. An
hotel was found for her at Westbourne. She inspected it, found
fault here, praised there, and gave them a list of her requirements. Of the weeks which followed she looked back as one
looked back on a nightmare. Her plans were all made, her
stores were all ordered, beds arrived with no bedding. No fuel
had arrived, and only one cooking-stove. She lived on the
telephone, the authorities grew impatient, and—so did
Antonia. Finally everything was ready, and her first intake
arrived. She questioned them all. They were inclined either to
giggle or to be sour.

"Private 'Urchinson," for she still had difficulties sometimes with her aspirates, 'you can cook, no?"

"Ah can boil a pertater, 'appen Ah can cuke a chop or summat o' that, but Ah'm noa cuke, m'am."

"Private Smithers, can you cook?"

"Not reely as yew might sai—cook. Mum alwais says my rock cakes are a treat, but I'm not so hot at what you mite call—plain cooking."

"And you, Private Finnis?"

"M'am, I'd be fair affronted not to be able to cook a guid dinner for onny man! I'll no say fancy-like things, but guid homely food, why, aye, I've cooked iver since I can mind."

And so it went on. But slowly order emerged out of chaos, and she found women who were reliable, hard-working and intelligent. She taught them well, with efficiency and imagination; at intervals she allowed them to make something which was slightly—but very slightly—more elaborate than the ordinary dishes.

From time to time there were inspections, when Antonia urged her girls to do their very best, to give a meal which should enhance their reputation and hers. Other schools were opened, and she visited them all in turn. She had found teachers who were capable, energetic, and intelligent, she trusted them and they repaid her trust.

She had never worked so hard, had never known how tired she could be and still—go on. She surmounted difficulties, she overcame obstacles, and she had that quality of making her girls respect and admire her. Never a martinet, except in matters appertaining to hygiene and complete economy, she gave her girls to understand that she trusted them, but that once that trust was forfeited—their career as an army cook was over so far as Antonia Winnerton was concerned.

The war—which had seemed as if it must go on for ever—ended, and the various cooking schools were closed. It was suggested that Antonia might continue to train cooks, but she refused.

"It's a grand job you've done, and there is still work to be done. I wish that we could persuade you to go on with it."

She shook her head. "Sir, I am flattered that you wish this, but I am a cook. I am ambitious for myself and my success. Also, it is necessary that I return to Italy for a short time. I wish to bring back pictures painted by my husband. You understand; I have missed their presence."

The colonel with the red tabs and numerous medal ribbons sat stiffly upright. "I say, you have some pictures of his, Mrs. Winnerton? I don't wish to be impertinent, but I suppose there are none you—well, none you wish to dispose of, eh? I'm a great admirer of his work—that is, your late husband's."

She smiled at him, and he thought what an attractive woman she was, not very young, but with the most beautiful eyes he had ever seen, and hair which, while not being gold, shone like polished metal. Her skin looked so smooth and soft, and when she smiled she showed teeth which were delightfully regular and white.

"There are three which I need for myself, sir. How many others—I am not sure. It is so long since I saw them. Let me have an address which will find you, and when I return I shall acquaint you with how many there are—for sale. They are none of them very large. The largest he ever did was of Venice. All said that it was very beautiful."

He nodded excitedly. "I know it! I've seen it. It belongs to old Emmanuel Gollantz, or it did. It now belongs to his son. It's a lovely picture. I'd give my eyes to possess a picture like that."

With a little air of dignity which was charming, he thought, she said, "It is pleasant to hear you speak in this way. He was a very lovely person, Francis. Our life together was—well, something which was almost too perfect. I shall not forget, sir. Good-bye."

She had gone to consult Grayson, grown old and white-haired. She had sufficient money; she had never touched any of the income which Francis had left her. She made an offer for the empty hotel at Westbourne, and it was accepted. She visited Italy, saw her mother and Ferrari, visited Count Zevio and his wife and collected the pictures. The three which she loved she kept. The rest—which she could not really understand, and still regarded as a mild eccentricity on the part of dear Francis —she sold at prices which were far beyond her expectations.

Then with the hotel cleaned, refurnished, with the most modern cooking appliances installed, with bedrooms furnished charmingly, she opened her School of Cooking and Domestic Training.

She gathered round her women who were specialists in not only cooking, but needlework—particularly mending and repairs—household management and domestic economy. She charged high fees and did not deny it.

"It is not an ordinary college," she told prospective clients, "it is—different. All bedrooms are very nice, so are the sitting-rooms. The girls are treated as sensible people; they are given liberty. If that liberty is abused, then they must return home; I do not want them. They will be able, on leaving here, to manage the houses of their husbands—but perfectly— if they have made good use of their time."

She was given the D.B.E. and had not the slightest idea what it meant or why it had been given to her. "For valuable work in training cooks for the Army."

"But I did nothing," she told Margaret Finnis, who had come to her as second in command when she obtained her release. "I had to do some work for the war, and that was all I knew how to do."

Miss Finnis returned, "Ach, never mind the whys and

wherefores, madame, it 'ul look grand on the prospectus, think on."

Now in her own sitting-room she knew that she was a success. Her school was full, there was a long waiting list. The girls were nice young things, and keen on their work. Antonia herself enjoyed every day as it came.

John had served with some distinction. She had followed his career as closely as possible, and thrilled with pride when she heard men speak well of him. Tomorrow she was to see him again. She refused to allow herself to speculate as to what might be the outcome of their meeting—she only knew that she still loved him. She had cut herself away from him for what she had believed was his good; she had suffered, and now she just—waited. After twenty-two years.

iii

Antonia had arrived too late for the reception, she had done that purposely. She could not have borne to have come face to face with John, to have bowed, and passed on. She made her way to the top table, and slid unobtrusively into her seat. He was six places removed from her. The Mayor's wife sat next to him, and Antonia could hear her voice as she chattered to him. How that woman chattered!

John, older, his hair completely grey, but still erect and slim, examined the menu.

"I'm afraid, Madame Mayoress, that I appreciate good food, and this menu promises excellent things. I don't think that I have ever known a *salade Boulonnaise* served before at a luncheon of this kind."

She laughed. "Ah, we hoped that it might be a surprise for you! We have all sorts of surprises in Westbourne."

Later he turned to her and said in a tone which was almost

startled, "This *sole en surprise*! I tasted it last—like this—in the South of France—many years ago. It is admirable."

It was when the *chaudfroid of sweetbreads* was before him that he demanded rather than asked, "Tell me, Madame Mayoress, who is responsible for this luncheon?"

Her smile widened. "Our local wonder—our D.B.E.—Antonia Winnerton."

"I should like to meet her again. I knew," his voice sounded strained and harsh, "her many years ago. Her husband was a friend of mine."

"Of course, Your Grace, how delightful that you are old friends." She babbled on, telling him of Antonia and her college, of her success, and of her popularity. When luncheon was over, he said again that he wished to be presented.

She thought, "Presented! Fancy a Duke using that expression!" The guests were dispersing, and Mrs. Whitegift took him to meet Antonia. "Mrs. Winnerton—Dame Antonia, I should say—the Duke—I mean, Your Grace, this is Dame Antonia."

John saw a woman who was dressed with great care, met her eyes, still that bright gentian blue, and saw her lovely mouth curve into a smile. Antonia saw the man she had known twenty-two years ago; the same slim figure, the same kind eyes, the hair quite white, and new lines graven on his lean, sunburnt face.

"This gives me great pleasure," he said, and took her hand in his.

"I hope that you enjoyed the luncheon, no?"

"I have always enjoyed—good cooking," he said. "This is a most fortunate meeting, Dame Antonia. I have two daughters who wish to learn to cook, to understand domestic management, in short to equip themselves as perfect housewives. Owing to the modern trend it seems likely that in the near future no one will be able either to find or afford domestic help. They wish to—be prepared. Most meritorious, I think."

The Mayoress said, "Dame Winnerton, if His Grace has time, why not ask him to walk round and see your college? No time like the present."

Antonia said, "It is only three minutes' walk. I shall be most happy."

Together they left the Town Hall and walked in silence.

Antonia said, "Here is the place—an hotel at one time, you understand. Now, I have seventy girls! It is very much work, but I enjoy work."

He smiled. "You always did! Antonia, let me come in and talk to you. Don't make me go round and see things. I only want to see—one thing. My dear, twenty-two years. Why did you treat me so badly? I tried—to find you, although I was angry and resentful that you had gone as you did. . . ."

She held out her hand impulsively. "John, I did not know what else to do. If you had come back and I had still been there, I should have been weak, given in. I dare not do that. Try to understand, my dear."

They entered the large paved hall, and together walked up the wide, low stairs. The whole place, John noticed, had an air of prosperity, it shone with cleanliness and much polishing. It was typical of Antonia to have the place kept so immaculately.

"Here is where I live," she said. "I must sometimes have quietness, be alone. It is a small apartment, you see—what is called self-contained. Now I shall telephone for tea—yes, it will be Earl Grey."

He stood looking about him, then his eyes lit on the pictures. She heard his sudden exclamation, and having hung up the receiver, came over to where he stood.

He looked down at her. "How wonderful to see that lovely picture again," he said. "I'd almost forgotten how beautiful it was. And the small Aramis—I am afraid that he must be gathered to his fathers, eh? And Francis's little joke, that he painted especially for you. I didn't realize that I could be so glad to see any pictures again! But the one of you is the jewel."

Antonia made him sit down, pushed a silver cigarette-box towards him, saying, "They are the kind which you once told me you preferred."

"How like you to remember."

"I don't forget many things. Now tell me about—you. I was sad that your wife was taken from you. And your children? I read about them when they were born. The girls—*gemelli*, eh?—must be twenty, nearly twenty."

"I was very fond of my wife," John said. "She was essentially kind and understanding. The girls—yes, they're nice girls. If you'll have them, I think they'd like to come here. The boy—John—because the eldest son is always called John— Anthony Francis. Nice names, don't you think—John Anthony Francis? He's a fine fellow, clever, hard working. Refused to consider the Army or Navy, decided that agriculture was his line of country."

Smiling, Antonia repeated, "John Anthony Francis. That is very sweet, a nice thought—the three of us."

He lay back in his chair, his long legs stretched out before him. She thought that he looked tired, and wished that she could keep him with her, look after him, and lavish affection on him. She listened to his deep, quiet voice, and when tea was brought poured it out for him exactly as she remembered he liked it.

He said, "Ah, you must still be the only woman, other than British, who can make drinkable tea, 'Tonia."

"Of this Earl Grey," she said, "I like the perfume, but I shall never like tea very much to drink. I remember thinking how strange it was that you and Francis—you remember when you stayed with us at Morano—two grown-up men—could drink tea early in the morning, and seem to like it a great deal. Do you still have 'early morning tea'?"

He nodded. "Yes, I've not changed. Antonia, when will you marry me? My dearest, listen, we are neither of us very young, I am nearly sixty. I've worked hard—very hard—for twenty years, more, for I was learning to work when we were in France together and you practically drove me to it. I'm regarded as a good landlord, I've tried to do my duty to the estates. Tony will carry on when I've finished with it.

"The whole world is changing. There are new conditions everywhere, new values are set on things. Some of the stupid old shibboleths have been discarded. The future is going to be a strange business. I want at least to make my future safe and secure, and I can only feel that it is both if I have you with me. I've always loved you, dearly and sincerely. Growing old can be a very lovely thing, if you grow old with the person who matters most to you. It can be a very lonely thing, too—my girls will marry, Tony will marry, and men of my generation lost most of their friends in the first war, the remainder—in the second." He rose and came to her side. " 'Tonia, you're not crying, my dear!"

"If I cry it is to shed tears of gladness," she told him, dabbing her eyes. "But, John, my business, this place?"

"Still terribly practical. My sweet, Rivermead is only fifteen miles away, you can come over and remain the—what shall we call you?—the directress. Maybe you can turn one of my girls into a worthy successor, eh? Antonia, you've not answered my question. When will you marry me? If you don't answer me soon, and not insist upon discussing your tedious business, which can very well take care of itself, I shall think that you have no love left for me."

She sprang to her feet and put her hands on his shoulders. "You could never think that. It would prove that you were not only growing old but foolish! Do I love you? Ever since I knew that you were coming here, I have planned for this luncheon. I chose dishes which would—remind you, yes, remind you of Morano, of France—of—me."

"Then," he put his arms round her, "you will marry me?"

She lifted her face and he stooped and kissed her, saying, "Oh, my Antonia, how wonderful it all is, how wonderful it is all going to be! Even though you have practically admitted that you are nothing more than a schemer!"

How splendid it was to feel his arms round her again, to be able to relax in the realization that they were together again. She sighed.

"I sigh for happiness," she said. "It is so long since I felt your arms round me, your kisses on my cheeks. Twenty-two years—a long time—now you have come back, and they are forgotten. It is as if I had sat for a long time in a room which was slowly growing dark, but because I had been there so long I had not noticed that the darkness was increasing. Now you come in, you switch on all the lights and for a moment my eyes are dazzled, I don't see quite clearly."

"Do you imagine that I don't feel exactly the same, my 'Tonia?"

"Sit down," she ordered. "I think you look tired. I shall—see how English I have become—mix you a drink. Yes, I always have it here, when mayors and councillors come to see me. I discovered that if they take a drink they talk more easily. There! See if I have prepared it correctly, my dear."

She watched him as he sipped his drink, giving her a smile of appreciation. "John, when we are married, shall you mind what people will say?"

"What will they say?"

"They'll say, 'Oh, he only married her because he is a *gourmet*, and she makes the best sauces in the world!' That's what they will say."

"And I shall answer that although it is true, and you do make a very passable sauce——"

"Passable!" she cried. "Oh! How dare you!"

"Let me finish," he said. "Yes, very passable sauces, but what really staggered me, left me dazed and scarcely accountable for my actions, I shall tell them, was her astonishing conceit. Under those conditions I asked her to marry me, she accepted me—and then I fully recovered consciousness."

"You can take back your offer, then I shall take you to the court and demand reparation for what they call—oh, I have forgotten—no, I remember—breaches of promises. Are you afraid, my dear John?"

"Having found you again, having heard you promise to marry me, I am afraid of nothing."

Gardone Riviera.
June 1954.